MEASURING LIVES

A Thriller

Tom Foley

BARRICADE BOOKS, INC./NEW YORK

Published by Barricade Books Inc.
150 Fifth Avenue
New York, NY 10011

Design and page layout by CompuDesign
Printed in the United States of America.

Library of Congress Cataloging-in-Publication Data

Foley, Tom (Thomas C.)
        Measuring lives / by Tom Foley.
                p.   cm.
        ISBN   1-56980-091-X
        I. Title.
    PS3556.03918M43   1996
813'.54—dc20   96-21041
                                                                  CIP

First Printing

For My Parents

February, 1993

John Geddy pulled the curtain aside and looked out the window. Across the city street, he could see a small group of homeless men huddled under the marquee of an adult movie theater, trying to keep out of the rain. A woman wearing a jogging suit and holding a red umbrella walked down the sidewalk, paused for a moment, then continued on her way. Geddy searched the dark windows across the street, then the roof of the building, but he did not notice anyone watching him. Then, just as he was letting the curtain fall back into place, something caught his eye.

An old red pickup truck pulled up and double-parked directly in front of the motel. A short man wearing a black baseball cap rushed out. Geddy watched the man run toward the entrance to the motel, then he hurried to the door to his motel room and put his ear against it.

A minute later he could hear the door at the end of the long hallway open and slam shut. He could clearly hear the footsteps echoing down the corridor. He counted each step. One, two, three....

The sounds of the footsteps eventually stopped. Twenty-eight steps. It had only taken Geddy twenty-five steps when he counted off the distance the night before, but he was six foot two, and he could tell the man who drove up in the truck was short and would take shorter steps. He knew that the man would be standing directly outside of his door. A moment later he heard the man knock four times on the door to the room across the hall—the room Geddy had registered under his real name.

Geddy's mouth dropped open. His heart was pounding and the sweat began to trickle down his face. In all of his thirty-three years, he had never been as confused as he was right now. He looked around the room, unsure of what to do. Climb out the window to the fire escape? Wait and see what the man in the hallway did? Call for help?

Who could he trust?

"Hey, Geddy," he heard a voice shout at the door across the hall. There was more knocking. "I've come to get you."

He decided this was it. For the first time since he had realized he was being followed, he had the advantage. It was time to go on the offensive. He threw open his door and rushed at the stocky figure standing a few feet away. He didn't wait for the other man to turn around. He rammed the startled man's head against the door and threw him to the floor. The black baseball cap flew backward onto the ground. Immediately Geddy was on top of the man, grabbing him by the hair, ready to smash his head against the tiled floor until he was no longer a threat. Then he'd drag him into the motel room to find out once and for all who was after him.

Before he had the chance, he got a good look at the man's face. He wasn't a man at all, but a boy, no more than seventeen years old.

"Who are you?" demanded Geddy.

"I'm a runner for the state attorney's office," the boy cried. "Your secretary sent me."

"She was supposed to come get me herself!" The boy struggled to get up, but Geddy held him down. "I told her not to tell anyone where I am. Is she all right? What happened to her?"

The boy's voice was filled with anger. "She said you're out of your mind! Everyone in the state attorney's office knows it. She said you were paranoid, and that there was no reason for all this running around and hiding. Besides, did you really think she was gonna come to this crappy neighborhood all by herself to get you?" The boy slapped Geddy's hands away. "What are you doin' in this dump anyway? What the hell's your problem, man?"

For the thousandth time, Geddy asked himself the same question. He slid off the boy and stood with his back to the wall, trying to catch his breath. "Sorry, kid."

The boy shakily pulled himself to his feet. "Just get to the courthouse, asshole," he said as he walked away, swearing at Geddy.

Geddy opened the door the boy had been knocking on moments earlier, revealing several packed boxes stacked against the wall and a closet full of clothes. He grabbed his navy blue suit and went back to his other room, the one registered under a false name. He put on the suit, combed his golden blond hair, and hastily made himself presentable for court. After looking out the window one last time, he rushed down the back stairway to an alley where his old Ford was parked. He was only five minutes from the court-house.

•   •   •

When the guilty verdict was announced, there was the usual uproar caused by the media and the public seated in the court-room. Standing behind the prosecution table, John Geddy was immediately the center of attention. Any cameras not focused on the defendant, known as the South Beach Butcher, were focused on Geddy.

It took several minutes to regain order, poll the jurors, dismiss the jury, and take care of the defense's posttrial motions. The judge ordered the defendant chained from his ankles to a steel collar around his neck. Six armed Miami police officers surrounded him, not only for his protection from the outraged public, but also for the protection of those in the courtroom. There was no telling what the man found guilty of seven of the most brutal, bloody murders in memory was capable of doing.

Though he could barely move a muscle, the serial killer—whose name was James Hoffer—twisted his head in Geddy's direction and shouted threats using the most obscene language imaginable. Geddy did not look at him. He was trying to decide what he should say to the media.

"There will be a sentencing hearing three weeks from today, at ten o'clock," said Judge Resnick, rising from behind her judge's bench. "The defendant shall be remanded into the custody of the Department of Corrections until such time. That will do it, ladies and gentlemen. Court is adjourned." She started to throw down her gavel, but suddenly remembered something. "Mr. Geddy, I want to see you in chambers. Immediately, please. The press can wait." The gavel finally fell, causing the reporters to surge toward Geddy.

He slipped around the prosecution table and headed for the hallway to the judge's chambers. Just as he reached the door, James Hoffer shouted one last time, "I'll kill you, Geddy! I'm gonna cut your heart out!"

Geddy watched as they dragged him away then went directly to Judge Resnick's chambers.

"I'm sorry I was late getting here today, judge . . ." He stopped midsentence. Seated behind the judge's desk was the Miami state attorney. The judge was nowhere to be seen.

Geddy could not hide his surprise. "Where's Judge Resnick?"

"Sit down, John," the state attorney directed, as nicely as he could. Years ago, before he became the state attorney, he had been like a big brother to Geddy. "The judge was kind enough to offer her chambers so I could talk to you." He nodded at a seat, but Geddy chose to remain standing.

"Don't be alarmed, I'm here to congratulate you. You put on a hell of a case. A conviction of a serial killer is the ultimate prize for any prosecuting attorney. You've been a credit to the office."

Geddy looked his boss right in the eye. "I'm really getting sick of your bullshit."

"I'm being perfectly honest. We hate losing you."

"You've been trying to get rid of me for weeks," said Geddy.

"Get rid of you? I found you a cushy job in a prestigious law firm in Naples, one of the wealthiest, most beautiful cities in the country. I thought you'd be grateful."

"You know I want to stay. I want to continue prosecuting."

"I think you know that leaving is the best thing for you."

"How many times do I have to tell you I can handle the pressure?" asked Geddy. "And I'm not paranoid. Somebody has been following me for months. I'm not imagining it. Something is wrong with this case, and somebody out there knows it. . . ."

"We offered you protection," said the Miami state attorney. "Round the clock surveillance. We checked out everything you told us, but nothing came up. Nobody's out to get you. You're imagining the whole thing. Hoffer killed those seven girls, you proved it yourself and the jury agreed. There's no conspiracy, and you're not being watched. I think, deep down, you understand that. Why else would you turn down police protection?"

Geddy hesitated before answering. "It's possible that it's been the police who have been following me."

The state attorney shook his head. "That's exactly what I'm talking about, John. Your paranoia is clouding your otherwise excellent judgment. I can't have my most visible prosecutor making crazed allegations of a conspiracy. You're the best trial attorney we have, but the pressure of the South Beach Butcher case got to you. Frankly, it's amazing that you lasted this long, considering what happened with your parents. . . . "

"That has nothing to do with this."

"Then why wouldn't you accept counseling? I was willing to let the doctors decide."

Geddy refused to discuss that again. "What's really on your mind? Are you worried that I'm going to go out to that mob of reporters and tell them what I really think about this case? Is that why you're here now? To keep me from going to the press?"

The state attorney shouted his reply. "As of this moment, you are no longer an assistant state attorney, so you no longer have immunity for defamatory statements! I advise you to watch what you say! I've tried to be patient with you, but enough is enough!" An uneasy moment passed, and he softened his voice. "Do yourself a favor and don't talk to the press. Forget about this case. Start your new life, John. Get out of Miami and pull yourself together."

Geddy stared down his former mentor. "Is that a threat?"

"No, it's not a threat. It's good advice from an old friend who's worried about you," the state attorney told him. "I'll handle the press. What would you like me to tell them?"

"It doesn't matter what I want. You'll tell them what you want them to hear," said Geddy, who abruptly turned and walked out of the judge's chambers toward the rear exit.

"Maybe I should tell them the truth," the state attorney called after him. "Maybe I should just tell them you lost your nerve."

2

A few days after winning his final case as a prosecutor, Geddy was driving through the most charming quarter of Naples, a secluded tourist community nestled against the Gulf of Mexico on the south-western tip of the Florida mainland.

In Olde Naples, there are very strict zoning ordinances requiring certain kinds of signs, storefronts, and types of stores. The result is an antiseptic, classy small-town ambiance with a pervasive air of wealth. The shopping district is five blocks long, followed by two blocks of pretty cottages and bed-and-breakfasts. Then Fifth Avenue, like every avenue in Olde Naples, culminates in a cul-de-sac where beach-goers park and take wooden steps over a sea wall to peaceful sandy beaches that stretch north and south for as far as the eye can see.

The Hirt, Harrington office in Olde Naples was just a short drive from his room in a boardinghouse and only two blocks from the beach. John Geddy took the glass elevator up out of the dark underground garage into the sunlit-bathed Third Street Plaza, where he could see out over the entire shopping area. The Plaza was immaculately kept, with marble walkways and winding rows of exclusive shops and restaurants lined with palm trees and modern but tasteful sculptures and fountains. It was a flawless scene, except for the clock in the tower which was always set several minutes too fast.

He stepped out of the elevator and made his way along the outdoor tiled walkway and stood in front of the door to his new office. In large, scripted gold letters against the dark tinted windows was the name, "HIRT, HARRINGTON, BURKE & ROBB, P. A. "He stepped into a reception area with oak walls and brass fixtures and a gold-flecked green carpet.

"Hello, Ms. Grimes," said Geddy to the receptionist, whom he had met at his interview two weeks earlier.

"Mr. Geddy. Welcome to Hirt, Harrington," she replied professionally, if a bit coldly. "We've been expecting you. You're late, so Mr. Burke asked me to bring you right in. Please come this way."

Geddy followed her though the main corridor to the right of the reception area, passing several offices before reaching the last one on the right. The receptionist announced him, and Geddy stepped inside.

David Burke was a pencil-thin seventy-two-year-old man with thin gray hair and badly sun-damaged skin. With an effort, he stood, offered his hand, and told Geddy to make himself comfortable. Geddy felt obligated to apologize for being late.

"The man responsible for putting that lunatic behind bars need not worry about being a little late," the senior partner of Hirt, Harrington told him.

"Do you mean James Hoffer?"

"Of course I do. Who else would I be talking about?"

"I specialized in lunatics," replied Geddy.

"Oh yes, I heard all about them. But none were as big as the South Beach Butcher case. You certainly pulled some surprises during the trial to get that conviction. Frankly, I don't know why the state attorney let you go. He said you were the best young prosecutor he'd ever seen."

"If you don't mind, I'm a little tired of talking about it."

"Then get over it, because you're going to be hearing a lot more about that case. Have you read the *Naples Daily News* lately? They did a feature on how you were leaving Miami and coming to Naples to work for Hirt, Harrington. You're practically a celebrity around here now. The trial, the protest outside the courthouse, the way you tripped up Reverend Johnson on cross-examination. The *Miami Herald* said you're the best at putting an innocent man behind bars."

"They never said that."

"Not in so many words," said Mr. Burke, smiling. "Relax, it's good press. In fact, your fame has already brought us a new client."

"My fame?"

"Ms. Grimes got a call for you on Friday. Since you hadn't started here yet, I took the call. This woman—Cynthia Dole—read about you and the Hoffer case in the *Chicago Tribune* last week. The article mentioned how you were moving to Naples to work for Hirt, Harrington, so she wants you to look into a problem she's having with a trust fund that's located here. She told me that you were just the man who'd be able to get her money for her."

"I've been prosecuting killers for the last five years, Mr. Burke. I hardly remember anything about trusts from law school," confessed Geddy.

"I thought of that, but don't worry. Faith Williams—our associate who takes care of most of our trusts and wills—can handle it. You just need to be at the meeting and pretend to know what's going on, let Cynthia Dole think you'll be looking into it. It's Thursday at four o'clock, your secretary already has it penciled in on your calendar."

Geddy rose from his seat and stood in front of a window which took up nearly the entire south wall of the bright office. He looked out over the red Mediterranean-style roofs and the walkways below, teeming with tourists.

"It looks like I really am out of the murder business," he said almost to himself.

"I know what you're thinking, John. You're a young man, a talented trial attorney. Right now you miss the excitement of a murder trial. That's good. I'm glad to see that you're so hungry for the courtroom. We handle some very complex litigation here, some very tricky multimillion-dollar lawsuits. It might appear to be boring to you at first, but I can guarantee you'll be challenged. And if it really is that important to you, maybe we'll consider letting you take on a few criminal defense cases. . . ."

"No," said Geddy. "I don't defend killers."

Mr. Burke laughed. "It's just as well. I wouldn't expect much criminal defense work anyway. This city is as crime-free as any in the country—if you don't count white-collar crime."

"Bring on the rich clients and three-martini lunches," said Geddy unconvincingly.

"Now don't start thinking that what we do over here in Naples is any picnic," warned Mr. Burke. "Some of these wealthy people are, let's just say, out of touch. Especially when it comes to wills and trusts, because you're usually dealing with your client *and* your client's family. And when family's involved, anything can happen."

• • •

By Thursday afternoon, Geddy was finally settling into his new job. He had been given several run-of-the-mill property-dispute cases to work on, a couple of mechanic's lien foreclosures, and a few of the other types of cases that his friends in Miami said would bore him to death.

A light on his telephone lit up. "Mr. Geddy, your four o'clock is here," said Ruth Creighan through the intercom. Ruth was a diligent but humorless fifty-five-year-old secretary who was always sure that if anything could go wrong, it most surely would, and she would probably be blamed for it. He pulled on his suit jacket and made his way down the hall to the reception area, where another young associate from the firm was talking with a richly dressed woman, who he assumed was their new client.

Cynthia Dole was in her late thirties, he guessed. A tall woman with an attractive figure, she sported a great deal of make-up on her astonishingly thin face. The skin under her jaw was pulled painfully tight and her fashionably curly, dyed blonde hair was bunched on top of her head, which she held rigidly, as if she were afraid the slightest look down would cause the piled locks to topple over. By far her most compelling feature was her long, arrogant nose, which drew attention from the rest of her face.

"There you are, John," said Faith Williams in a professional voice, not the Southern drawl she used during casual conversation. Faith was two years younger than Geddy and had been with Hirt, Harrington for three years. She was almost six feet tall, with dark brown eyes that looked out over a tiny nose. Her hair was cut extremely short, almost like a boy's. Faultfinding women might not call her beautiful, but Faith had a certain undefinable quality—the shape of her face, perhaps, or the curve of her lip that made men want to look at her.

"Please meet Ms. Cynthia Dole. Ms. Dole, this is John Geddy."

"How do you do," said Cynthia Dole imperiously. "I have read so very much about you. You should be congratulated on your handling of that serial killer. Miami is simply going to pieces, isn't it? Such nasty business."

"It's a tough town," he replied.

Just to the left of the reception desk was a narrow hallway that led to a conference room, the law library, a small kitchen, and a file room. Geddy held open the door to the long sunlit conference room that looked out over a few cheery cottages on Broad Street. They sat in high-backed green leather chairs around an oval rosewood table, with paintings from local galleries of sailboats and sunsets lining three walls and a large portrait of the deceased Mr. T. J. Hirt looking down ominously from the fourth.

"Ms. Dole, you mentioned your situation briefly over the telephone," began Faith, "but maybe you could explain it again now, so John and I can get a full understanding of the situation."

"Certainly, darling. I am a beneficiary of a trust fund that was set up by my grandfather, Adam Gentry," said Cynthia importantly, pausing to let the name sink in. The name meant nothing to Geddy, but he could tell Faith recognized it.

"My brother Curtis is the other beneficiary. The trust is worth, oh, I don't know," she said then waved her hand as if she would throw out her best guess, "thirty million dollars. Currently, my brother and I receive distributions from the trust. For the last few years, I have been allotted close to two hundred thousand dollars annually with these distributions. Needless to say, I would rather have my half of the principal of the trust, which would come to approximately fifteen million dollars, to do with what I want. However, the trustee refuses to give it to me."

"Do you have a copy of the trust with you?" asked Faith.

"No, that is one of the problems. You must understand, my grandfather set up the trust years and years ago, well before I became a beneficiary. So I have never been given a copy. I'm not sure what my rights are. That's why I want you," she said, pointing at Geddy, "to find out when I can get my money."

Faith wanted to speak, but the client had turned toward Geddy and put her hand on top of his.

"Could you tell us the name of the trustee and where we can reach him?" he asked. From behind Cynthia Dole, Faith was shaking her head *yes*, indicating to him that it was a good question.

"The trustee is a woman. It's unseemly, really. Her name is Morgan Gentry, she's my cousin," said Cynthia, who huffed in disgust before resuming. "If I can't get my money now, I want her removed as trustee. Is that possible?" From behind the client Faith shrugged her shoulders.

"It depends," said Geddy, who didn't know what he was talking about, but hid it well. "Without reading the trust agreement, it's better not to speculate." Faith smiled at him.

"Of course, I understand. I've written down the trustee's name and the number I have for her. She's very often out of town, but I'm sure she'll be at the Phil, so try to reach her tomorrow and this weekend. You'll be attending the Phil, won't you?"

What the hell is the Phil, he wondered?

"Why, of course he will be," answered Faith on behalf of Geddy, realizing from his expression that he didn't know what the Phil was. "John and I will be both at the Philharmonic tomorrow night."

He hadn't heard anything about any Philharmonic, but he found himself saying, "I'm looking forward to it. Will you be there?"

"Of course. *Everybody* will be there." She looked at a watch so bejeweled it was nearly impossible to tell the time, then stood suddenly, surprising Geddy with her abruptness. "Now, you've been very kind, but I must be going." Faith stood to leave also, so Geddy assumed that she had all of the information she needed for now. They followed Cynthia out to the lobby where Faith held open the door that led outside.

"One last thing, Ms. Dole," said Geddy. "How do we get in touch with you?"

"I will be in Naples until next Wednesday, then I fly home to Lake Forest." Geddy had heard of the well-to-do suburb of Chicago. "When in Naples I always stay at the Ritz-Carlton. You can reach me there until next Wednesday. Before I leave, I will give you my home address." She started to walk away, but Faith stopped her.

"It may be a good idea to meet again before you leave, after I've gone over the trust. We can discuss our fees and a retainer then," said Faith smoothly.

"I thought I made myself clear over the telephone, but you obviously don't understand. Mr. Geddy is the lawyer I want working on this matter. As for meeting again before I go home, I would be happy to meet with Mr. Geddy, but I see no need to ever see *you* again." Cynthia brushed past Faith. "Thank you again, Mr. Geddy. I shall see you tomorrow night."

"I'll be looking out for you."

The door was about to swing closed behind her when Cynthia Dole turned around quickly. Faith had already stepped inside, so Geddy grabbed the door and held it halfway open.

"One last thing," said Cynthia, as if suddenly remembering something. "If there's a way to prevent my brother from getting any money, that would be splendid."

On Friday evening, Faith Williams pulled her car past a puzzling silver sculpture and under the majestic horseshoe-shaped porte cochere in front of the twenty-one-million-dollar Naples Philharmonic Center for the Performing Arts. The Phil was built in 1989, a beautiful neo-gothic monument to fine music, where plays and symphonies and art exhibits were featured year round. After explaining to Geddy that the partners would expect him to attend this important social event, Faith mustered the courage to ask him if he'd like to go with her. They took her car because she knew the paparazzi would be making a fuss as guests arrived that night, and there would have been sneers from the aristocrats if they went in the beat-up wreck he drove.

Naples is home to many Fortune 500 executives, entrepreneurs who made it big, old money, and the most widely known Wall Street types. Though it has its share of famous homeowners, many of the rich and famous prefer the east coast of Florida, or Sarasota, for their winter homes. Headliners such as Donald

Trump flock to Palm Beach with its old money and high society, but the millionaires of Naples hope to avoid the spotlight, and the city accommodates them. The Valentine's Day Ball is the most important night of the season, however, the one cultural event which attracts even the most reclusive winter residents.

Limousines dropped off glamorously dressed and jeweled occupants who were greeted by photographers and other smiling attendees sipping champagne. Next a Bentley or a Rolls would pull up, or perhaps an Excalibur, and deferential young valets hurried to open doors for the notable and fashionable guests. As Faith and Geddy exited her car and made their way along a red carpet, they beheld tanned, gray-haired men in tuxedos escorting women in sequined gowns with elaborate hairstyles. Faith handed an invitation to a tuxedoed man at the door, who welcomed them with a bow and a sweep of his top hat. Inside, the buzz from a hundred conversations echoed throughout the lobby, where the air was alive with gossip and innuendo.

"Well, here you are. What do you think?" asked Faith, switching out of her natural southern accent to a typical Yankee tone as soon as they were out of the car. She was wearing a simple blue gown with very thin straps which showed off her impressive figure, high heels which made her almost as tall as Geddy, and a modest string of pearls to complete the picture. Faith was usually careless in her attire, so the effect of the dress was to transform her. She had become impressively elegant.

Before he replied, Geddy admired the spacious antechamber with its lofty ceilings and marble floors, its solemn decor conferring an air of urbanity to the interior. The heavenly balcony provided commanding views to the couples who looked down curiously at the hubbub below. A photographer or two interrupted groups of people to get a photo for the social newsletters, causing the invitees to pose briefly with practiced ease.

Geddy frowned at the spectacle. "I think I need a drink."

Faith pulled him close so she could whisper in his ear. "Now John, tonight you're going to meet some of the snobbiest people you've ever met, but it's important to at least *act* like you don't hate them."

"Is that what you do? Is that why you hide your accent? You're putting on an act?"

"Around these people? That's exactly what I do. They'd kick me out of here if I acted naturally."

He nodded in understanding. "At least big parties are easy. It's the smaller ones that are too much work. Where are you from, Faith?"

"Just outside of Knoxville."

"What made you move here?"

"Money," she said, as if that should explain it. "I grew up poor, but it doesn't mean I want to stay that way."

"I get the impression that you don't like it here in Naples."

"I don't. I hate it. I guess I just don't feel like I fit in. The only reason I stay is because the money is so good. My plan is to stay here until I can't take it anymore. Naples is a beautiful city, it's just that there's so many rich snobs, they drive me nuts. You're probably used to those types, but I tell you, I'm going to want to slit my wrists before this night is through. What brought you here?"

He hesitated before replying. "Can you keep a secret?"

"No," she said, beaming, and rubbed the back of her neck. Geddy noticed she did that often, as if she were unconsciously reaching for long locks of hair that had been cut off long ago to achieve the professional look which was expected of her.

"Well in that case, I won't tell you."

"Oh come on, I'm just teasing. You've been here a week, and you haven't told me anything about yourself. What is it? You have family here I bet. You're a Kennedy, right?"

"Hardly."

"A Rockefeller or a Vanderbilt? Or, I don't know, you're from one of those rich families. A cousin, right?"

"Faith, did I tell you that you're the prettiest woman here?"

"You're just trying to change the subject," she said, blushing.

"What kind of a name is Geddy anyway? It sounds familiar."

"I don't know."

"How can you not know? Haven't you ever asked your parents?"

"It's a long story."

"Well there's nobody else I'd rather talk to," she said and held his hand affectionately. Then she spotted someone over his shoulder. "But speaking of people I'd rather *not* talk to, your boss is right over there."

Geddy turned and noticed Jeffrey Robb, the forty-eight-year-old litigation partner at Hirt, Harrington. He was a tall, well-built man with black hair that was graying at the temples. Jeffrey walked with a pronounced limp, the result of a foot wound he received during his first and only day of combat in Vietnam in 1971.

"Let's get a drink," said Faith. She led Geddy past buffet tables covered with all of the expected delicacies before stopping in front of a bar with a brass rail. "What do you want?"

"Thanks, Faith, but I'll get it. What are you drinking tonight?"

"I really want a beer, but I better settle for a glass of wine. And I'm buying. I do have a job, you know." She shouted, "Two white wines!" over an older man's shoulder, causing the man to turn and leer at her. She smiled at the man. When he saw that she was an attractive young woman, he smiled back and initiated a conversation.

While Faith was busy with her new admirer, Geddy watched as uniformed waitresses weaved through the crowd with silver platters perched precariously in their hands high overhead. He smiled knowingly at those guests who moved about most rapidly. They were undoubtedly politicians or salesmen. He was critically observing the groups of prominent Neapolitans, many of whom talked at once, with a blatant disregard for so much as a syllable that did not come from their own mouths, when his eyes met a woman's. She was standing in front of a collection of Cugat paintings, a remarkably beautiful young lady wearing an elegant pink dress revealing a slim, attractive figure. The first thing he noticed was her blue-eyed stare, then her wavy red hair that reflected the light as wisps fell and teased her shoulders. She was about his age, and there was no mistake, she was looking right at him.

When she realized that Geddy had caught her looking at him, she coyly turned back to the group she was standing with, but gazed toward him again almost immediately. Just as the beautiful woman began to blush, she quickly turned away when Faith returned, startling him.

"Here you go, one white wine. I asked if they had beer but the bartender . . . what are you looking at?"

With an effort Geddy took his eyes off the other woman. "Nobody." Just then they both heard a voice cry out his name. "It's Cynthia Dole," said Geddy and nodded toward her. "Purple dress, little crown on her head."

"That's a tiara, but I know what you mean. I think she's going for the Princess Di look."

Geddy agreed. "She looks like a caricature."

Cynthia Dole roared hello and staggered over to them, wrapped her arms around Geddy, and brushed her cheek against his. "My knight in shining armor, you look positively edible! It is so nice to see you." She looked behind herself briefly and noticed Faith but did not acknowledge her. "Have you managed to have an enjoyable time without me, Mr. Geddy?"

"Call me John."

"Only if you call me Cyn. C-Y-N. Cyn, I insist." He couldn't suppress a smile. She was obviously looped. "Have you contacted that nasty witch of a trustee yet? I really am anxious to get this whole matter resolved."

"I've left a few messages but haven't talked to her yet. Have you seen her here tonight?"

"Oh yes, she's here. She was talking with Dick Didier, the surgeon from Switzerland. Follow me, I know she must be around here somewhere." Cynthia Dole held his hand impersonally and led him through the crowd, leaving Faith behind.

They paused briefly next to a bony woman with translucent

skin, who put her hands on either cheek of her drawn face and cried, "Yes, business has been grand! I've sold three homes in the last two weeks." The saleswoman lowered her voice as she spoke to the three ladies surrounding her. "My commission will more than cover another facelift and a tummy-tuck, not to mention my trip to Rio!"

Cynthia pulled him away again but stopped short, causing him to almost stumble over her. Next Geddy heard a man explain, "The Howard Crosses of Philadelphia are here tonight, and so are the Lawrence Packards of St. Louis. Bob Donovan is here, too. He's nobody, but I like him anyhow."

"I have her!" exclaimed Cynthia, tearing Geddy away from the anonymous tycoon. "Come, before she gets away." Cynthia pushed her way through now without bothering to excuse herself until she stopped in front of the beautiful young woman in the pink dress.

She was even more stunning up close. She wasn't particularly tall, but she carried herself like a statuesque model. Her skin was perfectly fair, the kind that comes from a lifetime of expensive lotions and makeovers, the kind that comes from the stress-free comfort of prosperity.

"Morgan, I want you to meet someone," demanded Cynthia aggressively. "This is John Geddy. He's a lawyer, the one from the papers. Since you never return my calls, I had to hire him to get to the bottom of this trust situation. John, this is Morgan Gentry, the trustee."

Morgan Gentry smiled pleasantly and remained well-mannered even in the face of Cynthia's rudeness. "It's a pleasure to finally meet you, Mr. Geddy," she said, stressing the "finally." "I thought I noticed you before from your picture in the newspaper."

Well, that explained why she was looking at him. He extended his hand. Morgan seemed to embrace it with her own. "The pleasure's mine. I'm sorry if we interrupted," he said with dignity to Morgan and the rest of her group.

"There's no need to apologize, Mr. Geddy," replied Morgan.

Cynthia made a face and said with mock politeness, "Don't worry Morgan, I won't impose myself on you any longer. John, I will leave you to business." Cynthia walked away and latched onto another unsuspecting victim.

"She's such a phony," one of the women in Morgan's group exclaimed.

"She's a phony, but she's a genuine phony," remarked Morgan whimsically.

Geddy took a couple steps backwards. "Look, I don't want to bother you with business tonight . . ."

"Please don't go, we all know Cynthia. It's not your fault. We were just chatting, would you like to join us?" Morgan turned to her group. "Dick, this is John Geddy. If you read the papers, you'd know he's a big sensation. He's a former prosecutor and . . ."

"Ah yes, the lawyer from Miami. The man who prosecuted the South Beach Butcher. Pleased to meet you, Mr. Geddy."

"You too, Doctor," replied Geddy, remembering that Cynthia said he was a surgeon. The doctor introduced Geddy to everyone in the group. There was an inebriated financier and his wife, another doctor and her domineering husband, and a retired British Army colonel and his wife.

"I'm so excited to meet you," the financier's wife told Geddy in a grating voice. "We have something in common."

Geddy had no idea what that could be.

"I'm a bit of a serial killer buff," she said. "I find them fascinating. So cruel, like animals. That's what they are, animals. I've been interested in the New Moon Murders for years. It's a little hobby of mine. You must have heard of them. They took place in Naples years ago. Perhaps we can do lunch some time and discuss them?"

Geddy shrugged as if they were both out of luck. "I never eat lunch," he lied, and she believed him.

Dr. Didier smiled at him, liking him. "We were all about to find our way to the balcony and make unmercifully cruel comments about everyone here," he said with a German accent as he gestured overhead. "It should be quite entertaining. Won't you join us?"

"Actually Dick, I need to speak to Mr. Geddy for a moment," said Morgan, and she started to walk away with Geddy. "I'll rejoin you all later."

"Find us after the symphony," called Dr. Didier after them. "We're going to do great, terrible things tonight!"

Geddy half-smiled then turned his attention to Morgan. "He's sure enjoying himself."

Morgan frowned. "It looks like it, but I know he's faking. He's been very depressed lately. His wife's dying. She's a great friend of mine."

Geddy didn't know what to say to that. "I didn't mean to take you away from your friends . . ."

"Please, take me away," pleaded Morgan, smiling at him. "Besides, I know it's not your fault. I've known Cynthia for quite some time, so I know how she can be. She never changes. Chardonnay," she said politely to the bartender. "And for you, John?"

"The same."

The bartender nodded and poured the drinks. Geddy slipped forward to pay without a word from Morgan, who let him do so. He handed Morgan her glass. She thanked him as she raised it in a toast.

"Welcome to Naples, John," she toasted him in a cheerful, blissfully feminine voice. They both tipped their glasses back ceremoniously. "Well, what is this about a problem with the trust?"

"There's no problem. Cynthia just wants to know the status of the trust, and she doesn't have a copy of it. I left you a few messages, but I haven't been able to get through to you. All I need is a copy."

Morgan waved a hand at him. "Is that all? That will be no problem, could you call me late next week? Friday? You can pick it up then."

"I'd like to have it sooner. Cynthia's leaving Naples on

Wednesday, and I'd like to look it over and talk to her before she goes."

"Hmm," muttered Morgan, frowning. "The problem is I'm flying out early tomorrow to New York, and I'll be there until Thursday night. I'm afraid anytime before then will be impossible."

"Is there any reason I can't pick it up tonight?"

His question caught her off guard. "Won't your date mind?"

"You must mean Faith Williams. We work together. She's not my date," he told her casually.

"Well, there are some parties after the Phil. . . ."

"After the parties then."

She was blushing again, bringing his attention to her high cheekbones. She was absolutely stunning. "It would be strictly business," she told him.

"Of course. What else would it be?"

Morgan laughed nervously. "All right then. I live at 105 Venetian Villas, the red building. Shall we say two?" she said before she turned to go. Geddy nodded then watched as she walked slowly up the stairs and melted back into her party above him, where he thought she looked as far out of his reach as the stars.

● ● ●

The Venetian Villas compound is built on stilts out over Venetian Bay, just off Gulf Shore Boulevard. It is a highly exclusive collection of twenty European-style row houses with a Norman tower thrown in for good measure. It looks like a small section of Amsterdam or Copenhagen, or of course, Venice. Each townhouse at Venetian Villas is a different color—red, yellow, blue, white, pink—and each is built right up against the next. They are all very narrow with red Mediterranean roofs, each with a slightly different design to give the appearance, as in Europe, that the townhouses were built at different times rather than all at once according to a master plan. There is nothing haphazard about them though. The villas are an interesting blend of ordered chaos and architectural presence.

Geddy drove over a short causeway and stopped at the guard station. He was allowed to pass and drove along the red-tiled driveway past a couple of Porsches and a Ferrari. He parked in between a long black Mercedes sedan and a pink two-car garage on the opposite side of the lot from the villas. Geddy walked up to Morgan's door and rang the bell, still dressed in his rented tuxedo. When there was no answer, he rang the bell again, then waited. Again there was no answer, so he assumed that he had missed her. As he was recrossing the courtyard, a white convertible roadster in mint condition pulled up between Geddy's car and the Mercedes. At once Geddy noticed Morgan's radiant red hair.

"I hope I haven't kept you," she said as Geddy made his way to her car and held open the door. "I found myself listening to some man's never-ending story about the gold standard and couldn't get away."

"Old guy, drinking mint juleps?"

Her white skin seemed to glow in the darkness. "You too?" Geddy nodded. "I don't know why I go to those things," said Morgan as she guided him to her door and admitted him to a grand room of noble proportions. The villa was three stories high, very narrow, and had a cathedral ceiling on the first floor. A royal-blue carpeted stairway swirled upward, but Morgan had already slid back the wrought iron gate to the indoor elevator.

"Make yourself comfortable while I get the documents you need," she said as she stepped inside the elevator. "Wait for me on the veranda. I'll fix us both a cup of tea after I make copies of the papers you need. Then perhaps we can discuss them."

Geddy pretended to let her talk him into it. When she was gone, his eyes flashed about curiously as he surveyed the great room, from its intricate plasterwork on the lofty ceiling to its elegant woven carpet in ruby-red and pale champagne. In between, the walls were painted blood red and provided the backdrop for an unusual portrait gallery. Mahogany shelves bulged with antiques and marble busts and potted plants. Geddy stepped carefully, as though he were in a museum, to the far end of the room. He opened the French doors which were built into the center of an oversized arched bay window and looked out over Venetian Bay.

Carrying a silver tea tray, Morgan finally joined him outside. They took their seats on cushioned white wicker rocking chairs that creaked. She placed the tea on the table, then handed him a manila envelope from the tray. "Here you are, John, this is a copy of the trust. You may look at it now if you like, and I'll be happy to answer any questions you might have."

"I don't know too much about trusts. I'm only helping one of our attorneys. Maybe you could explain it to me."

"There's so much to explain. Where should I begin?"

"Why don't you tell me why my client can't have her money?" suggested Geddy, smiling.

"All right, that's as good a place as any." She smiled back at him warmly. "The first thing to remember is that it's not up to the trustee to decide when to give the beneficiaries the money from the trust."

"That reminds me," interrupted Geddy. "You're not exactly what I pictured when Cynthia told me about her wicked trustee. How did you get the position?"

"It's a long story, believe me. Suffice to say, the trustee is entitled to a nice little salary for managing it, so the trusteeship has been kept in the family. Cynthia is my cousin. My grandfather set up the trust and was the first trustee. My father took over when my grandfather died, and I took over three years ago, after my father died."

"Did your grandfather leave anything to your father, or to you?"

"He left my father the family business, which was worth more than the trust in its day. However, my side of the family can never become beneficiaries of the trust. My grandfather set up the trust in 1952 for his daughter, my aunt Victoria. That's Cynthia's mother. Only descendants of Victoria Gentry's side of the family can ever become beneficiaries. The beneficiaries are listed as, here, let me read it."

"Victoria Braden Gentry, the only daughter of the trustor, and any descendants of Victoria Braden Gentry, more specifically described as children, grandchildren, great-grandchildren, great-great-grandchildren, etc. In the event of a failure of descendants of Victoria Braden Gentry, the sole beneficiary shall be the University of Tampa, an institution of high learning."

"What this means," said Morgan, putting down the trust, "is that only descendants of my aunt Victoria can be beneficiaries of this trust. Even if her line dies out, nobody from my side of the family can become a beneficiary."

"Too bad for you," said Geddy.

"It hardly matters. Cynthia and Curtis, Victoria's two children, are alive and well. If they die without children before the trust vests, the University of Tampa will become the beneficiary."

"Well, that's simple enough to understand," he said, wondering what the confusing part was.

"The confusing part," she said as though she could read his mind, "and the part that Cynthia doesn't understand no matter how many times I tell her, is the part of the trust that describes when it terminates. Even if I wanted to terminate the trust and give Cynthia and her brother Curtis the money, I couldn't. Of course I don't want it to terminate, so even if I could end it, I wouldn't."

"Why not?"

"Because then I would lose the trusteeship and the money I earn from it."

"Right. Well then, when does the trust terminate?"

"That's where the Measuring Lives come in," she said, rolling her eyes. "You see the trust has a puzzling device to ensure that it will last as long as legally possible. In the old days, wealthy people loved to set up these huge trusts for their family to live off of rather than just give the money to their families outright. Rich people often leave their fortunes in trust funds after they die, so that their children and grandchildren can't get their greedy little hands on the money all at once and waste it. But there's one legal

rule that prevents someone from leaving their money in trust forever. Do you remember from law school a legal rule called 'the rule
against perpetuities'?"

"Vaguely," he admitted.

"Well, the purpose of the rule against perpetuities is to limit
the duration of trusts, so that wealthy people can't tie up large
amounts of money after their death by leaving it in trust forever
and ever. Under this rule the maximum permitted duration of a
trust is measured *not* in terms of years, but by the life span of the
people who are named in the trust. The trust can only last as long
as the life span of these Lives-In-Being, as they are called, plus an
additional twenty-one years after the death of the last surviving
Life-In-Being."

"I remember now," said Geddy. "Any person named in the
trust is a considered a Life-In-Being, right?"

"Yes. So the more people named in the trust, the better
chance you have that one of them will live a long life. When you
add twenty-one years from their date of death, you can make a
trust last fairly long, more than a hundred years if at least one
Life-In-Being lives long enough. My grandfather wanted the trust
to last as long as legally possible so that generations could live off
of it, and also to ensure that aunt Victoria's husband couldn't run
off with her inheritance. But there were only two people named in
the body of the trust agreement: My grandfather, Adam Gentry,
and his daughter Victoria. So since Adam Gentry was dying, the
trust could realistically only be expected to last until twenty-one
years after Victoria died."

"When did she die?" asked Geddy.

"1972."

Geddy added twenty-one years from 1972. "That's great
then—for Cynthia, at least," he added, remembering that if the
trust was terminated, Morgan would lose the valuable trusteeship.
"Since Victoria was the last living Life-In-Being and she died in
1972, the trust will terminate twenty-one years later, in 1993.
This year. So Cynthia and her brother will get the money from the

trust this year."

"No. Because Victoria wasn't the last Life-In-Being to die."

"But you just said . . ."

"One moment, you didn't let me finish. A clever way lawyers have devised to make a trust last as long as possible without violating the rule against perpetuities is to simply list the names of several newborn babies in the trust agreement, thus qualifying them as valid Lives-In-Being. Therefore, the trust will last until twenty-one years after the last baby dies. One of these newborn babies could live to be eighty, ninety, maybe even one hundred years old. If the last one of them, the last Life-In-Being, dies at age one hundred, for example, the trust would last for one hundred and twenty-one years. They even pick baby girls as these Lives-In-Being since women have a longer life expectancy. It's a simple way to try to ensure that the trust will last for as long as possible under the rule."

"Let me make sure I follow you," said Geddy. "What date did Victoria Dole die?"

"I think it was March 4, 1972."

"All right. If we forget about adding a list of babies—baby girls, I should say—the trust would terminate and the money would vest in Cynthia and her brother twenty-one years from Victoria Dole's date of death. It would vest March 4, 1993. A few weeks from now."

"Yes."

"*But*, there is this list of names in the trust," he said, then turned to Appendix A and read the following names, birthdates and places of birth:

APPENDIX A

Gabrielle Smith
Born, July 10, 1952
Naples Memorial Hospital

Julieanne Cherube
Born, January 3, 1952

Barron Collier Hospital, Naples, Florida

Angelica Savasta
Born, May 23, 1952
Fort Myers Hospital

Sally Baumgartner
Born, December 27, 1951
Thomas A. Edison Hospital, Fort Myers Florida

Deborah Moore
Born, August 11, 1951
Naples Memorial Hospital

"These girls are also valid Lives-In-Being, so the trust won't terminate on March 4, 1993. It will terminate twenty-one years from the date of death of the last one of these girls to die."

"Exactly," agreed Morgan.

"They were all born in 1951 or 1952. That would make them, what, forty-one or forty-two?"

"Yes."

"So out of these five girls, it's almost certain that at least one is still living," said Geddy.

"I would say definitely at least one, if not all of them."

"So Cynthia has to wait."

"Yes. It's not up to me to decide when to end the trust," concluded Morgan.

"Have you been keeping tabs on these five girls?"

"Not yet, because I know the trust has to last until at least March 4, 1993, which is twenty-one years after my aunt Victoria died."

"Well, it's February 14—15," he corrected himself, looking at his watch. "March 4 is only a few weeks away. I think it's time to find these Lives-In-Being. I'll let you know when I find them."

"That would be very kind," she thanked Geddy. "But let me correct you on one little thing. Once you determine that a person is a valid Life-In-Being, it's not really accurate to continue to call them a Life-In-Being. Since their life span measures the duration of the trust, they're called the *Measuring Lives*."

The office was dead quiet and completely empty on Saturday afternoon, so Geddy was dressed in his most comfortable pair of Levi's, a blue T-shirt, and his basketball sneakers. He had been at his new job for only one week, but already he was falling frighteningly far behind in his work, so far behind that he wouldn't have time for the haircut Jeffrey Robb had suggested he get.

He opened the manila envelope Morgan had given him earlier in the morning and slid out the eight-page document. On the top of page one were the words "TRUST AGREEMENT." He sank back in his chair and kicked up his sneakers on his desk. He read every page slowly and carefully, keeping in mind everything Morgan told him.

When he finished, he rubbed his eyes and arched his back, then settled in his seat and considered the trust. He remembered little about the rule against perpetuities, only that it was historically a difficult rule, one that even the most competent trust attorneys approached with extreme caution. He pulled a book on trusts from his bookshelf and looked up the rule. When he found it, he read it aloud, slowly. It rang a bell.

"No interest is good unless it must vest, if at all, not later than twenty-one years after some Life-In-Being at the time of the creation of the interest."

He recalled that the basic problem with the rule was that if it was violated, the trust might not be valid. One technique lawyers devised to ensure trusts wouldn't violate the rule was to insert a "savings clause" into the trust. He reread the savings clause from page three of the Adam Gentry Trust:

Notwithstanding anything herein contained to the contrary, the provisions of this Trust Agreement shall not postpone the vesting of the trust property or any portion hereof for a period of more than 21 years after the death of the last survivor of the persons living at the time of execution of this document listed on Appendix A, attached hereto and made a part hereof by reference.

That was all it took, that and the list on Appendix A, to make the five baby girls valid Lives-In-Being. Therefore, he concluded that the trust would terminate and the money would vest in the beneficiaries twenty-one years after the last of the five babies listed on Appendix A to die. Geddy sat up and scribbled, *"Gentry Trust—Need to find the Measuring Lives, right?"* on the outside of the envelope, replaced the documents, and left them on Faith's desk for her review.

• • •

On Monday morning, Faith found Geddy in his office and closed the door behind her. The balloons and streamers hung to welcome him had long been removed by his secretary. His office was neat and bright, decorated with the formality that clients expected from the firm. Geddy had not contributed a single thing to his home-away-from-home. No family pictures, no diplomas or awards on the wall, and no framed newspaper clippings.

"I have something for you." Faith handed him two sheets of paper.

He looked at the two computer printouts. On each page was

a girl's name and some biographical information. "Let me guess," he said. "You enrolled me in a computer dating service?"

"Not on your life! Don't you recognize the names?"

Glancing at them again, he remembered. "Oh yeah, the Lives-In-Being. I mean, the Measuring Lives."

"I'm very impressed with you, John; you figured out the trust all by yourself," she said, teasing him a little by using the tone of voice one uses when speaking with a child. "You were exactly right, we need to track down the five Measuring Lives. I ran their names through an on-line computer subscription service we use to track down heirs of wills, or long lost relatives, or witnesses or whatever. The problem is only two of them came up."

"Well," he began, looking at them, "let's see. Julieanne Cherube, born in Barron Collier Hospital, January 3, 1952 . . ." Geddy stopped and reread the next line of information. "Died, June 12, 1972." He looked up. "Well, what do you know. That's one down."

"Read the next one," instructed Faith.

Geddy turned to the second page and began reading aloud again. "Sally Margaret Baumgartner, born December 27, 1951, died . . . July 11, 1972. Is this right?"

"It should be," she said, shrugging her shoulders. "It's kind of weird though, they died only about a month apart."

"Well, Cynthia would be happy to hear it," he said, thinking out loud. "This means twenty-one years after the later of them to die would be . . ." he looked down at the papers again. "July 11, 1993. This summer. If these were the only Measuring Lives, the trust would end—would vest—this summer."

"That's right," she agreed. "All it really means though is that you have to look for the three other Measuring Lives until you find one that's living, or at least one that didn't die so long ago."

He tossed the printouts on a stack on his desk. "A month apart, huh? Maybe Cynthia killed them," joked Geddy. "Imagine that? Queen Cyn, a ruthless murderer?"

"Oh sure, I can see it now," laughed Faith. "Imagine Cynthia pulling a switchblade on these poor unsuspecting girls in a dark alley. 'Do not make a move, dahling, or I shall kill you,'" she said, imitating Cynthia's voice.

When they finished laughing, Geddy suddenly had a thoughtful look on his face.

"*Now* what?" asked Faith, expecting another joke.

"She would have a motive, you know."

"Sure she would."

"No, think about it. She gets periodic distributions from the trustee, right? Obviously Cynthia's not satisfied with her allowance, she wants it all now. If the Measuring Lives were all dead for twenty-one years, she'd split the thirty million with her brother. She'd have fifteen million dollars cash all to herself."

Faith wasn't buying it for a second. "That would mean she would have had to kill five girls in 1972 to get fifteen million dollars in 1993. I don't think so, John."

"Why not? If you're nineteen or twenty years old, let's say, and you knew if you managed to kill off five twenty-year-old girls you'd get fifteen million dollars when you were forty-one years old, you wouldn't do it?"

"Are you kidding? Of course I wouldn't," answered Faith honestly. "Would you?"

"No. But then again, it's easy to say no when you don't have the option. I damn sure know you could find a lot of people who *would* do it."

"Only a prosecutor could turn a simple trust matter into a murder case. You spent too much time in Miami, John. This is Naples, remember? Murder's not part of the vocabulary over here."

Geddy laughed at himself. "Yeah, I know, but I'll tell you what. I have to call Cynthia this afternoon. Maybe I'll just ask her if she killed the Measuring Lives."

He got up and walked away, laughing. When he was halfway down the corridor, Faith called out to him from behind.

"While you're at it, ask Cynthia if her brother might have killed them!"

• • •

Later that day, Geddy had a chance to turn his attention once again to the Gentry Trust. If he wanted to have an answer for Cynthia Dole about the trust by Wednesday, he had to track down the remaining Measuring Lives.

Geddy looked at the computer printout that Faith had run for him. The computer search had found one of the Measuring Lives who was born in Naples and one who was born in Fort Myers. He pulled the Naples telephone book from his bottom drawer and began looking for Deborah Moore. No luck. She's probably married and had her name changed, or maybe she moved away from Naples, he thought. He would have tried calling some other Moores to see if they might be relatives of hers and might know of her whereabouts, but there were more than two pages of Moores.

He pulled out the telephone book for Fort Myers, a larger city about thirty-five minutes up the coast. He checked the list again. Angelica Savasta. There was only one Savasta listed, under the name Anthony Savasta, so he tried it.

"Good morning, I'm sorry to bother you, sir. My name is John Geddy. I'm an attorney in Naples. I'm trying to find a woman by the name of Angelica Savasta, who was born in Fort Myers Hospital on May 23, 1952. I thought she might be related to you. Do you know her?"

"What's this about?" was the suspicious reply.

"Her name came up in a case I'm handling. I just need to speak with her for a minute," explained Geddy.

"What case? What's this about?" the man demanded.

"It's a little confusing."

There was silence at the other end. He heard the man take a deep breath, then another pause. "Angelica's no longer with us," the man finally said. "She's been dead for over twenty years now."

Geddy hung up the phone and a second later was out the door

• • •

Later that afternoon, Faith was in her cluttered office working on her computer when she heard a familiar knocking on her office door. She turned to see Geddy rush in slapping a piece of paper on her desk.

"What's this?"

"Something I just dug up at the Naples Office of Records," he told her in a hurry. "Someone's killed the Measuring Lives."

"John, I . . ."

"It's a death certificate for Gabrielle Smith. Read the date."

"June 11, 1972."

"1972, Faith! The two Measuring Lives you found with the computer search died in 1972. I confirmed another has been dead for twenty years. Now this girl, Gabrielle Smith, died during the summer of 1972 as well. Somebody's killed the Measuring Lives!"

She was speechless at first, then finally managed to whisper, "But you only found four. There were five Measuring Lives."

He stood and closed her office door, then crouched right beside her and asked eagerly, "What do you know about the New Moon Murders?"

• • •

It took them only five minutes to get to the Naples Public Library on Central Avenue in Olde Naples. Its Jeffersonian brick exterior gave the impression that it was an historic site, but like so many buildings in Naples, it was fairly new, built during the 1980s' construction boom. They walked up to the large square information center and were promptly greeted by a little white-haired woman eager to help.

"We want to look through some old newspapers," said Geddy. "The *Naples Daily News*."

"What dates are you interested in?" she asked sweetly.

"The summer of 1972."

The librarian's expression turned to one of contempt. "Would this have anything to do with the New Moon Murders?"

Geddy and Faith looked at each other but neither could speak.

"Don't tell me you've never heard of them," the librarian scoffed at Geddy. "I've worked in this library for eight years and in the original Naples Library for sixteen, and it seems every few years somebody wants to dredge that horror up again. What is this fascination with those terrible murders? What are you, a reporter?"

"No, I'm not a reporter. I'm a lawyer," he told her, which didn't help. "Where are the newspapers?"

The librarian looked down her nose at him. "Whatever. I can't keep you from seeing them, but if I could have my way, I'd never let another word be uttered about that business again. Let those girls rest in peace."

"Girls?" exclaimed Faith.

The librarian didn't care to discuss it further. "Follow me," she said. Geddy's heart was racing as he followed her to a small room in the back of the library. The librarian explained that back issues of the *Naples Daily News* were all on microfilm. She showed them how to use the machine, where to find the microfilm they were interested in, then she walked away. Geddy hurriedly picked out a roll of microfilm for the *Naples Daily News* covering the month of June 1972.

Faith pulled a seat alongside Geddy's. "Don't bother searching day by day," she told him. "Start by checking the Sunday editions first."

He fast forwarded until he found the first Sunday edition. "June 4, 1972." Geddy scanned the pages looking for any mention of murder. "There doesn't seem to be anything here."

"Try June 11," suggested Faith, her voice filled with excitement.

Likewise, June 11 came up empty. But when they reached the June 18, 1972, Sunday edition, a chill whipped through Geddy's body. The headline read: **POLICE BAFFLED BY BEACH KILLINGS**.

The cover story summed up the two murders that occurred late on the evenings of Sunday, June 11, and Monday, June 12. It took only a few sentences to get the names of the two victims.

Gabrielle Smith and Julieanne Cherube. They were both Measuring Lives.

"Holy shit! Move over, John. I can hardly read it from this angle."

"You have to look at it head on. I'll read it out loud."

By Nick Farley
Daily News Staff

NAPLES—Police have yet to make an arrest in connection with the murders that took place on the beach last Sunday and Monday nights. Gabrielle Smith, a graduate of Naples High School, age nineteen, was found early Monday morning by Mr. and Mrs. Lawrence Frankfurt as they took a morning walk along the beach near Fifteenth Avenue South. Police believe Miss Smith was attacked from behind and had her throat cut in the night, and was left for dead on the beach.

Similarly, two unidentified elementary schoolchildren found the body of twenty-year-old Julieanne Cherube early Tuesday morning, this time on the beach near Third Avenue North.

Police Chief Timothy McShane confirmed reports that, at present, police have no suspects. "There appears to be no motive," Chief McShane stated. "Nothing was stolen from the girls, and there is no evidence of sexual abuse. We're still investigating and are confident the killer will be caught."

The police are reluctant to release any information to the public, and Chief McShane would not confirm that the girls were killed by the same person. But the similarities may prove too striking to conclude otherwise. Both girls had their throats slashed, and in both cases, the murder weapon was found near the scene of the crime. There is no evidence of a struggle, and the girls' clothes were not torn or otherwise damaged.

FOR MORE ON MURDERS,
please turn to page 3.

"Turn to page three!" exclaimed Faith as Geddy hit the rewind knob on the microfilm machine.

"We can go back to it," he told her, the shortness of his tone betraying his excitement over their discovery. "First, I want to see about the others. Get me the film for July 1972."

Faith found the film. Geddy quickly threaded it into the machine and searched for the next Sunday edition. Again, the first two Sunday editions had no reports of any murders other than follow-up stories on Gabrielle Smith and Julieanne Cherube. However, the headline for July 16 hit Geddy like a sledgehammer.

FOUR MURDERS WITHIN MONTH—"NOT THE LAST"

"Fuckin' A," cried Faith. "Read it."
The front-page story summed it up.

By Nick Farley
Daily News Staff

NAPLES—The two latest victims of the so-called New Moon Slasher, "Not likely to be the last" victims, says Naples Police Lieutenant Dennis Edwards. All four of the murders occurred within a night of the new moon—the night the moon is not out. Hence the name, the New Moon Slasher.

"Unfortunately, with the kind of psychopath we're dealing with here, he probably won't stop until he's caught," Lt. Edwards explained. "And it's also unfortunate that, other than the knives, there's not much hard evidence." Lt. Edwards asked that any persons who might have knowledge of the killer please contact the police immediately.

Angelica Grevey, twenty, wife of Robert Grevey, was found Monday night in the parking lot behind her office on Fifth Avenue. Like the murders that took place last month, she was found with her throat slashed, the murder weapon found nearby. The Naples Daily News has learned that Mrs. Grevey was apparently changing a flat tire when the killer came upon her. The flat tire may have been caused by the same knife used to slit Mrs. Grevey's throat.

Then, Tuesday evening, Sally Baumgartner was found in an empty parking lot behind Chamonix Restaurant off Tamiami

Trail North. In a gruesome departure, Ms. Baumgartner, age twenty, was stabbed perhaps a dozen times before having her throat slit. The knife was found next to her body. There was no evidence of rape or theft.

> FOR MORE ON MURDERS,
> please see pages 2–5

"I don't remember an Angelica Grevey from the trust," said Faith. She looked pale.

Geddy was furiously working the dials of the machine. "No, but there's an Angelica Savasta. Let me flip to page two . . . there, you see?"

"What? I told you I can hardly read it."

He swallowed hard. "There's a quote from Angelica Grevey's father. His name is Anthony Savasta. I talked to him a few hours ago on the phone."

"Oh my God!" cried Faith, actually sounding scared.

Geddy sat back, his mind blown. Four deaths. Four Measuring Lives. It all seemed unreal to him, that he must be dreaming or imagining this, but he knew he wasn't so he tried to tell himself that it must be a coincidence.

"Faith, you don't look so good," said Geddy suddenly. "Are you okay?"

"Just keep looking, there's one more to go. Deborah Moore, the one we haven't tracked down yet."

Geddy finished scanning the newspapers for July and then replaced the microfilm with the August 1972 film. It didn't take him long to confirm what he suspected. He expected to find that Deborah Moore was murdered in early- to mid-August—the next new moon. When he came to the Sunday newspaper for August 13, he found what he expected: **MURDERER OF FIVE STILL AT LARGE.**

By Nick Farley
Daily News Staff

NAPLES—The New Moon Slasher continues to baffle police one week after he took his fifth victim.

Early Thursday morning, Deborah Moore was found decapitated outside of her own home. Police admit the similarity of this most recent killing to the four murders that took place earlier this summer, specifically the similar age of the victims and method of killing, not to mention that all five murders took place during the new moon.

Police concede there is a serial killer stalking young women in Naples. The victims appear to be chosen at random. Other than the girls' ages, the police can find no other link.

"You want a link," Geddy said to Faith, their faces inches apart. "Well, I got a link. A thirty-million-dollar link."

Geddy and Faith stayed at the library until nine o'clock, reading over every article they could find relating to the New Moon Murders. There were very few details disclosed in the newspaper stories. The most important fact they discovered was that there was never a suspect.

"I want to take a look at something," Geddy told Faith as they were getting into her car. He had her drive him to the beach at Fifteenth Avenue South.

"This is where the first murder took place," muttered Faith as they got out of her car and looked about warily.

The area was well lit by a streetlight centered at the end of the cul-de-sac. There was a bench on either side of a wooden stairway and a public telephone on the right. A bicycle was stashed off to the left side in a rack.

They took the wooden stairs down to the beach. After walking twenty or thirty yards in the sand, the light from the street faded, making it very dark. The moon was almost full so there was some light to see by, but if it had been a new moon, it would be pitch black. Ahead about a hundred yards they could see the street-light from Sixteenth Avenue South shining out towards the water. There wasn't a person in sight.

"It's only about nine thirty. In the early morning hours there'd probably be no one around," remarked Faith, who had to almost shout over the sound of the crashing waves. "Especially not in 1972. Naples was a lot less populated then."

"Who knows if these beachfront houses were here then? And what about the street lights? I wonder what year they were installed? As we look into them we have to keep in mind that these murders took place twenty years ago. A lot has changed since then."

"Look into them? John, I admit that something strange is going on with these Measuring Lives but we won't be looking into the murders. You're not a prosecutor anymore."

"We're going to look into them all right. Faith, we're on to something here. We can catch the killer."

"It's not our job to catch him, John."

"Do you mean to tell me that if someone connected to the trust killed these five Measuring Lives, it has nothing to do with us?"

"How could it?" she asked.

"What about the Murder-Inheritance Statute? Doesn't it say that anyone found guilty of murder can't inherit from their victim? If we find that the killer was a beneficiary, that beneficiary could be disqualified from receiving the money from the trust."

"No John, that's not right. Yes, it's true the Murder-Inheritance Statute does say that a killer can't inherit from his victim, but in this case, the killer wouldn't be inheriting from his victim. The five Measuring Lives were the victims, and the beneficiaries don't inherit from them."

"Well, there must be some way to prevent someone who kills five girls from being rewarded with millions of dollars."

"It's possible that the killer had nothing to do with the trust," said Faith. "Maybe it really was a serial killer."

"Do you honestly believe that? That out of all the nineteen- or twenty-year-old girls in Naples in 1972, some psychotic serial killer just happened to pick the five Measuring Lives from the trust?"

Faith reluctantly shook her head no. "All right, I agree there must be a connection with the trust. But who exactly do you think killed these girls? Cynthia?"

"It's possible. And like you said earlier, maybe her brother, Curtis Dole. He's the only other beneficiary."

"We were just joking around about that," said Faith.

"I know, but I was serious when I said a lot of people would be willing to kill five strangers when they're twenty years old to receive fifteen million dollars when they're forty-one."

"But this is Cynthia Dole we're talking about," argued Faith. "And her brother is probably some snobby-ass socialite, too. They don't go around murdering people."

"There might be some other possibilities. Maybe one of them hired a killer, or maybe they got together and both hired a killer."

"John . . ."

"The point is there's a lot we don't know yet," Geddy said finally. "But don't you understand how valuable the information we just stumbled onto is? Now we know the killer had something to do with the trust."

"Look John, I know you're probably getting a little restless with your foreclosure cases and that divorce case you've been stuck with, but you're out of the murder business, remember?"

"I know I won't be able to handle the trial, but that doesn't mean we shouldn't investigate. We spend a little while figuring out who had the best motives and find out more about the murders. Once we narrow down our suspects, we'll turn the information over to the Naples state attorney. I'm just talking about a week or two, that's all. You're the expert on all of these trust issues. I need you. Just help me narrow down the suspects."

"What if Cynthia is the killer? Our own client. We might be

ethically bound not to turn her in."

"Then . . ." Geddy thought for a moment. "We have to tell Cynthia about the Measuring Lives."

"What!" she cried.

"She's our client, Faith. She has a right to know what's going on. More importantly, if Cynthia tries to order us not to look into it, we'll know there's a good chance she's involved."

It was a warm sunny day as Geddy cruised slowly up the oval drive in front of the Ritz-Carlton. He was running late, so he stopped in front of the valet at the main entrance. A doorman in a top hat and tails opened his door without looking at him, signaling for a valet. He looked at Geddy's car distastefully, careful not to touch it. Geddy started to walk away, knowing from his days as a valet not to tip until his car was returned, when the doorman asked snidely, "Would you like me to have your car washed for you?" He had the snootiest way of speaking that Geddy had ever heard, worse even than Cynthia.

"Don't bother," replied Geddy.

"In that case, would you *mind* if I had your car washed?" the man asked. Geddy didn't hear him. He hurried over oriental carpeting through the richly decorated massive front hall of the hotel and out the elaborate French doors in the rear. Then he crossed a large marble veranda and stepped onto a palm tree-lined wooden walkway that took him over the sand and seagrass until he came to a tiki bar overlooking the beach, where tables were set up for lunch. Liberated from the embarrassing attachment of his car, Geddy was an impressive sight in his olive suit, cordovan wingtips and tortoise-shell Wayfarers. He was shown a table and waited, his golden hair blowing in the gentle gulf breeze.

At twelve-fifteen, Geddy watched as Cynthia Dole emerged from under one of the many brightly colored beach umbrellas and strolled up the beach and the wooden stairs. She had a sarong that matched her bikini top wrapped around her waist, and wore a wide-brimmed straw hat with a pink band that read "JUMBY BAY" in white letters across the front. There was a small dab of sunblock on the end of her long nose. Geddy thought about telling her about it, but he enjoyed seeing her look ridiculous.

"Mr. Geddy, so nice to see you again. I apologize for being late, but it couldn't be helped." She spoke with that accent that wasn't British, but wasn't American, either. Where does someone get that kind of accent, he wondered?

"No apology necessary, Cyn," he replied as he stood and held her chair for her.

"What? What did you call me?" she demanded as the sunblock started to run down to the point of her nose.

He should have known that she was drunk the other night and would forget she told him to call her Cyn. C-Y-N. "I said don't apologize, Cynthia."

"Well as long as you're calling me Cynthia," she said as though it offended her, "I may as well call you John." She finally noticed the sunblock and wiped it away self-consciously.

They ordered lunch and ate, talking primarily about their travels in and around Europe; he on a motorcycle, she first class. After they had finished their meal, Cynthia brought up the trust.

"So John, do I get my money or am I at the mercy of that bitch?"

"You mean Morgan Gentry?"

"Of course," answered Cynthia. "It's not right that I have to answer to her. She gets a hundred thousand dollars a year just for keeping the books, half what I get, and I'm the beneficiary, for God's sake. It's scandalous! Do you think that's fair?"

"Of course not," he said to soothe her and then tried to explain it. "But this is a 'Support Trust,' it was set up to simply provide *support* to the descendants of Adam Gentry, not give you a pool of money to live off. You see, the intention of your grandfather was that his daughter and her descendants should *work*, and this trust would supplement whatever . . ."

"Work? Do you know how ridiculous that sounds? There are millions of dollars in the hands of that classless bitch that belong to my side of the family, and she's only giving Curtis and me two hundred thousand dollars a year apiece!"

"That sounds like more than enough for your support."

"But can't I get more? There is so much money in the trust. Can we sue her?"

"Yes, we could try, but we don't have to," announced Geddy triumphantly. "By August you'll be the proud holder of about fifteen million dollars."

Her eyes lit up and her mouth opened in amazement. "Really, John? It's all mine?"

"It will be. The trust will terminate in August, so you and your brother will split whatever it's worth." Her happiness was contagious. It was fun telling someone she would soon be handed millions of dollars.

"And Morgan? She's out of the picture?"

"By September, she'll be just another person looking for a job," he said for Cynthia's enjoyment.

"That is fantastic! Thank you, John! I knew when I read about you that you were the right person to get my money." She stretched her hand across the table for him to hold, but he jerked back without thinking.

"Cynthia, you also wanted to know if there was a way to keep your brother from getting any of the money. Do you mind if I ask why?"

"Because I hate him, of course," she said matter of factly.

Geddy looked at her until she explained. "I've hated Curtis since my mother became ill. He was so uncaring, and he rarely saw her. He didn't visit her during her last days and didn't even go to her funeral. I could never forgive him for that, so we haven't spoken to each other for years and years. I suppose it's sad, we are brother and sister, but family is always a complicated matter. And there is another reason I don't care to discuss. Suffice to say, I don't think he's fit to have any of the money. Why do you ask?"

"Well, I have a great deal more research to do, but there may be a way to keep Curtis from getting his share of the money from the trust. It's a long shot, but if it pans out you could get it all."

Geddy thought Cynthia was going to faint. Her head swayed a little backwards, and her skin became momentarily gray. "Oh, you are a miracle worker, John!"

"It would mean accusing Curtis of the New Moon Murders," he said bluntly.

She wasn't sure she understood him correctly. "Did you say murders?"

"Do you remember the New Moon Murders from 1972?"

"Why, yes," she said, a frown crinkling the tight skin between her eyes. "It's been so long, but yes, I remember. What do they have to do with this?"

Geddy began to explain about the trust and the rule against perpetuities and the savings clause and the Measuring Lives. Cynthia was concentrating on what Geddy was saying and appeared to follow him so far.

"When I tried to track down these five girls," he continued, "I discovered they were murdered in 1972. Every one of them was killed by that New Moon Slasher. That's why the trust is ending this August. August 10 will be twenty-one years from the date the last of those five girls was killed."

She gasped and watched him wide-eyed as he continued.

"Obviously, I can't help but think that this is more than a coincidence. I don't believe that the five girls were randomly murdered by a psychopath. I think it was a brutal and vicious way to bring an end to the trust. I've been looking into it, and from what I can tell so far, Curtis is the most likely suspect."

"Nonsense! That can't be!" She continued to shake her head in disbelief until the possibility of it could sink in. "Even . . . even if it were true, why couldn't he receive his half of the trust?"

"In Florida, like all states, there's a law which says that someone who is adjudicated guilty in a court of law for killing someone else can't inherit from the dead person, the person they killed. It's called the murder-inheritance statute. Now in our case that law doesn't control, because Curtis wouldn't be inheriting from the people he killed. But that law was enacted pursuant to a long recognized concept in the law: a killer should not be permitted to benefit from his criminal act. We would provide this information to the Naples state attorney. He would charge and try to convict Curtis. If Curtis is convicted, he'd be disqualified as a beneficiary, leaving all the money to you."

Cynthia Dole couldn't speak right away. She took a sip of her daiquiri and gazed into it thoughtfully. Finally she asked, "Are you certain Curtis killed those girls?"

"No, far from it. I've only just begun to look into it. There's a lot more investigation that needs to be done, not only by me. If we give the Naples state attorney this information, he will certainly reopen the case, and anyone connected to the trust would be an initial suspect. Including you," he said, trying to read her expression. "From what I can tell so far, you and Curtis are the only logical suspects. However, I don't know enough about the murders or Curtis yet. He might even have an alibi, or he might have been living somewhere else at the time. Who knows, I might discover that Curtis isn't responsible."

"And let me guess. You're wondering if I might have had anything to do with it?" asked Cynthia.

Geddy returned her gaze without blinking. "Did you?"

"No. I was going to school in Chicago back then and spent the entire summer there. Besides, I knew nothing about any Measuring Lives."

"Then this is something you'd like me to pursue?"

"For another fifteen million dollars, are you joking? You look into it, John. Do whatever you have to do." She reached over the table, grabbed his hand, and lowered her voice. "If you pull this off and get me all of that money, you can write your own ticket."

7

In his office Friday morning at around ten-fifteen, Geddy dialed a telephone number, made sure it was ringing, then put the receiver down on his desk and began to organize the files in front of him. Thirty seconds later, as the phone continued to ring, Faith Williams popped her head into his office. "Hey, want a coffee break?"

"I'd love one, but I'm making a call." He nodded to the receiver lying on top of his desk.

Faith looked at it with a puzzled expression but didn't ask. "So, John, have you had a chance to look over my research on the trust? You know, the stuff about a killer not being permitted to benefit from his crime?"

"Yes, and it looks great. You really know your stuff, you . . ." He put up one finger as a signal for her to wait as he heard a voice come through the phone.

"Nick Farley?" asked Geddy into the receiver.

The sleepy, gruff response was slow and grumpy. "Who the fuck is this?"

"Sorry to bother you. The person who gave me your number said that I'd have to let the phone ring awhile before you'd answer."

"There's a reason for that. I was sleeping," the other man grumbled angrily.

"Yeah, well, I just thought you might be interested in something I recently stumbled upon. I might know who the New Moon Slasher is."

"Who the hell is this!" was the startled reply, and Geddy thought that Nick Farley must have jumped out of bed.

"My name is John Geddy, I'm an attorney in Naples."

"Geddy? G-E-D-D-Y?"

"Yes," replied Geddy, wondering why Nick Farley spelled his name.

"Yeah, you're the guy who tried James Hoffer, the South Beach Butcher. I covered that story," Nick Farley said. "You got the wrong guy, you know. Hoffer was a killer, all right, but he didn't kill those prostitutes."

"I didn't call for your opinion," snapped Geddy, who had to fight the temptation to say more. "I've got the secret to finding the New Moon Slasher. I assume you remember the New Moon Murders? In Naples, twenty years ago?"

"Of course I remember," Nick said. "What's this information you have?" Now that he was awake, Nick's voice had settled into a slow, nasal twang, but it still had an edge to it.

"I thought you might be interested," said Geddy. "I'll tell you when I see you. I want you to come to Naples."

"Why?"

"Like I said, I might know who the New Moon Slasher is, but I need to prove it. I read every story you wrote about the murders in 1972. You seem to know more than anyone else does about the details. I tracked you down through a friend of mine at the *Miami Herald*."

"Who?"

"Mimi Feinstein," answered Geddy.

After a pause and a few more questions, Nick Farley reluctantly agreed. They set a time and place to meet, and Geddy hung up.

"What was that all about?" asked Faith.

"Remember Nick Farley, the guy who wrote a lot of those old newspaper stories we read about the murders? I thought he could help us."

Faith shook her head, still reluctant to be involved. "Come on, I'll buy you a cup of coffee," she said. They started walking down the hallway.

"It'll have to be a quick coffee break. My ten-thirty appointment will be here in a few minutes."

"Who are you meeting with?" asked Faith.

"Didn't I tell you? I'm meeting with the trustee of the Gentry Trust in a few minutes."

"No, you didn't mention it . . ." began Faith.

"Oh, there you are, John," the receptionist interrupted as Faith and Geddy entered the front hall. "I just buzzed your office. Your ten-thirty is here." She nodded to Morgan Gentry, who was seated to the side on a couch in a cream-colored suit, her red hair pulled stylishly over one shoulder.

"Morgan," he said, not hiding his pleasure at seeing her again. "It's nice to see you. You're early."

"It's nice to see you again, too, John," said Morgan as though she truly meant it, something that didn't escape Faith, who looked at Morgan with barely concealed rivalry as she rubbed the back of her neck nervously.

•   •   •

To say that Geddy had the attention of everyone in the conference room would be an understatement. He had just finished telling all the lawyers in the firm about the trust, the Measuring Lives and the New Moon Slasher. So far, he could tell Mr. Burke seemed cautiously optimistic. Jeffrey Robb, Geddy's demanding supervising partner, was shaking his head doubtfully, and Josephine Harrington, a slick real estate attorney, hadn't tipped her hand yet. Faith, his reluctant partner, hadn't said a word, either.

"We want to hire an investigator," continued Geddy after laying out his theory. "Faith and I need to get as much information on the murders as possible. We anticipate the Naples state attorney's office will initiate their own investigation, but we don't want to rely on them."

"You think they're going to give you access to their files?" inquired Jeffrey Robb, implying by the tone of his voice that he doubted it.

"We're sure they'll investigate, and we're hopeful they'll give us access to their files. We plan to work together with them on this. The Naples state attorney is a friend of yours, I understand. I was hoping you would talk to him."

"Maybe, but I'd have to know a great deal more before I get dragged into something like this," Jeffrey said.

"What more do you need to know? The trust is the key to the New Moon Murders."

Jeffrey clearly didn't appreciate Geddy's tone, but he let it pass. "Look, John, I'm just saying we shouldn't rush into anything. We have our reputations to protect. Frankly, I think you're getting carried away. Your name's not on the letterhead yet, but you can't wait to play private prosecutor. I know you want to crack the case, solve the mystery, but you really don't know a thing about Curtis or Cynthia Dole. You can't conduct this thing like a witch hunt."

"He's just eager. Who can blame him?" said Mr. Burke in Geddy's defense. "Besides, all he and Faith are asking is to look into it. Why the reluctance, Jeffrey? You'd think they were accusing you."

Jeffrey tossed his pencil onto the table and shook his head skeptically. "I just don't buy it. Killing five people to inherit money twenty-one years later? Sorry, I don't believe it. It's too far-fetched. Curtis and Cynthia Dole had everything to lose. They could count on what, a hundred, two hundred grand a year for life? That isn't bad for doing nothing . . ."

"Stranger things have happened, Jeffrey," interrupted Mr. Burke. "There are plenty of real-life outrageous schemes that involve relatives knocking each other off to get at the family fortune. I read about a case where a husband and wife were eighth in line for an inheritance of a wealthy older widow. Over the course of six years, they murdered everyone who stood in line before them then knocked off the widow. Well, I probably don't have to tell you they were the first and only suspects, and they were convicted and never saw a cent. The point is they thought they could get away with it. People will do extreme things for this much money."

"True, but how do we know it's not just coincidence? And what if Cynthia Dole did it?" reasoned Jeffrey. He looked at Geddy. "What will you do if you find it was your own client?"

"I talked to her today. She was in Chicago for the entire summer. She can prove it," replied Geddy. "She couldn't be the killer."

"There might be other possibilities. If there's no descendant of Adam Gentry, the money goes to the University of Tampa. Maybe someone associated with U.T. killed them and are planning to knock off Curtis and Cynthia to get the money that way," tried Jeffrey. "Then what are you going to do, accuse the entire university of murder?"

Mr. Burke glanced sideways at Jeffrey. "Aren't you on the Board of Trustees at U.T., Jeffrey? Maybe you could sniff around?"

Faith finally spoke up. "Mr. Burke, I'm afraid that someone from U.T. being involved is the most unlikely of all the possibilities. If someone from the University of Tampa were going to kill Cynthia and Curtis, they wouldn't wait until six months before the trust vests. They would have done it a long time ago and collected the distributions every year."

"Did you consider Cynthia's father?" asked Mr. Burke.

Faith nodded. "Benjamin Dole, who married Victoria Gentry in 1953, was alive at the time of the murders. He died in 1983. But he had no interest in the trust; only his wife and his kids did. The kids would get the money, not their father. In addition, he was in Chicago all summer."

There was silence for a half minute before Mr. Burke finally spoke. "It sounds to me like there are two reasonable possibilities. And I exclude coincidence as a possibility," he added, looking at Jeffrey. "Either Curtis Dole did it, or Cynthia Dole paid someone to do it."

"That's what I think, too, Mr. Burke," agreed Geddy. "Other than the possibility that Cynthia hired someone, Faith and I agree it has to be Curtis. There's no other logical suspect. So you see, all we have to do is investigate those two possibilities, either Curtis or Cynthia."

"For the record, I disagree," stated Jeffrey. "How do you know it wasn't me who killed those girls? I lived here in 1972. Maybe it was Burke, or . . . it could have been anyone. It could have been . . ."

"It could have been me," laughed Josephine Harrington in a deep voice, the first words she had uttered at that meeting.

"But the point is that the killer had to have an interest in the trust," argued Geddy. "It's too much of a coincidence otherwise."

After more deliberation, it was clear that only Jeffrey was against investigating further. "Very well, you two, look into it," announced Mr. Burke. "You have carte blanche. But be discreet. You may find that Curtis Dole isn't the killer, and it could even turn out to be Cynthia." He tapped Geddy's arm with his pen. "I have a list of investigators in my office. I'll help you pick one out."

"I appreciate that, but I have someone in mind. A reporter who covered the stories back in 1972."

"Hire whomever you feel is best, just don't lose your head," said Mr. Burke, then surveyed the room. "If there's nothing else, we can adjourn . . . Josephine, you've been quiet, do you have anything to add?"

Josephine Harrington, a very tall, hard-working spinster with a normally serious disposition, was content to just sit back with a smile and observe. "I think it's a neat case," she said as she ran a hand through her short gray hair.

8

On Friday night after work, Geddy packed his baseball glove and cleats and rushed off to Heckscher Park. It was dark already, so the softball fields stood out majestically under the lights as ballplayers and friends and families made their way happily to their respective sides, where the players started warming up. Geddy hung around until the city league games were about to begin, watching intently until he found what he was looking for: a short-handed team. He eagerly volunteered and was inserted at third base and played a doubleheader.

After the games, his teammates and their family and friends broke out a half keg of beer. Geddy joined them. They laughed and joked good-naturedly and recounted the highlights of the games. Geddy, whose borrowed uniform shirt was covered in dirt from a few dives and several slides, was complimented on his fine play and asked if he was available to be a regular on the team. He jumped at the chance, and they handed him a schedule. He had made his first friends in Naples outside the firm.

About an hour and a half later, the keg was dry, and everyone headed home. Since it was his first time there and he had not known the best place to park, Geddy had to walk to the far end of the field. He walked alone as the field lights suddenly flashed off. He was in total darkness.

It was quiet now. He could hear the crickets and night bugs, then a jet flew overhead to the nearby airport. He looked up to see the lights of the airplane, but it was a cloudy night so he couldn't see a thing. No plane, no stars. No moon. As the jet raced away it became silent again.

For some reason, he remembered the Cardillo case. That was the one where the homeless man was found in the park with two pencils sticking out of where his eyes used to be. It was one of dozens of brutal murder cases he worked on in Miami, but for some reason he couldn't get the picture of that homeless man's corpse out of his head. It was the first dead body he had ever seen. Well, the first one as an assistant state attorney, he reminded himself.

Suddenly he heard a click behind him. Instantly he was on guard. Geddy spun around and squinted in the darkness but could see nothing. He stood motionless for a full minute, but could not see or hear anyone.

Maybe the state attorney was right, he thought. Maybe he really was going crazy.

He resumed walking and tried to laugh it off. After only a few steps, he walked straight into a soccer goal post, hitting it so hard with his head, he heard a faint metal clang. It didn't hurt, but it took him by surprise, and he gasped loudly, staggering a step or two before slowly regaining his direction, now with his hands held out before him in the darkness.

Only a few seconds later, after taking only a couple of steps, he heard another faint metal clang. He stopped, whirled around and peered into the darkness. His heart began beating uncontrollably when he made out the dark outline of a man only a few feet from him, silhouetted against the street lights on the other side of the park.

"Who's that?" demanded Geddy. The silhouette became completely still. There was no reply.

It was happening. Just like he always knew it would.

Geddy had to open his mouth now to breathe. He started taking steps backward. There were no lights on the horizon behind Geddy, so the silhouetted stalker would not be able to see him. The stalker must have been following him by sound. He had been following Geddy's footsteps.

Geddy's heart thumped relentlessly. He continued to take small steps backward until he stepped on what sounded like a discarded plastic fork. It snapped loudly in the otherwise complete silence. He saw the silhouette rush into action and come towards him. When the dark figure sprang at him, Geddy's instincts took over. He rushed forward also, surprising the stalker, and tackled him hard. But as he was on top of the attacker and ready to punch the man's face with his right fist, he felt a stinging pain in his cheek under his right eye. He sprang backward to avoid another swipe of the knife blade.

Geddy rolled away and searched for his assailant. His head darted in every direction looking for the silhouette. When he was sure he couldn't see it, he dropped to his stomach in order to make himself harder to see. He kept completely silent, listening intently, but he couldn't hear anything over the sound of his heart pounding as if it would burst through his chest.

It seemed an eternity passed before he decided the man who had stalked him must have fled after his initial attack was unsuccessful. Geddy slowly pulled himself into a crouch, held his breath and listened. He didn't hear a thing. Then he stood, and after a few seconds carefully stepped backward. When all remained silent, he took a few more steps, quick and watchful, and continued this way until he felt his car, slid along the side of it. He frantically jumped in and started the engine.

He hit the headlights. They shone out over the field toward the soccer goal. There was nothing else there, other than his glove and his cleats lying a hundred feet away where he had dropped them. He walked out to the middle of the field, where the attack had just taken place. There was no one to be seen. He could feel the blood running down his cheek. He searched the ground for clues but found nothing, so he picked up his glove and cleats and returned to his car.

He turned on his inside light and could see the blood dripping onto his purple softball jersey. He looked up into his rearview mirror and saw the bloody two-inch gash. He was almost glad to see it. Now he knew he hadn't been imagining everything. Someone really was after him.

• • •

A few hours later Geddy was back in his room at Mrs. Lovett's boardinghouse, which was all he could afford after years of paying off college loans with his modest assistant state attorney's salary. The small rustic residence was located near the city docks at the end of Naples Bay, a poor address by Naples standards, but compared with his old place in Miami it was a safe, quiet location. He had one small room with a kitchenette, his own private entrance up steep wooden stairs, and he shared a bathroom with the other boarders.

Geddy flopped down onto his cot and within minutes his phone was ringing. It was Nick Farley.

Nick explained that he was in Alabama and couldn't drive down to Naples on some wild goose chase. He wanted to know what Geddy knew about the New Moon Murders, to make sure it was worth his while. Without naming Curtis, Geddy told him everything about the trust. Nick Farley was blown away. He agreed to meet Geddy the next night.

"Nick, before you go, let me ask you something. You said James Hoffer wasn't the South Beach Butcher. Why?"

"I know serial killers, and he ain't one," Nick Farley replied. "What the fuck do you care, anyway? You won the trial. Screw Hoffer."

"I was attacked tonight, and I can't understand why. I think it might have something to do with the South Beach Butcher case."

Nick demanded to know what happened. Geddy told him.

"Hoffer's in jail, kid, so it wasn't him."

Geddy exhaled loudly. "There are some other possibilities. There was a lot more going on in that case that nobody will ever know."

"I'd like to hear about it sometime."

"I'd like to tell you, but I don't know," admitted Geddy.

"Whatever you say, Chief. But you know, you're workin' on this New Moon Murder case now, right? Maybe your attacker has somethin' to do with the New Moon Murders."

"Impossible."

"Who knows what you're up to?"

Geddy sighed. "Just Cynthia Dole, Morgan Gentry, Faith, me, and now you. Believe me, it wasn't a woman who attacked me. I was on top of the guy, and I saw his silhouette."

Nick grunted in agreement. "No one else knows?"

"Well, no," said Geddy slowly, then added, "except for the partners in my firm. I told them all about it today."

Nick Farley was laughing hysterically. The bartender and a few patrons looked over at him to see what was so funny. "Hey Red, another round!" he called out through his laughter to the red-headed barmaid.

Faith, Geddy, and Nick Farley were seated in a restaurant-bar across Naples Bay from Tin City, another tourist-trap shopping plaza in Olde Naples. Rosie's Waterfront Cafe is a laid-back place located in a wooden structure under a thatched roof with Jimmy Buffet piped ceaselessly over the loudspeakers. Large open windows dominate three walls. The fourth side has no wall at all, providing an unobstructed view of a paddle-wheel fun-cruise boat docked alongside in Naples Bay. The first few minutes of the meeting were spent by Geddy explaining to Faith that his stitches were simply from a softball injury. Then Nick told them all about some serial killer he once covered in New Mexico. They took their drinks to one of the few remaining tables and ordered dinner. Nick immediately asked for round number three.

"Man, I love this song!" Nick exclaimed suddenly, then began to sing along. "Whyyyy, don't we get drunk, and screwww . . . !" Nick sang a verse until the next round of beers were delivered.

"John tells me you're sort of a serial-killer expert," said Faith, wanting to get the ball rolling. Nick Farley was in his midforties and had thin brown hair, a flat nose, and pig's eyes. He was sloppily dressed and unshaven, typical of many freelance journalists. Like many people who have no one to answer to, Nick had no reservations about speaking his mind, even to the point of offending people. He simply didn't care what people thought of him.

"Nick's a freelance journalist," said Geddy, whose stitched cheek throbbed. "He got his start right here in Naples."

"That's the plain truth," Nick agreed. "Good old phony Naples. It gets worse and worse every year. I swear someday the whole damn place is gonna turn into one big old goddamn snobby-ass country club. The people get fatter and more sunburned every time I'm here. Do you know what Naples's number one industry is? Tourism. Know what's second? I don't either, nobody does. They don't do a damn thing here, the place was a goddamned swamp fifty years ago. But somehow, everywhere you go, people are just throwing away money left and right. You know why they got so much money if there's no industry here? Because nobody's from Naples! Everyone's from somewhere else." He downed half his beer. "What's a couple of smart kids like you doin' here, anyway? This ain't the place to make money, this is the place to blow it. It's the most unproductive place I've ever been."

"People are from here," said Faith. "Those five victims of the New Moon Slasher were all born here."

"Oh, they got their locals, their lifers, but they don't count. They're just here to serve the Yankees."

"Are you originally from Naples?"

Nick jerked his head back. "Hell no. Norman, Oklahoma. I'm a Sooner. But I got my first paying newspaper job down here in '71. After the New Moon Murders, I was offered a job out in Texas with a *real* newspaper. But I went out on my own after a while, started freelancing. Seems the only thing I'm good at's murder."

"There wasn't enough murder in Texas for you?" asked Geddy.

"Oh, they got murder there. There's murder everywhere, don't get me wrong. It's just that serial murders are the thing I like coverin'."

"Why would anyone want to do that for a living?" asked Faith, who ran a hand through her close-cropped hair and rubbed the back of her neck.

Nick sat up excitedly. "Okay, say there's a murder. Most of the time, it's in the local papers for a day or two, then it's gone. If the killer's caught, it's news for another day or two. But a serial killer, why they're damned celebrities! I can show up to cover a killer in New Mexico and rent an apartment for a few months, settle in, find myself a nice waterin' hole or two to hunker down in. I get to know the cops workin' the case. I know the details by heart. I can pump out story after story. Papers all of the country are dyin' for my stuff. I can't write enough about 'em. Then for years to come, I can do follow-up stories when I need the cash. I got editors all over the U.S. who're callin' me night and day asking what I got on the latest serial killer cases. They're bigger than the Beatles!"

"So that's what you do?" asked Geddy. "You go wherever the serial killers are?"

"Hell yeah. I was in Alabama when you called. They got some guy out there who's doin' the old hitchhiker thing."

"What do they call him?" asked Faith.

"He doesn't have a name yet. That's a specialty of mine, though, makin' up names. I've hung more than a few nicknames on killers in my time. I named that South Beach Butcher Mr. Geddy here thinks he took care of."

Geddy was looking out over the bay. "Hoffer was the killer."

"Yeah, and I'm gonna win a Pulitzer Prize."

Faith looked confused. "You don't think Hoffer did it?" she

asked Nick.

"The jury said he was guilty," insisted Geddy with finality.

Nick put his elbows on the table and leaned towards Geddy. "Well, you better hope he was the killer, and you better pray the appeals court doesn't reverse the conviction." He turned to Faith. "When they were takin' Hoffer out of the courtroom, he kept shouting that the first thing he was gonna do when he got out was cut John's heart out."

Faith winced. "Yeah, but I bet those guys say stuff like that all the time."

"The problem is, Hoffer's the kind of guy who'd do it," Nick told her, then added, "but that doesn't mean he killed those prostitutes in Miami."

"Did you name the New Moon Slasher?" asked Geddy, wanting to change the subject.

"No, I can't take credit for that. The locals around here started that one. First they were calling him the Werewolf because of the connection with the moon. It didn't stick though, since werewolves are supposed to come out when there's a *full* moon." He took a long pull of his beer. Nick always seemed to take a long pull, never a sip or a taste. "Now, what's this about solving the New Moon Murders? I have to admit, you got me interested. I never solved a serial murder myself. I just report them, try not to get emotionally involved."

Though Geddy had told Nick almost everything on the phone the night before, he and Faith told Nick again, in more detail, about the trust and the Measuring Lives. Geddy asked Nick if they could count on his help.

"I don't know, I usually work alone. What makes you think I won't just go public with the story right now?"

Faith spoke up immediately. "You can't do that! There's still too much we don't know yet."

"There's enough for a story. What are you gonna do, sue me?"

Geddy looked Nick dead in the eye. "I'll kick the crap out of you."

Nick grinned. "So, you're a tough guy, huh? What's the tomboy's role in all this?"

Faith immediately threw a punch at Nick's face, but he pulled away, causing his chair to topple over. Geddy was on his feet in an instant in case Nick tried to retaliate. But Nick just shook his head and laughed.

"Damn broads!" Nick cried. "I was just havin' some fun, darlin'. Don't go gettin' all pissed off."

"Don't call me darling!"

"Okay, easy now, girl, don't go raving at me with that feminist crap. I'll knock it off. I thought you had a sense a humor, is all." Nick sat out of Faith's range and got down to business. "Yeah, I'm in, we've got a deal. I'll keep things under wrap until you're ready to go public. You have my word. So tell me, exactly who do you think killed the five girls?"

Geddy hesitated, but finally decided to trust him. "That's what we need to find out, but it seems there are really only two possibilities. Our client's brother or our client."

"Un-fuckin'-believable!" Nick raised his glass and finished his beer. "What do you want me to do?"

Geddy leaned forward now on his elbows. "We need to know everything about the murders, but there's an unbelievable shortage of information about them. Other than your stories from 1972, we can't seem to find out any details."

"Yeah, the cops were mighty tight-lipped," Nick agreed.

For the next hour, Faith, Geddy, and Nick discussed the murders. Then Geddy began rattling off a list of things for Nick to begin looking into, and Faith wrote everything down so Nick wouldn't forget. After dinner Geddy paid the bill, they left Rosie's, and together they all walked through the parking lot.

"Well, this is me," Nick said as they arrived at his old, faded black van.

Faith handed him five hundred dollars cash. "This is for

expenses for now. We'll set up an expense account next week. We consider you our investigator for now, so you'd better keep your promise not to write about any of this until the state attorney makes an announcement. We'll draw up a contract for employment on Monday."

"As soon as the state attorney charges someone, you'll have the exclusive," added Geddy.

"Fine with me." Nick climbed into his van. "When do we get started?"

"Do you work Sundays?"

"Sure, every day's the same to me."

"We'll meet you tomorrow morning, at the site of the first murder."

Nick waved and started to drive off as Geddy walked Faith to her car. "Wait, there's something else I want him to do," said Faith. She hurried over and was able to reach the van before Nick pulled out of the parking lot. Nick rolled down his window obediently and playfully covered up as if she were going to try to hit him again. She ignored it.

"I thought of something else for you to check on, but you can't tell John," she said so seriously that Nick immediately took out the pad and pen she had given him earlier. "The trustee's name is Morgan Gentry. She lives in Venetian Villas, here in Naples. Find out everything you can on her. Everything," she repeated.

• • •

It was now past eleven. Geddy was walking on the docks of a local marina. After his meeting with Faith and Nick, he went back to his room in the boardinghouse and found two messages on his answering machine. The first one was from the Naples police, telling him that they still had no leads on the attack on him the night before. The second message was from Morgan Gentry. He listened to it twice before deciding not to call her.

He went into his kitchen and pulled out the Swiss army knife he had been using to open his canned goods, flipped out the long blade, and concealed it in the inside pocket of his Levi's jacket.

Then he left the comparative security of his room.

It was ordinarily a peaceful five-minute stroll to the nearest marina, and under any other circumstances, he would have enjoyed the cool quiet night, the soft breeze, the crickets chirping, and the stars shining. He loved the sea and boats and often walked the narrow docks between the yachts and cabin cruisers at night when the nightmares came. The sea always calmed him. It had permanence, it was always there, and it kept coming, wave after wave.

But this night he was tense and wary, breathing lightly and listening intently for even the slightest sound. He had to admit it to himself, he was scared. Someone had tried to kill him—who wouldn't be scared? He didn't trust anyone, including the police, so he decided to go out that night and invite his stalker to try again. He wanted to get it over with, once and for all. He had to find out who tried to kill him. After about half an hour of walking through the marina, Geddy sat on the end of a dock, facing the sea, exposing his back to his stalker, daring him to attack, if he were there.

After some time passed without incident, he decided there would be no confrontation that night. He was on guard during the entire walk home, ready for whomever might be lurking there for him. As he turned the corner by the mailbox and walked up the sidewalk toward his boardinghouse, he noticed Morgan Gentry's vintage white roadster parked in the street.

He stepped to the side out of the light and watched as Morgan descended his stairs, crossed the sidewalk, and opened her car door.

"And I thought I had nothing better to do on Saturday night," he said, coming out of the shadows.

"Oh John! How terrible of you to frighten me like that!"

"Sorry, I wanted to be sure I knew who was coming down my steps."

"Who did you expect? Didn't you see my car?"

"I didn't notice it," he lied. It was impossible not to notice that car.

"I called you tonight. Why didn't you return my message?"

"I had something to do."

"What? Take a walk?"

Geddy genuinely liked Morgan, but he wasn't in the mood for banter. He had other things on his mind. "What are you doing here, Morgan?"

"I . . . I don't know why I came. Sometimes I just do things on a whim. Call me impetuous, just stop laughing at me."

"You're not even faintly impetuous."

"Well then, if you know me so well, why am I here?"

"You must need a lawyer."

She laughed, a slight, dignified laugh. "Wrong again."

"Then I don't know."

"I guess . . . I guess it's because I've been thinking about you a lot. Too much, probably. I thought if I saw you, I could put you out of my mind, and . . ." She stopped suddenly. "John! What happened to your face? Are you all right?"

"I played softball last night," he told her.

"Did you get socked by the ball?"

He managed a laugh. "Socked?"

"I'm trying to be nice."

"I know, you need to see me long enough to get me out of your mind."

"I didn't mean just seeing you. I meant—you know . . ."

"Are you trying to ask me out?"

"No! I have never asked a man out."

"Are you trying to *ask me* to ask you out?"

She tired to hide her embarrassment, but her pale cheeks flushed. "I just thought we could go for a ride?" she suggested and jingled her keys.

With a little more cajoling, Morgan ushered him into the driver's seat, and he was speeding off in her little classic convertible.

He took her down Gordon Drive to the Port Royal area, where every house seemed to have a yacht docked behind it on a canal that led to Naples Bay, and each estate was worth well over a million dollars. His troubles seemed to fly away as they roared up and down the palm-lined streets blaring their music, awakening the prosperous residents as Morgan perched herself precariously on the back of her seat, letting her red hair down to blow freely in the wind.

Morgan directed Geddy to the south end of Port Royal, past a row of boathouses and into a parking lot. At the end of the lot was a gas station for boats, then Gordon's Pass, and on the other side of the narrow strait was Keewaydin Island. They jumped out of the car, sat on the dock, and watched an occasional boat return to harbor after a late night cruise. Geddy made sure his Swiss army knife was still stashed securely in his jacket. They talked for half an hour, laughing a lot, enjoying each other's company. Then the conversation turned more serious.

"So, I've resigned myself to the fact that the trust is ending. I have to find a job," said Morgan.

"Well, it's not so bad. Most of us common folk do it," he said.

"You're no common person," she replied, then added in mock anger, "and I'm no stranger to hard work."

"I didn't mean it that way . . ."

"And I've worked hard for what I have," she said, slapping him on the shoulder.

"All right, you're a real rags-to-riches story. Just don't hit me again."

"I admit my father always had money, and we always had a nice home, but I didn't just sit around and eat grapes all day. I was accepted to Stanford and got my joint JD/MBA. That was no picnic. Afterward, I worked in investment banking on Wall Street."

"How did you like that?"

"I didn't. I hated every minute of it." Her hair seemed to float on the sea breeze. "I promised myself I wouldn't be a slave for the rest of my life, so I moved to Switzerland and decided to take a couple years to learn French, ski, travel, and meet interesting people."

"How was that?"

"I absolutely loved it. The Swiss Alps are the most beautiful place on earth. I never wanted to leave. But when my father died, I received the trusteeship, so I had to move back here."

"You could go back to Switzerland now."

"No, I'm getting too old for that. There are other things I want to do now."

"Like what?"

"Like have children."

"You should probably get married first."

She looked at him, unable to suppress a smile. "Maybe I'm working on it."

Just then two dolphins surfaced a few feet away, temporarily breaking the spell she cast over him. "Tell me about these Measuring Lives, Morgan." At their meeting at his office the day before, Geddy had broken the news to Morgan that she would soon be losing her trusteeship when the trust terminated. He also told her about the murdered Measuring Lives. While distraught about the five girls, she was also concerned for her future, since her only income came from being the trustee. "Where did Adam Gentry get them? Are they relatives or beneficiaries?"

"First of all, Adam Gentry didn't choose the five baby girls, his lawyer did," she explained. "But I'm afraid I don't know where his lawyer found them. They aren't relatives though, he probably just chose them some random way. They could have been daughters of friends, or he could have seen their birth announcements or baptism or christening announcements in the newspaper, or gone to hospitals or nurseries looking for five healthy baby girls. It really doesn't matter where he found them, just that they were added to the trust. I'm sure they didn't even know about it. There's no reason for them to know. They're not beneficiaries. They have no interest in the trust. They're like human clocks.

Their life spans determine when the trust vests, that's all."

Geddy looked at her gravely. "You've been the trustee for how long? Three years? You grew up in Naples. You were thirteen years old when the murders took place, right? But you didn't notice that the Measuring Lives were the New Moon Murder victims? Your father was in possession of the trust in 1972, and he didn't notice either?"

"Well, I think I can speak for my father as well as myself. We simply never had to concern ourselves with the Measuring Lives. As I explained to you the other night, we didn't have to track down the Measuring Lives until March 4, 1993, twenty-one years after Victoria Dole died, because she was a valid Measuring Life, too. That's a couple weeks away. I suppose I would have had to get to it soon, but I never dreamed that these girls would all be dead. They should only be forty-one or forty-two now."

"Didn't those names ring a bell?"

"No. I probably looked at them when I took over the trust and read it over for the first time, but that was in 1990, eighteen years after the murders. This is a tourist town, John. They don't exactly advertise their serial murders. I hadn't even heard their names for years."

"That's understandable, but what about your father? He had the list of girls in his possession then. Why wouldn't he have noticed?"

"He'd been trustee since 1952. He probably hadn't looked at the trust agreement for years when those murders took place. All you have to do as trustee is keep track of the money, the invest-ments, and the distributions. You don't refer to the trust agree-ment for anything after you understand what your duties are."

Geddy nodded. What she said made sense.

Morgan looked sideways at him. "John, what are you getting at? Do you think my father did something wrong?"

"No, it's just that this is a strange situation. I'm trying to understand everything." He felt badly for interrogating her, but he was relieved to have those questions answered. "So, where will you be jetting off to when the trust terminates? L. A.? New York? Paris?"

"I told you, I think I should stay in Naples."

"Why?"

"Because I could be a good influence on you."

He moved closer to her. "You know, I think you might be right. But there's something you should consider."

"What?" she asked.

He placed his hand behind her neck and began to pull her close. "I might not be such a good influence on you." With that Geddy kissed Morgan softly, a tender inquiry, which built in intensity.

They continued to kiss on the dock until a car pulled into the lot, alarming Geddy, who had not forgotten that someone might still be stalking him. He was concerned about putting Morgan in a potentially dangerous situation, so he stood, took her by the hand, and walked her back to the coupe. They drove off, with Geddy at the wheel again. When they neared his boardinghouse, Morgan called over the rushing wind and the roar of the engine, "I think I'd better go home now!"

"You need to find out if you're able to stop thinking about me, is that it?"

"Don't make it sound silly. I'm old-fashioned, is there anything wrong with that?" She looked away as if to hide a blush, or a smile. "What are you doing tomorrow?"

"I thought you didn't ask men out."

"I don't. I only asked what you were doing tomorrow."

Pulling in front of his boardinghouse, Geddy finally asked with feigned calm, "Morgan, will you have dinner with me tomorrow night?"

She pretended surprise. "Why, I don't know if I can. I might be jetting off to L. A. or Paris, or somewhere."

"Forget it then," he said with a shrug.

"Oh come on, you know I'm teasing. I'd love to have dinner with you. Don't you worry about a thing. I'll even make the arrangements." She kissed him on his left cheek and gave him a hug. Geddy detected that this was his good-night kiss and stepped out of the car. Morgan climbed over the gearshift and into the driver's seat. "I'll call you tomorrow," she called out excitedly and sped off into the night.

10

On Sunday morning after church, Geddy was standing on the beach at Fifteenth Avenue South. He was wearing denim shorts and a gray sweatshirt. He slipped his sneakers off and waded in the warm water up to his knees, enjoying the feeling of the wet sand. There were few people on the beach at nine A.M., but he knew the crowds would be coming soon. He would enjoy the relative tranquillity while he could.

He looked back towards the street and admired the mansions that lined the beach for miles in each direction. Every house along the beach in Naples has picture windows that look out over perfectly manicured yards, the beach, and finally the gulf. It was very quiet. He couldn't tell if the residents were sleeping or if the houses were empty while the owners spent time in another exotic location. The French Riviera maybe, or the Caribbean, or Aspen? Maybe they lived in New York or Chicago or Boston, and these million-dollar beachfront estates were merely vacation homes to them.

Just then he heard what he thought was Nick's old van pulling up at the end of the cul-de-sac. Moments later Nick appeared, wearing his customary dark brown pants and beat-up work boots. He had on a plain gray T-shirt under an unbuttoned flannel shirt that blew open when the wind caught it just right. Geddy noticed for the first time how thin Nick was. As he approached and smiled faintly, more of a smirk than a smile, Geddy noted his hollow cheeks covered with an ever present dark stubble. He decided he liked Nick. There was nothing put-on about him. He was obnoxious, sure, but basically he seemed fun loving. Geddy didn't always laugh out loud at Nick's jokes, but he was always amused.

"Where's Faith?" asked Nick, without saying good morning. He looked around eagerly.

"She'll be here."

He frowned and rubbed his chin. "I don't have much time. I'm flyin' out to Boston in a couple of hours."

"I thought you were sticking around for a couple of weeks to help me dig up some information for the state attorney?"

"I'm goin' there to talk to a possible witness, Barbara Keenan. She lived behind the real estate office where the third girl was killed."

"You tracked her down already?" Nick shook his head yes. "You aren't wasting any time."

Nick shrugged. "What the hell else have I got to do? I don't have a pretty face like you, it's not like I got any hot dates lined up. I mean, even those stitches look good on you. Now you're not such a pretty boy anymore, you look tough, you know? With that blond hair and a scar you look like a Swedish hockey player or somethin'."

Geddy paced a little in the light surf, then turned back to face Nick. "Why do you insist James Hoffer wasn't the South Beach Butcher?"

"Hey, I'm not the only person who thinks you got the wrong guy," Nick replied.

"There was plenty of evidence."

"It was all circumstantial."

"Circumstantial evidence is still evidence."

"Susceptible to a whole bunch of different interpretations," Nick pointed out.

"What about the newspaper articles they found at James Hoffer's apartment, the ones about the decapitations? He wallpapered his apartment with them."

"No shit. If you killed seven whores, would you go home and wallpaper your place with newspaper clippings about them?"

"You have to admit, Hoffer was sick, a sociopath," argued Geddy.

Nick frowned. "People throw that word around too lightly. A true sociopath is a rare thing, my friend, and they aren't always so easy to spot. They're not like in the movies when they're ugly and have scars and really psycho eyes and little pointy beards like the devil, and they don't work for drug smugglers like Hoffer did. No, Hoffer was a killer, but he was no sociopath. He didn't commit *those* murders."

"What's this about Hoffer working for a drug smuggler?" asked Geddy.

Faith suddenly called out to them and rushed down the beach. She was wearing sandals and cutoff denim shorts and an orange T-shirt that read, "TENNESSEE VOLUNTEERS," in white block letters. "Sorry I'm late," she said, stepping into the surf next to Geddy in her sandals. "What did I miss?"

"Not a thing," replied Geddy.

Nick stuck his neck out in her direction. "I was just about to begin telling the Swede here how the Slasher ripped the hell out of the first girl's throat and watched her blood spurt out and then flow and ooze . . ."

"Are you gonna be like this?" asked Faith angrily, as Nick laughed at her. "Why do you have to be so offensive? If you think you're funny, you're not."

Nick led them up the beach near the sea wall in front of a stately white mansion with bright blue shutters. It was the same spot that Faith and Geddy had come to talk after discovering the newspaper articles on the New Moon Murders.

"This is where it all started," Nick began. He toed the sand with his foot. "Gabrielle Smith. Numero Uno. I know she was at a bar on Fifth Avenue earlier that night, but that's all I know about that. She was found in the mornin', lyin' on her back. The old grandma and grandpa who found the body thought when they first saw her that she was sleepin' on a red beach blanket. Turns out, it was the blood that had gushed out and ran down around her."

Faith blanched. Geddy signaled to Nick to tone it down.

Nick nodded. "When they found her, there was a man's size thirty-two-inch belt wrapped around her arm, and a heroin needle sittin' right next to her. The girl's fingerprints were on the needle, but none others."

"Was any blood recovered from the heroin needle?" asked Geddy.

"The cops never gave out that kind of information, but we're sure she did the heroin. She had needle marks up and down her left arm. So it would've been her blood."

"Unless she shared the needle with the killer," said Faith. "We'll need to verify it to prove it in court."

"The state attorney's office should have lab reports," Nick pointed out. "Anyways, junkies usually wrap somethin' around their arms like a tourniquet, to make it easier to find a vein. So it looks like the killer was here with her for a little while, because he loaned her his belt and she tied it around her arm. Now, come over here." They followed Nick to the sea wall. "Right up here is where they found the knife. It wasn't buried or nothin'. The killer left it pretty much out in the open." Nick leaned against the sea wall. "Okay, that's the first one."

"That's it?" cried Faith. "You're the expert, and that's all you can tell us?"

"That's all there is, babe, other than lab reports. It's common knowledge that the killer didn't leave any prints on the knife. What else is there to know?"

"What about footprints?" asked Faith.

Nick pointed down the beach. "Tell me, Einstein, which prints are yours, mine, and John's?" Faith looked for a few seconds but didn't reply. "You can't tell whose is whose in the dry sand."

"Did any neighbors report seeing anyone?" asked Geddy. "Cars parked on the street, people hanging around? Anything at all?"

"Nobody saw a damn thing. It was pitch black that night, a new moon, remember?"

Nick answered a few more questions before getting impatient. "Okay, I'm runnin' outta time, let's talk about the second murder. It took place about ten blocks down the beach, but I don't have time right now to show you. Basically, the location was identical to this one, maybe a little closer to the stairway."

"What do you mean, you don't have time? What do you think we're paying you for?" asked Faith angrily.

"Nick's going to interview an important witness up in Boston," explained Geddy.

Nick smiled at her victoriously. "If there are no further interruptions, let me tell you about Julieanne Cherube. She was discovered by two little brats. They saw these sea gulls sittin' on top of her and just thought that was the neatest thing they ever seen, until they saw she was splattered with blood. There was a paper cup that she had carried with her from down the beach, where there'd been a keg party. I'm pretty sure she'd been boozin' it up that night. She was lyin' flat on her back, just like the first victim, blood all over the place. This time, the killer didn't use a knife. He used a straight-edge." Nick continued as they followed him up the steps to the cul-de-sac. "The straight-edge was found up the stairs, in some bushes next to the street. The killer probably just dropped it on his way out. Again, no prints were found on it."

"Then the killer was wearing gloves," concluded Geddy.

"Not yet."

"How can you say that?" asked Faith. "What do you think the killer did? Slash their throats and then calmly wipe the weapons clean before running off?"

"Yes, that's exactly what he did," Nick answered. "The knives recovered in the last three murders had lots of blood on them, mostly on the blade. But in the first two murders, there was hardly any blood on the knife or the straight-edge. That means the killer wiped the weapons with somethin', his shirt probably, then left them behind, probably so he wouldn't be caught with them later. But by the third murder he was wearin' gloves, so he didn't have to wipe the prints off, which explains all the blood that remained on them."

"Cute, Nick, but you forgot one thing. Someone sure would look conspicuous walking around during the middle of the hot Florida summer wearing gloves all around town."

"Not if nobody sees you in the dark, you smart-assed little . . ."

Geddy told them both to be quiet. Nick walked to his van. Geddy and Faith followed.

"There's one last thing about that second murder," Nick told them when they reached his van. "Julieanne Cherube was sittin' with someone on the beach. You could tell by the way the sand was moved around where their asses and feet must've been. You know how you sit on the beach and push the sand out in front of you with your feet? Well there were two mounds. That means there's a good chance she was sittin' with the killer. When her body was found, her lipstick was smudged somethin' awful, which leads me to believe the victim and the killer were kissin'."

"Oh my God!" exclaimed Faith, as if she might be sick. "I can't handle this stuff, John. It really creeps me out."

Geddy felt the same way, but concealed it.

"Look, I gotta go," Nick said, looking at his watch. "Sorry to cut it off so short. We can talk when I get back."

"Call me as soon as you get back to town. Thanks a lot, Nick," said Geddy. Nick drove off, leaving Geddy and Faith alone.

"Any objection if I let you and Nick handle the murder details?" asked Faith.

"I'll let you off the hook if you handle the legal aspects. The murder-inheritance statute and all that stuff."

"Deal," she gladly agreed. Faith looked about nervously, obviously with something on her mind. "John, now that Nick's gone, I'd really like to ask you . . . do you . . . I was wondering, if you might want to go out with me tonight. If you're not too busy."

She caught Geddy totally off-guard. "I can't tonight."

She looked disappointed. "Okay, I understand."

"Look, I . . ."

"You're going out with Morgan Gentry, aren't you?"

He raised his eyebrows in surprise. "As a matter of fact . . ."

"I thought so. I knew it by the way she looked at you at the office the other day."

"No, Faith, you don't understand, I haven't been seeing her, it's no big deal . . ."

She opened her car door. "You don't have to explain, really. It's probably better this way. I always heard you shouldn't date people you work with." She put up a good front but he could tell she was disappointed.

"Look, Faith, I'd really like to go out sometime . . ."

She narrowed her eyes. "What do you think I am? You think I'm going to go out with you when I know you're seeing her?"

"I'm not exactly seeing her. We're just going out tonight for the first time . . ."

But Faith got in her car. "I don't need any mercy dates, John. I'm a big girl, just be a man and say no." With that she drove away.

• • •

By the time Geddy pulled up through the guardhouse and walked up to her door on Sunday night, Morgan had already come out of her villa and was waiting for him. He climbed the steps as Morgan smiled at him, looking beautiful. She wore a tasteful designer outfit and her long red curls were tied back with a white bow. Geddy was resolved to play it cool, but as soon as he reached her, she threw her arms around him and gave him a big hug. Geddy hugged her back.

"I hate to hurry you out, but we really should get going." She took Geddy's arm and led him through the parking lot. "Do you know how to drive a boat?"

"A powerboat, sure, but I can't sail," he admitted.

"Fine. I always get a little scared maneuvering through the harbor," she said, but before Geddy could ask her what she meant, Morgan led him right past the parked cars to the edge of the parking lot. They looked out over Venetian Villas' docks, which were between the stilted islandlike foundation of the villas and Gulf Shore Boulevard.

"Your ship, Captain," said Morgan, gesturing toward a twenty-seven-foot Mako. "It was my father's fishing boat." She handed Geddy the keys.

"Where are we going?" he asked when they were on board.

Morgan pulled a bottle of champagne and two glasses from the cooler. "You're the captain but I'm the pilot, so don't worry about that. It's a surprise." She gave him a mischievous look before going to work on the champagne bottle.

Geddy fired up the engines, and after a short warmup, they were off. Morgan stood beside Geddy with a hand on his shoulder as they rode over the wakes of large yachts and sipped expensive champagne. She pointed out beautiful houses and fantastic boats, the homes of famous or powerful people, and the correct path out to the gulf. After traveling less than a mile south through Venetian Bay, they turned west, headed out Doctor's Pass, and were in the Gulf of Mexico.

Once in the open water, Geddy threw down the throttle. They raced south at more than forty knots through the rougher gulf waters, paralleling the beaches of Naples. On their right and just ahead, the sun was a red ball falling in the horizon, surrounded by pinks and reds canvassing the sky, moving Geddy to initiate a kiss.

"What was that for!" she asked over the sound of the engines and the rushing wind as she nestled closer to him.

He smiled but didn't bother to answer. Morgan stood on the seat behind him and wrapped her arms around his neck. They passed the one-thousand-foot Naples Pier and waved to the people fishing or just milling about at the end, then drove for another mile or two, just past Gordon's Pass, where they had sat and kissed the night before.

"With your permission, Captain," said Morgan, saluting him. "I'll take over for a minute."

Geddy moved out of the way as Morgan eased herself in front of the wheel without a bit of hesitation. She turned the boat directly at the beach and raced toward it. As they got closer and closer, Geddy waited for Morgan to slow down, but she charged ahead, unblinking. Thirty feet to shore and they still sped on. He thought about taking the wheel from her. Twenty feet, ten, and then she yelled, "Hold on!" as she pulled all the way back on the throttle and clicked it into neutral. They both jerked forward. By the time they repositioned themselves, the boat had partially coasted up the sand. It was a perfect beaching.

"Well, what do you think?" asked Morgan.

"Very dramatic," he tried to say casually.

Geddy jumped out the front of the boat with the anchor and dug it into the beach in case the tide came in. He helped Morgan down, and she led him up the beach in the impending darkness to a path cut through the palm trees and bushes. She explained to him that they were on Keewaydin Island, where there were no homes and no buildings except for a small hotel with an excellent restaurant. They picked their way through the growth until they ran into a shell path which led to the Keewaydin Club.

A quaint building, Key West style, it fit perfectly into its natural surroundings, with plenty of trees, vines, and bushes for camouflage. As they neared it, the sound of voices and the bustle of a hotel grew louder and louder. It was extremely busy that night—this was tourist season after all—but Morgan knew the manager, so they were shown to an outdoor table immediately. After dinner, Geddy purposely turned the conversation to the trust and Morgan's family.

"As you know, Cynthia and I are cousins," began Morgan. "Adam Gentry was our grandfather. When Grandfather died in

1952, he left a sizable estate to his two children. He left his son Mark, who was my father, a real estate company which consisted of properties scattered throughout Florida. Grandfather left the trust to his daughter Victoria, Cynthia's mother. The company and the trust were worth about the same, but there was a reason Victoria wasn't given the money outright.

"You see, about the time Grandfather fell ill and began to plan his estate, Aunt Victoria was engaged to Benjamin Dole, whom she later married. My father and grandfather didn't trust Uncle Benjamin. They thought that he was after my Aunt Victoria's money, which is quite possible because Adam Gentry was a wealthy, dying man. Also, Aunt Victoria was sweet and charming, but she had no concept of money. She was terribly spoiled. So when Grandfather Gentry created the trust, he named himself as the trustee for life, to manage the money in trust for Victoria's benefit. The trustee is directed to give the beneficiary periodic distributions from the trust, but only enough money for the beneficiary to live in a reasonably comfortable way."

Geddy nodded. "So that way Victoria and Benjamin Dole had enough to live on after they were married, but Benjamin couldn't get his hands on the entire trust principal and run off with it."

"Exactly," she said. "Another provision in the trust directed the trustee and all successor trustees to name their successor in their will. Adam Gentry named my father, Mark Gentry, to succeed him as trustee. In 1990 after my father died and had named me to succeed him, I became trustee. I in turn have named my successor."

"What kind of salary do you earn as trustee?"

"It's not really a salary, it's a commission on the income generated by my investments of the trust principal. The better I invest the trust monies, the higher my commission is. Last year I made about a hundred thousand dollars. And believe me, it's not a very difficult job, especially not for someone with a master's in business and a law degree. I work out of the office in the villa, only a few hours a week."

"Cynthia and Curtis are lucky to have someone as qualified as you to run the trust."

Morgan was happy for the compliment. "I do pretty well, but it's easy when you have forty million dollars to play with."

"Forty million? Cynthia said the trust is worth thirty million."

"Believe me, she never knows what she's talking about," said Morgan matter of factly. "Most of it's in safe investments, blue chip stocks, T-bills. But I've pulled off a few coups in the three years I've been managing the trust. I invested a few million in some psychiatric hospitals which have turned a hefty profit, and I have a few more million in some venture capital deals that are really starting to pay off."

Geddy looked suitably impressed. "Too bad you can't become a beneficiary of the trust and put the money to work for yourself. Why didn't your grandfather provide that the money should go to your father's side of the family if your aunt Victoria's side died out? Why did he make the University of Tampa the contingent beneficiary?"

"My grandfather made his fortune in the 1930s and 1940s in real estate, mostly in the Tampa Bay area, where he lived. He was a real Florida pioneer and was obsessed with the expansion of the state, so the university was important to him. He gave them so much money, they named a building after him. Besides, he provided for my father by giving him the real estate company, so he didn't think it necessary to make him a beneficiary of the trust. I guess, as much as I loved my father, it was his own fault for ruining the company. He blew it, ran the company into the ground, and was left with nothing but the villa and the trusteeship."

The rest of the evening they chatted comfortably, Morgan regaling Geddy with stories of people she had met and places she had been. On the boat ride home, she stood next to him with one hand around his waist, the other on his chest. Whenever he felt courageous enough to pull his eyes away from the dark sea in front of him, they kissed passionately. As they cruised through the bay on the way back to her dock, she squeezed beside Geddy in the driver's seat, put her head lazily on his shoulder, and dozed off. She awoke just as Geddy was ready to dock and nimbly jumped out, securing the bow while Geddy fastened the stern line. Then he walked Morgan to her door. It was 1:30 A.M.

"Would you like . . ."

"Thanks for a great first date," he interrupted. He had made up his mind not to come in, even if all she meant to do was offer him coffee or tea. He was beginning to realize that Morgan was special, so he didn't mind taking it slow.

She didn't hide her surprise. "I usually have to chase men away at the end of a night," she said as he unlocked the door for her and opened it. He handed her the keys and stood back silently, admiring her. "Thank you. It was lovely, and I can't wait for the next time."

With that they kissed and said good night. Geddy was just turning to leave when Morgan tossed him a couple of keys on a ring.

"Why don't you take the coupe? At the risk of sounding like a snob, I don't want my boyfriend picking me up in some old clunker all the time." She smiled at the look of surprise on his face.

"No, I couldn't."

"Oh, go ahead. I always use the sedan anyway. If it would make you feel more comfortable, consider it a trial period. If you like it, maybe you'll want to buy it from me. I do have to watch my money now, you know."

He stepped forward and gave her another soft kiss. "Thanks," he said, trying not to appear too blown away. "I'll call you tomorrow."

Almost two weeks later, Geddy was sitting in his office gulping down cup after cup of coffee, scrambling to finish up a complaint on a laborious contract case. When he finished, he left the draft on his secretary's desk and rushed out the door, down the steps, across the Plaza, and through the maze of expensive boutiques until he came to the Olde Naples Pub. Seated at the bar with two beers in front of him was Nick Farley.

Geddy frowned. "Two-fisted at two in the afternoon? I thought we had a deal, Nick. No beers on the expense account."

"Relax, Chief, one of these is for you." Nick slid one of the beers down to Geddy.

Geddy sat next to Nick at the bar. "Are you going to tell me where you've been for the last two weeks? I thought you skipped out on me."

"I wouldn't dream of it," Nick said through his trademark smirk. "I've been lookin' into things. Where should I start?"

"Did you check up on Curtis?" Nick indicated he had. "Tell

me everything you know."

"Adam Curtis Dole. He goes by the name Curtis," Nick began. "He's forty-one years old. He would've been twenty at the time of the murders in 1972. His mother was Victoria Gentry-Dole, a crotchety old bitch who died when she was fifty-two of Hodgkin's disease. Obviously, there's no chance of foul play in Victoria Dole's death."

Nick flipped some papers and continued. "Victoria Dole was married to Benjamin Dole, who was from a real blue-blood Chicago family, but they lost most of their dough, so Benji's family wasn't rich anymore. They had two kids, Curtis and Cynthia. They both went to a fancy boarding school in Chicago, but they visited home a lot. Cynthia loved Chicago, but Curtis hated it. He liked sailing on the Great Lakes though, and he went to college at Brown University in Rhode Island mostly so he could be near Newport, which is like the sailin' capital of the world. Cynthia went to college in Chicago. Curtis was really smart, but he wasn't much for studyin'. He got great grades though," added Nick and he slid Curtis' college transcript in front of Geddy.

"Okay. So the summer after his sophomore year, Curtis came home to Naples just like he did every summer. That was 1972, the summer when the murders took place. He was home by about the middle of May. Plenty of time to plan and commit the first murder, which was," he flipped another page in his notebook, "June 11. Curtis didn't work at all that summer. His mother had croaked that March, so he lived in the house on Green Dolphin Drive in Naples all alone. The house is owned by the Adam Gentry Trust. Curtis's father spent the summer in Chicago with his family, and Cynthia was in school up there that summer. Curtis and his father weren't talkin' to each other at the time, but I'm not sure why. By this time, the summer of 1972, his mother was six feet under so he was a beneficiary and was gettin' distributions from the trust."

Nick paused to take a long pull of his beer, smacked his lips, slammed his mug down on the table, and resumed.

"So he didn't have to work, he just entered sailing races all the time, but they were only small, local races. Later he turned into a big shit racer. Raced in two America's Cups in the 1980s and a few of those Whitbread races—you know, the around-the-world race? He was in one this year, as a matter of fact. The boat he was in started sinkin' tryin' to get around the southern tip of South America, and they had to quit the race. So he went up to Newport, where he just left a few days ago in some rich guy's yacht. He's sailin' it down to the rich guy's winter house in Palm Beach.

"When he's not out at sea he lives in Naples in the house on Green Dolphin Drive, all by his lonesome since his father died in 1983. His housekeeper says he's due home in a week or two, and then he's supposed to spend a little time in Naples before headin' to San Diego, then Japan and Australia for a good six months, at least."

"What does he do when he's here?" asked Geddy.

"Not too much. Just hangs out and sails around until he finds another race to enter. He's also into skiing and mountain climbing and scuba diving and parachuting, a real adventure guy. He's also really into art. He paints a little, but I've seen some of his stuff. He sucks, if you ask me. He's part owner of a gallery in, let me check this, Waterside Shops In Naples."

"Waterside Shops is a pretty pricey shopping plaza in the north part of Naples," said Geddy.

"Whatever. Anyways, people who know him personally—I said I was a reporter for *Sailing Magazine,* and I was doing a story on him—say he's real laid back, fun lovin', and always looking for somethin' to do. He always seems to have money, from the trust I guess, and he's real generous, always picks up the tab, you know? Speakin' of the tab, can I get another?"

Geddy ordered two more beers.

"He's never been married, no kids . . ."

"Never married?" repeated Geddy.

"Uh, no. He's a homo."

"Gay?" exclaimed Geddy but then tried to hide his shock. He

wasn't the most liberal-minded person around, but he was still disappointed with himself for being pleased that Curtis Dole was gay. He thought it might help their case, and he was ashamed for feeling that way, but the fact was that most jurors would hold homosexuality against Curtis Dole.

Nick, however, was even less tolerant. "Yeah, I know. Fuckin' gay! A regular first-class fruit. Well whatever, don't get me started. That was real hard to find out. I don't think a lot of people know. For some reason Curtis hasn't come out of the closet."

"Does Cynthia know?"

"I don't know, ask her yourself. She's gotta know though."

"Tell me more about what Curtis did during the summer of '72."

"There's not a lot to tell. Curtis lived in Naples, Cynthia was in Chicago, and so was their father. She was gettin' money from the trust too, so she might have been able to afford to hire a killer. But you'll be happy to know, I confirmed that she never came home to Naples that summer. She hates the hot weather, apparently."

"I just don't buy this hired killer theory," said Geddy. "Hiring someone makes it too messy. Who can you trust? One more person knows, and do you really risk going to jail as an accomplice to murder by hiring some brain-dead thug to commit five murders for you? I just think it's much more likely that Curtis did it. Besides, I don't think Cynthia is smart enough to even think of it. From what you tell me, Curtis was the intelligent one."

"Whatever you say, Chief. Anyways, Curtis hung around with this one girl in 1972, Donna Canty, who was kind of a friend. She had the hots for him back then, but after puttin' the moves on him one night, he told her he was gay. I guess he wasn't . . . up for it, if you know what I mean. She says she used to go to his house or they'd ride his dirt bike around, hang out in the few bars they had here back then, sometimes go to parties on the beach, bonfires and that sort of thing. She said he didn't drink much, but he smoked a lot of marijuana."

"Really?"

"Don't be surprised, John-Boy. It was 1972, remember?" He laughed a slow, nostalgic laugh before resuming. "Curtis tried other drugs, too. LSD, heroin, cocaine . . ."

"Heroin?"

"Yeah, I thought that might interest you. Gabrielle Smith was doing heroin on the beach when she was killed." Nick finished his second beer. "Okay, so Donna Canty said he was really smart and funny, and lookin' back, Donna thought that since he was gay, it made it easier for him to talk to girls. Since he wasn't thinkin' about getting laid all the time, like the rest of us, he was just real nice and they liked him. But he never did anything with them," Nick said with a wink.

"All right," said Geddy. "Is that it on him?"

"Yeah, for now. I'll keep digging."

"That's not bad. You've obviously been working hard. Now, what about Cynthia?"

• • •

Cynthia stayed in Chicago after college and married her college sweetheart, Donald Preston, in 1974. Donald Preston made it big in the commodities exchange in Chicago, and as soon as he could afford to, he divorced her. They had no kids.

In 1984 Cynthia remarried, this time to a much older gentleman named Lawrence Tuloch, who died two years later at age sixty-three. She inherited very little thanks to a pre nuptial agreement. Since 1986 she remained single, though there had been proposals.

She lived in a large elegant home in Lake Forest, Illinois. In 1983 Mark Gentry agreed to have the trust purchase a house in Lake Forest for Cynthia to live in since Curtis pretty much had the run of the Naples house. She traveled in a circle of fashion designers, food critics, artists, and others along those lines. She didn't have to work because she received the money from the trust. Cynthia dated fairly often, and while seeing a man, she was completely monogamous. Every man she dated was filthy rich. She was only forty years old and had had a face lift, liposuction, and collagen shots in the skin around her eyes, all of which helped to explain her flawlessly youthful appearance.

Nick explained that Naples had many highly regarded plastic surgeons since so many rich older women could afford them. Other than for those three surgeries, Cynthia never came to Naples. When Geddy asked why Cynthia came to Naples two weeks ago, Nick admitted he had no idea.

Geddy asked what Naples was like back in 1972, so Nick explained that Naples began to boom in the mid-seventies. A construction epidemic swept the region, as the Third Street Plaza and many other shopping and commercial areas were being built, more hotels, more restaurants. Younger people trickled in to work in the new banks, medical offices, hotels, and restaurants that were springing up on every corner. Tourism began to grow exponentially, and many tourists bought and developed land for vacation homes. As air conditioning became more widespread and Florida became more livable, demand for land and homes in Naples grew. During the 1980s Collier County was the fastest-growing county in the country, and that boom continued virtually unabated into the 1990s.

When Geddy got around to asking about the murders, Nick shook his head.

"What I got out of that old broad in Boston was the only additional information I've been able to find. There's nowhere else to look."

"We don't have enough," said Geddy. "We need to give the state attorney more in order to convince him to investigate. I'm meeting with him this afternoon. What did the woman in Boston have to say?"

"She lived next to one of the murder scenes. I'll tell you all about it when I show you and Faith where it happened."

"Faith won't be going to any more of our meetings. She's handling the paperwork."

"I'll miss Faith," Nick said thoughtfully. "She's got one helluva nice, perky body. She should let her hair grow out instead of trying to be Miss Professional Big Shot, but oh, I love those perky bodies.

Just as well though, she's got it bad for you. You get any of her action?"

"Maybe I'll be able to get some leads from the families," said Geddy, ignoring Nick's comments. "After my meeting with the state attorney, I should be able to get access to the police files."

Geddy took the long way to Morgan's place, enjoying driving her car. He put the top down for the first time in a week to enjoy the magnificent evening. It was early March, a beautiful time of the year in Naples, about sixty-nine degrees with low humidity. He pulled up to the Venetian Villas, where the guard opened the gate for him. Geddy passed through and parked next to Morgan's Mercedes. When she answered her door, she was dressed in cream-colored pants and a green silk blouse. But the eye-catcher was the red apron she was wearing.

Morgan flashed a smile and they kissed. "It's so good to see you, honey. I've been waiting for this all day. I hope you're hungry, dinner is almost ready."

"It's great to see you, too. You look particularly stunning tonight."

"Yes, I pulled out all the stops." She did a little twirl in the doorway. "You really like it?" she said, playing along with him by modeling the apron.

"I have a feeling it'll become wildly popular."

Geddy helped her carry dinner out to the table on the ter-race. Out over Venetian Bay, it was twilight, Geddy's favorite time of day. Boats were slowly making their way back to their docks. A private jet flew overhead as they constantly did in Naples, most likely flying its owner down for a weekend of golf, sailing, and fine dining.

Over tea and dessert, Geddy told her all about his meeting with Nick. Morgan had grown accustomed to the idea of the trust terminating in August and didn't mind discussing the Dole case with Geddy. In fact, she had volunteered to read through the reams of documents pertaining to the trust that had accumulated over the years.

"How did your meeting with Charles Warren go?" asked Morgan, referring to the state attorney.

"Not as well as I'd hoped it would. First he thought I was out of my mind, but I managed to convince him I was on to some-thing, and he agreed to investigate. He wasn't happy though. He's just a lazy civil servant. He thinks it's going to be one big headache for him."

Morgan frowned. "You need him though, don't you? If you find out Curtis Dole is the killer, you need him to prove Curtis guilty at trial in order to disqualify Curtis from the trust."

"That's right, I'm at his mercy. He won't even give me access to the New Moon Murder files so I can investigate myself. We almost came to blows over it. I sort of lost my head. I guess the pressure's starting to get to me. You see, Nick found out that Curtis will be coming to town soon, but only for a few days. Then Curtis will be out of the country for at least six months, maybe longer. If Charles Warren doesn't move fast, Curtis will be gone before they can take him into custody. Then this whole thing gets really messy."

She patted his hand reassuringly. "Well, let me get the papers I told you I wanted to show you. They might be able to help." Geddy watched Morgan walk away and climb jauntily up the winding staircase. When she returned from inside, she was carrying a large file folder which she placed on the wicker table. The folder was stuffed with six black binders.

"In these binders and some others upstairs are all of the documents concerning the trust over the years. My father took careful pains to document everything concerning the trust." She laughed. "Trustees are a paranoid lot. We have this duty to keep everything in order. If there are any mistakes, we can be found liable if there are any losses, so I continued his practice of recording everything that occurred and keeping copies of everything. Every communication of any significance concerning the trust is recorded, including letters between the trustee and the beneficiaries, accountants, or lawyers. We even note and summarize our meetings and important telephone calls."

She handed Geddy one of the journals. "I don't really know what you're looking for, but I think I found something interesting. Look at the period for April, 1972."

Geddy scrutinized the binder. It was simply labeled: *Gentry Trust—April, 1972* on the front. It was a chronological collection of notes and letters concerning the trust, rather unofficially compiled, with each page dated and containing the trustee's brief description of whatever action had been taken on the trust. Occasionally there were letters to the trustee or photocopies of letters from the trustee to others. Geddy flipped through the papers until he reached a brief, neatly typed note.

April 10, 1972. Curtis Dole called today. He insists on receiving his first distribution as soon as possible. I told him it would be in the mail to him shortly, he must be patient. It has only been a month since his mother passed away, and there are some administrative details I must attend to. He also demanded a copy of the trust. I assured him there was no need for that, but he insisted.

NOTE: *send him a copy of the trust with his first distribution check.*

Geddy skimmed through a few more entries until he came

across a photocopy of a letter dated April 30, 1972. It was from
Mark Gentry to Curtis, who was still at Brown University in Rhode
Island. It began:

Dear Curtis,

As you requested, I have enclosed your first distribution
check from the trust. I hope you understand the delay in getting you your first check. Please be assured the checks will
arrive from now on, quarterly, without fail.

Reluctantly, and only because you are lawfully entitled
to it, I have also enclosed a copy of the trust. There has never
been any need before for anyone other than myself to have a
copy, and I hope you do not intend to cause trouble with it.
As I have explained to you and Cynthia, it is in my sole dis-
cretion to determine your needs, as this trust only requires
me to provide you with the support you reasonably require.

I am not inclined to provide you with the extravagant
amounts you are requesting, and a judge will surely agree that
I am providing you with more than enough support. You are
young and it is important for you to work and better yourself.
I urge you not to simply live off the trust. You are an intelligent young man, and you have a promising future. I would be
happy to help you find meaningful summer employment here
in Naples, or perhaps some other city if I can.

There are a few other matters I wish to bring to your
attention. You may recall . . .

That was the end of page one. Page two related to other,
unimportant matters, and was signed "Mark Gentry, Trustee."

When he finished, he looked at Morgan. "So, what is it? I
don't see anything earth shattering."

"Listen to this. In going over these indexes for all the years
of the trust, 1952 until now, I noticed there are no other requests
for a copy of the trust. The trustee always simply kept sending the

money so there was never any need for the beneficiaries to have a copy. But Curtis requested one. A couple of months before the murders took place."

"Now I get it," he said, the realization sending a bolt of excitement through him. "If Curtis is the only person who ever requested a copy of the trust, he's one of the only people, outside of you and your father, and some lawyers maybe, who knew who the Measuring Lives were. He's the only person with a motive to kill the Measuring Lives who could have known who they were!"

"Exactly!" declared Morgan, excited now as she saw how pleased Geddy was. "Curtis requested the trust agreement in April, and at the same time that he received it, my father denied his request for more money from the trust."

"Curtis must have been furious," said Geddy, extending their logic. "He didn't want to work, to have to earn a living. He wanted to sail, go mountain climbing, skydiving."

"So after reading over the trust," Morgan picked up the cue, "Curtis discovered the Measuring Lives clause and realized that if something happened to them very soon, twenty-one years later he would be in sole possession of somewhere around twenty million dollars. He could sail through those intervening years living on the trust distributions, comfortable with the thought that by the time he was forty-one-years old, he would be rich."

"So it couldn't be Cynthia," pronounced Geddy. "She couldn't have hired anyone to do it because she never knew who the Measuring Lives were!"

"I didn't even know you were considering that possibility."

"Sure I considered it, but I didn't consider it likely," he replied.

"It couldn't have been her, or anyone she hired. Cynthia Dole never requested a copy of the trust, and she never received one. If she did, it would have turned up here," said Morgan, patting the file folder.

"Since your side of the family was expressly prohibited from any interest in the trust, your . . . uh, father, wouldn't have done anything to them. Once the trust ended, so would the profitable job of being trustee. So we're down to two possibilities. Either Curtis Dole killed the Measuring Lives, or it's one colossal coincidence that these five Measuring Lives were murdered by a serial killer."

"Nobody in their right mind would believe it's a coincidence," she said for both of them.

Geddy tried not to get too carried away but couldn't help jumping out of his seat. "It must be Curtis!" He was ready to celebrate, until he noticed the smile on Morgan's face had just a trace of sadness in it. "Morgan, I'm sorry. I've been so wrapped up in this that I forgot. The end of the trust means you lose your trustee's salary, and here I am happy about it."

"Listen, I understand. I've resigned myself to the fact that the trust is ending. I'm just glad I can help you." She stood and kissed him meaningfully.

Geddy held her at arm's length and looked at her gravely. "You know, as the trustee, you should really be neutral in all this. It's going to look bad if the lawyer for one beneficiary is dating the trustee."

"I think," she interrupted, fitting her body up against his, "that you're making too much of it. As trustee I'm supposed to oversee the fair and disinterested business of the trust. If one of the beneficiaries kills five people to bring about an early termination of the trust, my duty is to the trust. To ensure that that person doesn't benefit. So don't try to use that excuse to get rid of me," she teased provocatively. She was flush against him, moving her hips and breasts against him as she spoke, her words almost a whisper.

Geddy put his hands on her hips and held her tightly. He kissed her with growing passion as their hands at first roamed politely over each other, then with more intensity. Morgan started kissing Geddy's neck, then unbuttoned his shirt and kissed his chest.

Geddy was ready to take their relationship to the next level. "Which is the fastest way to the bedroom, the elevator or the stairs?"

"I'm afraid," she breathed excitedly, "that neither way is terribly fast."

Geddy swept her up and gently laid her down on the floor. They stayed there until morning.

• • •

"Another Sunday morning spent at another murder scene," Nick lamented as he and Geddy walked to the rear of Naples Realty, located on Fifth Avenue. It was part of a long strip of shops that had been renovated several times since the murders, cleansed of death, and dolled up like the rest of the town to display its facade of perfection.

In the rear of the building, there was a small, secluded parking lot. They walked down the driveway leading from the street and stopped as Nick pointed upward. "See that light," he said, indicating a light that looked like a streetlight but was attached to the side of the building and hung a few feet over the lot. "That light was workin' only an hour before Angelica Grevey was murdered. But when they found her body sometime before midnight, the light was busted."

"Stopped working or shattered by someone?" asked Geddy.

"Shattered by someone. The victim's car was parked over here, by the back door. When the police got here that night, they found the lot in total darkness. Remember, it was a new moon. Her tire was flat, and her trunk was open. The spare tire and the jack had been moved but weren't taken out of the trunk yet."

"The flat tire was caused by the killer, right?" asked Geddy, remembering that detail from one of Nick's old newspaper stories.

"Yeah, the knife that was used to kill Angelica was dropped next to her. Like I told you a few weeks ago, by murder number three, the killer was wearin' gloves, so he didn't wipe the knife clean. It was full of blood, as you can imagine, but some rubber from the tire was still stuck in the jagged edges on the top of the knife."

Geddy took a deep breath. "How was she found? Just the usual, on the ground, covered in blood?"

"Yeah, and that's it except for what the Boston woman,

Barbara Keenan, told me." He walked away from the building towards the back of the lot and looked through the bushes where there was a small, neatly kept white-brick house. "See that house right there? In 1972 Barbara Keenan and her husband lived there. She seems like one of those nosy neighbors, always knows what's goin' on in the neighborhood, you know? She said she was in her kitchen when she heard a woman shout out, 'Shit, stupid car!' from somewhere in this lot. But it was dark, so she didn't see anything. A few minutes later she looked out again. She saw a flashlight and heard a man's voice as well as a woman's voice."

"So the killer slashed her tire, then when Angelica came out, the killer offered to help."

"And then he slashed her, too. First he knocked out the light, though."

Geddy was nodding his head. "This one seems pretty carefully planned, like the killer knew who he was going after."

They both climbed into Morgan's coupe. Nick directed Geddy down Fifth Avenue, then left onto Tamiami Trail. They traveled seven or eight blocks until reaching a four-star restaurant on the left side of the road. Nick told Geddy to park in the back. They got out of the car, and Nick guided Geddy over to a house with an iron fence, two well-kept gardens, and a gravel walk.

"This house wasn't here in 1972," Nick explained. "It was a small dirt lot that they used for overflow parkin' for the restaurant, like on weekends and stuff. Sally Baumgartner's car was parked in this lot, about forty feet from the street. It was pretty dark in the lot, but apparently she was meetin' a date here so maybe it doesn't seem so stupid to park in such a secluded, dark spot with a serial killer on the loose. I don't know, it was pretty dumb if you ask me."

"She's the one who was stabbed before her throat was slit, right?"

Nick shook his head yes. "With a steak knife. Twelve times, as best as they could count 'em."

"Well, what's the story?"

"The cops got a call around nine at night. An anonymous call, from a man who claimed there was a dead girl in the lot. When the cops got here, they found her car over there, with the driver's side door open. It was one of those seventies' muscle cars, a two-door Monte Carlo, I think. The door was open and the driver's seat was pushed forward. Her purse was on the floor in the back. There was a stack of books on the passenger seat. She had told her parents she was goin' to the library, but she obviously lied. She'd made a reservation at the restaurant for two people at eight-thirty."

"Where was she killed?"

"Well, there was a foot mark on the side of her car. It was made by her. Apparently the killer came up from behind and tried to slash her neck, but she pushed off with her leg against the car, and they fell backwards a few feet. She wasn't stabbed until they got over there, about ten feet from the car." He pointed at a spot in the yard. "She put up a fight so the killer must've stabbed her in desperation. Whatever the case, he still slit her throat before leavin'. Nothin' else interesting to report except for the footprints."

"They found footprints?" asked Geddy with great surprise.

"Yeah, the killer wore a size ten-and-a-half."

Geddy had been pacing but stopped in his tracks. "Why the hell didn't you tell me that before! I'm tired of your screwing around, Nick, this is elementary! All we need to do is find out if Curtis wears size ten-and-a-half shoes!"

"I already checked on that," Nick said, and he wore a crooked smirk. "I got my hands on the records from his draft-board physical, from 1970. He wore a size thirty-two inch belt, and a size ten-and-a-half shoe."

Immediately upon arriving back at his office after a meeting with Charles Warren, Geddy received a call from Morgan. She told him that she had just talked to Curtis Dole. He was in Beaufort, South Carolina, en route to Palm Beach, and he needed her to wire him some money. She did so and said nothing about what was happening. Curtis also told her that he'd be in Naples in a few days and would be staying for a week before heading to Australia.

After hanging up with Morgan, Geddy walked into Faith's office and slumped down in a chair. "It's all over, Faith."

"What are you talking about?"

"I just came from Charles Warren's office. In no uncertain terms, he refuses to prosecute Curtis Dole for the New Moon Murders. He says there's no evidence. He won't even let us look at his files."

"That fat bastard!" cried Faith, who was finally convinced Curtis Dole was the killer. "How can he say there's no evidence? With what we already know, we could build a decent case against

Curtis, not to mention what we're bound to turn up. We have to subpoena those records!"

He shook his head in defeat. "It's no use, Faith. Without Warren to prosecute Curtis, there's nothing we can do. He absolutely refuses to charge Curtis. I almost got in a fight with him over it. Believe me, he's not going to change his mind. It's out of our hands."

"What do you mean?"

"In ten days Curtis will be out of the country for at least six months," explained Geddy. "Without the state attorney's files, we'll never get a case together in ten days, so we'll never convince Warren to prosecute. By the time Curtis is back in the country, the trust will have vested. He'll already have the money. It will be too late."

Faith narrowed her eyes. "So what? We can go with the civil trial. I'll draft a lawsuit, and we'll serve it on Curtis before he leaves the country."

"What are you talking about, a *civil* trial? The law is clear, the alleged murderer has to be found guilty before being prevented from inheriting. If the state attorney won't try Curtis, it's all over."

"It's not over. *You* can try Curtis. You John, personally."

It took Geddy a moment to figure out what she was talking about. When the state, through the prosecuting attorney, charges someone for murder, the resulting case is a criminal case. In a criminal case, the penalties are jail or probation or other punishments. But in a civil case, it is one party versus another. No one goes to jail. Usually what is at stake is money or return of property or an injunction or some other remedy from the court.

"You're the one who brought up the murder-inheritance statute, I thought you knew," explained Faith. "A defendant has to be 'adjudicated in a court of law' in order to be prevented from benefiting from their crime. It doesn't say anything about it having to be a criminal trial. It can be civil or criminal. If we think Curtis killed the Measuring Lives, we can file a suit on behalf of Cynthia accusing him of the murders. Dole versus Dole. If you win the trial and prove Curtis guilty, he won't go to jail, but Cynthia will end up with the entire forty million. I can't believe you didn't know this."

"Why would I bother with Charles Warren if I can handle it myself!"

"I thought you were hoping to look at the state attorney's files," she answered.

Geddy felt the pressure on him instantly, but also a charge of excitement, a thrill he could never duplicate other than when he was going after a killer.

"What are we waiting for!" He jumped out of his seat and grabbed Faith's telephone. "Ruth, get Nick Farley over here right away!" He slammed the phone down. "Faith, I need you to get started on drafting the lawsuit. Just throw in as many facts as we can allege for now." He turned to rush out.

Faith was startled at his sudden transformation. "Where are you going?"

He forced a smile. "We've got one week, Faith. I'm back in the murder business!"

•   •   •

Three days later, Nick Farley was sitting in Geddy's office. "Curtis Dole got to town yesterday. I stayed up all night following him around," the reporter said proudly.

"Why did you follow Curtis? The murders were twenty years ago. What did you expect to discover? He didn't see you, did he?"

"No, I'm a pro," Nick answered confidently. "I just thought maybe he'd do somethin' interesting, like slit some girl's neck." Nick chuckled.

"What did he do?"

"Not a damn thing. I found him in the afternoon at his house in Naples, in an area called Port Royal. Anyway, he went out to eat with a married couple, the Jensens. It was just the three of 'em, they went to a little place in Tin City and stayed 'til ten. Then Curtis went to the beach."

"Which beach?"

"Down around Eighteenth Avenue South. He had a couple

fishing poles. He cast out into the gulf and stuck 'em in the sand and sat there drinkin' a couple beers he brought along and listened to a talk show on the radio. He didn't catch anything, went for a swim, and then straight home. I waited outside his house all night to make sure he didn't go out again. He didn't. I think he went right to bed."

"Don't waste your time following him anymore," said Geddy. "We have less than a week to find out if Curtis Dole killed those Measuring Lives. After that, it'll be too late. That means no more screwing around, Nick. We can't accuse the guy of murder unless we know we can prove it."

"Relax, Chief, we've got plenty of time. I even got a lead on another possible witness, but she can wait. I'm beat. I hardly slept last night. I knocked on your door this mornin', but you didn't answer."

"I was at Morgan's," said Geddy. "If I'm not home or at the office, you can try to reach me there." He gave Nick the number. "Don't be a wise guy if you call there."

Nick made a face to indicate he knew better. "Hey, how you've you been? Anybody pull a knife and sneak up on you lately?"

"No, I haven't had any problems. I don't know what to make of it."

Nick leaned closer and glanced over his shoulder before whispering to Geddy. "Have you considered the possibility that Curtis didn't do it, and now that the real killer knows you're going after Curtis, he, or she, has decided to leave you alone?"

"Nick, there's no question Curtis killed those girls."

"It looks like it, but watch your back, kid," Nick warned him. "Don't trust anyone. There's a lot of fuckups out there."

One week later, Geddy walked into Jensen's Designs alone. The art gallery was located in the Waterside Shops pavilion in North Naples, tucked within the interior of the exclusive collection of boutiques and studios and restaurants. There were several people milling about looking at the paintings that hung on the walls. An incense candle burned in one corner, giving the gallery a bohemian atmosphere, almost mystical.

Standing on a ladder in the narrow east wing of the gallery was a man wearing faded jeans and a colorful paisley button-down shirt. He was about Geddy's height, but very thin, particularly in the face. Geddy noticed the resemblance between Curtis and Cynthia by the nose. They both had that thin, prominent nose.

His short black hair was receding from his temples, and his face was a mixture of scars and sun-inflicted wrinkles, particularly around the eyes, which didn't make him look older than his forty-one years, just more rugged and weather-beaten. He was changing a light bulb in the small chandelier than hung just above him.

Geddy watched Curtis as he worked, waiting to be noticed, taking this opportunity to size him up. He caught a brief look at the callused palm of one of Curtis' hands and knew it must be from the work on the boats. He grew excited and adrenaline pulsed through his veins when he saw Curtis's boat shoes stepping down the ladder.

"Hello," Curtis Dole said to Geddy, a little startled to find someone staring at him.

Geddy was dressed in his newest, darkest suit, a chalk-striped charcoal-gray number with a stylish blue tie and shiny black wingtips. He just stared back at Curtis.

"Can I do something for you?" asked Curtis with a friendly, but puzzled tone.

"Curtis Dole?"

"Yes, I'm Curtis Dole. What, is there something wrong? Who are you?" asked Curtis, beginning to realize Geddy was not there to buy a painting.

Geddy turned to look out the window where a Collier County sheriff was watching. He nodded, and the sheriff immediately headed for the front door.

"You're a killer, and I'm gonna prove it."

"What the hell are you talking about?" replied Curtis, raising his voice a little. "Get the hell out of here!"

At that moment the sheriff walked up to them. "Curtis Dole?" he asked, his uniform making any introduction unnecessary.

"Yes. What's going on?"

"I'm authorized by law to serve this complaint and related documents on you." The sheriff handed the documents to Curtis, who took them, dumbfounded.

"Complaint? What's this all about?"

"I think you know, Curtis. You did a lot of planning twenty years ago to get away with those murders," said Geddy, maintaining his attitude, "but you didn't plan on me."

"What the hell are you talking about?" cried Curtis incredulously, but Geddy wasn't fooled. Surely, Curtis must have known this day might come.

"I just wanted to see you, Curtis, and I want you to get a good look at me, because just like you hunted down those five girls, I'm coming after you." Geddy spoke softly but with deadly seriousness so that Curtis could make no mistake about it.

Geddy walked away with the sheriff following him out. Customers turned to see what was happening as Curtis shouted after them. "I don't know what the hell you're talking about! What is this? I don't understand! What's happening?"

The night before the trial began, Geddy lay awake in Morgan's bed, his right arm under her head. He watched her as she slept and marveled at how she had been able to put up with him over the course of the last few months. He'd been moody and short tempered and an overall bundle of nerves ever since the trial date had been set. He was fortunate if he got a couple of hours of sleep a night. The trial preparation was taking a toll on him, but she was always there to help. He swore he'd make it up to her after the trial.

The trial.

His thoughts turned to the trial again, as they always seemed to do. When he left Miami, he thought there would be no more murder trials. Maybe he should have left it that way. Even before he was forced out, his six-year experiment with the Miami state attorney's office couldn't be considered a success. He would never get the sight of his parents' bloody bodies out of his head. He would never forget finding his sister lying in the bathtub, blue face, white lips, eyes mercifully closed. *Mercifully* because he didn't think he would have been able to handle it if she had stared back at him that morning, asking him how he did it, how he always seemed to carry on as if their parents' deaths didn't affect him. Deirdre had reached the point where she wouldn't leave the house because she was so frightened of what might be waiting for her outside.

Geddy had those same fears when he was younger, but he took it upon himself to confront them. From the day he started law school, he knew what he was going to be. A prosecutor. He'd get those madmen in the courtroom, and he'd enjoy watching them squirm, making them cry on the stand, begging for mercy. He wouldn't be ruled by fear like his sister was. The killers would be afraid of *him*.

For six long years, he thought that was true. He became the most feared prosecutor in the most violent city in the country, but in time he learned it didn't mean a thing. He never could seem to do enough. There were so many of them. They had hungry eyes and hard faces, and they always denied the murder or the rape or the drug dealing, or they bragged about it, but they were never afraid of him. Even after he proved their guilt, they would go kicking and screaming, threatening to kill him or the judge or the cops just as soon as they got out, which was usually after serving only a fraction of their sentence. He learned it was pointless, but he couldn't bring himself to get out, to try to move on and live a normal life. He couldn't give up what he knew he was meant to do.

Then came his last case.

The three months he spent working on the South Beach Butcher case were the toughest of his life. The media attention was overwhelming. The pressure from his superiors unrelenting. Everywhere he went, people asked him about the case. The families of the victims were demanding justice, they were demanding the death penalty. The police kept screwing up. Evidence was lost. Other evidence somehow appeared out of nowhere. The state attorney and the mayor called him into their offices. Geddy wasn't

convinced James Hoffer was guilty. He was worried that the police
had manufactured the case, that they had set up James Hoffer to
take the rap. Geddy tried to prove that, but he couldn't. He wanted
to withdraw from the case, but it was an election year and the case
was too big, the state attorney needed his top man working on it.
Geddy couldn't sleep. He lost weight. He received death threats
saying they knew where he was, so he cleared out of his apartment and moved from motel to motel. It didn't help. He knew he
was being followed, but nobody believed him.

Then after he won the case, he was sent away.

Now, a year later, he received word that James Hoffer's conviction had been reversed on appeal. Maybe that was justice,
because James Hoffer might, in fact, be innocent. Whether he was
innocent or not, they were going to set free the man who Geddy
proved committed the most brutal murders he'd ever seen.

Other than his parents' murders.

Why had he been so excited last year when he discovered that
the Measuring Lives had been murdered? he asked himself. It was
because he missed it. It was only a few weeks after he left Miami,
but he missed the hunt, he missed putting the case together,
missed being hot on the trail of a killer. He knew this case would
be all his, too. No state attorney, no mayor, no police. He was calling the shots this time, so there would be no politics involved. He
always knew he was too emotionally involved and stressed out and
he didn't miss the politics, but the truth was he loved it. A psy-
chologist would tell him his life has been dedicated to avenging his
parents deaths. He'd never catch their killer, but he sought
revenge on others just like him. He didn't realize it before, but
maybe that's really what he was after all the time. Revenge.

Most people would give anything to live in a place like Naples,
have a girlfriend like Morgan, make a lot of money, drive a beautiful car, go out on the boat, eat at the best restaurants, and attend
all of the society functions. But nothing charged him up like the
power he felt when he got just a little bit of revenge.

Could he ever get enough revenge for what happened to his

family?

Don't think about them.

He made himself think about the trial. Was he ready? Maybe. No. He didn't know. What about the photographs and the coroner's reports and the lab reports that were missing? Charles Warren said they got lost over the years. Was the state attorney lying? No, why would he lie? Besides, Geddy didn't care if he was lying or not. No doubt that evidence would have helped the case, but he didn't think he could have handled it. The photographs of the victims must have been gruesome. The lab reports weren't always bad, but the coroner's reports were so hard for him to take. Stomach contents, bodily fluids, the depth of the stab wounds, the details of the decapitation. No, he wasn't up to all that.

The sight of his parents' bodies flashed before his eyes.

Stop!

Morgan awoke and rolled over to face him.

"Is everything all right, John?" she asked sleepily.

"Everything's fine. Go back to sleep."

16

On February 27, 1994, just over a year after Geddy had arrived in Naples, the trial of *Dole v. Dole* began.

"Mr. Geddy. Opening statement," called Judge Frost from his lofty perch behind the massive judge's bench. Behind him was the seal of the state of Florida in bronze, flanked by an American flag and the flag of the state of Florida.

Geddy stood with some trepidation, then approached the jury slowly, the tapping of his shoes echoing like trumpets announcing his arrival. He had lost weight, his eyes were puffy, and the scar under his right eye stood out prominently against the paleness of his skin.

The courtroom was new, modern, bright, packed with spectators and media. Geddy took a brief look at Curtis Dole, who was wearing a standard blue suit and blue tie, looking remarkably innocent. Beside him was the debonair Earl Blue, Curtis's attorney, looking as dapper as ever, and next to Earl Blue was a young attorney named Fred Lee. They tried to stare Geddy down, like prizefighters before a bout, but Geddy didn't blink.

What a perfect jury, he thought as he stopped before them. Naples took its jury pool from the list of registered voters. Since most of the rich people in Naples didn't live there year round, they were registered to vote in their places of residence up north. That meant the jury pool was made up of retirees who lived in Naples year round but weren't wealthy, and of locals. As Geddy had learned from his buddies on the softball team, the locals hated rich people.

He took a deep breath and began, his speaking voice clear and true. "Have you ever watched the game show *Concentration*? Well, in case you haven't, the game centers around a large board which is divided into numbered boxes. Each contestant picks two numbers, which flips those boxes around, revealing a prize. If the prizes behind the numbers picked match, the two squares are flipped again, revealing a part of a puzzle. These puzzles are usually cleverly designed, but they're not difficult to solve when you see the entire puzzle, especially when the host explains it after the puzzle is solved. In fact, most contestants solve the puzzle long before all of the squares are turned. That is, they solve it when only a *part* of the puzzle is revealed."

Now Geddy started pacing, sometimes with his hands by his side, sometimes using them to make a point, and very often with his hands clasped behind his back. He looked very relaxed and confident. He was not.

"This trial will be a little like that. *Concentration*. Only, this isn't a game. This is a very, very serious matter. You see, this is basically a murder trial, ladies and gentlemen, and the evidence will show that Adam Curtis Dole," he said, walking to the defense table and pointing briefly at Curtis, "is a very clever, calculating killer. For over twenty-one years, he got away with the murders of five young, innocent, unsuspecting women, and he only left us enough clues to see a *portion* of the puzzle. I don't mind telling you, we may not see the entire puzzle at the end of the trial. But we will know more than enough for us to solve it."

Geddy briefly described each murder and what was found at each murder scene. He purposely did not get into details. He simply wanted to enlist the jurors' aid in helping him solve this mystery, and he didn't want to tip off the defense any more than necessary.

Finally, he announced in a loud voice, "Ladies and gentlemen, now, over twenty-one years later, after the police have given up, frustrated without a motive to link the murders, we know who the killer is. Not only that, but the killer's motive is now crystal clear: twenty million dollars!"

Geddy then explained at length Curtis Dole's motive. He told the story of Adam Gentry and his children and grandchildren. He went through the ascendance of Morgan's father and then Morgan to the role of trustee. He read relevant portions of the trust aloud to the jury. He pointed out who the beneficiaries were and how much money they received per year. Most importantly, he instructed them on the rule against perpetuities and explained the savings clause.

Then he explained the significance of the Measuring Lives and made sure the jury understood that Curtis and Cynthia couldn't receive the money from the trust until twenty-one years after the Measuring Lives were dead. He then slowly walked back to the plaintiff's table and picked up the trust. He took his time returning to his spot in front of the jurors, letting the curiosity build.

"Now, here's the rub," he said almost in a whisper, as if he were sharing a secret with the jury. "The names of those five young women are Gabrielle Smith, Julieanne Cherube, Angelica Savasta, Sally Baumgartner, and Deborah Moore. They were the five victims of the murders during the summer of 1972. And get this." He paused again for dramatic effect. "The five Measuring Lives are listed in the trust in the exact same order in which they were killed!"

There were audible gasps from those seated in the audience. At least two jurors' mouths dropped open.

"Curtis Dole killed them! He killed them in 1972 and intentionally made it look like a serial murderer was loose. Curtis knew that if even he were charged with the murders when the trust connection was found, nobody could prove him guilty beyond a reasonable doubt. But Curtis Dole fouled up there. You see, this isn't your typical murder trial, and I don't have to prove Curtis Dole guilty beyond a reasonable doubt.

"Just go ahead and erase that phrase from your mind, it doesn't apply here. This is a civil trial. I'm not a prosecutor. I represent the other beneficiary of the trust, Cynthia Dole. If you find Curtis Dole guilty, he will not go to jail. But to a spoiled, greedy, cold-blooded killer like Curtis Dole, we can do the next best thing: if you find him guilty of those five murders, he won't see a penny of the money he killed for. His half of the trust will go to his sister, Cynthia Dole.

"This is a civil trial, ladies and gentlemen, and that's very important for another reason. You see, the burden of proof is different in a civil trial, it's not 'beyond a reasonable doubt.' There's a lesser burden of proof in a civil trial, it's easier for us to find him guilty. The burden of proof in this trial is 'clear and convincing evidence.'

"What is clear and convincing evidence? It's somewhere between 51 percent and beyond a reasonable doubt. That's not a very specific definition, but I want you to think back to the game *Concentration*. How much of the puzzle do you need to see to be sure of the answer? Only enough for you to be clear about what the answer is, not the whole thing. There will be things we can't explain, because only Curtis Dole knows them. But if I can give you enough of the puzzle for you to see that Curtis Dole committed those murders—just enough for you to solve the puzzle, you don't need to see the whole thing—then you can find him guilty.

"As the trial proceeds, I will present witnesses who will begin telling you the details of the trust and the details of the murders. This entire time, there's one thing you must keep in mind. It is the most important aspect of this case, the part of the case that cannot be questioned, the part of the case that's similar to flipping over most of the puzzle in *Concentration*: Curtis Dole is the only person with a motive who could have killed the five young women! He's the only person who could stand to benefit from those murders who could have known who the five Measuring Lives were!

"It becomes very simple, ladies and gentlemen." Geddy paused and looked briefly at each juror. "Either the killer was Curtis Dole, or it's a tremendous coincidence, a billion to one shot, that a serial killer that summer just happened to kill the five young women named in the trust. Think about it. The odds against a psychopath picking these particular five young women randomly out of the entire population of Naples are astronomical.

"It had to be Curtis Dole. So what I request of you for the next few days is your concentration. Look for the clues that Curtis left behind, look at his motive and his ability to commit all five of the murders. *Concentration*. Let's not permit a greedy, vicious killer to be rewarded with twenty million dollars.

"Thank you for your attention, and thank you in advance for your concentration."

Geddy turned and slowly walked back to his chair, seeing the somber faces of the families of the victims, as well as the lawyers from his firm, other than Jeffrey, sitting in the gallery behind the plaintiff's table. He then took his seat next to Faith, Cynthia, and Morgan. Morgan had been brought in as a nominal plaintiff in order to safeguard the assets of the trust, as was her duty as trustee. Geddy was seated with the three most important women in his life.

• • •

The judge invited Earl Blue to give his opening statement.

"Good morning. As you know, my name is Earl Blue, and I'm the attorney for Curtis Dole, sitting over there." He nodded in Curtis's direction, momentarily halting his monotonous and standard introduction. Earl Blue was a dignified forty-five-year-old gentleman who was always dressed to the max, his hair always slicked just right. But he was what Nick Farley called a pretender:

all style, no skill. He was filthy rich, always well tanned and thought of his law practice as a respite from his jet-setting lifestyle. He had made his excellent reputation by settling most of his cases and taking only sure winners to trial. In addition, he once represented a celebrity's son. Though he lost the case, simply being hired enhanced his reputation in Naples legal circles.

"Mr. Geddy would have you believe that Curtis Dole is the only person who could have committed these murders. Good people of the jury, there are at least two other equally plausible possibilities. First, that it's just a coincidence the five New Moon Murder victims were the five girls named in the trust. Do not simply discard this possibility, as Mr. Geddy tried to persuade you to do. You will hear an expert on serial killers testify that these murders were classic serial killings and not the only murders the real New Moon Slasher ever committed.

"The second possibility, and one that we will prove is just as possible, if not more probable than Curtis Dole killing the five girls, is that the plaintiff, Cynthia Dole, paid to have the five girls killed."

This caused a small stir among the onlookers, and surprised even Geddy.

"What you'll see, members of the jury, is that the reason Mr. Geddy is talking about *Concentration* and missing pieces of the puzzle is because he really doesn't have any pieces of the puzzle. He has a few coincidences, that's all. Circumstantial evidence. He has no fingerprints. No blood samples. No eyewitnesses. He has nothing that links Curtis Dole to the murders.

"I, too, want you to concentrate. Concentrate on the murders themselves. Is there any evidence to prove, clearly and convincingly, that Curtis Dole committed those murders? If you concentrate, members of the jury, you'll find that Curtis Dole did not kill those girls."

Earl Blue looked down at his notes for a few seconds. He always carried a yellow legal pad with him when he addressed the jury or examined a witness and would frequently pause to refer to it. He flipped a page and continued on in his dull, patrician tone.

"Let's look at the murders, shall we? The first one was . . ." he paused and looked down at his notes. "June 11, 1972."

He continued on, discussing each murder and explaining what the jury could expect to hear from the witnesses. He was extremely boring and very long winded, but after hearing his opponent's opening statement, Geddy was concerned that somehow Earl Blue knew something Geddy didn't know. That somehow Earl could prove that in 1972 Cynthia knew who the Measuring Lives were and therefore could have had them killed.

•   •   •

The rest of that first day was spent on Geddy's first two witnesses, Dr. Paul Davidson and George Casserly. Dr. Davidson was a former New York University Law School professor of Geddy's and was called to explain the intricacies of the Adam Gentry Trust: who the beneficiaries were; the fact that neither Morgan nor her father could hope to receive money through the trust, other than the trustee's percentage; who the trustee had been and currently was; and the fact that it was a support trust and the amount of the distributions was controlled by the trustee alone. Dr. Davidson also explained the rule against perpetuities, the savings clause, and the Measuring Lives. He made Curtis's motive quite clear.

The second witness was George Casserly, a former Naples police officer who worked on the New Moon Murder investigation in 1972. George Casserly was called to introduce what was found at every murder scene. This was where Geddy offered up his most tantalizing toys of the case: the knives. The faces of the jurors grew astonished as Geddy let them handle the three hunting knives, the straight-edge, and the steak knife. They were holding the actual knives that they had heard so much about twenty years ago.

Otherwise, George Casserly simply told the jury the details of the murders, much as Nick had told Geddy almost a year before. Nothing George Casserly said seemed to point towards Curtis. George was just the set-up man.

17

The next morning back at the courthouse, after another sleepless night, Geddy called his third witness.

Gregg Smith was the brother of Gabrielle Smith, the victim who was found on the beach with a belt tied around her arm and a heroin needle beside her. He was five years older than his deceased sister, which put him now at age forty-five.

Geddy began by asking Gregg Smith to describe his sister. He told the jury Gabby was extremely pretty, that she could have been a model if she wanted. She had long brown hair and was very thin. Her friends called her Twiggy. Geddy let Gregg Smith continue to talk about Gabby for a few minutes, to gain sympathy for her from the jury. Then he asked about the heroin.

"Yes, she'd started getting mixed up in heroin," said Gregg Smith somberly. "It was 1972, and she was nineteen. I guess all of her new friends had been doing it, so she got involved, too. Unfortunately, I'd just started graduate school in Atlanta and wasn't there all year to protect her."

Geddy was standing at the end of the jury box opposite the witness stand so the jury would not focus on him, but on the witness. "How did you find out about her heroin use?"

"A friend of hers, one that wasn't into heroin, called me in Atlanta. She said Gabby had stopped hanging around with her and was spending her time with a different crowd and was shooting heroin, smoking marijuana."

"What do you remember about the night she was murdered?"

"I was home for the summer. I wasn't married yet, so I went out with a couple of old friends to Lindy's Pub, on Fifth Avenue. It's not there anymore, but it was where the young people used to go. Lindy's served alcohol to minors. It was Ladies Night, so all women drank for free. A lot of girls would show up and therefore, a lot of guys, too."

"Was Gabby at Lindy's Pub that night?"

"Yes, she was there with her new friends. I didn't like them at all and told Gabby that, but she laughed it off. She was pretty drunk by the time I showed up. I was disappointed in her."

"Did you spend time with her at the bar?"

"Only briefly. Like I said, I was disappointed with her and told her I didn't want to be around her when she behaved the way she was behaving. Those were the last words I ever said to her." The witness began to choke up.

"What happened?"

"Well, I stayed at the bar until closing. It was getting pretty empty, and I didn't see Gabby, so I assumed she left. I found one of her new friends, who told me Gabby made a score and left."

"Made a score?"

"Yes. She found somebody who had heroin, and she left to go do it."

"At the time, did you know where they went?"

"No."

"Did you ask who she went with?"

"Yes, but her friend didn't know. Gabby never said. She just said she made a score and headed for the door."

Geddy paced a little. "How did you find out about the murder?"

Gregg Smith took a deep breath. "It was the next day. My parents and I got a call from the police. They told us . . ." He choked up, just short of crying. "They said she'd been murdered. Her throat had been slit open. On the beach. She was dead . . ." Geddy paused to allow Gregg Smith to try to regain his composure. "It didn't make sense," the witness continued emotionally. "She was a good girl. She got a little mixed up in drugs, but she was a good person. Until you told me that some rich son of a bitch used her in that trust . . ."

"Objection!" shouted Earl Blue.

"Thank you, Mr. Smith," said Geddy before the judge responded. "That's all I have, Your Honor."

Earl Blue's cross-examination failed to elicit anything noteworthy, and the witness was excused. Gregg Smith walked shakily away from the witness stand, stealing a last look of disdain at Curtis Dole, who twisted uneasily in his chair.

• • •

Geddy's next witness was Margaret Brennan, an old friend of Julieanne Cherube, the second victim. As George Casserly had explained to the jury the day before, it appeared Julieanne had been sitting next to someone on the beach that night and that the police believed she kissed the killer before being slashed with the straight-edge.

With tears in her eyes, Margaret Brennan described Julieanne Cherube as the kindest and funniest person she had ever known. Though Julieanne was extremely boy-crazy, she wasn't particularly pretty and didn't get many dates. Margaret explained that she and Julieanne began the night at Margaret's house, where Julieanne had arranged a surprise birthday party for her. The party was a huge success. Most of the young people in the small town showed up. After a few hours, the party moved to the beach, a few blocks away. There was already a slightly older group of young people partying around a bonfire, so Margaret, Julieanne, and the rest of their party joined in. Margaret got drunk and lost track of Julieanne.

In the morning, the police arrived at her house and told her that Julieanne Cherube had been murdered on the beach, ten blocks from where the party had been the night before.

After another long and uninspired cross-examination, Geddy called Robert Grevey, the husband of Angelica Savasta-Grevey, the Measuring Life who was killed behind her real estate office. Robert Grevey didn't have much to add since George Casserly already testified about the killer's smashing of the parking lot light, the slashing of the victim's tire, and the hunting knife found beside the victim. Geddy put Robert Grevey on mainly for sympathy and also to explain that Angelica had dinner with a few coworkers on the evening she was murdered, then returned to the office, and called him to say that she would be working late.

Geddy then started with his next witness. "Please state your name for the record," he asked.

"Barbara Keenan," the sixty-three-year-old white-haired woman answered with a distinctive Boston accent.

"Tell us please, Mrs. Keenan, where you lived during the summer of 1972?"

"Five-five-four Fourth Avenue South. It looked right out over the back parking lot of Naples Realty, where that poor girl worked."

Geddy guided the witness through several minutes of questioning until they came to the night Angelica Grevey was murdered.

"Oh yes, I remember it perfectly. My husband Jack was in the den listening to a ball game on the radio. I had just finished putting away the dishes when I heard something in the parking lot."

"Could you see anything?"

"No. It was too dark."

"Was that unusual?"

"Yes it was. There was usually a light back there, and I could always watch the comings and goings from that office. Not that I'm a busybody or anything, but we had a window over our kitchen sink that looked out over the lot. I remember wondering why the light was out that night."

"Did you hear anything that night?"

"I heard a woman's voice. You'll have to pardon me, I never swear, but she said the 'S'-word."

"The 'S'-word?"

"S-H-I-T."

"Yes, thank you. Anything else?"

"Oh, I almost forgot. I heard her say, 'Stupid car'! She practically yelled it."

"What did you do?"

"I thought she was probably having car trouble so I went into the den to get Jack to help her. But he just said, 'Not now, Hammerin' Hank's up!' That was his favorite ballplayer. So I went back to the kitchen to get a flashlight to help her myself, but when I looked out the kitchen window again there was already someone out there helping the girl."

"How did you know that?"

"First, because I saw a light. Then I heard voices. The woman's voice and also now a man's voice. And no, I can't identify the man's voice."

"All right, tell us about this light. What did it look like?"

"Just a light. I assumed it was a flashlight."

"Did the light move or was it stationary?"

"I only saw it for a few seconds. It didn't seem to move while I was looking."

"Are you sure it wasn't moving?"

"For the few seconds I was watching, I don't remember it moving."

"Thank you. What did you do then?"

"I thought the girl had help, so I went into the den with Jack."

"What's the next thing you remember happening that night?"

"A couple of hours later the whole police force showed up in that back lot and I gave a statement. I had to go to the station. It was terrible."

"Thank you, Mrs. Keenan. I have no more questions, Your

Honor."

"Mr. Blue?" asked Judge Frost. "Cross-examination?"

Earl Blue began his cross by establishing that the distance from the Keenan's kitchen to the parking lot was about one hundred feet. He drilled her on the fact that she never saw the man and couldn't identify the man's voice. When he came to the part about the light, he was clearly puzzled.

"Mrs. Keenan, about the light you saw. What, again, did you see?"

"A light."

"Like a flashlight, you said?"

"Yes."

"Was there anything sinister about this flashlight?"

"No."

Earl Blue scratched his head and told the judge he had nothing further.

After pushing through the reporters and leaving the courthouse, Geddy and Faith went immediately to the Hirt, Harrington office to spend the hour-and-a-half lunch recess preparing for the next witnesses. They worked in the conference room, which they had converted into a war room for the duration of the trial. There was a knock at the door, and when Faith opened it, Nick Farley was standing there with his arms held wide and the customary smirk fixed on his face.

"Look what the cat dragged in," said Faith gloomily.

"Hey, pardner," Nick called out in his high-pitched drone, which irritated Geddy's frayed nerves. "I just rode back into town. I thought I might be able to help you out, cowboy."

"You've got to be kidding," said Faith.

"What's the problem?" Nick said innocently. "We're a team."

"We *were* a team, until you started writing those trashy articles!" cried Faith. "You called me a Southern shrew. You made me sound like some emotionally bankrupt, asexual, all-business old maid."

Nick feigned an apology. "I did? I'm sorry, I didn't mean to. You're not old."

"I'm gonna call security," she said and hurried to the phone.

"Hold it, Faith." Geddy sighed and turned to Nick. "We don't have time now, Nick."

"Hey! I got a story to write, I was hopin' for a little of that insider's information you guys owe me."

"Owe you!" exclaimed Faith furiously. "After the stuff you've written, we're not telling you anything."

"Listen here darlin', you wouldn't have a case if it weren't for me. Besides, we made a deal."

Geddy's headache was getting worse. "He's right, Faith, we had a deal. But Nick, we really don't have the time. I'll meet you later for a little while, all right?"

"Fine, I'll let you buy me dinner. But before I go, I have some information for you." He walked over to Geddy and whispered in his ear. "You probably know that the Third District Court of Appeal reversed the Hoffer case a few days ago. What you probably *don't* know is that the Miami state attorney isn't retryin' him. He was released last night."

"What!" exclaimed Faith, obviously eavesdropping. "Reversed? Why didn't you tell me, John? Why did they reverse, on what grounds?"

Geddy didn't answer, so Faith looked at Nick. "Hey, I'm no lawyer," he said. "I don't understand all of that technical legal crap. But I know one reason was that the search of Hoffer's apartment was ruled illegal, so the evidence of the newspaper clippings wasn't gonna be allowed if there was a retrial."

"That's ridiculous!" she said to Geddy. "The police had a warrant!"

"Yeah, that's right, that was the problem," Nick remembered. "They say the cops lied on the affidavit they gave the judge to get the warrant. I guess that made the warrant illegal or somethin'. Does that sound right?"

Geddy slumped back into his chair, wanting to get it over with. "The Appeals Court made the right decision. So did the state attorney. Without the newspaper clippings, they don't have a chance in a new trial. That's why they had to let him go. Without the evidence the police seized from Hoffer's apartment, they'd never get a conviction in a retrial."

"He had some pretty nasty things to say about you," Nick said. "I'd watch my back. Like I said to you before, he's not the South Beach Butcher, but he's a killer all right."

"You don't think he'll come after you?" asked Faith, obviously concerned.

Neither Geddy nor Nick answered her.

The first witness of the afternoon session was Gus Baumgartner, the father of the fourth victim. As George Casserly had testified, Sally Baumgartner was killed in an empty lot behind the Chamonix Restaurant. Gus Baumgartner described his daughter. She was twenty years old when she was murdered, wanted to be an elementary school teacher, was very quiet and a very good daughter. He could not add much to what was already known about his daughter's murder. He was another sympathy witness.

"Please state your name for the record," said Geddy to his next witness.

"Constance Bass," the pug-nosed, thirty-one-year-old woman answered. A large silver crucifix hung from a chain around her neck.

"What is your maiden name?"

"Moore. Constance Moore."

"All right Mrs. Bass, could you please tell us why you're here?"

"That man killed my sister," she said, pointing at Curtis Dole.

"Objection!" shouted Earl Blue.

"Sustained," ruled Judge Frost. "Strike the answer."

Geddy asked Connie about her sister, Deborah Moore. Connie explained very clearly and slowly with just the right amount of emotion that she and her sister were very close. She described Debbie's long black hair, her freckles, and her smile. She talked about what a great big sister Debbie was, her love clear to everyone in the room, even after all those years.

"Do you remember what Debbie was doing the night she was murdered?"

"Yes. She was going on a date."

"With whom?"

"I don't know his name."

"Did she describe what he looked like?"

"No, she just said something like he was 'really smart,' and he was 'mature.' She said he was nice. Oh, and that he had his own place, but that was it."

"Tell me, do you know of any men, young men, that your sister went out with who had their own place?"

"No."

"Was Debbie popular with the boys?"

"Well, actually, she was. She, um . . . she slept around."

"Slept around?"

"You know? With guys."

"She had sex with them?"

"Yeah."

"Did she say if she planned to sleep with this man?"

"I don't think she said it, it was just sort of, like, implied. Debbie was gonna sneak out of our bedroom window and meet him at the end of the driveway where he would pick her up. She planned on staying out all night."

"Did Debbie drive?"

"No, and she didn't have a car."

"Why was she sneaking out? She was twenty years old, wasn't

she?"

"Our mom was strict, and everyone in the town knew the killer might strike that night. It was a new moon. Debbie was the same age as the other four girls who were killed, so my mother didn't allow her out."

"Wasn't Debbie scared that night?"

"No. She expected this guy to pick her up, so she probably felt safe since she wouldn't be alone. She didn't know that her date, Curtis Dole, would kill her."

Earl Blue nearly jumped over the defense table. "Objection! The witness already testified her sister never told her who she was going out with that night!"

"Sustained!" the judge replied and then went on to admonish the witness. Geddy suppressed a smile, pleased that Connie was performing just as he had coached her.

"Is there anything else you remember?" asked Geddy. "About that night?"

She thought for a moment. "No."

"What happened the next morning?"

Connie swallowed hard. "Well, she didn't come home, but that didn't surprise me. She always brought a bag with her uniform in it to go right to work the next day. So I was having breakfast and was probably just gonna hang around. Then the dog started barking. He was going crazy out by the end of the driveway. My mom sent me out there, to quiet down Woodstock, our dog." She started having difficulty talking, and the tears rolled down her cheeks.

"I know this is hard, but I need you to just, briefly, tell me what you saw."

Connie cried freely now as she answered. "I walked up to Woodstock and told him to be quiet. I remember I was mad for having to walk out there to shut him up. He was jumping around barking like crazy, right by the mailbox. . . ." She stopped and cried some more before resuming. "When I got closer I saw the blood on the driveway. I stopped for a second because it scared me, and then . . . then I saw the knife . . . like a hunting knife, at the edge of the bushes. I looked at the bushes and I could see . . . there was something in there. I walked a little closer and noticed Debbie's bag, it was, like, on top of her legs. I started to say her name. *Deb? Deb?* Woodstock was just going nuts."

She couldn't speak for a few seconds, and her chest heaved in attempts to catch her breath. "I saw her face. It was all gray and bloody . . . her mouth was open, her eyes were open, just staring. But then it hit me . . . I could see . . . her head wasn't . . . it wasn't . . . connected . . . to her body. . . ."

Connie grasped her silver crucifix with both hands and cried for a full minute.

"She . . . was looking . . . almost right at me. It looked . . . I couldn't get . . . any . . . words out." Geddy waited for her to say more. "Blood was all over her face . . . oh God! Why Debbie?"

Geddy watched as Connie cried and cried, giving her a chance to say more if she wished. Earl Blue didn't dare object. "After a little while, I started screaming. Not words, just scream-ing. I must have just been hysterical. I don't even remember the rest. My mom . . . they had a doctor come see me, but I don't even remember . . . I was only ten years old! Ohhh!"

The jurors were uncomfortable watching her, but that was fine with Geddy. He needed them to want to punish the man who caused all this, and it was difficult to believe they couldn't sym-pathize with Connie Bass. In time, Geddy walked up to her and put his hands on the rail of the witness stand. He didn't say any-thing because he knew it would sound corny. He just waited. Eventually, Connie stopped enough for Geddy to continue.

"I'm almost done now," he said gently. "If Debbie didn't have a car, how did she get to work every morning?"

"She walked."

"Walked? How far was it to work?"

"About four miles."

"She walked four miles to work every morning? Sometimes without any sleep?"

"Yes."

"Because she didn't drive, right?"

"Yeah."

"Did she have a bicycle?"

"No. She was scared of bikes."

"Scared of bikes? Why?"

"When she was like twelve, she was riding a bike and got hit by a car. She almost died. She was in a body cast for, I don't know, like, months."

"What about a moped then? Why didn't she buy a moped to use to get to work?"

"No, she was too scared. She wouldn't even get on a bicycle, so she wouldn't dare get on a moped."

"Or a motorcycle?" asked Geddy slowly, with great interest in his voice.

"No way. She wouldn't do it. She was real scared of anything like bikes or motorcycles."

"Are you sure? She wouldn't accept a ride on a motorcycle?"

"Never."

"Thank you, Mrs. Bass. Thank you very much." Then to the judge, softly, "I have no further questions."

Geddy's next witness was Donna Canty, an attractive thirty-nine-year-old widow wearing a low-cut blouse who sneaked a look over at Curtis as she ambled up to the witness stand. She was sworn in and explained that she was a friend of Curtis's during the summer of 1972. He was home from college and didn't have any friends in Naples other than her. She said he was handsome, and very sweet, easy to talk to, and that they had sailing in common.

"You had some sort of a crush on him, right?"

"Objection! Leading!" shouted Earl Blue for no good reason.

"I'll rephrase the question," said Geddy calmly. "Did you have a crush on him?"

"Yes, I had a crush on him."

"Did you ever . . ."

"Did we ever get romantic? Sleep together?"

"Yes."

"No. We never even kissed."

"Whose choice was that?"

"Uh, his. He's gay."

There was a commotion from the back of the room. Curtis sat unwavering, unashamed in his seat at the defense table. The judge called for order, and Geddy turned as if startled by the disturbance, which of course he wasn't.

"What did you do together?"

"Sometimes we went to bars and parties, but not much. He didn't like to party much."

"Was he too clean cut?"

"Ha! Far from it. We did heroin together." This revelation caused another stir in the gallery.

"How often did you and Curtis do heroin?"

"Whenever we could get it. It was hard to come by, it's illegal, you know? But Curtis had this guy he knew in Fort Myers Beach who could get it. Some days when I wasn't working, we'd sail up there on his boat and Curtis would buy it. We'd do it together."

"What else did the two of you do together?"

"We'd sail or go to the beach. Like a lot of people we'd go to the beach to watch the sunsets, bring a couple of fishing poles, cast them out into the water, and stick the rods in the sand. Sometimes we'd have a joint. You know, marijuana. We did coke once. That's about it."

"All right. Tell me, what kind of car did he drive?"

"Well, sometimes he drove his mother's old Cadillac, like when he was picking stuff up at the store, but he usually liked to ride his motorcycle."

"Motorcycle?" repeated Geddy to the jury.

"Yeah, he loved it. It was nothing special, it was like an old dirt bike."

"Did he wear a helmet?"

"Yeah, but he only had one, and he usually wore it. Said he needed to keep the bugs out of his eyes when he drove, so I didn't have a helmet when I went with him."

"Tell me something, Ms. Canty, and please, think hard about this next question. It's crucial."

"Okay."

Geddy took a short walk, then returned to her. "When he was driving his motorcycle, did he wear gloves?"

She thought for one full second. "Yes, I'm sure of it." The courtroom buzzed with understanding.

"When he was wearing these gloves, he wouldn't leave any fingerprints, would he? If he was holding a knife . . ."

That last question enraged Earl Blue. "Objection! Objection Your Honor!"

"What grounds!" Geddy yelled back.

"Order," the judge demanded.

"It's, it's prejudicial!" insisted Earl Blue.

Geddy held up his hands. "Of course it is. It's supposed to be. She's my witness!"

"Quiet, both of you. Not another word." Judge Frost tried to calm the two lawyers. He liked to keep things moving, and he hated sidebars or resorting to chambers. "Order! Sit down, Mr. Blue." He turned to Geddy. "That was uncalled for. I want that question stricken from the record."

"I apologize to the court," said Geddy. "Let me rephrase the question. Did these motorcycle gloves cover his hands and his fingers entirely?"

"Yes."

"And did he wear them even during the summer? When it's so hot?"

"Sure. Whenever he was driving that motorcycle, he wore his gloves."

Geddy nodded his head to emphasize the point. "One more thing about the motorcycle. Did it have a headlight?"

"Sure it did."

"Was it round? Square?"

"Round."

"Tell me, if it were a dark night and the motorcycle was

parked facing you, and you were, oh, a hundred feet away, and you looked up for a couple of seconds, could the headlight be mistaken for a flashlight?"

"Sure," answered Donna. Once again people seemed to shuffle in their seats.

"Thank you. Now, do you remember what you were doing the night of June 12, 1972?"

"Sure, I was at a birthday party at Margaret Brennan's house."

"How do you remember?"

"Because it was the night a girl in my high school class was murdered. Julieanne Cherube."

"Did you go alone?"

"No, I went with Curtis Dole," answered Donna. Geddy had to wait until the gallery settled down before telling the judge, "No more questions."

"Cross?" asked Judge Frost.

Earl Blue stood and faced Donna Canty. He clearly had been surprised about the gloves comment and the motorcycle headlight.

"Ms. Canty, do you remember last summer when I took your deposition?"

"Yes."

"Did you ever mention gloves or a motorcycle?"

"No."

"Why not?" he asked accusingly.

"Because, Mr. Big-Shot Lawyer, you never asked." There was laughter all around.

"Tell us, Ms. Canty, since Curtis Dole was gay, he wouldn't want to kiss a girl, right?"

"Objection!" exclaimed Geddy, standing. "Witness has no basis . . ."

Despite Geddy's objection, Earl Blue continued before the judge could respond. "So he didn't kill Julieanne Cherube on the beach because *she* kissed the killer!"

"Objection!"

Judge Frost pounded his gavel. "Mr. Blue! That's enough. You know better. I won't stand for any more from either of you. You're supposed to ask questions, not make statements."

"What about these gloves?" Earl Blue went on. "You don't have to ride a motorcycle to wear gloves, do you?"

"No, but you sure would look silly in Naples in the summertime with gloves on," she said, just as Geddy had coached her.

Earl Blue was becoming angry with the witness. "You were with Curtis the night of Julieanne Cherube's murder, right?"

"Yeah."

"But the two of you didn't go to the beach when the party at Margaret Brennan's broke up, right?"

"Curtis said he didn't want to, but I bet he went back to the beach after he dropped me off at home."

The lawyer gritted his teeth. "Did you see a knife or other weapon anywhere on him?"

"I wasn't looking for one."

Earl Blue picked up the straight-edge that was used on Julieanne Cherube. "Do you really think he could've been carrying this straight-edge and you never saw it?"

"Maybe. It folds. The blade tucks into the handle. Here," she reached out and snatched it out of his hands, showing how it could be collapsed to a much smaller size. "He sure could have hid it if it was like that, don't you think?"

Earl Blue was seething, but finally realized he was only making things worse. "No further questions," he said angrily.

"Redirect?" the judge asked Geddy.

"No thank you, Your Honor."

"I think it's time now to adjourn for the day . . ." began Judge Frost.

Geddy interrupted. "Actually, Your Honor. If I may . . . my next witness will be very brief."

"Mr. Blue?" the judge asked.

"Fine with me." He didn't like to end the day on such a bad note.

• • •

Geddy's next witness was Paula Affatato, whom Nick had discovered a few months earlier. She was a tiny woman in her early
fifties with big brown eyes and dark red lipstick. When she was
sworn in, her shaking voice betrayed her nervousness.

"Ms. Affatato, I don't want to take too much of the court's
time. We're all getting a bit tired. Could we just go directly to the
night of July 11, 1972?"

"Okay."

"What happened that night?"

"I was a maid, a live-in maid, at the Doles' house here in
Naples. I had a little room over by the garage. That summer
Curtis's father and sister were living in Chicago, so it was just me
and Curtis in the house. I was reading the newspaper that night
when I heard Curtis pull up. It was around ten-thirty."

"Was this strange?"

"No, he was out of the house a lot. But that night he didn't
come home for dinner, so I just thought I'd see if he wanted anything because there was a lot of leftovers from the dinner I fixed
for him."

"What happened?"

"I stepped outside of my room, and Curtis was just coming in
from the garage. He was soaking wet."

"Wet?"

"Uh-huh. He didn't have a shirt on, and he was wearing only
some red gym shorts."

"Where were his clothes?"

"I don't know. I didn't see them."

"What happened?"

"Nothing. I asked him what he was doing, and he said he was
at the beach, fishing. He said he stripped down to his shorts and
went for a swim."

"Anything else?"

"No, he just said he wasn't hungry and went upstairs, to his
room."

"Ms. Affatato, why do you remember this so well?"

"Because someone I knew was killed that night. Sally Baumgartner."

"Do you remember how she died?"

"She was killed by that New Moon Killer. He, you know, slit her throat."

"What else do you remember about the way she was killed?"

"I . . . I don't know, she was in a little lot, near Chamonix . . . she was stabbed twelve times . . . it was very bloody. . . ."

"Very what?"

"Bloody," repeated Paula. People where beginning to understand now.

"I guess the killer must have got some blood on him, too . . ."

"Objection!"

Geddy headed back to his seat to give the witness a chance to remember where he was going with this line of questioning. Then just before sitting, he asked one more question. "When you saw Curtis that night, was there any blood on him?"

Geddy could see the light go on over her head. "No, but if he did get any blood on him, the water would have washed it off."

After the second day of trial, Geddy met Nick Farley in a little sports bar by the docks, near the room Geddy still kept in the boardinghouse. He spent most of his nights with Morgan, but he wanted to keep up the appearance that they were not living together. Besides, he had been working so hard over the last couple of months, it was nice to stay in his own room once in a while to get a good night's sleep. He could have forsaken the boardinghouse for a nice condominium on the beach, but he anticipated moving in with Morgan after the trial, so he thought it wasn't worth the hassle and the cost.

Nick was sitting next to Geddy on a bar stool. They'd just been served a couple of steaks. Nick was talking to the pretty, young waitress, who had a lot of free time since the place was nearly empty.

"You call that a birthday?" Nick asked in an overly astonished voice, teasing her. "Hell, I'd puke if Lionel Ritchie sang to me on my birthday. You want to hear about my best birthday?"

"I bet you can't beat mine," the waitress said. She was playing along, having fun. Nick had charmed her, as odd as it seemed to Geddy.

Nick playfully pulled down the bill of her New York Yankees baseball cap. "I would have to say it was 1978. My birthday just happened to fall on the day my beloved Yankees played the Red Sox in a one-game playoff at Fenway. I was dating a model at the time, and some big cosmetics company offered to fly us up to Boston and gave us seats right next to the Yankee dugout."

"What model?" the waitress asked.

Nick ignored her. "Anyways, the Yanks were losing, when late in the game Thurman Munson leaned out of the dugout and asks me, 'Who ya rootin' fer?' I told him the Yankees, so he says, 'Come on in, maybe you'll be good luck.' So there I am, sittin' in the dugout with Munson and Nettles and Jackson and Chambliss, when Bucky Dent comes up to Reggie and says, 'Reg,' he says, 'There's somethin' wrong with my swing, you notice anything?'

"Well Reggie didn't notice anything, but I says to him, 'Open up your stance, try to pull the ball more.' Bucky thinks about it and says he will. Now that I got his ear, I told him to move forward in the box, and I told him to visualize. The mind can be a power-ful thing, I told him. Picture hittin' the ball out of the park, just over the Green Monster. He says okay. Then I told him some other stuff, and he goes out, and he's in the on-deck circle, and I see he's visualizin', and he's foolin' with his stance, just like I told him. Oh yeah, keep your butt down I told him, so he's doin' that, too."

"Is this really true?" the waitress asked in a cute voice. Geddy couldn't tell if she actually believed the story or was just playing along.

"Sure it is, I swear on my mother's grave it's true. Well, I don't have to tell you, Bucky goes ahead and pulls the ball just like I told him, right over the Green Monster, one of the greatest home runs in baseball history, and the Yanks go on to win! I have a baseball signed by the whole team to prove it."

Geddy would not have been to surprised to see Nick take a

ball out of his pocket with twenty-five forged signatures to confirm his story.

"Well, this was a nice break from the trial, Nick, but I have some work to do," Geddy said as the waitress walked away.

"Hold on, you haven't touched your food, and I haven't had a chance to pump you for information," Nick said.

"You're wasting my time."

"All right, she's gone. I'll get down to business. Come on, you gotta give me a few minutes at least. Finish your steak."

"I have too much work to do."

Nick grabbed him by the arm and pulled him back to the barstool. "You're gonna have a nervous breakdown if you don't relax awhile."

"Being with you is relaxing?"

For ten minutes Geddy answered most of the reporter's questions. He told Nick that Morgan would be his final witness the next day, then he would rest his case.

"What about Cynthia?" Nick asked. "She's not gonna testify at all?"

"What can she add? Nothing worth putting her on the stand. The jury would hate her, and . . ."

"Geddy!" a loud voice suddenly called from behind. Geddy and Nick both whirled around on their barstools. It was the hulking figure of James Hoffer.

Geddy didn't speak.

James Hoffer's fists clenched and unclenched repeatedly down by his sides. "You fucked me over, Geddy! I'm gonna rip your fuckin' face off for settin' me up!"

Everything in the bar stopped. Geddy remained seated and did not say a word. His calm only made James Hoffer more angry. He swore at Geddy and began moving forward.

"I wouldn't, cowboy," Nick said.

But he kept coming and suddenly he rushed forward and took a swing at Geddy. Geddy was much quicker and ducked the punch easily as he slid away from the bar. James Hoffer came after him with another roundhouse right, but Geddy ducked it again. Now James Hoffer realized that he needed to get hold of Geddy, so he lunged for him. Geddy sidestepped away like a matador, but James Hoffer followed and would have had him if Geddy hadn't overturned a table, knocking his attacker to the floor. As James Hoffer lay red with rage, his eyes focused on a steak knife that had fallen from the table.

He picked it up and stood, brandishing the knife. The waitress screamed, and a few people fled the bar. Nick had hardly moved.

"No knives!" warned Geddy. "You want to try to kick the crap out of me, fine. But don't lose your head. Put it down."

But James Hoffer was far from clearheaded. For over a year he had been in prison, no doubt dreaming of his revenge on the man he held responsible for putting him there. He screamed in fury and charged again.

Geddy readied himself, hoping to use his leverage to send the rushing man sprawling. Then Geddy would have to run. James Hoffer would keep coming until he was dead, so Geddy's only alternative was to kill *him*. But, he wasn't prepared to do that. He had to make a stand just long enough to get a chance to rush for the door at the far end of the bar.

James Hoffer suddenly stopped and made a violent sweep toward Geddy's eyes with the knife, but Geddy jerked his head backwards like a boxer and avoided it. James Hoffer hadn't rushed blindly this time, as Geddy had expected, giving Geddy no chance to knock him aside and run. Geddy could only retreat into a corner.

When Geddy had nowhere else to go, James Hoffer drew the knife back to his right ear and prepared to plunge it into Geddy's heart. Geddy landed a quick combination of punches that drew blood, but it wasn't nearly enough to stop the larger man. The knife kept moving toward Geddy's heart. Geddy caught the hand with the knife, but James Hoffer was a huge man. Despite using all his strength, the knife inched inexorably toward Geddy's chest.

In one quick movement, Geddy released his hold on the

killing hand and jumped to the side. With a thud, the knife was buried in the wall. Before James Hoffer had a chance to pull it out, Geddy grabbed a dart that was sticking in a dartboard next to his head and rammed it into his attacker's right forearm. James Hoffer doubled over and howled in pain as his blood spurted out. Instinctively, Geddy jerked the knife from the wall, held it tightly in his fist, and rammed the hard, heavy handle into James Hoffer's skull. Once. Twice. Three times. James Hoffer went down. Geddy jumped on him, turning the knife around in his hand, readying to deliver the death blow. Then Nick came out of nowhere and tackled him.

Geddy threw Nick aside and pulled himself to his knees, but his fury had subsided just enough to realize that his attacker was no longer a threat. As he gasped for air, he stared at James Hoffer's motionless body. Nick kneeled next to Geddy, whose knuckles were white around the knife handle, and slowly pulled the knife from Geddy's hand.

"It's all right, he's probably not dead," Nick said matter of factly. Geddy struggled to his feet and made his way past a crying woman to his place at the bar. Still breathing heavily, he leaned over the bar and grabbed a telephone. Nick joined him and sat on his bar stool.

"Thanks for the help," said Geddy angrily as he dialed.

"I called the cops while you were fighting," Nick told him.

Geddy stopped dialing, then slammed the receiver down. "You might as well have called an ambulance, too! He was trying to kill me, Nick! Where were you?"

"I told you, I was callin' the cops."

Geddy didn't bother to say anything. He sat down and rested his head in his crossed arms on the bar.

A minute passed and Geddy did not move. "So what's the deal, are you gonna eat that or are you done?" Nick asked him. When Geddy didn't answer, Nick quietly reached over to Geddy's plate and cut himself a piece of Geddy's steak as sirens began to scream.

• • •

An hour later at the police station, Geddy and Nick were sitting in a hallway waiting to give their statements. Geddy was drinking coffee and had hardly spoken, while Nick kept getting up, demanding that the police let them go. Then he would sit down again and complain to Geddy about how long it was taking.

"What's *your* hurry?" asked Geddy finally, with a touch of anger in his voice.

"I got a story to write," Nick said. "'Geddy Gets Hoffer. Again!' I can see it now, an eyewitness account. It'll make front page. It should go great with the stuff I found out about your past."

Geddy tensed up, but made himself relax, hoping Nick was bluffing. "My past? Pretty boring."

"Oh, I don't know. I think people would be interested to hear that your parents were murdered by a serial killer."

Geddy jumped out of his seat, his jaw muscles flexing spastically. "That's none of your business, Nick! If you print . . ."

"Why do you think I haven't printed it before?" Nick interrupted. "It's because you're my friend, that's why. Don't lose your sense of humor, Johnny, I was kidding. I figured there was a reason nobody knew about it, so I never wrote about it."

Geddy grudgingly returned to his seat.

"Well, what about it?" Nick asked. "How come it's such a big secret? It's nothing to be ashamed about."

"I just don't like thinking about it. Most of all, I don't like talking about it."

Nick shrugged his shoulders. "Understandable. Nine-year-old-kid and his sister discover their parents' dismembered body parts piled up in the kitchen, their blood splashed all over the walls by the killer . . ."

Geddy stood and grabbed Nick by the shirt collar, hoisting him to his feet. "You should know I take this very seriously."

"Years later you discover your sister, slit wrists and all, layin' in the bathtub. Yeah, now I can see what got a pretty boy like you into this racket . . ."

Geddy threw Nick hard to the ground, but Nick didn't stop talking. "They never caught the killer, so you think by prosecuting other psychos you can get back at him, is that it? Well, judgin' by your continuing obsession with murderers, it hasn't done you much good." Geddy was on top of him, and cocked his fist. "That's it! That's more like it! Take it out on me like you wanted to take it out on Hoffer! Winning trials isn't enough to satisfy you, is it? You tried to kill Hoffer tonight! You would have, too, but I stopped you!"

Geddy thought hard about it, but he didn't throw the punch. He stood abruptly and began walking down the hall.

Nick called after him. "You can talk to me about it, John! I'm your friend!" Geddy didn't turn around, he kept walking away. "Maybe I should have let you done it, but you know why I didn't? Because you're the best friend I've got!"

Geddy burst through the door at the far end of the hall without looking back. Nick picked himself up, walked over to a secretary's desk and grabbed a pad and pencil. He began writing his story about James Hoffer's attack. He didn't mention anything about Geddy's past.

The next morning back at the courthouse Geddy had to literally fight his way through the mob of reporters. He'd been up all night answering questions at the police station, then was overwhelmed by a crowd of reporters waiting for him as he left the station that morning. The morning newspapers put James Hoffer's attack on Geddy on the front pages, displacing the trial for the time being as the top story. He was relieved when he finally made it into the courtroom, where the pressure of the trial was a welcome respite from the demands of the press and the queries of the police. Faith was already at the plaintiff's table, along with Morgan. They had both been waiting for him that morning when he came out of the police station, so he'd already endured their questions and expressions of deep concern.

When Morgan was called to the stand all heads turned. Geddy noticed that once a few of the men in the jury caught a glimpse of her they stared at his girlfriend longingly. That pleased him. Morgan was something special, he thought. She was dressed in a conservatively tailored blue suit, which fell just below her knees. Geddy stood before the jury and quickly went through the preliminaries before addressing their relationship.

"Morgan," he said, using her first name rather than the more formal Ms. Gentry, "before I begin, allow me to inquire into your personal life. Could you please tell the jury the name of the man you're dating?" Geddy smiled to the jury. Most of them already knew from the newspapers.

"I'd be delighted." She smiled and told the jury, laughing slightly. "John Geddy, this very John Geddy, is the man I've been seeing for the past year."

The women jurors smiled, noticing that Morgan was clearly a woman in love. The men looked at Geddy with admiration and envy.

"Could you tell the jurors how we met?"

"You mean you don't remember?" she said, obviously joking. Even the jurors laughed and smiled. "We first met a little over a year ago, at the Valentine's Day Ball at the Philharmonic in Naples."

"Is it a coincidence that I happen to have a case that involves a trust that you are the trustee of?"

"No, because that's why we met." She turned to the jury. "We met because John was working on this case, and he needed information on the trust. So naturally we had several meetings, then a few dates, and now, well, I love him."

The whole room was so giddy with admiration for this seemingly perfect couple that nobody noticed the astonished look on Geddy's face. It was the first time she had ever said she loved him.

He had to struggle to get back on track, but he smiled in spite of himself. She smiled back at him. "Uh, Morgan, is there . . . is there any possibility, however remote, that our relationship could prevent you from being a completely honest and unbiased witness?"

"Not at all. And besides, everything I've ever done relating to the trust is fully documented. Not to mention that the murders involved in this case took place in 1972, well before I became trustee."

For the next two hours Geddy led Morgan through her testimony. She explained how she became trustee, how much she earned for being trustee, and that she could never become a beneficiary of the trust, therefore she had no motive to kill the Measuring Lives. Then she explained about the trust journal that she and her father kept, and read aloud the letter she showed Geddy a year ago, establishing that Curtis found out who the Measuring Lives were just months before the murders. She also made it clear that Cynthia never received a copy of the trust.

Earl Blue then cross-examined her. "Ms. Gentry, your boyfriend, the person you care for perhaps more than anyone else in the world, is the lawyer for the plaintiff, correct?"

"Yes. As I explained, I've been seeing . . ."

"Cynthia Dole's lawyer, yes. You wouldn't want to see your boyfriend lose a big trial, would you?"

"Everything I testified to is well documented. If you're suggesting I've lied about anything, it should be easy enough to prove. So go ahead and try to prove that anything I said is not totally, absolutely, 100 percent the truth, Mr. Blue." Morgan was poised and sounded very confident.

"What I am suggesting, Ms. Gentry, is that you could have doctored the books . . ."

"Tell us how then. Specifically. Come on, Mr. Blue, don't make these bald-faced accusations and then not back them up."

"Ms. Gentry, I'll ask the questions . . ."

"The letter that my father wrote to Curtis Dole in April 1972 was signed by him. I couldn't have doctored it. Isn't that the only real issue here? What else have I said that could damage Curtis Dole?"

Earl Blue was livid. "Your Honor, could you please instruct the witness to only respond to my questions?"

Judge Frost admonished her in a stern voice. "Ms. Gentry, I don't want you to speak again unless you're responding to a question of Mr. Blue's, and then I only want you to answer the question."

Earl Blue decided to cut to the chase. "Ms. Gentry, you said that only your father and Curtis Dole could have known who the Measuring Lives were because the only copy your father ever gave out was to Curtis. Right?"

"Yes, that's right."

"But, isn't it true that once Curtis had his copy, *Curtis* could have given a copy to Cynthia?"

Oh no! Geddy screamed to himself. Faith looked perplexed. On the witness stand, Morgan was clearly speechless. Like the rest of them, she hadn't thought of that possibility.

"Ms. Gentry?"

Morgan tried to recover. "I . . . no. I don't have any record . . ."

"Ah, but that was not the question, was it? The question was, couldn't Curtis have given a copy of the trust to Cynthia?"

"I know he didn't," she said finally.

"How do you know?"

"She . . . she would have told me. Cynthia would have told me, and she would have told John."

"Not if she had the Measuring Lives killed, right? Or if she flew down to Naples herself and killed them. She wouldn't tell anyone then, would she?"

"Curtis wouldn't have given her a copy. They didn't like each other. They never even spoke."

"Well, we will just have to see about that, won't we?" said Earl Blue, feeling good about himself.

All of a sudden, Geddy realized that Cynthia could have had those girls killed. He also realized where the crucial part of the trial would be. When he cross-examined Curtis Dole.

●   ●   ●

"Mr. Geddy, is that the close of your case?"

"One moment, Your Honor." Geddy leaned past Faith and whispered to Cynthia. "Did Curtis ever send you a copy of the trust?"

"No, never. He's lying."

"Did he ever in any way give you a copy or send you a letter or discuss it over the telephone?"

"No," insisted Cynthia.

"Mr. Geddy?" asked Judge Frost impatiently.

"Your Honor, I would like to call Cynthia Dole for a few questions."

"No objection," said Earl Blue happily, expecting Geddy to call her now after Morgan's disastrous cross-examination.

The judge sighed. "You may call the witness."

Cynthia stood and walked to the witness stand with her head held regally, looking straight ahead. She was designer-dressed from head to toe, against Geddy's orders. He had scolded her discreetly when he saw her outside the courthouse that morning.

He kept it short and sweet. He didn't want the jury to see her enough to despise her, as he did. Just a few important points, then he had to get her out of there "Ms. Dole, did Curtis Dole ever mail you, or hand you, or in any other way give you a copy of the Adam Gentry Trust Agreement?"

"Never. I am absolutely sure of it."

"During the months of April, May and June of 1972, how many times did you speak to your brother?"

"I know for certain that I did not speak to him at all during those three months."

"What about letters, mail?"

"I had absolutely no contact with him."

"How can you be so sure?"

"Because after our mother died, our relationship was irreparably damaged when Curtis didn't go to the funeral in early March of 1972."

"Did you talk to him about that?"

"Immediately after the funeral, I called him and told him I would never speak to him again. I never have, and I never received any letters either. More specifically, I never received a copy of that trust from him. Why would he send me a copy? We haven't spoken since March of 1972."

"No more questions," said Geddy. He returned to his seat and crossed his fingers.

"Mr. Blue?"

Earl Blue approached the witness stand with confidence. "Isn't it true Curtis sent you a manila envelope with a copy of the trust and a handwritten note saying he wanted to sue Mark Gentry, the trustee, into giving the two of you more money?"

"He certainly did not."

"Didn't you later tell him over the telephone that you weren't interested in anything to do with him, and that you weren't interested in suing the trustee?"

"No, I did not."

"Ms. Dole, Curtis did mail you a copy of that trust, didn't he?"

"No! If he says he did, he's lying. Even if he really did, I never received it. Even if he says he mailed one, you can't prove I received it."

"Maybe you should take a moment to try to remember." Earl Blue walked a wide circle in the middle of the courtroom. "Didn't Curtis call you at school?"

"No."

"Didn't he call you at school to discuss the trust he sent to you?"

"No."

"Are you sure?"

"Asked and answered," demanded Geddy. "Twice, Your Honor."

"Please move on, Mr. Blue," the judge commanded.

"Didn't he confirm over the telephone that you received a copy of the trust?"

"No. He never mailed me the trust, and he never called me about the trust. We haven't spoken since the day after my mother's funeral."

"You hated Curtis, right?"

"Yes. And he hates me."

"In fact, after he told you he was gay, and after he didn't show up for your mother's funeral, you probably wouldn't have cared if he was dead. Right?"

Cynthia raised her head defiantly. "Maybe not."

"And isn't it true that during the months after your big falling-out with Curtis, you wouldn't have had any misgivings about framing him for those five murders?"

Geddy shouted. "Objection! There's no basis for that question."

"Overruled. The witness will answer."

"Mr. Blue, I was nineteen years old. I was receiving thousands of dollars a year in distributions from the trust. I was in college, living in Chicago. I didn't need more money, and I didn't socialize with hired killers. I didn't have those girls killed."

"But if you knew who the Measuring Lives were, it would be possible for you to have them killed, correct?"

"*If* I knew who the Measuring Lives were, but I didn't."

"But Curtis sent you a copy of the trust, so you did know."

Geddy rose quickly. "We've heard this question twice, Your Honor."

"Actually that was a statement, not a question," the judge corrected him. "Either impeach the witness or move on, Mr. Blue."

"If Curtis did send you a copy of the trust, you wouldn't admit it now, would you, because it would raise the very strong possibility that you had those girls killed or that you killed them yourself?"

"I can't even answer that question because I in fact did not receive a copy of the trust. If Curtis said he sent me one, he is a damnable liar!"

Earl Blue looked very satisfied. "I suppose it will be your word against his."

Cynthia didn't answer. That was the close of Geddy's case.

In Judge Frost's chambers during the lunch recess, the lawyers argued fervently over Earl Blue's motion for a directed verdict, that is, a dismissal of the case for lack of proof. It was really just a formality, and as soon as Judge Frost denied the motion, Geddy hurried out to the halls of the Collier County Courthouse, followed closely by Faith. A Naples police department detective was waiting for him. Nick was there, too.

"There's the man!" Nick screamed as he pointed Geddy out to the officer. "He's the one who beat up poor defenseless James Hoffer!"

Geddy walked right up to them and leered at Nick. "Shut up, Nick."

Nick feigned fright. "Help me, officer, I've seen him in action. He's dangerous. He might kick the crap out of me, too."

Geddy shook his head and tried to ignore Nick. "Afternoon, Officer," he said. "How's Hoffer?"

"He's at the hospital. I hear he's going to be all right."

"What about John?" asked Faith. "Is everything all cleared up?"

"Oh sure, we talked to everyone in the bar," said the detective, a serious, strong-jawed man with close-cropped hair, like a marine's. "It's clear that James Hoffer intended to inflict great bodily harm . . ."

"Listen to this guy!" Nick said with a smile. "Hoffer was gonna carve a big hole in your chest, and he says, 'intent to inflict bodily harm.'"

"Nick, I'm not in the mood," said Geddy.

"Everyone told the same story," the detective continued, trying not to pay attention to Nick. "Hoffer had threatened you verbally and then brandished the knife in a threatening way as he was moving toward you, Mr. Geddy. You acted in self-defense. Hoffer will be charged with attempted murder. We have the statement you gave last night, but if we need more, we'll let you know. By the way, how are you feeling?"

"Better."

The detective turned to Nick. "I'd show a little more respect for the law if I were you, Mr. Farley." The detective walked away after saying good-bye to Geddy and Faith.

"Keep up the good work!" Nick called out.

"I guess you managed to piss him off, too, huh Nick?" said Geddy.

Nick got serious. "What's your problem? Are you mad at me or mad at yourself?"

Geddy thought about not saying anything in front of Faith, then decided it was all right if she knew. "You were right. I tried to kill him."

Nick punched him on the shoulder playfully. "It was the heat of the moment."

"What are you talking about, John?" asked Faith.

"Last night, with Hoffer. After I got the knife and he was hunched over, I tried to ram the blade into his head. It all happened so fast I didn't realize I was holding the knife upside down.

If I had hit him with the blade-side rather than the handle . . ."

"Don't take it so hard. It was human nature," Nick told him.

"To commit murder?" said Faith incredulously.

"Murder's the most natural thing known to man, after eatin', sleepin', and broads." Nick wasn't cheering Geddy up. "Look, you had no choice. You were a goner, my friend. Even if you got away from him last night, he would've come after you again, maybe by surprise next time like whoever gave you that scar."

Faith caught that, but she didn't ask.

Geddy knew what Nick was saying was true, but he couldn't get over it. "You know what bothers me the most? I enjoyed it. In the half-second it took to swing that knife, I felt the most incredible rush, some kind of surge of energy. When I thought I was ramming that knife into his brain, I felt so revved up, so powerful. I thought I was killing him, and I liked it."

There was silence between them, as if both men understood and there was nothing more to say.

Faith was furious with Nick. "I still can't believe you didn't help him."

"Hey, how many times do I have to tell you, I was callin' the cops. I thought he'd get away from Hoffer and run out of the bar. John would get away, but so would Hoffer and then he'd come after him again some other time, when John least expected it. I figured it was best to get the cops searchin' for Hoffer as soon as possible so they could haul his ass in before he got away."

"But Nick, what made you think John would get away? Hoffer is an animal."

"Hey, it's not like blondie here is one of these prissy society boys they got so many of in Naples. After his parents were killed . . ."

"That's enough, Nick!" demanded Geddy.

Faith couldn't help herself this time. "What? What's this about your parents?"

Nick looked surprised. "Shit, sorry, John. I figured she knew."

"Knew what?" cried Faith. Grudgingly, Geddy allowed Nick to tell her.

"John's parents were brutally murdered," Nick explained to an astonished Faith. "He and his sister grew up with his grandmother in the Bronx. They lived in a crappy neighborhood near Yankee Stadium. Johnny used to run with a gang until a few buddies of his got their heads blown off right before his very eyes in some territorial gang shit. He was the only one who got away. I knew he could take care of himself."

"Why didn't you tell me?" she asked Geddy, who didn't know how to answer. Faith turned to Nick. "How did you find out about all this?"

"His—I'd guess you'd call him a foster father—told me. John's grandmother died soon after his older sister committed suicide. His sister never got over the sight of their parents' bodies. This foster father guy was a teacher at John's school, and offered to take care of him until arrangements could be made for what to do with him. He took a liking to John, and took care of him until he went off to college. This guy was also the high school lacrosse coach, a real hard-ass type, who got John to straighten up and made him play on the lacrosse team. Three years later he was a high school All-American and Princeton came calling. By the time he got out of Princeton, he was so polished no one could tell he grew up a punk. He could have done anything he wanted, but he went to law school at NYU, then immediately to Miami to prosecute criminals rather than get the big bucks on Wall Street. That was something none of his law school friends could understand, but then, they didn't know who he really was, and they didn't know about his parents. They didn't realize what John was after."

"What is he after?"

Before Nick could answer, they suddenly heard the ding of the elevator. Seconds later the elevator doors opened, and a few reporters came out and spotted Geddy. Soon he was inundated with questions about James Hoffer's attack. Nick, too, was being asked questions, and microphones were being shoved in his face.

Nick pushed his way out, dramatically acting overwhelmed, which of course he wasn't, having stood in the reporters' shoes so many times before. "Vultures! Leeches! Be gone! Let me live in peace!" He ran off like a bashful starlet with the back of his hand held melodramatically over his forehead.

The last thing Geddy needed in the middle of the trial was this. Faith tried to protect him from the reporters, to no avail. He answered questions as patiently as he could and slowly made his way back to the courtroom. The lunch recess was almost over. He hadn't had a bite to eat.

Once the courtroom settled down after the lunch recess, Earl Blue began the defense case.

"Mr. Blue, call your first witness."

"Your Honor, the defense calls Dr. Reginald Holmes to the stand."

Dr. Holmes was a middle-aged African-American psychology professor from Boston University who was called to testify as a serial killer expert.

"Dr. Holmes," went on Earl Blue after the preliminaries, "could you please tell the jury the name of the book you have written?"

"Serial Killers, A to Z."

"Would you please turn to page three-eighty-seven, which has been marked Defense Exhibit One, and read the name of the serial murderer whose story begins on page three-eighty-seven, and ends on page three-eighty-eight?"

"Yes. It's the New Moon Slasher."

"And you wrote that this New Moon Slasher was responsible

for the five murders that occurred in Naples in 1972, correct?"

"Yes."

"Why did you classify them as serial murders?"

"Because they fit the profile perfectly."

"And what profile is that?"

"A series of murders by the same killer, often in the same geographic location, usually with similar victims and often with no apparent motive other than the desire to kill."

"Could you take each criteria and explain how it correlates with the New Moon Murders?"

"Certainly. The most obvious feature is that all the victims were the same age, nineteen to twenty. And they were all female. This is very common among serial killers. Often, they are compelled by a past event where they suffered some type of psychological trauma, and they commit murder to cope with it. For example, a young boy is sexually abused by his mother when he is eight years old and his mother is thirty. He then grows up and seeks out thirty-year-old women to abuse sexually and kills them."

"So with the New Moon Slasher, could something like this have happened?"

"It's very possible, but there are other possibilities. Their reasons are extremely varied. For example, there have been serial killers who killed simply because they had a deep-felt hatred of the police. By terrorizing the population and not being caught, they make the police look incompetent, and they derive satisfaction from that. In some cases, they're shunned by society and their victims resemble the type of people who have made them feel unwanted in the past. Also, in the overwhelming majority of cases, the serial killer came from a broken family and was often illegitimate or adopted. Then there's the more frightening possibility: a psychotic driven by a blood lust."

"You mean killing for pleasure?"

"In a manner of speaking. Some, but not all, serial killers suffer from mental disease, some kind of psychiatric or genetic abnormality. They can be intensely obsessive and irrational. Others think they're possessed by evil spirits or the devil himself. But in most cases, they just seem to gain a deep inner fulfillment from killing, some kind of intense gratification. It often manifests itself at an early age, such as a child who derives pleasure from killing animals."

"So they're psychotics?"

"Yes, most are either psychopathic or sociopathic. A psychotic personality is characterized by emotional instability, perverse and impulsive behavior, inability to learn from experience.

"What is a sociopath?"

"A psychotic personality whose behavior is aggressively antisocial."

"Then they must be easy to spot."

"No, not at all. They may or may not exhibit the symptoms. Take Ted Bundy, for example. He was almost always described as a handsome, charming young man. He was a law student. But underneath that facade, he was just as deranged as Charles Manson. He traveled from coast to coast murdering young women. John Wayne Gacy used to dress up like a clown and perform at children's birthday parties. Of course, some serial killers do exhibit their antisocial feeling, but most of the time, once a serial killer is caught, you hear the same old stories. Their friends and family thought they were just nice, normal people. I personally interviewed a serial killer who had been a doctor for over twenty years. There has even been a serial killer who was a practicing lawyer."

Earl Blue held up his hands in jest, letting everyone know it wasn't him. "In fact, the notion of serial killers has become almost entertaining to our society today, hasn't it? Children can even buy trading cards, like baseball cards, with pictures and biographies of serial killers. But just how common are they?"

"There are many more than the public would like to believe. There may be as many as 100 in this country alone, taking thousands of victims, and there will be many more."

"What are some other characteristics of a serial killer?"

"They most often come from the lower class or perhaps the lower middle class, and they usually feel excluded from the upper class they so desperately want to join. They feel no regret, no remorse or pity. In fact, they're proud of their murders and take trophies from their victims. Most serial killers enjoy the attention they receive in the papers. They enjoy the notoriety they attain, the immortality that comes with it."

"Explain to the jury what trophies are."

"Often a killer will cut off a finger or an ear or some other body part, or take the victim's driver's license, jewelry, clothing, or even take a photograph of their victim after the murder as trophies, souvenirs, of the murder. Something to remember the murder by."

"Tell us, are serial killers imbeciles, or are they capable of carefully carrying out murders that may never be solved?"

"Very often they're of at least normal intelligence. One well-known serial killer, Charles Starkweather, even wrote a rather impressive autobiography while he was in jail. They're often very artistically talented. Killing for them is a kind of misplaced creativity."

"What about sex? Is sex a prime motivating factor?"

"Some killers are sexual deviants and necrophiles, that is, they do kill for sex. For example, they believe if they want to have sex with a woman, they have to kill her first. But for the majority of serial killers, sex is not a major motivating factor."

"What are some common ways of killing employed by these serial killers?"

"It could be anything, but some of the most common ways are strangulation, stabbing, decapitation, slashing the throat, shooting, and beating the victim to death."

"What do you think happened to the New Moon Slasher? Did he just disappear? Stop killing?"

"There's no explanation. It's possible he moved on to other killing grounds though. Serial killers often move about a great deal, from town to town, job to job. There's a theory that one man is responsible for many of the unsolved serial killings over the last twenty years. A sort of Super-Killer. It's an interesting theory. However, there's little documented evidence to support it. It answers a lot of questions though. It's possible for, let us say, a series of strangulations in Texas to be related to, say, the slashings in Miami or the recent series of murders in Alabama."

"And perhaps even related to the slashings here in Naples?"

"Yes. I mentioned in my book that the New Moon Slasher could be the same killer who has committed over a hundred unsolved murders across the country during the seventies, eighties, and nineties. In these unsolved murders, there was often no sexual molestation and no trophy taking. A sort of Super-Killer who has never been caught."

"Then you're telling us that after all of your research, your years of schooling and from what you heard here at trial, the New Moon Murders were committed by a serial killer?"

"I have absolutely no doubt that they were."

"And is it your opinion that the New Moon Murders were committed by this so-called Super-Killer?"

"Yes."

"No further questions," said Earl Blue.

Geddy rose to his feet and asked only one question. "Dr. Holmes, when you wrote your book, did you know that the victims of the New Moon Murders were the five Measuring Lives of the Adam Gentry Trust and that they were killed in the exact same order as they were listed in the trust?"

Dr. Holmes reluctantly admitted, "No."

Geddy threw up his hands and laughed. "No more questions."

• • •

For the rest of the afternoon, Earl Blue paraded a whole slew of character witnesses in front of the jury. First was a college professor, then Curtis's college sailing instructor. Next was a minister who testified that Curtis was involved in charity work. Then the captain of a Whitbread sailing ship Curtis had sailed on testified about Curtis's excellent work ethic, and finally a friend of his, a doctor from Fort Lauderdale, spoke of his decency. They were all there to show that this nice, decent fellow couldn't hurt a fly.

Geddy never put much stock in character witnesses. You could find a half-dozen people who would tell you that the Son of Sam was a charming sort who always helped little old ladies cross the street. Geddy didn't ask one question of any of them. When Earl Blue was finished, Geddy would simply say in a bored voice, "No questions."

When the day was over, the judge asked Earl Blue how many more witnesses he would have. He replied one. The judge said they would take care of the final witness and closing arguments the next day, then the jury would deliberate.

When court adjourned, Geddy heard a whisper in his ear. "John, could I talk to you?" It was Earl Blue. "Curtis and I would like to invite you and Cynthia to Curtis's house this evening. For dinner. We think if just the four of us can talk in less adversarial surroundings, maybe we could work something out."

"You don't have much confidence in your case, do you?"

"Come on, John, don't give me that. You put up an admirable fight so far, but it's all going to change tomorrow. Besides, you know as well as I do that once it gets to a jury, who in the world knows what's going to happen? Remember, you have to convince every single juror. They know there's a chance Cynthia hired someone to kill those girls or that she did it herself. Don't you think at least one of those jurors isn't convinced it had to be Curtis? If they're not unanimous, it's a hung jury. That's as good as a win for Curtis."

"No it isn't. We'll bring it to trial again," said Geddy. "But I'll tell Cynthia about your offer. I'll call you in an hour." He didn't want to settle, but it was his ethical duty to inform Cynthia of the offer.

"Good enough. But John," added Earl Blue seriously, "please try to talk her into it. It might be the best for everyone if we could work it out."

24

Geddy and Cynthia rode in silence down Green Dolphin Drive through the Port Royal area, but the silence didn't make either one of them uncomfortable. Cynthia was too self-involved to believe she had any obligation to be polite to Geddy, her employee, and Geddy knew that Cynthia was so far out of touch with reality that he didn't care what she thought of him.

Cynthia was very short with Geddy when he picked her up that evening. He was still in his work clothes. Cynthia had changed into yet another elaborate outfit. They cruised down Green Dolphin Drive in Morgan's roadster with nothing but the roar of the engine and the scenery of the million-dollar Port Royal houses to fill their minds. They reached a cul-de-sac and stopped in front of a wrought-iron gate. Geddy noticed the bronze plaque on the stone pillar that read "South End," obviously the name of the house.

The Dole homestead, South End, was a beautiful replica of a French chateau. The wrought-iron gateway opened when they pulled up. Geddy pulled into the circular cobblestone driveway and parked next to a colorful front garden. Twin Doberman pinschers ran up to the car and bared their teeth viciously. Geddy was thankful he had decided to put the convertible top up for Cynthia, though he knew the dogs could tear right through if they wanted.

Ivy grew on the light yellow exterior of the house, making odd turns to avoid the hunter green-painted shutters and arched windows, which were symmetrically arranged on each floor on either side of the marble-stepped entranceway. The front door opened. Curtis stepped outside holding a cocktail. Geddy heard him shout, "Halt!" and the dogs sat on the cobblestones. "It's okay to come out now," he said pleasantly, stepping onto the driveway and opening Cynthia's door.

Geddy hesitated, not liking the idea of being at Curtis's mercy with the dogs.

"Cynthia. Mr. Geddy. I'm very happy you decided to accept. Please, come in." Curtis moved aside to let them enter under the carved entrance arch and led them through a long gallery, past a cantilevered wood staircase, which was a sculpture in its own right. They strolled through a living room with cathedral ceilings and with oil paintings on every wall, decorated as though it were a wing at Versailles. Magnificent double doors led outside to the patio, where Earl Blue was seated on an old Italian wooden chair. His gin-and-tonic rested on a marble sundial inexplicably placed in the shade of the awning overhead. Curtis excused himself to check on dinner.

"Evening, John. Ms. Dole. Thank you for coming tonight. It certainly is beautiful, isn't it?" said Earl Blue as he swept his hand at the view.

South End was at the tip of one of the fingers of the Port Royal development that jutted out into Naples Bay. Looking out over swaying palms and beyond Curtis's thirty-five-foot sailboat tied to the dock at the end of the backyard, Geddy could see the mangrove-lined bay and the boats heading toward nearby Gordon's Pass. He also caught another glimpse of the two Dobermans, who were patrolling the backyard.

"It certainly is," agreed Geddy. "You were fortunate to grow up here, Cynthia," he said to her, hoping to get her involved in the conversation.

Cynthia folded her arms. "When this trial is over, I want you to sell the house right away. I don't care what you get for it."

"Well, don't get ahead of yourself, Ms. Dole," counseled Earl Blue. "The trial's not over yet, and frankly, we aren't very concerned. Especially with Curtis testifying tomorrow."

"So he's gonna testify," said Geddy, ending his own speculation about whether he would or not.

"Yes, he will, and to tell you the truth it's going to break the case wide open. That's why we wanted to talk to you."

Curtis returned at that moment. "We can talk business after dinner. It's on the table. Shall we?" Curtis was in a very cheerful mood, especially considering that his sister had accused him of multiple murders and could soon be taking everything he had away from him.

Dinner was fantastic, served on elegant china with exquisite silver settings in Curtis's beautiful Regency dining room. The cook was a young man named Philip, who silently brought the food out to them on ornate silver trays. Geddy didn't know if he was a live-in cook or just hired for the night, but everything was delicious.

Curtis controlled most of the conversation, and when it became apparent that Cynthia didn't wish to participate, he directed his attention to Geddy. They spoke about attending Ivy League schools, Brown and Princeton. From that nucleus, the conversation spun out into every direction, encompassing topics ranging from their shared love of motorcycles to Renaissance art. Earl Blue was mostly silent, and when he did add anything, it was always a serious observation rather than lighthearted small talk.

After dessert they talked about college football. "I noticed the name of the house when I drove in," said Geddy, suddenly remembering. "South End. That sounds like South Bend, as in Notre Dame."

188

Tom Foley

"Very good, John," he said, nodding. "Not many people put those two together. Yes, my father thought it was pure genius when he thought of that name. He loved the double meaning. This house is, of course, at the south end of Naples, and Notre Dame is in South Bend, Indiana. He went to Notre Dame and thought the name was very clever. I leave it there because it reminds me of happier times."

"That reminds me, John," spoke Cynthia, her first words since dinner was served. "Before you sell this place, take down that ridiculous plaque outside. It's an embarrassment."

"Cynthia . . ." Curtis started to say in an apologetic tone. He seemed to want to patch things up with her, but every time he tried, she rebuked him.

At that moment, Philip appeared and asked if they wanted any more dessert or coffee. They all accepted more coffee, and Curtis stood, looking like he was ready to make an important announcement.

"Cynthia, I know you don't approve of my lifestyle. I know that my homosexuality and the fact that I didn't go to mother's funeral has caused this rift between us, but I don't hate you. You're my sister, and I love you. There's nothing I would like more than for us to make up."

Cynthia huffed but her lips formed no words.

"I want you to meet somebody. This is Philip, he is my . . . roommate."

Cynthia looked ill. Curtis had his arm on Philip's shoulder as Philip stood nervously next to him holding the coffee pot. Philip was extremely tan, with thin black hair parted in the middle and brushed to the sides. He was handsome, Geddy supposed. At least he thought that women would find Philip cute, if not a little scrawny, especially compared to Curtis, who was bigger and more rugged.

"I want you to know that I'm not some kind of male whore and that I don't hang out at sleazy nightclubs and sleep around. Philip and I have been together for three years. I want you to see that we're just like anyone else, we're not an embarrassment. I hope that you can see that I'm still your brother, and I'm not . . ."

"How dare you," hissed Cynthia as she stood up. "How dare you! You *are* an embarrassment! Every time I think of you, I feel ashamed. Do you know what it's like when I meet somebody who knows that my brother is gay? You're revolting. You detract from me!"

Curtis looked pleadingly at his sister. "Cynthia, listen to yourself . . ."

"And I will never, ever forgive you for not coming to mother's funeral."

"She didn't want me to! When I told her I was gay, she said she never wanted to see me again. She actually said 'Don't even come to my funeral,' and she said if that trust money was hers, she'd disinherit me! Do you know how that made me feel?"

"Do you know how you made her feel? And Father? He was ashamed, too!"

"But they were wrong. It's nothing to be ashamed about. It's who I am. I thought that now with all of the changes in people's ideas about homosexuality you'd change your mind. But you haven't. You're just as narrow minded as ever!"

"If you are going to make personal remarks . . ."

"Why don't we all calm down," pleaded Earl Blue. "Please, just sit down. This is doing nobody any good."

Curtis sat, and so did Earl Blue. Geddy had never stood. Knowing he couldn't control Cynthia, he didn't even try. Philip slipped ghostlike back into the kitchen, unnoticed. Cynthia remained standing.

"John, take me home," she demanded.

Geddy didn't move.

"Take me home now!"

"Calm down, Cynthia."

"I don't want to hear anymore," she said to Geddy, then realized he still wasn't moving, so she turned to Earl Blue. "If you have a settlement offer, make it now!"

Earl Blue stood up while Curtis remained seated. "We'll settle the whole thing right now for sixteen million dollars. You get four million, Curtis gets sixteen." Cynthia would make an additional four million dollars over the twenty million that was her half of the trust.

"Your offer is rejected. Take me home, John," demanded Cynthia before turning and heading for the front door.

"You know something, Cynthia," Curtis called after her. "The money's not even what's so important to me. I just want to tell you something. I don't know how all of this got started, and I swear I don't know who killed those girls, but it wasn't me! I swear to God, it wasn't me! How can you not believe your own brother?"

Geddy remained seated. "What are you waiting for?" Curtis screamed at him. "Get out! How could you do this to me? I'm innocent, I didn't kill those girls!"

"The hell you didn't."

Curtis regained his composure. "You better think this settlement over, because tomorrow, I testify."

Geddy finally stood and calmly warned Curtis. "You're the one who's in trouble, Curtis. You *don't* want to be cross-examined by me."

"John, I think you should leave," suggested Earl Blue strongly. "Now, please. Curtis, don't say another word. John, tell your client five million. She gets five million, Curtis gets fifteen million. It's more than fair, she's already got twenty million."

"I'll tell her, but she won't accept," said Geddy, still surprised at Curtis's violent outburst.

"It's our final offer," cautioned Earl Blue.

Curtis threw down his napkin. "Forget the five million, I'll see you on the stand, Geddy. You're gonna blow it! I was just willing to give Cynthia an extra five million and the two of you blew it!"

"That's a hell of a temper you have, Curtis. You look like you could kill me right now." Geddy turned away and walked outside, where Philip was keeping the dogs at bay. He slipped behind the wheel and turned the ignition. Cynthia gave him a nasty look.

"John . . ." she began.

"Shut up. Just shut the hell up," he ordered her, shocking her. "I want you to listen to me. They're too confident, they're up to something. I have to know if Curtis ever sent you a copy of that trust!" He screeched to a stop at the gate, waiting for it to open.

"I told you, no."

"If he did and you're lying to me, we could lose this case. If you tell me the truth, right now, maybe I can still salvage it. But I have to know, now!" Geddy accelerated quickly through the gears until he was doing sixty in a twenty-five-mile-an-hour zone without even realizing it.

"John, I swear to you, he never mailed me a copy of that trust, and I never spoke to him about it."

"Fine," said Geddy as he pushed his favorite rock tape into the deck. Soon the sounds of screaming guitars and drums filled the car.

"I didn't appreciate . . ."

"Cynthia, I have a lot to think about, so could you just be quiet. I have to take you right back to your hotel so I can plan for Curtis tomorrow and get a little sleep for a change. For once don't be a pain in the ass!"

They didn't speak again until Geddy drove up in front of the Ritz. Cynthia was helped out by a uniformed valet. Then she bent down and spoke with all the rage she'd built up on the ride there. "Curtis is lying, and if you are anywhere near as good as you are supposed to be, you'll prove he's lying."

Geddy pulled out just as she closed the door.

Why was he so mad at her? Sure, she was rude all evening and was too close minded about her brother, but that wasn't really it. He was angry because he had to trust her, and he didn't.

There was a bit of a stir when Curtis was called as a witness, since he had not been expected to testify. Earl Blue knew that right now the jury could go either way, but if the defense could prove the possibility that Cynthia could have hired a killer or killed the Measuring Lives herself, Curtis had an excellent chance for at least a hung jury, if not a not-guilty verdict.

The room fell silent as Curtis was sworn in. He looked good, in fine spirits, totally relaxed. He would be a tough nut to crack.

Earl Blue guided him through the preliminaries. Curtis came across as a regular guy, a bit of an adventurer as he talked about his sailing exploits, his love of climbing and sky-diving. He wasn't the least bit arrogant, unlike his sister. Despite the outburst the night before, Geddy had grown to like Curtis, and he was sure the jury was beginning to feel the same way. Eventually, Earl Blue came to the heart of the questioning.

"Mr. Dole, let me just come right out and ask the question we all want answered. Did you commit the five murders that took place in Naples during the summer of 1972?"

"No, I didn't," answered Curtis firmly.

"Do you know who did?"

"No, I don't."

"Well, do you have an alibi?"

"No."

"Not even for one of the murders."

"No."

"Why not?"

"Because they occurred more than twenty-one years ago. Who remembers where they were on a given night twenty-one years ago? Besides, most nights I was probably all by myself. I didn't have any friends in Naples."

"You do remember one night, don't you? Which one?"

"That's right. The night of the second murder, I was at a party with a girl. I guess she was sort of a friend, Donna Canty. But we left by eleven o'clock. I took her home and then went home myself, and I probably went right to bed."

"You used to have a maid. What was her name?"

Curtis actually drew a momentary blank, the first hint that he was nervous. "Paula Affatato."

"She testified that the night of the fourth murder, that of Sally Baumgartner, you came in at around ten-thirty soaking wet, wearing nothing but sneakers and gym shorts. Do you remember this?"

"No, but I believe it. I did that a lot. You see, I often go fishing alone down at the beach. Especially back then, since I didn't really have many friends. And there's nothing weird about it. Go to the beach any night, and you'll see people with poles stuck in the sand. Sometimes I stripped down to my shorts and took a swim."

Earl Blue asked Curtis some other questions that really weren't very important, other than the fact that Curtis was simply admitting that while he wasn't the murderer, he couldn't explain his whereabouts. It was very believable, and the jury was surely thinking, "Well, I don't blame him. I don't remember what I was doing twenty-one years ago either."

"Mr. Dole, there has been testimony that you requested a copy of the trust agreement a few months before the murders. Is that true?"

Curtis shifted uneasily, not taking his eyes off Earl Blue, and Earl Blue likewise never stopped staring down at Curtis. It was an awkward moment, as if they were having a battle of wills. Eventually, Curtis said, "Yes."

"What did you do with it?"

"I looked it over. Then I sent a copy to Cynthia."

The courtroom burst into mumbling and grumbling as the onlookers acknowledged the importance of this testimony. The judge called for order.

"Did she ask for a copy of the trust?"

"No, we weren't speaking to each other at the time. I sent her a copy along with a letter explaining an idea I had. I thought if we stuck together, we might be able to sue the trustee in order to get more money distributed to us."

"Did she respond?"

"She never got back to me."

"Well, maybe it got lost in the mail?"

"No, I called her. She told me she received it."

There were more murmurs now. A man in the gallery behind Geddy whispered to the woman beside him. "This is it. That bitch is gonna get nailed."

"When did you call her?" asked Earl Blue.

"I don't remember the exact date I called. I received the copy of the trust and my first distribution check during finals week, the first week in May. It was shortly after that, when I came home for the summer."

"So you're sure she received a copy of the trust? Before the Measuring Lives were killed?"

"Yes. I know I didn't wait long before calling her, it must have been a good month and a half or so before the first murder. When we spoke on the phone, she said she got the trust but wouldn't discuss it with me. She said she never wanted to talk to me again."

"Mr. Dole, can you prove that you called your sister in the middle of May of 1972?"

"Well, I tried. I went to the telephone company to try to get a printout of all my calls for that month, but they didn't have the records."

Earl Blue picked up several pieces of paper that were waiting on a corner of the defense table. He handed one set to Geddy, one to the clerk, and one to Curtis. "Your Honor, I have a signed affidavit from the Naples Telephone Company, which we obtained just yesterday, which confirms there are no records available from 1972."

Great. That was Geddy's last hope. Ask for a recess and check the telephone records. He was really sunk now. They had established that Cynthia knew who the Measuring Lives were before the murders, if the jury believed Curtis—and he did come across as believable. At the same time, he had made Cynthia look like a liar.

• • •

Geddy slowly walked to the middle of the courtroom, almost dragging himself up there. He appeared to actually shrink two inches. Geddy was no longer swaggering like an unbeatable gunslinger walking confidently through the center of town. He appeared terribly mortal now.

"Mr. Dole, you're a homosexual, aren't you?" He decided his only chance was to use the jurors' probable prejudice against homosexuals. He had nothing against gay people and he hated doing this to Curtis, but he was desperate.

"Yes. There's nothing wrong with that," answered Curtis.

"A lot of people wouldn't agree. Isn't it true you live with . . ."

"Your Honor?" said Faith suddenly. Geddy turned to see her standing. What was she doing? This was all Geddy had. He had to use Curtis' homosexuality against him.

"Yes," the judge answered.

"May I speak to counsel for a second?" requested Faith.

The judge said yes, and Geddy hurried to the table. "What are you . . ."

"Sshh! Look at what Morgan has."

Morgan handed it to Geddy like she was handing him the key to victory. Geddy needed to look at it for only a brief moment before he understood. He took a few seconds to think and turned back to Curtis Dole.

"Your Honor, I'd like to strike my first question." Geddy stood in the center of the courtroom, ten paces from Curtis. "Before we get to your alleged mailing of a copy of the trust to your sister, I have a few details to get through, but it shouldn't take a minute. During the summer of 1972, did you own a motorcycle?"

"Yes."

"Did it have a headlight?"

Curtis hesitated. "Yes."

"Did you wear motorcycle gloves when you drove it?"

"Most of the time," he admitted.

"Did you do heroin?"

He exhaled. "Look, I . . ."

"Yes or no! Did you do heroin!"

"A couple of times, but . . ."

"Did you ever buy heroin that summer?"

"Yes, once, but . . ."

"So occasionally you had heroin in your possession?"

A sigh. "Yes, two or three times . . ."

"What size belt did you wear in 1972?"

"I don't remember . . ."

"Do I have to introduce the records from your draft physical?"

Curtis sighed again. "I was a size thirty-two." There was an audible gasp in the courtroom. "But that must be the most common waist size for a twenty-year-old . . ."

"What size feet do you have?"

"Another very common size."

"What size!"

Curtis swallowed. "Ten-and-a-half." There was more whispering in the gallery.

"I'm trying to be brief. I want to get to the good stuff." Geddy was on a roll now. "You say that you received a copy of the trust agreement in early May 1972, correct?"

"Yes."

"And you also say that you mailed a copy to Cynthia in early May?"

"Somewhere around that time. Maybe it was the second week. How can I be expected to remember?"

"And you also stated that you're sure Cynthia received this envelope in the mail. How are you sure of that?"

"Like I said, because I called her."

"Are you sure she didn't call you?"

"Yes."

"Positive?"

"Yes."

"There's no mistake about it?"

"Your Honor!" objected Earl Blue.

"Move on, Mr. Geddy," ordered Judge Frost.

"What telephone number did you call?" asked Geddy

Curtis shrugged. "I don't remember the exact phone number."

"Would you remember if I told you?"

"No. It was just a phone number, and I almost never called her."

"Then how did you even know what telephone number to call?"

Curtis hesitated, thinking. "I . . . I called her from Naples, from the house. I'm sure her number was written down somewhere. The maid had it, I think. Paula had the number."

"You're sure you made the call from home?"

"Yes."

"When you say home, you mean 935 Green Dolphin Drive?"

"Yes."

"I see. Long distance, right?"

"Yes. Chicago is long distance, but don't tell me you have the phone records because Mr. Blue and I already tried to get them, and the phone company said it wasn't possible. It's a different phone company now, and the old company doesn't keep that information for more than a certain number of years," insisted Curtis.

"Yes, that's unfortunate. Because if we had the telephone records, your call to Chicago would have showed up, right?"

"I suppose so."

"And it was Chicago where you telephoned Cynthia?"

"Yeah, Chicago."

Geddy turned and quickly walked back to the table, his heart ready to jump through his chest. The case was over now.

"Your Honor, I have in my hands the trust journal for the month of May 1972. As you will recall, all the trust journals have been previously moved into evidence."

"Yes. Proceed," the judge said.

"May I have an opportunity to review the journal?" asked Earl Blue.

"Mr. Geddy . . ." The judge said, signaling for Geddy to carry it over to Earl Blue.

Geddy walked over to his counterpart with the three-ring binder. He blessed Morgan again, this time for reminding him that the house on Green Dolphin Drive was owned by the Adam Gentry Trust. Geddy pointed to something in the back of the binder, and Earl Blue almost fainted.

"May I have a sidebar, Your Honor?" Earl Blue managed to ask.

"No way . . ." began Geddy.

The judge cut Geddy off. "Mr. Blue, do you have an objection?"

"I . . . I would like to speak to my client."

"No way, Your Honor," demanded Geddy.

"Your request is denied, Mr. Blue. Proceed, Mr. Geddy." Earl Blue hesitated, wanting to do something. He reluctantly slumped into his chair and tried to breath.

"Mr. Dole, who owns the house at 935 Green Dolphin Drive?"

Curtis was nervous now, he could tell Geddy was up to something. His voice reflected his insecurity. "Actually, it's trust property. The trust owns it."

"And who pays the mortgage?"

"Well . . . the trustee does, I guess. Morgan."

"Who pays the bills?"

"Well, I don't. They, they must go to the trustee."

"Ladies and gentlemen," announced Geddy as he held the trust journal over his head, turning briefly to the gallery, then to the jury. "The trust journal for the month of May 1972, previously marked as Plaintiff's Exhibit Ten, contains the May 1972 long-distance telephone bill, along with all of the bills for that home for that month." The excitement grew as Geddy pulled the bill from the manila envelope in the back of the trust. "I'm placing the bill in front of you, Mr. Dole. Would you please point out your telephone call to your sister?"

Curtis couldn't speak. It took him a few seconds to even pick up the bill. His hand trembled slightly, and the bill fell into his lap. He looked down at it with a horrified expression.

There were several calls to Providence, two to New York, and one to Hyannis, Massachusetts. There were three to Newport and several to Fort Lauderdale, Palm Beach, and Miami. But there were no calls to Chicago.

"Mr. Dole? Where is that call to your sister?"

Curtis's head bolted upright, and he looked desperately at his lawyer. Earl Blue couldn't face him and rolled his head downward.

"Mr. Dole, there is no call to Chicago, is there? Yet you insisted—what, three, four times—that you called her? That's how you allegedly confirmed that she received the trust. But you lied. You never called her." Curtis didn't respond. "What is your explanation, Mr. Dole?"

Curtis looked at Geddy, frightened, then looked at the jury as if just realizing they were watching this entire spectacle. He leaned his elbows on his knees, buried his face in his hands, and pulled his hair as if he were trying to tear it out of his head.

"Mr. Dole, you must answer the question," the judge ordered.

"He won't answer because he has no answer!" exclaimed Geddy. "Isn't that true, Mr. Dole? You lied! You never mailed a copy to your sister, and you never telephoned her! You lied!"

Curtis didn't answer. When he looked up, his face was shattered.

"Mr. Dole, you had *better* start talking because I'm not going to go away without an explanation. You lied about the telephone call. Now admit you lied about mailing the trust, or I'll prove you lied. Answer me!"

"Answer the question, Mr. Dole!" the judge ordered. Earl Blue was conspicuously silent, and Curtis didn't even look up, much less answer.

"All right, if that's the way you want it." Now it was time to bluff. Geddy had him, it was time to rub it in while he could. "You want to go through this again? You want me to prove again that you're a liar? Fine! Tell me what post office you mailed the trust from! Tell me!"

Geddy gave Curtis half a second to answer then continued.

"What post office? What address did you mail it to? How much postage did you put on it? Did you mail it yourself? Who mailed it? What time of the day was it mailed? How big was the envelope? Answer me Curtis! Answer me!"

The young lawyer seated next to Earl Blue timidly rose to his feet. "Objection," said Fred Lee in a feeble voice.

Geddy whipped around and pointed at him. "You shut up! This is Blue's witness, not yours!" Geddy's instincts took over. He was an awesome sight, standing over Curtis, challenging him. As Geddy expanded, Curtis shrunk.

"Order!" The judge banged his gavel. "Order. Okay, that's far enough. Back off, John."

Geddy was racing with adrenaline, but he did back up a step or two and waited a good ten, fifteen seconds. Nobody moved a muscle in that courtroom except for Curtis, who finally looked up.

"I never got a copy of the trust," he said in a whisper.

"What?" asked Geddy, not sure he understood him.

"I never got a copy myself."

"You mean Cynthia never got a copy!"

"No, I didn't mail her a copy, but that's because I never got a copy."

"What? First you say you did get a copy from the trustee and that you mailed a copy to your sister. Now you're saying that you never even got a copy yourself?"

"I swear it."

"Then why would you lie?"

"Because we knew . . ." Curtis caught himself.

"We?" repeated Geddy. "*We?* Who is we? Do you mean Mr. Blue?"

Curtis just stared straight ahead without answering.

Judge Frost spoke now. "Mr. Dole, did Mr. Blue instruct you to lie under oath?"

Curtis was on the verge of weeping. "I told him I never asked for a copy, that I never received one. But Earl said it was documented and that no one would believe me if I said I never received it. So he told me to lie, to say that I got a copy but that I mailed a copy to Cynthia so it would look like she could have hired a killer."

There was a prolonged commotion now. Even the judge was shocked and didn't call for order.

Geddy pressed ahead. "The only thing we know is that you lied! It's over, Curtis. Admit it. Tell us that you killed those Measuring Lives."

The room fell silent as everyone waited for Curtis' dramatic confession.

"No!" he screamed out. "I swear I didn't kill anyone! I can't explain it! I don't know who did it, but I didn't do it!"

Everyone in the room stared at him with disgust, including Geddy. "Your Honor, I think he's through."

Geddy walked proudly back to his chair, cognizant of the fact that Faith, Cynthia, and Morgan looked at him with near-reverence. He sat without looking at them, aware that all eyes were still on him.

"Does the defense have any more questions?" the judge asked.

Earl Blue didn't move, he just stared at the floor in the middle of the room. Fred Lee hesitated, thought for a moment, and finally replied, "No, Your Honor."

"Does the defense have any more witnesses?" asked Judge Frost angrily again.

Earl Blue said nothing. Unsure of himself, Fred Lee said, "No, Your Honor. The defense rests."

The courtroom erupted in the excitement generated by knowing that the trial was all but over now.

"Mr. Geddy, any rebuttal witnesses?"

He stood. "I don't think that will be necessary, Your Honor."

"We will adjourn for lunch. We'll meet back here at two o'clock for closing arguments. Bailiff, take the jury out!" When the jury was out of the courtroom the judge yelled at Earl Blue. "Mr. Blue, I want to speak with you in chambers. *Now!* Mr. Geddy, you may attend if you wish. Court is in recess until two o'clock." He threw the gavel down and swept off, forgetting to let Curtis know he could step down from the witness stand.

As the room emptied, the families of the five victims crowded around Geddy, slapping him on the back and shaking his hand. Curtis remained seated, as if in a trance. Earl Blue slowly marched off to the judge's chambers, past Curtis, without looking at his client.

26

"All rise!" the bailiff called out as Judge Frost walked hurriedly to the bench. The judge wasn't in a good mood and said, "Mr. Geddy, closing argument," before he was even seated. Geddy waited a couple of seconds for things to settle down, then rose and walked to the center of the room. It wasn't until that moment that he noticed only Curtis and Fred Lee were seated at the defense table. Earl Blue was not in the room.

Geddy began by explaining once again about the motive. He reminded the jury that Curtis Dole stood to receive twenty million dollars in 1993 if he killed the five Measuring Lives. Geddy also told the jurors that only Curtis had both knowledge of who the Measuring Lives were *and* a motive to kill them. Having once established that, all that was left for him to do was to explain *how* Curtis carried out the murders.

Geddy walked right up in front of the jurors and put his hand on the oak railing of the jury box. "On the night of June 11, 1972, Curtis Dole followed Gabrielle Smith to Lindy's Pub on Fifth

Avenue. He didn't know much about her except—like everyone who knew her—that she was addicted to heroin. This was perfect because Curtis did some heroin and he knew where to get it. So he waited for her to come outside or go to the ladies' room, sometime when not many people would notice him. He told Gabrielle he had some heroin, why don't they go to the beach and get high? She accepted, and they drove off on Curtis's motorcycle without anyone knowing.

"They went to the beach on Fifteenth Avenue South. Curtis parked his motorcycle off the street, probably behind some bushes where it wouldn't be noticed. That's why no cars were seen parked on the side streets that night near where the victim was found. Curtis and Gabrielle found a nice stretch of beach between the two streetlights from Fifteenth to Sixteenth Avenues, and he took off his belt. He wrapped his belt around her arm—you will recall Curtis admitted that his waist size back then was thirty-two, the same size as the belt found around the arm of Gabrielle Smith—and then handed Gabrielle the needle, which she stuck in her arm. She pulled it out and dropped it next to her while Curtis Dole walked behind her and slit her throat. Then he tossed the knife over the sea wall and hurried off, leaving the heroin needle and his belt.

"Curtis didn't have to worry about fingerprints. You see, as he admitted, he always wore motorcycle gloves. That, ladies and gentlemen, is why he didn't look odd wearing gloves in Naples in the summer. He simply left them on for the few minutes between the time he got off his motorcycle and the time he killed his victim.

"The next night, Curtis Dole killed the second girl listed in the trust—Julieanne Cherube. This time it was easier. Curtis was at Margaret Brennan's party. When it broke up and everyone went to the beach, he took his friend Donna Canty home. He said he was going home, but he didn't. He went back and found Julieanne Cherube.

"Now, Curtis is gay, but you can't tell that by looking at him. Donna Canty, in fact, had a crush on him all summer. Curtis was good looking, charming, obviously intelligent, and very well-mannered. It was easy for him to lure the boy-crazy, not very pretty but certainly very drunk Julieanne Cherube ten blocks down the beach, where he even went so far as to kiss her in order to get her in a position where he could easily kill her. In the heat of passion he moved behind her, pulled her head back and slit her throat.

"Then, as he did with all of his victims, he left her somewhere where she would be discovered fairly soon. He needed the bodies to be found right away. No burying them or dumping them in the Everglades or in the Gulf. He wanted them found because, remember, he gets his money twenty-one years after their date of death. He didn't want them pronounced 'missing,' and not dead for another seven years as the law provides when no body is found. If that happened he'd have to wait that much longer to receive his money from the trust.

"Over the course of the next month, Curtis realized he would have to change his method of killing. The police were all over the beaches. So on July 10, 1972, he followed Angelica Grevey back to her office after a dinner with some coworkers. She went inside, and Curtis went to work. He broke the single light that illuminated the parking lot and slashed one of her tires. Then he waited around the corner for Angelica Grevey to come out. What she found was a flat tire, and Mrs. Keenan heard her say, 'Shit, stupid car!' But seconds after Mrs. Keenan walked into the other room, Curtis pulled up on his motorcycle and offered to help. Maybe it was odd for somebody to pull in back there at that time of the night, but he was nice, polite, and she could use the help. She accepted.

"He parked his motorcycle behind the car a little, facing the flat tire so that Angelica would believe it was to better see the flat. Mrs. Keenan looked out and thought she saw a flashlight, but she only looked out for a second. What she really saw was Curtis Dole's motorcycle headlight.

"Angelica opened the trunk and began moving things out of the way so they could get to the spare tire. Curtis pulled out a knife, pulled her head back by her hair, and slit her neck from behind. He let her slide to the ground without a sound and dropped his knife next to her. He fled the scene, and when Mrs. Keenan looked outside again, all she could see was darkness. If the lot were lit up, she would have been looking out over the pool of blood running from the neck of the third Measuring Life listed in the trust.

"Sally Baumgartner was a college student home for the summer. Sometime in the days leading up to July 11, 1972, Curtis Dole made it a point to meet her and ask her out. He didn't give his real name, of course, in case she told anyone. She eagerly accepted and spent the day of her death at the hairdresser's, buying a new dress, and making dinner reservations at the best restaurant in town. Curtis told her to meet him in the back, in that empty dirt lot behind the restaurant where there were no lights.

"He was waiting for her and probably opened her door with his gloved hand, which explains the smudges on the door handle. A real gentleman. She got out and greeted him, then turned and reached into the back seat of her car for her purse. Curtis saw his opportunity. Keeping her chin up by pulling down on her beautiful blonde hair from behind, he tried to slit her throat. But Sally was a fighter. She put her foot on the car, leaving a mark, and pushed them both down. We know they scrambled a bit in the mud, but then he stabbed her in the stomach, which slowed her down. He stabbed her furiously eleven more times, then finally, mercifully, slit her throat.

"You'll recall, too," said Geddy as he turned and walked back into the middle of the courtroom, "that was the night that Paula Affatato, the Doles' maid, saw Curtis come in at around ten-thirty, about two hours after the murder, soaking wet. His clothes were nowhere to be seen, and he was wearing only his gym shorts. At the time she believed him when he said he took a swim that night while he was fishing, but now we know better. He was washing Sally Baumgartner's blood off before he went home. He no doubt,

as Officer Casserly testified, had blood spurted on him while he
repeatedly stabbed her.

"By August, Olde Naples was a war zone. Police and volunteers patrolled the streets waiting for the now-named New Moon
Slasher to strike again.

"Curtis learned how much easier it was to arrange a date with
his victim, because then he could get her wherever he wanted to
and kill her. Besides, the girls in town were no longer going to be
such easy targets. So he arranged to meet Deborah Moore and
asked her out, impressing her with his maturity, his intelligence,
and the fact that he had his own house. She accepted his invitation to spend the night, but it would have to be late because her
mother wouldn't let her out after midnight, and he would have to
pick her up because she didn't have a car. Debbie told Curtis to
pick her up at twelve-thirty in the morning, after her parents were
asleep so she could sneak out of her house. Perfect for Curtis. She
sneaked out and met him at the end of the driveway. For Curtis,
it would be simple. Take her to a nice quiet spot and kill her.

"But there was a problem. Debbie wouldn't get on his motorcycle. She was almost killed while riding a bicycle when she was
a child, and she was terrified of bikes, mopeds, and motorcycles,
not to mention that Curtis only had one helmet. So Debbie Moore
refused to get on Curtis's motorcycle.

"Curtis was so close. He had already killed four, and he desperately wanted to get this last murder over with. So he got off the
bike, and one way or another, he got behind her, pulled her head
back by her hair and began to slit her throat. He was so overcome
with adrenaline at finishing his murder spree that he cut right
through her neck. The body slumped to the ground, leaving Curtis
holding her head in his hand by the hair.

"He tossed her head into the bushes and dragged the body
there, too. Again, he left the knife. Yes, he was covered with his victim's blood, but it was late and Naples was much smaller then, so
there was far less traffic at night, and he could always pull off the
road on his motorcycle if any other cars approached. In addition,

he could have carried extra clothes in his saddlebags or could have made his way directly to the beach for a swim in order to wash off the blood.

"After he made it home that night, all five murders were completed. Now he would live off the distributions until 1993, when he could expect about twenty million dollars. He thought he had it made.

"As I'm sure you now understand, it's ridiculous to think that Cynthia Dole hired someone to kill the Measuring Lives. Not only is it clear in light of the facts as I've just explained them, but keep in mind, Cynthia Dole never knew who the Measuring Lives were, so it would be impossible for her to have them killed.

"Curtis tried to convince you of that, but you saw what happened. You saw Curtis and heard him admit that he lied. His lawyer told him to lie. Who knows what else they lied about? You see, Curtis realized how damaging this part of the case was. He needed to be able to try to convince you, the jurors, that it was just as likely that Cynthia killed the Measuring Lives. He knew how ridiculous the so-called serial killer expert sounded and how absurd it is to think it was all just a coincidence. These weren't serial killings. Curtis and Mr. Blue knew it and knew that you would know it, too.

"So he lied, but we caught him, and now it's time for you to decide. Remember *Concentration*? Did I flip over enough of the puzzle for you? Do you see it? Do you see that Curtis Dole had the motive? Twenty million dollars. That he was the only person who knew who the Measuring Lives were who could gain from the murders? Do you see it? Because ladies and gentlemen, Curtis Dole saw it, which is why he lied. By lying he unwittingly put the last nail in his coffin. Now we all know he is a liar, and we all know he is a killer.

"So as you go back to deliberate, look at the pieces of the puzzle and think of your choices. Was it Curtis Dole, or was it the most unbelievable coincidence any of us have ever heard? Please find Curtis Dole guilty, so we can all be proud of securing a little bit of justice for those five young women and their families.

"Thank you again for your time and for your consideration. Thank you for your concentration."

* * *

After Fred Lee delivered an awful closing argument in place of Earl Blue, Geddy knew that it wouldn't take long for the jury to make its decision, so he didn't leave the courtroom. He also didn't want to go outside to face the press about the James Hoffer incident or the trial, and he didn't want to answer questions from Morgan, Cynthia, and possibly even Faith asking, "What do you think our chances are? Maybe the jury will think this? Maybe they'll think that? If they deliberate for a long time, is that good for us, or does that mean they're not convinced?"

He knew he was going to win, so there was nothing to talk about. A couple of hours later, Nick walked into the courtroom. It was empty except for Geddy, who was sitting deep in thought in a juror's chair.

"There you are," Nick called out as he made his way over. "Are you all right? You don't look good."

"I just wanted to be alone."

"Well you don't have a thing to worry about, you know. You're going to win."

"I know."

"Then what's the matter? You don't think Curtis is guilty, do you?" Nick asked.

Now Geddy looked really annoyed. "I'm not in the mood, Nick."

"You're not alone. I don't think he's guilty, either. But you sure put on one hell of a case, just like you did with Hoffer. You've got a talent, kid. It's not easy to prove an innocent man committed murder. You think somehow Cynthia did it, right?"

"No."

"Well, then you're finally right about something. It wasn't Cynthia, either."

Geddy scoffed at Nick. "Who do you think then?"

"What I thought all along. A serial killer." Geddy laughed at him and didn't bother to respond. "Did you see my article?"

Geddy nodded. "Thanks, Nick. Thanks for not writing about . . . everything. Especially my parents and my sister."

Nick waved a hand at him. "It was nothing. I kind of liked the angle I took though. You like that quote from your old boss in Miami? 'You could see by the look in John's eyes that the Hoffer case would be his last. He was like a gunfighter who lost his nerve, but he knew he had one last fight.' " Nick howled with laughter. "I loved that quote!"

"That's bullshit, you know," Geddy told him. "I never wanted to leave. I think they got rid of me because they were scared."

"Of what?"

Geddy hesitated for a moment. "I'm not sure. Let's just say there's a chance you're right about Hoffer. He might not be the South Beach Butcher."

"Did you know that all along?" asked Nick.

"I still don't know if he's guilty or innocent, but I was never convinced he was guilty. Every time I went to the state attorney to tell him I thought something wasn't right, the next day more evidence of Hoffer's guilt would suddenly appear. I didn't like the way things looked. I wanted out of the case, but I was told in no uncertain terms I had to take it to trial and that I was expected to win."

"Did you resign because of that? Is that how you ended up in Naples?"

Geddy shook his head. "Like I said, I was forced out. Of course, they didn't put it that way. The Miami state attorney came to me with the Hirt, Harrington offer in hand. He went to law school with Jeffrey Robb, and he knew that Hirt, Harrington had an opening for a litigator, so he pulled some strings for me. I didn't want to go, but I was told that I was 'unstable' and that my memories of my parents' murders combined with the stress of prosecuting sadistic killers had become too much for me. They said it would be irresponsible of them to let me continue prosecuting. I knew the real deal, though. It wasn't an offer. It was a threat. Get out or else.

"So I took the job here, but before I started I contacted every state attorney in Florida looking for a position. They all turned me down. I had just won the most important trial in the state, and not one state attorney would hire me. Whoever was responsible in Miami arranged to shut me out. They obviously didn't want someone with my suspicions to have prosecutorial power. So I came to Hirt, Harrington. I figured whatever was going on was bigger than I had imagined, so I better get out of there."

"What were they so afraid of? These people in Miami, I mean."

"They must have been worried that I was going to figure out what was going on, Nick. I spent more time trying to find evidence that Hoffer was innocent than I did trying to find evidence of his guilt. I thought all along the case was manufactured, but I could never prove it. When I insisted they take me off the case, they not only refused, but I started noticing I was being followed. I even got a few death threats. By the time they realized I was suspicious, it was too late to replace me, so they did the next best thing. They arranged the perfect job for me in a fancy private firm at triple my former salary as a reward for keeping my suspicions to myself."

"Obviously. The big question is, who is 'they'? Who would want to make Hoffer look like a serial killer?"

"That's not much of a mystery. I just think since it was an election year the mayor or the Miami state attorney needed to nail someone for those murders, and Hoffer was picked. I wouldn't even be surprised if the judge were in on it. Of course, this is all assuming that Hoffer wasn't guilty, which I'm not 100 percent sure about." Geddy took a deep breath and exhaled. "I don't know. Maybe I'm imagining the whole thing."

"I don't know what you're doin' in here pouting. You did all you could. You tried to prove somethin' was goin' on, but when you couldn't, you did your job."

"I know, I could live with all that. There'll always be dirty politicians, I'm not on a crusade. I don't care about them. It's just that I don't like being run out of town, and most importantly, I wish

I knew for sure about Hoffer. If he was innocent, the real serial killer . . ."

The rear door of the courtroom suddenly opened. Geddy looked up and saw Faith peek in and look about.

"Oh! John, we thought we lost you," she said. "Have you been here for the last couple of hours? We've been waiting for you at the office."

"I thought we might have a decision by the end of the day."

"Well, you're right again. We got a call about twenty minutes ago telling us the jury reached a verdict. Everyone's on their way back here."

Nick was taken aback. "Really? Well, that was fast."

"You sound surprised, Nick. Didn't you expect it?" asked Faith.

"Nick thinks Curtis is innocent," said Geddy, implying with his tone and by rolling his eyes that Nick was out of his mind. "He thinks a serial killer murdered the Measuring Lives."

"Yes, I do think Curtis is innocent. But I think the jury will find him guilty," Nick added.

"How could it be a serial killer? Do you honestly think it's a coincidence that the victims were all Measuring Lives?" asked Faith incredulously.

"I guess so," Nick said. Both Faith and Geddy shook their heads at him as if he were out of his mind.

• • •

"Bailiff, bring in the jury," the judge said without hesitation. The bailiff opened a door and nodded to the jurors, who filed in and were seated. "Madam foreperson, has the jury reached a decision?"

A woman rose from her seat in the juror's box. "Yes, we have." The verdict form was passed to the judge, who inspected it briefly. Satisfied, the judge handed it to the clerk. "Please read the verdict."

The entire room fell silent, so silent that Faith held her breath for fear that she could be heard gasping for air as the moment of truth arrived. Curtis and Fred Lee stood rigidly as they watched the clerk look down at the piece of paper in her hand.

The clerk read from the verdict form. "In the case of *Dole v.*

Dole, case number 93-3917, we the jury find the defendant, Adam Curtis Dole . . . guilty of the murder of Gabrielle Diana Smith."

The courtroom erupted, particularly Faith, who grabbed Geddy and gave him a short, awkward hug. Geddy didn't move.

"As to the second question, we the jury find the defendant, Adam Curtis Dole . . . guilty of the murder of Julieanne Gloria Cherube."

Another outburst, not quite as loud, and Faith again grabbed him, now only with one arm. Geddy did not so much as blink.

"As to question number three, we the jury find the defendant, Adam Curtis Dole . . . guilty of the murder of Angelica Marie Savasta."

The crowd was a bit more settled, but there was steady crying from the assembled family members of the victims.

"As to question number four, we the jury find the defendant, Adam Curtis Dole . . . guilty of the murder of Sally Margaret Baumgartner."

Curtis's head was hung low, but he didn't cry. He obviously expected this.

"As to question number five, we the jury find the defendant, Adam Curtis Dole . . . guilty of the murder of Deborah Moore."

The courtroom was filled again with a hundred voices, and this time even Morgan and Cynthia hugged. Fred Lee was shouting something above the din.

Judge Frost tried to regain order. "Quiet down. Order! I'll get to you in a moment, Mr. Lee." Then after it had quieted down, the judge said, "Ladies and gentlemen of the jury, I want to thank you for your contribution over the last few days . . ." The judge explained that the bailiff had a certificate of appreciation for each of the jurors for fulfilling their duty and had the bailiff escort them out.

After the jury left and the crowd quieted down, Fred Lee cried, "Your Honor, the defendant moves to have the principal of the court-appointed trust remain in trust and not be distributed to Ms. Dole until after appeal."

"Your Honor . . ." began Geddy.

Judge Frost ruled immediately, obviously still very upset at Earl Blue and Curtis for what happened earlier in the day. "No need, Mr. Geddy, I'm denying Mr. Lee's request. I find that there's sufficient evidence to support the verdict. I do not see any basis for overturning the decision on appeal, and frankly, I am outraged at the behavior of Mr. Blue, who has obviously chosen not to be here today, and at the conduct of the defendant on the stand. You have the right to appeal, but this money—and this is my decision—this money that has been in trust by order of the court since last August is now deemed *vested* in the plaintiff, Cynthia Dole. Ms. Gentry?"

"Yes, Your Honor," replied Morgan respectfully.

"The court wants to thank you for managing the court-appointed trust until after trial. You are hereby ordered to give over to Cynthia Dole the entire trust principal, as the court ordered interim trust is now deemed terminated. The money and property are now the vested property of Cynthia Dole. Therefore, Mr. Lee, your motion is denied. There being no further court business, this courtroom is adjourned."

Geddy sank to his seat while everyone around him celebrated. But the happiness of Faith, Cynthia, Morgan, the families of the five victims, and the other Hirt, Harrington lawyers, all of whom were present now other than Jeffrey, was contagious. Finally, a grin broke through Geddy's melancholy. His contented grin eventually broke into a full-fledged smile as he stood up and hugged first Faith, then Cynthia, and finally and most enthusiastically, Morgan.

• • •

Geddy tried to get away unnoticed, but in the crush of reporters immediately following the verdict, he wasn't going to be permitted a quick exit. Microphones were thrust in his face, and the light flashes were blinding. On the courthouse steps, he was surrounded by Cynthia, Faith, Morgan, Connie Bass, Gus Baumgartner, Gregg Smith, Robert Grevey, Margaret Brennan, and other friends and relatives of the Measuring Lives. Most of the family members were crying out of joy, anger, and relief all at the same time.

Connie gained the media's attention by grabbing a microphone and making an emotional plea to the state attorney to charge Curtis criminally for the murders, so that he would finally get what was coming to him. Execution. She embraced Geddy and sobbed on his shoulder, and then Connie's mother hugged her. Robert Grevey joined in, and soon they were all one huddled mass, a group of victorious avengers.

By eight twenty that evening Geddy, Faith, Mr. Burke, and Josephine Harrington were seated at a large, round table in the magnificent main dining room of the Ritz-Carlton. The only member of the firm who wasn't there for the victory celebration was Jeffrey Robb, who regretfully declined the invitation. Morgan waited for Geddy at home where they would have their own celebration later.

"Don't you think someone should go get her?" asked Josephine irritably. She seemed to be in a hurry that evening.

"Oh, Cynthia's just getting all dolled up, I'm sure," said Faith. "She's superior to us, you know, so it's okay for her to keep us waiting."

"I want to propose a toast," announced Mr. Burke, not his first toast of the night. "To John Geddy, the bright young trial attorney of Hirt, Harrington. Your future is assured now, John."

"You bet it is," seconded Faith.

"Don't forget Faith, who did just as much, if not more, work than I did on this case," said Geddy, meaning it.

They all drank to Faith. "Thanks John, but you did it. You're the best I've ever seen."

"So what will Cynthia do now?" asked Mr. Burke.

Faith rolled her eyes. "She's flying back to Chicago tomorrow. The first thing she'll do is buy a condominium in the city, Chicago that is. 'The commute from Lake Forest to downtown is such an inconvenience,'" said Faith, doing her best Cynthia impression but only after turning around first to make sure she wasn't about to walk in.

"So is Ms. Cynthia ever going to show up? It's eight thirty. I have better places to be," complained Josephine from her seat in the middle of the most exclusive hotel in Naples.

Geddy stood up. "All right, I guess I should make sure she's still planning on joining us. I'll be back in a few minutes."

On the eighth floor of the Ritz-Carlton, Geddy stepped off the elevator and turned left, made a quick right, and then walked to the very end of the corridor. He knocked on the door of room 812, Cynthia's room. He waited a minute but there was no answer. He knocked again and waited and even called out that it was him, but still there was no answer.

Geddy went down to the lobby and asked the concierge if Cynthia left a message, but he was informed she hadn't. Puzzled, he went out to the valet station, where the same tuxedoed door-man who insulted Geddy's old Ford last year was standing.

"Hey Bobby," Geddy called out.

"Yes, Mr. Geddy. Your car is just around the corner, I'll have it in a moment. I put it in a special spot so it would be safe and . . ."

"I'm not leaving. I want to know if you noticed Ms. Dole leave the hotel tonight?"

"No sir, I haven't seen her since she returned from the cour-thouse. Maybe she's having dinner with her brother."

"Curtis?" Geddy laughed. "No chance."

"Well, he was here just a little while ago. I assumed it was to see Ms. Dole."

A terrible thought flashed through Geddy's mind. "Curtis Dole was *here!*"

The doorman nodded. "Sure, he pulled up in a green Jaguar. Hey Neil!" the doorman shouted to a valet. "You pick up a green Jag tonight?"

"Yeah, about ten minutes ago!"

Geddy ran over to the valet. "Was the Jag owner alone when he left?"

"Yeah."

Geddy didn't hesitate. He rushed past startled onlookers through the lobby of the Ritz and pounded on the elevator keys. The elevator dinged its arrival, and Geddy rushed inside even before the passengers had exited. He paced frantically in the elevator until it reached the eighth floor. He slid out the barely open doors, sprinted down the hall, and without stopping, lowered his shoulder into the door of room 812. It crashed open as Geddy nearly knocked it off its hinges. He fell into the room on his back and rolled over instantly, his shoulder stinging with pain. He recoiled in horror when he realized he was inches away from what remained of Cynthia Dole's face.

● ● ●

Geddy spent all night at the police station. He called Morgan at around ten. She rushed to be by his side, along with Faith and Mr. Burke and Josephine Harrington, but he knew it would be some time before the police took his statement, so he sent them all home. He ended up staying all night, hoping to be there when they brought Curtis in. But by the next morning, Curtis had still not been found. Geddy couldn't stand the waiting any longer, so he went to his office and bounded up the stairs past a few reporters who were waiting there for him.

When he walked in, everyone from the office came out to see how he was, to see what was going on. They had heard about Cynthia, but judging from the looks on their faces when they laid eyes on him they were more concerned about Geddy. Geddy answered their questions for a minute until Mr. Burke broke it up.

"Okay, that's enough. Let's get John a seat in the conference room before he collapses. John, come on in here. Jeffrey, Faith, you come, too." Josephine Harrington wasn't in the office that morning.

The four lawyers assembled in the conference room. "How did it go with the police?" asked Mr. Burke.

"Fine. They just asked a million questions."

"Okay, good. While you were at the police station, we've been discussing the case, and . . ." began Mr. Burke.

"What's to discuss?" asked Geddy. "Cynthia is dead, and Curtis did it."

"Yes, I know," continued Mr. Burke, "but the question is, what does this mean to your case?"

"My case? You mean Cynthia Dole's case. She's dead, it's all over. She's dead, and Curtis did it. But Curtis was already disqualified from the trust, so he won't get a dime. The University of Tampa gets the money. What is there to discuss?"

"John, you . . ." began Jeffrey.

"No, don't even try. You're going to say that yes, it's terrible that Cynthia was killed, but we have to think about the well-being of the firm and all of Cynthia's unpaid attorney's fees. That's all we ever think about in this office, but I don't care anymore. I'm sick of dealing with this case. I'm sick of all of these stupid fucking cases!" He rubbed his temples furiously with both hands.

"After I spent over a year proving that Curtis murdered those girls, what good comes of it? I win and my client gets killed, then the police tell me to watch out because they can't find Curtis. They think he might come after me!"

"After you?" asked Mr. Burke.

"The police think he went nuts. He went to the Ritz, had a valet park his car, walked right by the security cameras and took the elevator to the eighth floor and blew Cynthia's face off. Then he casually leaves like no one's going to notice."

"Then they're sure it was Curtis?" asked Mr. Burke.

"Hell yes. This morning they got a search warrant and found a gun with a silencer hidden in a storage compartment on his boat.

They've already confirmed it was the gun used to kill Cynthia." He shook his head. "I guess the police are right. He must have lost his mind to do something so stupid. He had nothing to gain!"

"John, I think there's something you don't understand," said Faith.

"Something I don't understand? Yes, that's right. I don't understand how Curtis could have thrown away a perfectly good life of sailing and doing all the other things he used to do to kill those five girls. And I don't understand, even after he lost the trial, why he would kill Cynthia and give up his chances on an appeal just to get revenge. I don't understand why someone would carve up seven prostitutes, I don't understand why my parents were killed, I don't understand why Deirdre killed herself, and I don't understand how people do it or why people do it or how it comes so easily to them!"

Faith tried to calm him even as she explained. "John, please relax, okay? There's something you're forgetting. Curtis isn't crazy, he had a motive. The trust is finished, remember? The judge ordered it vested in Cynthia. It has no effect anymore." Faith's voice soothed him a little. Now she tried to bring him back, to make him use his head. "Do you understand what that means? Remember, Cynthia had no will. She didn't set up any trusts, either."

It came to Geddy with a jolt. "My God! It makes perfect sense for Curtis to kill her. To get the money! She had no will, no trust. Curtis would be her legal heir!"

"Now you've got it," said Faith, still speaking in a low whisper. "Even though he was disqualified from getting the money from the trust, once the judge ordered the trust terminated, it no longer had any effect. Once the money became vested in Cynthia, it became all hers, free and clear of the trust. Curtis became just another heir."

"But then he killed her," said Geddy. "There's no question that he killed her, so he won't inherit now because as we all know, a murderer can't inherit from his victim. The murder-inheritance statute governs it. It's clear cut."

"That's right John, that's what I've been trying to talk to you about. Curtis won't get the money," said Mr. Burke, who didn't understand what was wrong with Geddy.

"So who gets all of the money?"

"I can't believe you haven't figured this out," said Jeffrey, incredulously. "Since Cynthia had no will, the money is passed according to the laws of intestate succession." Intestate simply means when a deceased dies without a will or trust. Intestate succession is the order of relatives the law provides for property to pass when the deceased leaves no will or trust.

"Since Cynthia didn't have a will," explained Faith slowly, "the intestacy laws govern who gets the money. First, it's the spouse. If there is no spouse, then the deceased's kids get the inheritance. If there are no kids it goes to the grandkids, or the great-grandkids, or the great-great-grandkids, on down the line. Now, Cynthia didn't have any of these, so lacking kids or other descendants, the money would next go to her parents. But as you know, Cynthia's parents are dead. If there are no parents, the next in line would be brothers and sisters."

Geddy blurted out, "But that would mean Curtis would get the . . ."

"Please, just listen, John. As we all know, Curtis killed Cynthia, so he'll be charged, tried, and with all of the evidence against him, he'll be convicted of killing Cynthia. As you said, the Florida murder-inheritance law would prevent Curtis from inheriting from Cynthia. So he doesn't inherit. The law treats him as if he had died before her."

Of course, Geddy thought. He started to take the logic further and go through the intestacy law, but Faith interrupted and did it for him.

"So since Curtis doesn't count, Cynthia has, for all intents and purposes, no brother or sister. She has no nephews or nieces who would be next in line, so next you go to grandparents. Adam Gentry and his wife are dead. So are Cynthia's paternal grandparents. No living aunts or uncles either, so we're down to cousins."

She paused and didn't say anything, thinking Geddy would finish for her, but he couldn't speak.

"I think you know who Cynthia's only cousin is," said Faith.

Holy shit! was all Geddy could think.

"Congratulations, kid," said Jeffrey. "Your girlfriend just inherited forty million dollars."

Early that same evening, Morgan and Geddy loaded up her boat with a large picnic barbecue Geddy prepared for them. He was waiting for the perfect time to tell her the news about the inheritance. It was obvious to him when he came home from the office that afternoon that she didn't realize she would inherit the money.

"John, it's so sweet of you to prepare this whole night. You're the best man a girl could ever hope for," she said from the dock as she handed him a basket of food.

"Do you really mean that?" asked Geddy.

"What a silly thing to ask."

"Well, it's been a crazy couple of weeks, and you've been great. I wanted to treat you to something special."

"Every evening with you is special," she said, smiling at him.

"This one will be the best," he promised and then turned the key, firing up the engines. He looked down at the gas gauge and got a sickening feeling. "We only have quarter of a tank. Think it'll be enough?"

She smiled slyly. "If not we'll be marooned on Keewaydin Island. We'll just have to find a way to amuse ourselves."

"Marooned or not, we're going to amuse ourselves," he promised with a grin.

Morgan wrapped her arms around him for most of the ride to Keewaydin Island, where they found a deserted stretch of beach to enjoy the fiery sunset. Geddy barbecued swordfish, they had a romantic dinner surrounded by oil lamps and soft jazz music, and after dinner they made love on the beach.

Finally, Geddy decided it was time. They were lying on a beach blanket when Geddy sat up and looked down at her. "I have something to tell you."

"Go ahead, *dahling,*" she joked, appearing very happy. "You have my undivided attention."

"Morgan, you know the money that Cynthia won in the trial?"

"Well, let me think. You mean the money you've been trying to win for her for over a year? The money that I held in trust for the last five years. Yes, I vaguely recall it."

"What I mean is, do you understand that Cynthia, now that she's dead, won't get it?"

"Of course, she can't get it."

"Cynthia didn't leave a will. So you see, the legal heir is determined by the Florida Intestacy Law. By law Curtis is her legal heir."

She sat up quickly. "That's right. I was under the impression that the University of Tampa would get the money. But the trust had already ended, so U. T. isn't entitled to it. Of course. So you mean Curtis will get the money after all?"

"He would have, except he killed Cynthia. By law, the murder-inheritance statute, a murderer isn't allowed to inherit from his victim."

"So who will get the money?"

"Well, if Curtis is found guilty of murdering Cynthia like he was found guilty of murdering the Measuring Lives, the next legal heir would inherit."

Morgan could only stare at him dumbfounded. When she finally spoke it was in short bursts.

"John . . . me? . . . I . . . I . . . all forty million? Is this true? When?"

"That's what I need to talk to you about. Mr. Burke . . . well, he wanted me to ask if you want me to file suit, to disqualify Curtis from inheriting. The state attorney has already got an arrest warrant out on Curtis, so once they catch him . . ."

She threw her arms around him. "John, do you know what this means? We have it all now! We can travel, buy houses, art, cars. You can have any cars you want! We have it all!" She threw her arms around him again and shook him, laughing with joy. Finally she pulled back and, seeing his face said, "Oh, John, I'm sorry. Here I am carrying on and I forgot all about those five girls who died, not to mention Cynthia, and it's only because of them that I'll get this money. You must think I'm awful."

"No. I think you're the sweetest woman I could ever meet."

"Well, thank you," she said, getting her giddiness back. "Then what's the problem? Whatever it is, we can work it out."

"I'm just worried that once you get the money . . ."

She stared at him with surprise. "Oh, John, I do love you, don't you know that? Didn't you hear me at the trial? I told the world—I was under oath."

He smiled. "You picked a hell of a time to tell me."

"I don't know why I couldn't tell you before, but I'm glad I did. I love you like I've never loved anyone before. I would be mad at you for even thinking that I'd leave you, but I guess it's understandable. After all we've seen Curtis do, money does do strange things to people. We can't let the money get between us, John. Tell me it won't."

"It won't, Morgan."

• • •

Geddy and Morgan arrived back at the villa at almost two in the morning. Morgan yawned sleepily that she was going to bed. Geddy told her he'd be up in a little while, since he still had some things to bring in from the boat, and he wanted to watch a replay of the eleven o'clock news that was rebroadcast at two A.M., to see what was new about Curtis. He kissed her and she thanked him again for such a beautiful evening. She reminded him of how great life would be together now that they never had to worry about money again. They said good night, and she took the elevator to the third floor.

Predictably, the trial and Cynthia's murder were the top stories and the focus of the first ten minutes of the newscast. The police were requesting that anyone who knew the whereabouts of Curtis Dole—his picture flashed on the screen—should contact the police at once. Apparently, this was the largest manhunt in the history of southwest Florida. Even in 1972, at the time of the New Moon Murders, there was never a suspect, so never a manhunt.

The last time he was seen was the night before, shortly after he returned home from the Ritz. Philip, his boyfriend, told police Curtis came home and immediately told him he was going out for a ride on his motorcycle, that Curtis said he had some thinking to do and needed to clear his head. Curtis never returned home. After the news about Cynthia's murder, the next report was on the trial, which was naturally still a big story. There was even a picture of Faith and Geddy walking out of the courthouse, answering questions.

When the reports of the trial ended, Geddy decided to bring in the rest of the things from the boat. He walked outside and admired the scene around him, the scene that he was still trying to get used to even though he had practically lived there with Morgan for the last five months. In a few months, after the probate of Cynthia's estate was concluded and they were filthy rich, would they live here or at South End? Or maybe leave Naples altogether? Who knows, they'd probably have a couple of houses. He wouldn't mind a ski house in Vail or Aspen, maybe a beach house somewhere in the Caribbean. And she was always talking about Switzerland. He could stand it there for part of the year, no problem.

He smiled at his good fortune.

Geddy walked across the parking lot, through the hedges and down the wooden gangway to the dock, then jumped onto the boat. There was a big picnic basket, a small barbecue, a few blankets, and some empty champagne bottles to bring in. He frowned, thinking that it would take two trips.

He was reminded that Curtis was on the loose when he heard police sirens wailing in the distance. Could Curtis still be in town? If he were smart he'd get out of town. Unless . . .

Unless Curtis was innocent.

No, Geddy thought. No chance. Curtis did it, that was clear. He looked down and saw the ship to shore radio and remembered it had a police band. He turned it on, hoping to listen to the police search for Curtis.

It was almost two-thirty, another perfect night. The lights from the street made it too bright to see many stars, but he could just make out the North Star and Orion's belt. An occasional car passed by on nearby Gulf Shore Boulevard, but it was late so it was fairly quiet. The moon was half full, and its lovely silver light reflected off the chrome of a motorcycle parked in the small lot on the other side of the short space between himself and the sea wall. It was what wealth was all about, he thought. Tranquillity.

He tuned the radio to the police band. After a little searching, he could hear the voices of officers as they coordinated the man hunt. He put his feet up, popped open another bottle of champagne, and relaxed.

It was so peaceful, other than the occasional sound of cars going by and the voices of officers on the radio. A single boat could be heard as it cruised through the bay, and crickets chirped steadily. He took a deep breath and smiled, silently toasting himself. He closed his eyes and tilted his head back with nothing to disturb his dreams but the sound of the radio and the hum of a nearby boat engine.

"This is NP-114. Still no sign of the suspect in Port Royal."

"Roger, NP-114."

"NP-224 reporting. No sign of the Harley on Tamiami near

the Coastland Mall. Repeat, no sign of the subject. Over."

Harley? Geddy jumped up and looked out across the water at the motorcycle he'd noticed there before. It was a Harley-Davidson.

He scrambled out of the boat and started to run back to the house, pulling out his keys as he jumped onto the wooden gangway. But by the time he made it halfway up the gangway, Curtis was at the top, waiting for him. He was pointing a gun at Geddy.

"Don't make a sound," whispered Curtis threateningly.

Geddy looked around and realized he was trapped by the railings of the gangway on either side of him. He considered jumping into the water, but he would have to climb over the railing first. If Curtis could shoot, Geddy knew he'd be a dead man.

When Curtis got closer, Geddy saw he was soaking wet. He must have swum the hundred feet from where his motorcycle was parked to avoid being seen by the security guard.

"In the house. Now!" demanded Curtis in a low but firm voice.

"No," answered Geddy. He didn't want to bring Morgan into harm's way.

"I won't hurt you, but I have to keep out of sight. They're looking for me."

"If you're not going to shoot me, then why are you pointing that thing at me?"

"I don't have time to discuss it. If I asked you nicely, would you go inside? No, you'd call the cops. That's why the gun. Now get up here!" he demanded, raising the gun to eye level.

"I'm not letting you in the villa." Geddy looked around one more time, hoping to think of something, but he soon realized his only chance to save Morgan was to sacrifice himself. "Go ahead, shoot!" said Geddy loudly. He knew that if Curtis shot him the guard would be alerted, and Morgan might be saved.

Alarmed by the noise Geddy was making, Curtis pointed the gun at him more menacingly. There was only fifteen feet separating them.

"Stop it! I didn't kill Cynthia, and I didn't kill those five girls. Something is going on here, and you must know what it is!"

Geddy realized that he could scream at the top of his lungs and the guard still might not hear him from inside the glass-enclosed air-conditioned hut, probably with the radio tuned to some damn talk show.

"You did commit those murders, I proved it!" said Geddy. He continued to look about hoping to find something, or somebody, that could help.

"Shut up, keep your voice down. I'm telling you the God's honest truth. I didn't—" Curtis turned to his left, thinking he heard something. Geddy had not heard a thing. There was nothing there. He's nervous, Geddy thought. His voice had cracked twice already, and the gun shook in his hands. From far off Geddy heard a police siren, but it was too far off to provide him with any hope of a rescue. He noticed Curtis tense up even more when he heard it. It must be a frightening sound when you're on the run, Geddy thought.

"In the house," demanded Curtis again. Geddy didn't move. "Give me those keys!"

Geddy looked down and remembered he was holding the keys. "You're not getting them."

"Toss them over here."

Geddy held onto the big black plastic part of the key to Morgan's Mercedes, stretched his arm over the railing of the gangway, and dangled the remaining keys out over the water. "If you shoot me, the keys are gone."

Curtis stepped forward. He was shifting his eyes back and forth erratically, unsure of what to do. For the first time, Geddy thought Curtis wouldn't shoot him. It was something in his eyes.

But then Geddy remembered the Measuring Lives, and he remembered Cynthia. They were all dead. Could that look in his eyes be something else?

Curtis cocked the gun and pointed it at Geddy's chest.

The time had finally come. He was going to die just like all those victims he saw in Miami. Sure, he caught the killers, but the victims were still dead. Now it was his turn. Curtis was going kill him, and there wasn't a damn thing he could do about it.

Don't give up!

Curtis was ten feet away now and coming closer.

Think!

Behind Curtis, in the parking lot, Geddy saw Morgan's car.

"You leave me no choice," warned Curtis, and he aimed at Geddy's head. "Give me the keys now, or . . ."

Geddy pretended to look over Curtis's shoulder. "Did you hear that, Curtis? Someone's coming. It's the security guard."

Curtis ignored him. "Why don't you just tell me my shoe's untied?"

"I'm telling you, the guard heard me before. He's got a gun. He's licensed to kill. He's an ex-cop, a tough son of a bitch." Geddy tried to think of other things to make Curtis worry. He didn't have to buy it. Geddy just had to get him thinking. Then he'd might be able to gain himself the second or two he needed to jump the railing and get into the water. "He hates gays."

"Get your ass up here, or I'll shoot you where you stand!"

Just then Geddy jerked his head sideways as if he saw something behind Curtis, then opened his eyes wide and in the next instant pushed the button on Morgan's key chain to de-activate the car alarm, causing three short but loud and startling beeps to sing out from the car.

Curtis jumped at the alarm's sound and inadvertently pulled the trigger.

"Click."

Geddy had already swung one leg over the railing, but he stopped suddenly when he heard the click. Curtis looked up like a deer caught in the headlights, and then they were running, Curtis up the gangway, past Morgan's car and then left, away from the guard station toward the end of the row of villas, with Geddy chasing after him. Curtis veered a little and headed between two garages at the end of the compound where he could dive into the water and hope to out-swim Geddy. But Geddy was too quick. At the last possible moment, he dove at Curtis's feet and got enough of Curtis's right foot to cause him to stumble forward just before the end of the platform. Geddy was on his feet in an instant and caught Curtis by the back of the shirt collar just as he was trying to crawl the last three feet to let himself fall over into Venetian Bay.

Geddy yanked Curtis up by the collar enough to cause him to gag. Then the young lawyer threw Curtis over backward away from the edge and was on top of him again before Curtis could react. With one blow to the face, Geddy broke Curtis's nose, and he slumped back onto the driveway, unconscious. Geddy sat on top of him as he tried to catch his breath, until he noticed the dark thick blood flowing out of Curtis's shattered nose.

Geddy hastily slid off him and walked back to where Curtis dropped the gun. He picked it up, opened the chamber and held the gun up to try to catch some light. Geddy couldn't believe what he saw. It didn't make sense. The gun wasn't loaded.

29

From his room at the boardinghouse, Geddy could hear Nick's van pull up outside. He walked down the stairs and sat on one of the bottom steps as Nick approached.

"I just came from the Naples state attorney's office," said Geddy. "Charles Warren is offering to waive the death penalty and will agree not to charge Curtis with killing the Measuring Lives in return for a guilty plea to second degree murder for killing Cynthia. Charles said Curtis's new lawyer jumped at it, though he still has to get Curtis to agree. I think you know what that means?"

Nick grinned at him. "Yeah, it's pretty simple. If Curtis pleads guilty, there's no need for a trial. Curtis won't be allowed to inherit from Cynthia. Morgan's going to get it all. I guess probate is the next step?"

"That's right. Faith's gonna handle it."

"How long before Morgan gets the money and the houses?"

"It depends on how long it takes her to figure out all of the assets of Curtis and Cynthia. Morgan's having the trust valued by her accountants and getting the deed to the house in Port Royal and all the papers on the cars and Curtis's sailboat. Then there's the jewelry, paintings. Everything."

"What about a deed to the house in Lake Forest?"

"Since that property is out of state, it has to be probated separately. Faith's getting a Chicago firm to handle the Lake Forest house."

"You really know how to pick 'em," Nick said. "Personally, I would have picked Faith, but . . ."

"What are you talking about?" asked Geddy.

"Oh come on, you could've had either one of them. Can't you see the way Faith looks at you, the way she does anything for you? I know I give Faith a hard time, but man, she's a piece of ass. Not as beautiful as Morgan, maybe, but she's got a hell of a lot of spirit."

"Are you saying Morgan doesn't?" asked Geddy with an edge to his voice.

"Look, I don't want to go pissin' you off. Maybe I don't know Morgan well enough, okay? I don't wanna fight, I just came by to say so long."

"Where are you off to?"

"Don't know yet."

Nick offered his hand.

Geddy stood and shook it firmly. "Thanks." Nothing more needed to be said between them. They had been through a great deal together in the last year, but neither was the type to go on about it. Nick suddenly began to laugh, then Geddy laughed along with him in ironic acknowledgment of what all their hard work together had finally accomplished.

"Don't be a stranger," said Geddy as he began climbing the stairs. Before stepping into his room, he turned to watch Nick go, a little bit sad to see his friend drive away.

In July the streets of Naples are empty, and there is no waiting for tables at the restaurants. If one wishes to go deep-sea fishing, there is no problem finding an available charter. Hotel rooms are easy to come by, and there is always a parking spot near the beach. But it is not a good season because it's always ninety degrees and the sun bakes the inside of cars and the black tops of streets and the skin of those who have to go out during the day. It's like winter up north. People stay indoors until they have no choice but to go out. Except at night. At night it is only eighty degrees, and there's no sun to deal with.

For residents of Naples, it is a slow, quiet time. It is a time to prepare for the next tourist season, which begins around November. It is a time to complete tasks that need to be completed.

For Geddy and Faith and Morgan, the summer so far had been spent pushing through the probate of Cynthia Dole's estate as quickly as possible. Once Curtis was finally convinced that he had no alternative but to accept the state attorney's final offer, he accepted the plea, but word was he cried. Geddy did not see Curtis cry, but he read about it. The entire city read about it. Nick Farley made it legend by recording Curtis' sobs forever in a bizarre newspaper story, even though Nick had not returned to Naples to hear them—an entire front-page story in the *Naples Daily News* dedicated solely to the lonely wailing and suffering of Curtis Dole, which might or might not have ever happened.

On that first day of July, Geddy, Faith, and Morgan were wrapping up their business in the well air-conditioned conference room at Hirt, Harrington, under the ever-watchful eyes of Mr. T. J. Hirt. They were dressed in suits, but the mood was relaxed. Geddy loosened his tie and took off his jacket, Faith unbuttoned her blouse a few buttons, and Morgan removed her silk scarf. They had just come from the courthouse, where the probate had finally been concluded. Once back at the office, Faith had Morgan sign several papers, and she explained where Morgan's newfound kingdom was scattered.

"The house on Green Dolphin Drive in Naples is all set," continued Faith. "I need to record the new deed in the public records, but that will be done today, so here are the keys." She passed them to Geddy, who handed them to Morgan without looking at her. "As far as the house in Lake Forest, the probate up there has already been completed and the new deed recorded. I'm expecting your copy of the new deed any day now. I'll give it to John as soon as it arrives."

"That's fine, but what I really want to know is, when can I have the money?" asked Morgan.

Faith handed Morgan a prepared list of all of the banking institutions where the money had been kept since the administration of the estate began. "Because it was such a large sum of money, I didn't leave it all in one bank, naturally, so it's been spread out. Here are all the banks and their addresses with the most recent balances and account numbers. You've already signed all the paperwork, so the money's yours now."

"I can do whatever I want with it?" asked Morgan.

"Whatever you want."

There were several other issues to discuss, then Faith packed up her papers. "Good luck with everything, Morgan," said Faith evenly. They had worked together without incident for the last few months, but Faith had never warmed to Morgan. "If you have any other questions . . ."

"I'm sure I won't," interrupted Morgan. "If I do, I can always ask John."

Faith walked past them and out the door. "I'll see you later," Geddy called out after her. "Don't you think you could have at least thanked her, Morgan? She went way out of her way to get this done as quickly as possible."

"She was well paid for it, too," replied Morgan, and pushed the Hirt, Harrington bill in front of Geddy to show him.

"Morgan . . ."

"John, please, let's not talk about her. I have something I want you to do," said Morgan. She searched in front of her for Faith's list of the banks which held her forty million dollars. "I want to consolidate all but a few hundred thousand dollars of this money into one account . . ."

"That's a very bad idea, Morgan, you know that."

"Of course I do, but managing money is my area of expertise, so please do what I say." Her tone was that of a mother instructing a child. "I want it all placed in a numbered Swiss account."

"Why would you want to do that?"

"Do you really want to know why? Do you want me to cite the tax code sections, do you want me to explain the confidentiality ramifications, do you really want to know all the reasons? Because if you do, maybe we should set up some time for another appointment, because it's going to take a while!"

He glared at her. It wasn't the first time in the last few months they had been short with one another.

"Don't look at me that way," she told him. "John, you know how stressful the last month or two have been. Just please, please do what I say. I'm sorry if I sounded mad, I'm just in a rotten mood.

I want this last thing to be done as quickly as possible so I can finally relax."

"Fine, Morgan. I'll have Faith get the papers . . ."

"No! Aren't you listening? I said you, John." Then she realized she had snapped at him again and said more mildly, "This is a lot of money, John. I don't want Faith or anyone else to know where it's kept and what the account numbers are. I just want to wipe the slate clean, consolidate the money, and then start investing it, after I've decided what to do with it all."

"Are you sure you don't want to transfer the funds yourself?" he asked. "You might not want me to know the number of the Swiss account."

She apologized with her eyes. "I trust you with all my heart, John. Not only do I want you to know the number of the new account, I want your name put on the account, right next to mine. Everything that is mine is yours." She was entrusting him with access to more than forty million dollars. There would be nothing to keep him from taking all of the money for himself.

"That's not necessary," he told her.

She reached out and took his hand. "John, since I've known you, we have had to deal with my losing the trusteeship, then your trial, then Cynthia's death, and finally the probate. We haven't had time to focus on *us*. I know we've had our share of arguments in the last few months, but now things will calm down and we'll have time to think about what we want, and when the smoke finally clears, things will be better than ever."

"I don't care about the money, Morgan."

"I know you don't, honey. That's why I know I can trust you."

• • •

Three days later it was the Fourth of July, and Morgan and Geddy were walking up the beautiful wide lawn of Donald Ordway's five-acre multimillion-dollar Port Royal estate. They had been down on the beach taking a long walk and had just stepped up the Ordways' beach stairs and into the backyard to rejoin the other 100 carefully selected guests of the Ordways' annual gala for those of Naples society who remained during the summer.

"Hello there! John, is that you?" Geddy looked up and noticed an older couple approaching.

"Sometimes I wonder why you want to come to these things," he whispered to Morgan, then put on a happy face. "Edgar! Violet! Nice to see you, where have you been lately?"

"We went on safari," said Violet, an older woman with ghastly colored hair, as she and her husband walked toward them. "Edgar got a lion. You should have seen him, he must have been within a hundred yards of the beast."

"Fourteen hundred pounds, John," bragged Edgar, a silver haired man in his sixties with bushy white eyebrows. "Fourteen hundred pounds of pure killer."

"Wow," said Geddy unconvincingly.

"We hear congratulations are in order," the woman said in a high-pitched squeal. "Cynthia's probate came through. Well, well, well, things have certainly changed for you two."

"The probate came through?" asked Edgar. "When did that happen? Why didn't you tell me?"

"Morgan got her money days ago," explained Violet. "If you weren't so busy with the taxidermist, maybe you'd have time to know what's going on around you."

"Fourteen hundred pounds," said Edgar again. "I'm having him stuffed."

When freed of their acquaintances, Geddy and Morgan continued on toward the house. Donald Ordway lived in the most expensive house in Port Royal, a tremendous pink marble mansion. In the middle of the backyard was a white gazebo, and beyond it most of the guests gathered on the veranda. Geddy led Morgan to a seat in the gazebo where they could be alone.

As the Fourth of July celebration began, Geddy reached into his pocket and pulled out a ring. Not an engagement ring, but to him it was just as important. It was his mother's ring, a family heirloom. Morgan saw it. Her eyes lit up as the fireworks began to explode in the distance, illuminating the gazebo momentarily until a sound like thunder signaled a return to near darkness.

"Morgan, I know things have been a little tense lately, and I don't always tell you how I feel about you. But I want you to have this . . ."

"No John, don't," pleaded Morgan, but he believed it was her emotions overcoming her and he continued.

This wasn't easy for him. He wanted to get it over with. "I want you to know what you mean to me . . ."

"Please," she demanded, and she rose to her feet as the fireworks display raged on. "I'm leaving, John. I'm leaving Naples."

Geddy stood but didn't say anything.

"I never knew it before, but I hate it here. I want to travel and meet interesting people. There's nothing here for me, John. I . . ."

"When did all this happen?" he asked her, and he saw her troubled expression for an instant against the colored light flashes.

"You want a normal life, John, but I don't. I never did. Until I got the money, I thought I could settle for it, but I can't."

"We don't have to stay here . . ."

"I've already decided, John. I can't see you anymore."

He couldn't speak.

"I'll be at the new house for a week or so before leaving town," she told him matter-of-factly, referring to Curtis's former Port Royal home on Green Dolphin Drive. "You can get your things from the villa this weekend. I know how much you love the car though, so I want you to keep it. It's the least I can do."

She started to leave, but he blocked her way. "What's going on?" he demanded.

"John, please, it's hard enough . . ."

"Don't give me that crap! You get the money and a few days later you walk out on me!"

"That's not what this is about. The truth is I've had second thoughts about us for months. I've even been seeing someone else. I tried to fight it, but I just don't . . . I don't think I love you anymore. I'm sorry." That left him speechless. She tried to step around him, but he blocked her way again. She sighed. "You've got no class, John. It didn't have to end like this."

Geddy finally let her go and watched her until she blended in with the rest of the Neapolitans. He turned around and slumped down on his seat in the gazebo. The sky lit up in a fiery red long enough for him to see his mother's ring again. Then, as silver sparkles fell from the sky, the ring fell from his fingers through the spaces of the wooden planks of the gazebo.

31

Geddy was a recluse on his first day of work after Morgan left him. He spent hours in the conference room with documents relating to the Dole case scattered all over the table and floor. He was in a foul mood, and Faith didn't make things any better. She could tell there was something wrong with him, and she wouldn't leave him alone until he told her what it was. Then he had to sit there and listen to her try to comfort him after he told her about Morgan. He didn't want comforting.

He was still at it in the early evening when Faith walked into the conference room yet again. Geddy was immersed in a flood of paper. "John. You're still here?"

"What!" he snapped back. "What now? Things will be all right, thanks, I know, good night."

If he had looked up, he would have seen the hurt in Faith's eyes. "Screw you, I don't deserve any of your crap. Why don't you give up on this crazy delusion of yours and admit she just decided she didn't want to be with you anymore. Why does it have to be such a big conspiracy? She dumped you, get over it."

"She used me, Faith. There's something going on . . ."

"Oh yeah, there's been something going on for a long time, John! You wanted little Miss Have-It-All, and you got what you deserved. I never told you, but I had Nick find out some things about her . . ."

"What?"

"I didn't trust her, I thought we might find something out to implicate her somehow . . ."

Geddy jumped to his feet. "You're right, she must have been up to something! I know it, it's the only explanation! What did you find out?"

Faith shook her head in disgust. "You're pitiful, John. She didn't have anything to do with those murders. Her past checked out just fine. It was her present that was interesting. Nick found out that Morgan had been seeing Dick Didier the whole time. He teaches half the year at the University of Miami Medical School. He would drive over to Naples every couple of weeks or so and get a room for himself and Morgan at the Marriot on Marco Island under the names Dr. and Mrs. Dick Didier."

"How do you know his wife wasn't with him? Nicole Didier was a friend of Morgan's."

"Nicole Didier died a year and a half ago."

Geddy tried his best to conceal his rage. "Why didn't you tell me? I thought we were friends."

"I wanted to, but Nick said it was none of my business." Faith rubbed the back of her neck. "He told me you made your choice, and I had to live with it."

"What are you talking about . . ."

"Why bother, I don't even care anymore," she cried out in a slightly higher tone. "I didn't come here to talk to you about Morgan. I just wanted to give you this." She handed him an envelope. "It's from the attorney who handled the Illinois probate of Cynthia's old house. I thought you might want to give it to Morgan yourself so you'd have an excuse to talk to her. As usual, I just wanted to help." He hardly noticed Faith storm out.

The office was quiet now, and it was beginning to get dark. He was in no hurry to get home. He was in no hurry to see the things he had retrieved from Morgan's villa the day before piled in the center of his room at the boardinghouse.

He had been at it all day, had looked at every scrap of paper in the room at least twice. He was ready to give up, then a thought struck him. He would have to confront Morgan. He could bluff, pretend he knew what she was up to. She was up to something. She had to have used him. It was the only explanation. Things had bothered him about the case before, but he couldn't put his finger on it. Now Morgan had the money, and she had no further need of him. It was unlikely she'd confess anything to him, but it was the only chance he had, he must confront her. His eyes caught the envelope Faith had just thrown at him. It was the deed. The deed to the Lake Forest house. It would be the perfect excuse to see her, to get the chance to confront Morgan face to face.

He picked up the envelope and opened it. He read the deed to himself without really seeing it, but he could tell it was the new deed, all right, passing title of the house to Morgan Gentry. Attached to it was a copy of the Adam Gentry Trust Agreement.

It was identical to the trust Morgan had first given him after the Valentine's Day Ball, other than the Official Records Book number, page, and date when it had first been recorded, along with the original deed, in the Lake Forest County Courthouse in 1983. This was what started everything—the Adam Gentry Trust Agreement. Thoughts of the last year and half ran through his mind. His arrival in Naples, his first client—Cynthia Dole—the Phil, Nick Farley, their investigation, the trial. And of course, those poor Measuring Lives. Lost in the whole crazy trial and then Curtis's murder of Cynthia was the fact that five innocent girls were brutally murdered, and for what?

"Money. It's all about money," he said aloud as he flipped to Appendix A. He looked at the names of the Measuring Lives.

The *ten* Measuring Lives!

A thousand thoughts flew through his head all at once. He jumped out of his seat and flew down the hallway. "Faith!" He screamed as loudly as he could. When there was no answer, he sprinted down the hall, burst through the double doors and shouted out over the Plaza, "Faith! Faith!" But she was already gone.

He ran to his office, ripped open a desk drawer, grabbed his keys, and started off again, running down to the basement garage. He screamed off into the night, down Gordon Drive and into Port Royal at sixty miles an hour. He didn't slow down until he reached the end of Green Dolphin Drive.

• • •

The white roadster screeched to a halt in front of the gate to the driveway of Morgan's new home, Curtis's former residence. Geddy rushed out of the car and, high on adrenaline, vaulted easily over the gate and charged ahead through the garden and tried the front door. It was locked. He pounded furiously until the door opened, allowing the sounds of a party to wash over him like a wave. A drunken Dick Didier opened the door with a pitcher of margaritas and stood in the doorway. Geddy quickly turned around and for the first time noticed the driveway was filled with cars.

"Well, funny seeing you here," said Dick Didier with a German accent. Geddy marched in looking for Morgan when Dick grabbed him by the arm. "I don't think you've been invited . . ."

Geddy pushed him hard with both hands and sent him backwards into the stairs, spilling the margaritas on the rug and hardwood floor. A few people standing nearby backed away from him as he walked with frightening purpose into each room on the main floor. Normally he would have been disgusted at the sight of these rich young people wearing expensive jewelry, talking loudly on cellular phones, chopping up lines of cocaine on the seventeenth-century mirror Curtis brought back from Florence, smoking marijuana or throwing back tequila shots. But he was too angry. He didn't see any of it. He was looking for Morgan.

He eventually found her in the crowded kitchen, sitting on the counter dressed like a high-priced prostitute, inhaling a line of cocaine.

"You switched the Measuring Lives!" he shouted at her from across the kitchen. She looked up, surprised at first, then laughed because she didn't hear what he said. She looked back down at the cocaine and finished what she was doing. "You switched the Measuring Lives!" he repeated, and he whipped the copy of the trust from his suit pocket, held it in his fist, and shook it at her. "You switched the Measuring Lives, and you set up Curtis!"

Several of Morgan's guests rushed to her side and began threatening Geddy, but he never took his eyes off of her. She calmly finished, wiped her nose, and told Dick Didier and the other men surrounding Geddy, "Leave him alone, he's just mad because I blew him off."

He went for her but was held back by several of her guests. "If you insist on seeing me, we can talk outside." She hopped off the kitchen counter and strolled out the sliding glass door onto the veranda. The men loosened their grip on Geddy, and he followed her out the door. She walked to the dock where Curtis's old sailboat was tied up.

He caught up to her there and faced her, shoving the trust at her. "You switched the Measuring Lives! It had to be you!"

"What's the matter with you?" she said condescendingly. "What are you talking about?"

"It's over, Morgan!" he shouted and then backed off, afraid he might actually hit her. "I found you out. You switched the Measuring Lives, now it's all over."

"John, look at you. You've got some serious problems. I can't deal with you right now, especially while I'm entertaining guests. Now either you . . ."

"No! Don't lie to me anymore. You've lied to me since the first time I met you! How could you do this?" he asked, his voice cracking from betrayal. He picked up the trust that she had let fall and waved it in her face. "How could you do this to Curtis?"

"Okay, slow down, let's take it step by step. Obviously something has upset you, but I assure you, I don't know . . ."

He threw the trust at her. "I know all about Appendix A,

Morgan. Take a look."

There was silence for a few seconds.

"John, what . . ."

"Take a look!" he shouted. "That's a copy of the trust that was filed in 1983, Morgan, in Illinois, along with the deed to Cynthia's house. Look at it Morgan. Look at Appendix A."

Morgan indulged him by picking up the trust and flipping the pages until she came upon Appendix A, where she saw the following ten names:

APPENDIX A

Helen Jean Alexiou
Born: May 10, 1952
Tampa General Hospital

Laurene Ellen Clark
Born: May 10, 1952
Tampa General Hospital

Teresa Elizabeth Crosby
Born: May 10, 1952
Tampa General Hospital

Nicole DiPaolo
May 10, 1952
Tampa General Hospital

Diane Vera Hawley
Born: May 10, 1952
Tampa General Hospital

Stephaney Bourdanay Herson
Born: May 10, 1952
Tampa General Hospital

Rachael Lea Linehan
Born: May 10, 1952
Tampa General Hospital

Pamela Marie Scherbak
Born: May 10, 1952
Tampa General Hospital

Donna Torresquientero
Born: May 10, 1952
Tampa General Hospital

Lori Kristen Zmijewski
Born: May 10, 1952
Tampa General Hospital

There was silence for a few more seconds, then the sound of Morgan flipping frantically through the trust. "John, what is this? How can this be? How . . . where did you find this . . . ?"

"You screwed up, Morgan. You thought nobody had a copy of the trust so you could switch the Measuring Lives. But you screwed up. This copy was recorded in Lake Forest Illinois—in 1983! Cynthia's house in Lake Forest was owned by the trust. In Illinois, when a house is owned by a trust a copy of the trust agreement has to be recorded in the public records along with the deed. It's called an Illinois Land Trust. Cynthia's house was probated by a Chicago lawyer. When he had the house signed over in your name as Cynthia's heir, he sent copies of all the documentation to Hirt, Harrington. This was the copy that was recorded along with the deed in 1983. That's how I know you switched the Measuring Lives. This 1983 version contains the real list of Measuring Lives. You switched Appendix A to be the New Moon Murder victims so that the trust would vest in 1993 and you could have Curtis disqualified!"

"John, why would I do that? The trust was all I had. I wouldn't get the money if . . ."

"That's enough! It's over, there's nothing you can do, it's all clear now."

"That's just plain silly." She turned her back on him and fixed her hair, which was being blown by the light wind.

"I haven't figured it all out yet Morgan, but I *know* you switched those Measuring Lives. Curtis didn't kill those girls, and you knew it! You knew they weren't the real Measuring Lives! You even used me when I became Cynthia's lawyer. You made sure I was on the right track and helped me get evidence against Curtis, like the letter from your father to Curtis, and the telephone bill during my cross-examination of Curtis."

Morgan turned and calmly handed the trust back to him and sat on the bow of the sailboat. "John, did it ever cross your mind that the trust you're holding is the one with the switched Measuring Lives?"

"These are the real ones," he insisted. "Take a look at these Measuring Lives. They were all born on the same day, in the same hospital. If you were drafting this trust how would you pick the Measuring Lives? I'll tell you how. It's so clear to me now. You'd go to your local hospital and find out the names of a bunch of babies born on that day. Adam Gentry lived in Tampa, so his lawyer probably did, too. When Adam's lawyer drafted the trust, he got the names from Tampa General Hospital. The victims of the murders—my God! There were three from Naples and two from Fort Myers. And their birthdays were all spread out. The only thing they had in common was that they were murdered by the New Moon Slasher."

Morgan didn't say anything right away. Then she tried, "John, didn't you consider that even if this crazy idea of yours was true, my father could have switched the Measuring Lives?"

Geddy knew she would never admit it. "I'll prove it, Morgan. I swear to God, I will prove you switched the Measuring Lives!"

She laughed at him. "Why don't you forget about this shit and join the party. You never did know how to have fun, you know."

Geddy couldn't stand to see her sitting there so calmly. She hardly resembled the witty and charming woman he had cherished. This was the real Morgan, and suddenly he realized he wanted to kill her.

He pulled her up by the collar of her blouse, partially ripping it. Her shoes fell off her feet as he backed her up against one of the tall wooden pilings of the dock. His hands were around her throat. He held her neck, fighting his urge to kill.

"Let go!" cried Morgan. "So help me, if anything happens to me, you'll be the first person they look for! You're the one who transferred the money to a Swiss account, not me! You can't imagine what you've gotten yourself into!"

Geddy didn't even hear her. He thought long and hard about giving into his hate and killing her. He imagined squeezing the life out of her, seeing her face turn from red to blue to gray, hearing her death gasps and feeling her body shake with the death throes. But when it came to actually committing the act, he could not. He had not lost his control the way he did with James Hoffer. He was furious, but he knew what he was doing. He could not take her life in cold blood.

"The gloves are off, Morgan," he said after putting his face right up to hers. "I found you out, and now I'm gonna make sure you pay for it for the rest of your life." Suddenly he yanked her away from the piling and shoved her with all his strength off of the dock and into the water. He held a part of her ripped blouse in his hand. When she came to the surface of the bay, she was scream-ing profanities at him. Geddy trembled with the effort it had taken him to overrule his instincts with reason.

There was nothing more he could do here. He dropped the piece of her torn blouse and hurried across the backyard to the side of the house. He heard the door to the veranda open and Dick Didier call out angrily, "Geddy! Where's Morgan?"

Geddy didn't bother to reply. He rushed around the side of the house, through the driveway, and over the gate, all the while considering his next move.

It was clear to him that someone had switched the Measuring Lives, the question was who: Morgan or her father? It seemed un-likely that her father would have done it. Mark Gentry would have been an old man in 1993, twenty-one years after the Measuring Lives died. He was sure it was Morgan, but he needed something else to bring to the police. After making everyone believe Curtis had killed the Measuring Lives, how easy would it be now to con-vince them that Curtis *had not* killed them? Morgan was too calm back there. She had something up her sleeve, so he had to be able to prove she did it. Besides, switching the Measuring Lives alone wouldn't gain her anything. In fact, she'd lose the trusteeship. No, switching the Measuring Lives was just the start of it, and he needed to find out the rest.

But there was one issue that was too pressing to wait. He had to get the money from the Swiss bank account before Morgan had a chance to disappear with it.

• • •

Geddy hurdled the passenger's-side door of his convertible and within seconds he was speeding down the streets of Naples. The top was down, and he felt the wind cooling him, his shirt damp from perspiration. In five minutes, he was downtown, where the streets were fairly empty, so even though he heard police sirens nearby, he was flying down Fifth Avenue, past the sight where Angelica Savasta had her throat slashed in the night by a serial killer. Then he was on Tamiami Trail heading north at well over the speed limit, past the restaurant that Sally Baumgartner had parked behind before she had been stabbed repeatedly with a long, steel steak knife. By a serial killer. A few miles past that was the street where Debbie Moore had met up with the serial killer who was so charged up that he decapitated her when he had probably only intended to slit her neck, like the others.

A serial killer.

He told the families of the victims he would catch the killer, but he didn't. Those victims weren't the Measuring Lives of that trust. Morgan switched the names on Appendix A and told him that she loved him, but all the while she'd been pulling the strings and he was her puppet. Not only that, he was a *great* puppet—he accomplished a very difficult thing. He proved an innocent man was guilty of murder.

It wasn't that difficult though, he thought. She fed him the evidence. She gave him what looked like an ironclad motive. She listed the New Moon Murder victims in the same order they were killed. Morgan must have had a good laugh over that one. He wondered if she thought that might be overdoing it a little, pushing her luck? He didn't know, but she did it and she fooled him, and then he fooled everyone else. Now he had to make it right.

32

Twenty-five minutes after his confrontation with Morgan, Geddy pulled up to the guard station in front of Venetian Villas. "Hello, Armand," he said to the guard, putting on a friendly voice. "I'm just here to pick up a few last things."

"It's a little late for that, isn't it?" replied the guard. Armand knew Geddy and Morgan had broken up. "Does Morgan know?"

"Sure, she knows. I left some important papers here for something I'm working on. It concerns her, she knows I'm coming."

"Did she give you a key?" asked the guard. "I can't let you in if you don't have a key."

"It's okay, Morgan gave me one," he lied, and produced the spare key he had used when he was practically living at the villa.

Armand finally waved him in, and Geddy parked in his old spot. He hurried to the door and let himself in, then locked the door behind him. He bolted for the safe, where he had placed the paperwork pertaining to the numbered Swiss bank account.

Taking the steps three at a time, he was there in an instant.

In Morgan's little office on the second floor, Geddy pushed aside her roll-top desk and yanked the portrait of her grandfather from the wall, revealing the safe. He hastily tried the combination that he knew from his days of being Morgan's supposed confidante. The safe wouldn't open. He tried it again, slowly this time, and thanked God when the steel door clanked open.

It was completely empty.

Geddy cursed Morgan and slammed the safe shut. He dropped to his knees and frantically searched the documents that had fallen out of the desk after he flipped it aside. Finding nothing, he checked the spare bedroom and the closets on the second floor. When he did not find what he was looking for, he raced downstairs.

He began knocking books off bookcases, overturning furniture, looking through drawers. He pulled the cushions off the couch and rolled up the rug to look underneath it. Then he checked every inch of the kitchen. He pulled pots and pans from the cabinets and tossed aside utensils and even flipped through the pages of the cookbook he bought Morgan when she expressed an interest in learning to cook.

Learn to cook! She never intended to learn to cook. She told him what he wanted to hear, and he ate it all up. He ate up her act and he ate up her horrendous cooking and complimented her on it even when it was barely edible. He was a sucker.

Frustrated and tired now, but clinging to a last hope, he climbed to the third floor.

It was as he remembered it, those endless nights with Morgan, sleeping together, waking up with her. She brought him breakfast in bed on the mornings of the trial. There was the jacuzzi they had shared countless times, the closet she had cleaned out for him to use, the sink and shower where he had begun his workdays.

The anger inside started to rise again. He fed off his fury and began tearing the room apart, growing more angry every minute because he was beginning to realize his search was hopeless. Nevertheless, he did not stop until he heard the police sirens.

"Armand," he said to himself. Geddy ran down the hallway to

a window overlooking the parking lot and saw two squad cars pull up and box his car in so he couldn't get out. Another one was racing down Gulf Shore Boulevard. He sighed in frustration, then returned to the bedroom and picked up Morgan's telephone. He dialed Faith's number and cursed when he heard her answering machine kick in.

"Faith, it's John," he said to her machine. "Look, I'm about to be arrested for breaking and entering. I'll explain everything later, just come down to the police station as soon as you can. You're gonna have to get me out of jail. Something's up with Morgan and . . ."

Faith picked up and interrupted him in a frantic voice. "How the hell could you call me! I can't help you now, John! Nobody can help you now!"

She wouldn't help? "Faith, what's the matter? Why are you . . ."

"How could you kill her?" exclaimed Faith. She sounded like she had been crying. "She wasn't worth it. How could you of all people do something so . . ."

"Kill who! What the hell are you talking about?"

"I know! The police know! They were just here. They're looking for you. Fifty witnesses saw you go out there with her, John. How could you expect to get away with killing Morgan? Did you lose your mind . . ."

"Kill Morgan! Faith, I just *saw* her an hour ago . . ."

"You just *killed* her an hour ago! Morgan's dead, and there are fifty fucking witnesses, John! How could you be so stupid?"

Suddenly there was a startling crash downstairs that made him drop the telephone.

"Move! Move!" he heard a man's voice bark, then the sound of many rushing footsteps. "Durkee, Glucksman, Frazier—check upstairs. Koshy, the kitchen!"

He shook off the initial shock and heard several men calling to each other, throwing open doors and screaming "Freeze!" each time they did. He heard a man call out his name. It was the police, all right, and judging from the way they were moving through the house like a SWAT team, he knew they weren't after him for breaking and entering.

He had killed her! The realization made him go cold. His mouth dropped open and he heard Faith calling to him but he could not speak.

He hadn't meant to do it. It was a mistake. He was furious, and yes, at that moment when he had her there on the dock and his hands were around her throat he could have killed her and in a way he wanted to kill her, but in the end he did not do it. He only threw her into the water. She could swim. She must be able to swim! She grew up on the water. She handled the boat like a professional. He thought for sure she could swim. He didn't mean to kill her!

The police were climbing the stairs to the second floor.

He would explain about the Measuring Lives. He could show the police the real Appendix A and could tell them he confronted Morgan, and he was mad with anger, but all he did was throw her into the water. Would they believe him? He thought of making something up. He'd say he confronted her about the Measuring Lives and she tried to kill him and it was self-defense and . . .

"Geddy!" an officer called out from second floor hallway.

Geddy started toward the closet, thinking he could hide. Halfway there, he discarded that foolish notion and looked back to the phone. Faith was still calling out to him. He looked left and right, then put his hands over his face in frustration and groaned. He was scared and confused. Worse, he was desperate.

He took a deep breath and gave himself a few seconds to think. The police were hurrying up the stairs to the third floor. He was concentrating and did not hear them. Suddenly, it came to him. The only logical explanation. Geddy rushed to the telephone.

"Did they find her body!" he asked Faith in a hushed but hurried voice.

Faith hesitated before replying. "Well, no. But the current . . ."

Geddy dropped the telephone again when he heard the police running down the hallway towards the bedroom. Instinctively, he hurried to the balcony and closed the door behind him. He knew he had only a minute before they would check the balcony. Could he climb to the roof? Probably. He looked down at the water. It was a pretty good fall. The roof would be safer.

Was it worth it to run? he second-guessed himself. Couldn't he count on the police to figure out what has happened? Couldn't he count on the state attorney, even though he hated Geddy, to clear his name?

Or would he just rot in jail, helpless, unable to save himself?

The key was the money. Morgan's Swiss account was in his name as well as hers. Somehow, he had to get to the money before Morgan. He knew now that she wasn't really dead. Once he told Morgan he had discovered she switched the Measuring Lives, she knew she had to disappear. If she was capable of switching the Measuring Lives and ending up with the forty million dollars after all the smoke cleared, she was surely capable of staging her own death to effect an escape.

Just then he heard a loud noise from inside. Now that they were in the bedroom he could hear them. "Geddy!" one called out. "Check the bathroom!" another shouted. "I'll look outside!"

It was time to decide. Should he turn himself in? Climb to the roof? He couldn't think straight, things were getting out of control . . .

He put his hand on the doorknob to go inside and turn himself in, but the voice of instinct spoke clearly to him from the recesses of his mind. It was telling him, ordering him, to jump. Don't be a sucker, it seemed to be saying. There was too much going on that he didn't know about. He had to get to that money before Morgan, or else he would surely never see her again and the world will think he killed her. If he could control the money, he could strike a deal with Morgan: she clears his name, and he lets her have the money. Then, when it was all over and he was free again?

Revenge.

Without the number of that numbered Swiss account, he

didn't know how he was going to get to the money. But one thing was certain. There was no way to protect the money and strike a deal with Morgan while sitting in jail.

It was over a three-story fall and he hit hard, landing awkwardly in the black water of Venetian Bay at night. Geddy didn't know which way was up, and he began to panic since the air was knocked out of him when he hit the water. Thinking he was going to drown, he started thrashing about wildly.

Stop struggling!

He forced himself to relax, and soon he was slowly floating upwards. As soon as he knew which way was up, he pulled for the surface, gasping for air as he broke through.

"I'm checking the roof!" he heard a voice call out from far above.

Geddy was in the bay, breathing heavily and looking about, still not sure what his next move would be. Suddenly the door to the terrace opened. The light from the first floor beamed directly on him like a spotlight. He knew he was caught, but his arms and legs started working, and after a few pulls through the water, Geddy was under the terrace, out of sight of the two men above him.

"See anything out here?"

"Nothing."

"Check the water, maybe he dove out the back when we came in."

In the light cast onto the water in front of him, Geddy saw the shadow of a man bend over the railing to look at the water. "Can't see anything, but it's darker than hell out there. We best call for the police boats."

"Can't do it. The tide's going out tonight, so there's a hell of a current out by Gordon's Pass. They've rushed the police boats out to Naples Bay to drag for the body."

A third man joined them on the terrace. "It's a mess up there, but there's no sign of him."

Finally the man who sounded like he was in charge said,

"Glucksman, you stay here, in case he comes back. The rest of us are gonna check the area in case he somehow got out of here before we came. His car's out front so he's on foot. Durkee, I want you and Frazier to go around to the other side of the bay, start combing the neighborhoods. It's possible he got out when he heard us and swam across." Venetian Bay was more like a river than a bay, and a strong swimmer could easily make the crossing.

"What do we do if we see him?"

The answer was given without hesitation. "Order him to stop. If he doesn't, take him down."

• • •

As soon as the three policemen walked back inside, Geddy began swimming for the center of the bay. Even dressed in his suit pants and shirt and tie, he made good time. When he was a child, his mother had taken him to the beach and taught him to swim. By the end of the summer he could swim to the first float and back. By the next summer he could swim to the fourth float and he would have showed his mother and she would have been proud but she was killed before he had a chance to show her and if he could go back now and show her she'd hug him and . . .

With an effort, he brought himself back to the present.

In five minutes he was in the center of the bay, where he tread water. He looked back at the villas and could see the faint flashing blue lights emanating from beyond them. In a minute, he saw a police cruiser pull away down the street, its lights flashing ominously.

His initial fright had left him as the realization sunk in that he was safe. Safe for as long as he could tread water. He could afford to relax a moment and think. He looked at both sides of the bay. He couldn't swim across the bay because he heard the police dispatch at least a couple men to patrol the other side, with more surely to come. They said the police boats were dragging Naples Bay, obviously for Morgan's body. That was good, because at least now he was safe on the water.

He tread water for close to ten minutes when finally a boat appeared far off and traveled towards him from the south, its red and green navigational lights growing brighter and brighter. He couldn't stay on the water like this all night, he knew, but neither shore was a friendly shore right now. As the boat came nearer, he saw it was a large cabin cruiser. He stayed just to the side of its path as it finally pulled by him at about ten miles an hour. He positioned himself to grab onto the large white bumper used to protect the side of the boat when tied up against a dock. It came towards him quickly, much more quickly than he expected. He grabbed desperately for it, but it was wet and slipped through his arms, hitting him hard on the nose. His nose stung, and he swallowed a mouthful of water as the large wake of the boat washed over him. He seemed to bounce as it lifted him up and let him down, lifted him up and let him down. Then he was in the white foam of the boat's wake when he saw that a rope extending from the stern of the boat was rushing by overhead.

He turned quickly and saw that a small dinghy being towed behind the cabin cruiser was coming straight at him. Instead of ducking under or jumping to the side, Geddy instinctively reached up for the pointed bow of the skiff. He had made his move too early but did manage to get his left hand around the last foot of the tow rope. The rope ripped his palm as it slipped through. He let go, and the boat struck him hard in the head. But at the last second, he grabbed the boat with his other hand and clung desperately to the bow where the rope was tied.

With the dinghy moving so fast and his legs dragging underneath it, Geddy couldn't pull himself up into the boat. He was losing his grip. He had to do something fast.

With his left hand, he went for the rope again just as his right hand slipped away. This time he held the rope tightly. Hand over hand, he struggled to pull himself backwards several feet away from the dinghy. His legs now bumped along in the surf just in front of the dinghy, instead of underneath it.

He couldn't hold the rope much longer. Besides, he knew he had to get into the boat. The small bridge at Park Shore Drive was coming up. He didn't want to be dangling from the rope in case police driving across the bridge should look down and spot him. He dove for the right side of the dinghy. He missed and it started to rush by, but then, with one last great effort, he grasped the side of the boat. He tried desperately to pull himself up. His muscles strained, and he was close to making it, but it was a high-sided skiff. He had exhausted himself with his swimming and treading water and hanging on to the rope. He couldn't lift himself high enough out of the water. He relaxed and rested his arms. After a couple of seconds, he tried to lift his right leg up and over the side. He struggled, but he couldn't get it high enough. The lower half of his body dragged through the water. He was almost at the bridge. He didn't have the strength to get in the boat. His hands were starting to slip away. They were going to spot him.

Use your head! Stop and think for a second.

Like a cowboy holding onto a saddle while being dragged by a runaway horse, Geddy thrust his legs out of the water just enough to kick them forward. As soon as his legs hit the water, they rushed beneath him and seemed to bounce off the top of the water. This gave him enough lift and momentum to swing his right leg high enough to get his heel into the dinghy. With his last ounce of energy, he pulled the rest of his body up and over the side. He fell exhausted into the dinghy, banging his head against the wooden bench. Gasping for air, he lay in the bottom of the boat for several seconds. When he opened his eyes, he saw the bridge rushing past overhead.

In a moment he righted himself and looked ahead at the cabin cruiser. There were two men on the captain's bridge twenty feet above the water. Apparently, they had not seen or heard him. The boat was heading north to the end of the bay just a quarter mile ahead. Geddy, however, needed to go south.

He scrambled to the bow of the skiff and pulled for slack on the rope that held him to the cabin cruiser. Then he untied the knot and threw off the rope. He was adrift on his own as the larger boat continued north, unaware of its loss.

On the stern was a small electric-powered engine. Geddy

started it, settled on the back bench and turned south. It was about one-thirty in the morning. The bay was quiet as he putt-putted at full speed, no more than five miles an hour. He slowed down just before the small bridge at Park Shore Drive. There was a chance the police could be driving or walking over it or maybe even had a man stationed there. He cut the engine, took out the single oar, and settled in the bow. As quietly as he could, he paddled underneath the bridge until he knew he would be out of sight.

Once past the bridge, he restarted the engine and stuck to the middle of the bay as he passed Venetian Villas again, still seeing the blue flashing lights, not so bright now, though just as hostile as before. In ten minutes he pointed his skiff out toward the gulf and made his way at a snail's pace through Doctor's Pass, then rode the rougher gulf waters uneasily until he was a hundred yards from shore and safe from view. His heart was beating regularly again. He was headed south.

• • •

Ten minutes later, Geddy cut the engine and listened. He gazed out over the water and took a good look at the condominium complex where Faith lived. No flashing blue lights. That was a good sign. He also didn't notice any movement, so he was put at ease. Why would the police expect him there? They already checked there earlier, and they thought he was over in the Venetian Bay area. Besides, he and Faith and were just friends, coworkers.

But he knew that Faith was more. She was a very good friend, and a very skilled co-worker. He trusted her and knew she would help him. Almost as important, he knew she *could* help him, and now more than ever he needed to figure out how he had gotten himself into this mess. The first step would be to gain control of the Swiss bank account, and for that, he needed Faith.

Don't go in there, the voice inside his head told him. Not tonight. Tonight things are too crazy. Play it cool tonight and regroup.

He wouldn't listen to that voice though, not this time. The prospect of a friend and ally and dry clothes and food and a beer—

oh, could he use a beer—overruled the voice of instinct.

He restarted the engine and made his way to shore, jumping out in the light foamy surf to pull his escape craft up the beach. Then he turned it around, in case he needed to make a quick getaway, and walked up the beach to the building, keeping low and staying in the shadows as much as possible.

The ten story building was called "Windsor By The Gulf" by a shameless developer who hoped to attract buyers with the promise of a touch of British gentility. Geddy entered through the doors on the beach side. As he stepped inside, he heard the Big Ben tune chiming away like a storekeeper's bell to let the security guard know someone was there. He straightened up and tried his best to pull himself together. His work clothes had dried only a little by then, and his wet leather shoes were squeaking on the marble floor as he walked the long lobby to the roadside entrance, where a security guard sat reading a magazine behind a desk.

"May I help you, sir?" the guard asked in an upper-class British accent, part of the royal treatment that Windsor By The Gulf promised. He was a thirtyish, dumpy-looking man wearing a blue blazer and red tie. His ears were long and large, and they jutted out comically from his head.

"I'm here to see Faith Williams," replied Geddy, trying to sound casual.

The guard's eyes widened. Geddy heard the inner voice of instinct trying to tell him something, but he shut it out.

"One moment, I'll ring her for you." The guard pushed three buttons and said into the phone, "Hello, Ms. Williams, Mr. Geddy is here to see you." The guard spoke slowly and deliberately, trying too hard to sound normal. "Yes, that is correct. It is Mr. Geddy."

Geddy suddenly realized he hadn't given his name, yet the guard referred to him as "Mr. Geddy." He reached out across the desk and grabbed the phone from the guard, put it to his ear, and heard a man's voice order, " . . . don't let him leave, stall him!" Geddy looked up to find the security guard pointing a gun at him.

He put the phone down.

"You don't know what's going on," argued Geddy. The guard looked unaccustomed to handling a gun. "I didn't kill anyone. Just let me go and I'll be out of . . ."

"The police said to keep you here!" cried the security guard, no longer with a British accent. "They'll be right down. Don't move or I'll shoot you. I will, too, I'll shoot you, so help me!"

Geddy knew he had no more than a minute before the police came downstairs, but he didn't panic. He knew he had plenty of time to think of a way out of this if he thought clearly. He could tell the guard was scared. Geddy could not afford to be scared.

"Take it easy," he said soothingly, putting up his hands to show he had nothing that could hurt the guard. "I won't give you any trouble. It's all a big misunderstanding. We'll just stand here nice and quiet, and wait for the police."

The guard was shaking with fear. Geddy, a study in calmness, slowly brought his hands down to rest by his side. His face was relaxed and completely unthreatening, though the scar on his cheek gave him a toughness he did not feel at that moment. He was scared, too, but he didn't let it show. He didn't make a sound. All Geddy could hear was the labored breathing of the security guard.

Geddy could tell the guard was near cracking. The gun was no doubt beginning to feel heavy in his hand. It started to fall just a little, but it was still aimed at Geddy.

The silence lasted only about thirty seconds, but he could tell the guard was a basket case. Geddy was thinking now. He didn't look like he was, but he was considering his options, none of which had any hope of succeeding, but he was thinking so he still had a chance. And he was calm, he realized. Genuinely calm. The police would be here any minute, there was a gun pointed at him, but he was calm.

He decided he had to wait. It wasn't a great plan, but it was better than rushing the guard and hoping he didn't get shot. It was better than trying to run away. He just had to remain calm. No matter how bad it looked, he had a chance if he could remain calm.

The guard whimpered a little, and Geddy grinned just to unnerve him. He knew it was going to be close, but he was resolved now. He'd chosen his course. He had to wait and let the silence work for him.

They stood there facing each other like gunfighters, each waiting for the other to draw—except Geddy was unarmed. That's the only thing that makes it a fair fight, Geddy thought.

Suddenly there was a "ding" from just down the hall announcing the arrival of the elevator. The sound, hardly noticeable most times, in this silence and with the security guard's frayed nerves, seemed as loud as a foghorn. It gave Geddy the split second he needed.

The security guard jumped at the sound and reflexively looked toward the elevator in hopes that it was the police. That was how Geddy expected him to react. He reached under the guard's elaborately carved wooden table and turned it over in one quick motion, causing the heavy table to fall over onto the guard's feet. The guard screamed in pain and stumbled backward onto the floor, his feet crushed under the weight of the table.

Geddy ran for the exit. Just as the elevator slid open, he rammed his shoulder into the front door. It wasn't until he was already through the door that the police fired their first shots, shattering the glass-enclosed entranceway. The shots spurred Geddy into running even faster. He raced out of the well-lit front courtyard down the side of the building and toward the beach again. He heard the police shouting as they came out the front, but by the time they reached the side, Geddy had veered toward the boat and was out of their gunsights. They chased him, and when he was halfway down the beach, he knew that in the near darkness they would see him pull out in the dinghy. Even if they didn't catch him, they could easily parallel his movements from the beach and keep tracking him until the police boats could be called in. So he abandoned the boat and sprinted down the beach, looking behind him only once. He couldn't see the police in the darkness, but he could hear them shouting to each other, so he knew they were not far behind.

Geddy knew that if he couldn't see them, they probably couldn't see him. There was no question in his mind that he could outrun them down the beach, but he knew they'd be calling for backup, and they might make out his tracks in the stand. So he made quickly for a hotel that was a quarter of a mile from Faith's condominium.

Just before running up the wooden stairs leading to the pool area of the hotel, he tore off his tie and wet dress shirt and T-shirt. As he climbed the stairs he kicked off his shoes, which were waterlogged and heavy. He stopped to look behind him as he ripped off his soggy socks and saw two figures roughly fifty yards behind. He ran off dressed only in his trousers, but he felt lighter and faster. He might also look more conspicuous, but he didn't exactly blend in with a soaking wet shirt and tie and dress shoes. At least this way he could run. Maybe live to see another day.

The pool area was deserted, as was the grass courtyard. He ran around the building and across well-lit Gulf Shore Boulevard, where the sounds of sirens could be heard in the distance. There were no people in sight at this early hour. He crossed the street and ran by the tennis courts and Pro Shop, then ran for the darkness at the center of the golf course. When he reached a green at the end of a long fairway, he was out of breath but safely cloaked in blackness, surrounded by dark, wide open spaces. He put his hands on his knees and gasped for air, looking behind and listening. He could hear no one. He must have lost the police at the hotel. There were any number of places he could have tried to hide, and the police were likely checking them all. He fell to the soft, trimmed grass and sprawled out in exhaustion as sirens continued to wail all around him.

33

For five minutes, John Geddy lay in the middle of the golf course. It was after two in the morning now, so he knew he had only about four hours until daylight. He also knew the dogs would be coming soon. They would start at the hotel and track him. He had to get moving. He had to find a place to hole up during the day, a place where he could regroup and consider his next move.

The golf course stretched east to west from Tamiami Trail back towards Gulf Shore Boulevard. Both were main streets and were too risky to take. The sounds of the sirens persisted, and every now and then, he could see the blue lights and hear the police cruisers screaming. In his bare feet, he jogged to the south end of the golf course, slipped through some bushes, and crossed a dark, quiet side street. Then he carefully climbed over a chain-link fence that enclosed a backyard. The house was dark, and there was a clothesline in the back, but no clothes hung there. There was a small shed, too, but the dogs would track him there, so he ran hunched over through the backyard and went over the stone wall in the back.

He found himself in another yard, but he didn't stop this time. He ran past the side of that house, across another side street, and behind yet another house, all the while making his way south. He needed water. That was the safest place for him. The dogs couldn't track him, and he'd be able to find someplace to hide on the water.

He'd have to keep moving south to get to the marinas, but to get there, he'd have to cross Fifth Avenue in Olde Naples, which he knew would be extremely well-lit and probably crawling with police. How would he cross that street? How would he even make it that far?

He stopped behind the next house because he saw a light. He crawled onto the patio and could hear through the screen door a sportscaster rattling off baseball scores. The Yankees had won. He allowed himself a brief smile. Then he remembered that he was creeping around in somebody's backyard in nothing but a pair of wet pants with the whole police force searching for him and half the town able to recognize him from the TV and the papers, so he had better concentrate on saving himself.

Geddy crouched and peered inside. An older man with gray hair and a very noticeable bald spot was sitting in his recliner, with his back to Geddy, watching television. There were more and more sirens crying out in the distance. Geddy waited until the old man got up. He carried a dirty plate and an empty glass with him.

Geddy opened the screen door slowly, carefully, trying not to make a sound. Naturally the door squeaked a little, but not loud enough to be heard. He carefully closed the door behind him. Geddy could hear the sounds of running water and dishes being put away, so the man was probably cleaning up. He saw a digital clock that read 2:25 A.M. He walked deeper into the room and began searching. He looked on the coffee table and on top of the television, then quietly hurried through the dining room to the front door, checking the settee in the front hallway. Then the sounds from the kitchen stopped, and so did Geddy.

He moved back into the darkened dining room and crouched behind the table. Eventually the television was turned off, then the lights, and he heard the back door shut and the man lock the deadbolt. Geddy crawled forward and could see the man walk to the far end of the house, most likely to go to bed.

In the dark now, Geddy crawled carefully back into the television room, where he could look down the hallway and see the light coming from under the closed bedroom door. He continued on, down on all fours, feeling in front of him to know where he was going. When he ran into a wall, he followed it until he reached the opening to the kitchen. He crept across its tiled floor, along the cabinets, until he found the refrigerator.

He leaned his back against the refrigerator to give the man time to fall asleep. He heard muffled voices from down the hall and assumed the man was speaking with his wife. In time the voices ceased. A few minutes later, Geddy felt that he had to get moving. He had to get out of the area fast. He was taking too much time.

Geddy opened the refrigerator to cast some light into the kitchen, afraid to use the overhead fixture in case someone were to awaken suddenly, leave the bedroom, and notice the bright light. In the gray light of the faintly illuminated kitchen, Geddy searched until he found a set of car keys on a hook next to the phone.

The phone.

He was going to need some help. When would he have another chance to make a call? He took two full minutes to carefully consider what he needed to do. When he was sure he had it straight, he dialed Faith's number and heard her voice.

"Faith, it's John," he whispered.

"Hello?" she said again.

"Faith, it's John," he repeated as loudly as he dared.

"John!" she cried. "Don't come here. The police are all over. And stop calling me! I'm not going to help you!"

The police must be there. "Are the police there now?" he whispered.

She replied quickly and angrily. "No, they're watching the out-side now, in case you come back." Then the tone of her voice changed to one of concern. "Don't you realize what kind of trouble you're in? I heard they shot at you. What are you thinking? You could be killed."

"How come you didn't tell me the police were still at your place?"

"You mean when you called me from the villa? Because they weren't here, they'd been gone for half an hour. But after you got away from the villa, the police heard me calling to you through the phone you dropped in Morgan's bedroom. I hung up when they asked who I was, but a second later they hit the redial button and I was too scared to pick it up. They heard my answering machine message and realized you called me, so they came back here hop-ing you'd come to talk to me in person. John, you have to give up. They'll catch you, if they don't kill you first."

He felt his heart constricting in his chest until he felt it would implode. "I can't talk. Have the trust that was recorded in Lake Forest along with the deed to Cynthia's house faxed to you first thing tomorrow. Take the 8 P.M. launch to the Keewaydin Club, then walk down the beach until I find you. One other thing. Look in my office for the file on Morgan's Swiss account. The account is in my name and Morgan's name. Contact the bank in Zurich and tell them you are my lawyer and the number of the account has been stolen so we need to freeze the account. Tell them not to let anyone withdraw a penny or else we'll hold them liable for the whole forty million. Tell them I'll contact the bank myself in a day or two to straighten everything out. Do you understand? Did you hear me?"

"I won't be your accomplice! Are you crazy . . ."

To shut her up, he pushed a button on the phone and let it ring for a few seconds. When he put his ear back to the receiver, she had stopped talking. "Don't let anyone follow you. Did you hear everything I said?"

"I heard you . . ." she began, but he hung up and stood silently,

waiting and listening to make sure no one in the house heard
him. When he realized all was still quiet, he went back to the refrigerator and saw the Toyota emblem on two of the keys. He shut the
refrigerator door and crawled painstakingly back to the front door.

He risked turning on the front hall light, knowing the bedroom was on the other side of the house, and looked for any sign
of a home alarm system in the front hallway. Finding none, he
carefully turned the lock, then the deadbolt, and slowly opened
the door. Immediately, he heard the sounds of many barking dogs
nearby.

• • •

Geddy hit the light switch and quickly but quietly shut the
door behind him. As he rushed outside he could hear the dogs
more clearly now. They couldn't be more than a couple of blocks
away. He rushed to the car parked in the driveway. It was a
Toyota, so he tried the key, but it didn't fit. The dogs were getting
closer. He tried the other key, but it didn't work either. Now he
could hear men's voices. They were retracing his route over the
fences between the houses. He knew that any minute now they
would appear from behind the house across the street. He dropped
the keys and began to run but took only a few steps before stopping suddenly. He did not yet see the officer, but he heard him
shout, "Let the dogs loose! There he is!"

The barking was louder now as the dogs appeared in the front
yard of the house across the street, running full out towards him.
The police hadn't emerged into the light thrown from the streetlights yet, but he could hear them shouting. He knew he couldn't
make a run for it. He was fast, but the dogs would be all over him
before he could reach the end of the block.

He took two seconds to think. It was all the time he had.

He looked around quickly, not knowing what for. Then he
found hope. Parked in the street in front of the old man's house
was another car. A Toyota.

He hurried back a few steps to pick up the keys where he'd
dropped them, then ran to the car on the street with the dogs

nearly upon him. The police were rushing across the front yard on the other side of the street. Flashlights bounced up and down and dogs raced ferociously, but his hand was steady. There was no fumbling with the keys when the first one didn't work. He kept his calm and quickly slid the second key into the lock. He jumped in and slammed the door. A savage-looking dog jumped at the window and stood on its hind legs barking at Geddy through the glass.

He was not out of it yet. The police were almost in the street now and were shouting at him to get out and put his hands in the air. He started the car, leaned over toward the passenger seat as as far he could, and spun the wheels as he accelerated ahead. He couldn't see because he was keeping his head down. The police fired at the car. The rear window shattered, but he was still crouched down to his right. A few seconds later, the sounds of the guns ceased. He pulled himself up, just in time to turn his headlights on and make the right turn onto Tamiami Trail. He was heading south again.

He knew it was only a matter of moments before the police with the dogs would radio his position and there would be a dozen squad cars rushing down Tamiami. So Geddy raced a few blocks, turned left down a side street, traveled a few more blocks, and turned right—heading south again on a less-traveled road, driving as fast as he dared. He could hear sirens now, but he couldn't stop. He had to get across Fifth Avenue.

He realized that once he made it close to Fifth Avenue he would be better off on foot than in the car the police would surely be looking for. After several more blocks, he pulled into the parking lot of a strip mall and abandoned the car behind a dumpster. In the dark of early morning, the parking lot was quiet and most of the stores were darkened, but there was some light coming from the supermarket night lights, so he sprinted toward the far end of the parking lot into the cover of darkness. He climbed a fence and ran hunched over through an abandoned lot, then jumped another chain-link fence and fell into a small parking lot. It hurt his feet to run on the gravel, so he slowed to a walk. This parking lot was smaller and hidden behind a brick building. He crept along the side of that building, then crouched in its shadow and found himself looking out over Fifth Avenue.

Cars rushed by intermittently, including several police cars. Occasionally the coast seemed clear, but it was so well lit, he wasn't sure he'd make it across the five lanes to the other side before one of the police cruisers, marked or unmarked, would suddenly turn the corner from Tamiami down the street, its blue lights flashing and its piercing siren screaming at him to give up. And it wasn't just the police he had to worry about. The entire city must know about the manhunt. He had to make it across the entire avenue without anyone seeing him. Five lanes, about forty yards, to the lee of the building on the other side. It would take him about five seconds. Five seconds in that light with that many cars on the busiest street in Naples was an eternity. Even at three in the morning, it was an eternity.

But he had to get to the water. The docks beyond Tin City were only a couple of blocks away now.

He realized that he was hungry and wished he'd taken some food from the refrigerator in the old man's house. When would he have another chance to eat? He certainly couldn't go out in the daytime. Food would have to wait.

He felt a breeze kick up, and he welcomed it. Though he was wearing only his damp suit trousers, he wasn't cold. It was at least eighty-five degrees. He wiped the sweat from his forehead with the back of his hand and checked Fifth Avenue again.

He saw that it was too risky, because police cars were speeding by, turning on and off too frequently. He wouldn't go back to the Toyota; it would be spotted easily. The police would soon figure out that he had turned off Tamiami and taken to the side streets, and they would be all over the place. He had to get moving. He was becoming anxious again, so he closed his eyes and made himself relax before deciding what to do next.

He hopped to his feet and retraced his steps for a block, then cut through a few empty lots until he was confronted by a thick marsh. He leaned into the heavy tropical growth that became more swampy with every step, pushing the tall reeds out of his way to keep them from scratching out his eyes. He could feel the sharp points of the reeds nick his feet like so many little paper cuts. It was like walking on needles and pins. Then his foot would sink deep into muck, and it was a struggle to pull it out. Presently he came to a small body of water that looked like a pond but was actually an estuary that met the mouth of Naples Bay at the bridge next to Rosie's Waterfront Cafe. Nick Farley had told him that he used to throw kittens off this bridge years ago. He wished Nick was still in Naples. He'd be able to help. Geddy could trust him.

He remembered what the police officer said back at Morgan's villa. The tide was going out that night. That meant he should be able to ride the current undetected under the bridge where the cars would be rushing down Fifth Avenue. He broke off a reed and tossed it into the water to make sure. It began floating toward the bridge.

He waded into the warm water. Slowly the current began to take him. Three cars passed overhead, two of them police cruisers, but there was no way they could see him. In a minute the current gathered strength as he was pulled under the bridge and out the other side, next to Rosie's on his left, the Tin City marketplace on his right. He swam to his right making hardly a sound, till he came upon the docks belonging to a condominium complex next to Tin City.

He remained in the water and pulled himself along the docks. This wouldn't do, he didn't like it. There weren't enough boats, and it was too close to the street. The owners of the boats in their condos lived too close. There was a better chance that they'd come out to their boats in the morning here than there would be at the city docks or one of the private marinas up ahead. So he swam a hundred yards around the foundation of the condominium complex, which was built right into the harbor, then he made for the more extensive city docks on the other side. He swam into the middle of the docks, underwater and underneath several until he lost himself in the center of the network of boats and docks and gangplanks. Then he chose a dark place to pull himself up.

It was quiet here, other than the relentless police sirens still searching Olde Naples for him. They probably thought he was headed for the office. He looked around, and not seeing any security guards or guard stations, he stood in the semidarkness. He found a sailboat that looked like it was rarely used and poorly cared for. He smiled at the name of the boat written on the stern. *Desperado.* The door to the small triangular cabin was latched, but he kicked it in and entered, closed the door behind him, and descended the few stairs.

The cabin smelled like low tide, and the floor was damp with a film of scum covering it, but this was just what Geddy was looking for. The next day would be Tuesday, so chances were that not too many boats would be used, but to be on the safe side, he wanted one that looked like it hadn't been used in months. He searched the storage spaces and captain's chest for food or clothing but found nothing useful. Underneath a bench, however, he found a gray raincoat, some type of sailor's foul-weather gear. He took it out and laid it on the long bench.

Next he covered the round little windows of the cabin with assorted boating supplies so that nobody could see in, then lay down on the thin-cushioned bench and huddled, wet and tired, for several hours, until he fell asleep listening to the still-screaming sirens of the entire Naples police force.

Geddy didn't wake until almost two o'clock the next afternoon. He was alarmed at first that he had overslept, but he accepted it and realized it was not a fatal error. The important thing was that Faith must have seen the list of the Measuring Lives by this time, so surely he had an ally. She would also have had the bank in Zurich freeze the Swiss account by now. That bought him a little time to try to figure out how to get the money without the account number.

He went to one of the portholes, pulled aside the life vest he had used to cover it up, and saw it was raining. He wasn't sure why, but the rain comforted him—the rain and knowing that if the police hadn't found him while he was sleeping, they wouldn't find him until he ventured out again and made a mistake.

He replaced the life vest and sat down where he had slept. He was covered with sweat. He realized he was famished. The more he thought about his hunger, the weaker he felt. He looked at his feet, cut and sore from all of his running barefoot. He second-guessed his idea to throw off his shoes and his clothes, but he quickly forgave himself. Whatever he did was all right, because he was alive and safe, for the time being.

He jumped up with a start and checked his pocket, then pulled out what remained of the copy of the trust with the real Measuring Lives. It was in shreds now and was still a little soggy. That was the least of his concerns. It was a matter of record in Lake Forest. It wasn't going anywhere.

He lay back again and considered his next move. Hungry and cold as he was, he knew he had to wait a few more hours for darkness to fall before he could venture out. Then what? All he knew about Morgan's supposed death was that they thought he did it. How could he prove his innocence?

He put that problem aside. He had made a mistake the night before that he needed to deal with first. He told Faith to meet him on Keewaydin Island so he could make sure she wasn't being followed. The trouble was, now he had to think of a way to get to Keewaydin Island by eight o'clock, in case she actually showed up.

By seven it wasn't dark enough outside to get moving, but he knew he would have to make a start at once if he were to have a chance to meet up with Faith. He donned the gray raincoat and pulled the hood over his head, then climbed out of the cabin and squinted at the faint light of the darkening sky. The rain was now a light drizzle, and there were few boats about. Several rows of docks away, he could see a group of people coming in for the night, securing their boat, and over to his right, through large bay windows, he could see patrons eating at a waterfront restaurant. He couldn't ask anyone for help because he was sure his face had already been plastered all over the newspapers and TV reports. He was on his own, and Keewaydin Island was three miles away, at the mouth of Naples Bay at Gordon's Pass.

●　●　●

On her return trip from the Keewaydin Club, Faith jumped off the launch before it had been secured and ran towards the red Volvo. Before she got there, she was grabbed from behind and dragged to the shadows, her mouth covered by her attacker's hand. She twisted away and kicked her assailant in the groin. When he was down, she kicked him again in the face. He rolled over, stunned and groaning.

"John!" she called out too loudly in her excitement, then knelt next to him and propped him up. "I thought they got you! When you didn't show up, I thought the police found you or you'd been shot!"

Her second kick had opened a small cut just above his left eye. He still had not recovered from her first kick, but eventually he managed to tell her, "I couldn't make it in time. I meant to get here before sunrise, but I fell asleep and didn't get up until this afternoon. After dark I managed to get here, but I was late and wasn't sure if you came. I didn't see your car. I figured I'd wait here and hope you'd show up."

"Of course I came. How could you think I wouldn't help you?"

"Did you see the trust? The one with the *original* list of Measuring Lives?"

"Yes, I got it." She looked around quickly, then helped him up.

"Did you get in touch with the bank in Zurich . . ."

Faith interrupted him. "Yes. I'll tell you about it later. First, let's get out of here. This is a dead end, and if the police come now, we're both in a lot of trouble."

They hurried to the red Volvo and with Faith at the wheel rushed north towards town.

"Where did you get this car?" asked Geddy.

"It's Philip Percy's," she told him. "Remember, Curtis's significant other."

"What the hell are you thinking? How can you trust him? After what we did to Curtis, he's the last guy who'd want to help me."

"Look, the police were following me everywhere. After your fool attempt to see me last night, they think you might try to contact me again. I needed a way to lose the police, and I needed a car they wouldn't be looking for. I drove to Curtis's art gallery in North Naples, where Philip works. As I expected, the police followed me. Philip gave me his keys, and I slipped out the back, and here I am."

Faith turned onto Fifth Avenue, so Geddy pulled the hood of his raincoat over his head. "But why would he help?"

"I told him we're Curtis's last chance. I told him we discovered Curtis didn't kill the Measuring Lives."

Ten minutes later, Faith checked them into a seedy motel in the part of town that was the real Naples. The buildings were old and neglected, a long way from the charm of Olde Naples. Far from the beaches, east of the interstate, this was where the service people lived. The waitresses and the mechanics, the policemen and store clerks. Reality reared its ugly head here and reminded the real people, the working class of Naples, that the reputation of Naples as paradise was a farce.

When Geddy came out of the shower, Faith had already returned with two bags of Chinese food and two six-packs of beer. It was too late for her to run out and buy him any clothes, so he sat on the bed in the small room at the Golden Gate Motel with a towel around his waist and a blanket wrapped around his back and shoulders.

"Feel better?" asked Faith as she began spreading the boxes of food across the bed. The cut over his eye hadn't stopped bleeding. When he sat down, the blanket opened enough for her to see the many cuts and scrapes on his chest and stomach, suffered while trying to get into the dinghy, sneaking through the marsh, climbing over chain-link fences, and pulling himself up onto the barnacle-encrusted dock.

"I've felt better," he grumbled as he closed his eyes and rubbed his head. "What degree black belt are you, anyway?"

"I played soccer in high school."

"I've been beat up by a female soccer player," he groaned. "Do me a favor and don't tell anyone."

"Well, it was a low blow," she admitted as she watched his muscles flex. "I promise not to hurt you anymore."

"Thank God for that," he said and then began eating ravenously.

"So, what's your plan?" she asked, handing him a beer.

"First, tell me what happened to Morgan."

"Didn't you hear, you killed her?" Her joke didn't go over well. "About fifty people at Morgan's party told police that you stormed into her house, knocking people over and shouting for her. They said when you found her, you screamed your head off at her until she calmly asked you outside. After a while, people noticed she never came back. Dick Didier went out to the dock where you and she had been fighting, and he found her shirt. It had been ripped, and it had traces of blood, her blood, on the collar. Didier called the police and told them about your fight. He told them that he saw you run away from the dock like you were in a big hurry. The police have concluded that you killed her in a jealous rage, dumped her body into Naples Bay, and took off."

Geddy was livid. "That's their proof? That's it? They shoot at me based on that!"

"It sounds like enough for me, especially after they discovered someone had transferred the forty million dollars. They assume that you've run off with it." She frowned at what she considered overwhelming evidence. "Not to mention that when they found your car, it was at her villa, and when they went inside, they saw that you had turned the place upside down and then took off when the police were after you. Then you broke into somebody's house and . . ."

Geddy realized that all signs truly did point to him. "I get the point. But tell me something. They never found her body, did they?"

"Police boats were dragging Naples Bay all night, but there's such a wicked current there at the end of the bay by Gordon's Pass when the tide's going out, they think her body was washed out to the Gulf."

"Do you believe that?" asked Geddy.

"I guess I did at first, but after seeing that list, I don't know what to think. It hardly matters though, John. You don't have to tell me anything, I'll help you."

"Faith, I'll tell you anything you want to know."

They stared at each other for a long moment. "Did you kill Morgan?"

"No."

"When did you find out she switched the Measuring Lives?"

"Yesterday. It was in the copy of the trust that the lawyers from Chicago included with the deed to the house in Lake Forest."

Faith nodded her head, knowing it made sense. "Do you love Morgan?"

He looked Faith square in the eye. "No."

She breathed a sigh of relief. "All right, then we have to figure out who killed her. And it might help me if you told me how you got that scar on your face. If you'd been hit in the face with a softball hard enough to cause that gash, there would have been a bruise. You might even have broken your cheekbone. What really happened?"

"You knew all along?"

She made a face like he was insulting her intelligence. He told Faith about being attacked after the softball game.

"Maybe the same person who attacked you killed Morgan."

Geddy shook his head slowly. "I don't think so, because I know who killed Morgan."

"For God's sake, tell me!"

"Morgan killed herself," he said matter of factly, causing Faith to raise her eyebrows.

"Suicide?"

"Not exactly. Once I found the Measuring Lives, Morgan knew she'd screwed up, she had to disappear. She knew I had just made a scene at her party, so that was as good a time as any. We had a fight and I ripped her shirt when I threw her into the bay. So she intentionally cuts herself, smears her blood on the shirt, and then swims across the little canal to the neighbor's dock so nobody at the party sees her leave. Then, one way or another, she gets out of town or goes into hiding until she has a chance to transfer the money. My guess is she got a car and headed through the Everglades to Miami."

"When did you dream this up?" asked Faith, sounding skeptical.

"I sat around all day in a sailboat downtown. I had nothing better to do."

"How are you going to prove it?"

"It's not going to be easy. We have a lot to do tomorrow. But the first thing is to make sure we get our hands on the money before Morgan does, otherwise she'll just disappear and I'm screwed. If we get the money first, she'll be forced to come out of hiding if she wants to have any chance of getting the money back. If I were her, I'd contact you, Faith. She'll figure that someone is helping me, and it's probably you. Then she'll use you as a go-between to cut a deal for the money. She clears me of her murder, and I give her the money. But in the meantime, we pull a double cross, and we nail her." Geddy was smiling, but Faith shook her head.

"What? What's wrong? There's got to be a way for us to get that money. My name is on the account, after all."

"I already told you, the money is gone. I verified it today. I told you, the police think you ran off with it."

"I thought you were talking about my transferring the money from the banks in Naples to the Swiss account . . ."

"No. I'm talking about the transfer of the money from the Swiss account to some other unknown account. The money has disappeared. I contacted the bank in Zurich just like you told me, but it was too late. The money was withdrawn the day after you deposited it. It's just plain gone."

He shut his eyes and swore beneath his breath. "She did it again. Morgan was one step ahead of me again. She took care of the money days ago." He gritted his teeth, jumped up, and paced from one end of the room to the other.

Faith broke a long silence. "Any more bright ideas?"

He sighed and shook his head. "I don't even know where to begin, Faith. There's so much more going on than you think. The whole plot started a long time ago. I think Cynthia was in on it."

"Cynthia?" she repeated. "What did she have to do with it?"

"Think, Faith. This whole thing starts with the Measuring Lives being switched. It almost had to be Morgan . . ."

"What if it was her father? She might not even have known that they were switched."

"Somehow, we have to prove that she did it."

Faith was pessimistic. "Why would Morgan switch the Measuring Lives? She would lose her trusteeship, which was worth about a hundred thousand dollars a year to her."

Geddy shrugged. "It's simple. She must have conspired with Cynthia. They were going to split the money."

Faith shook her head sullenly. "But Cynthia never did anything."

"Yes, she did. She did something very important. She hired me."

35

The next morning when Geddy awoke, it seemed like a dream. He lay in bed for some time before remembering what a disaster his life had become. When he finally tried to get up, his body was too sore, and he collapsed again in a heap. A minute later, he sat up with a groan and pulled himself out of bed.

Faith had refused to leave him alone and stayed the night in the motel room, but she left first thing in the morning to carry out Geddy's orders. She had much to do that day. She had picked up some clothes for him: a white T-shirt, Levi's, a pair of swimming trunks, and tennis shoes, just as he requested. She had also engaged another motel for them, this one on Marco Island, thirty minutes south, and left a key for him next to his new clothes. In an envelope, she left him one thousand dollars cash.

He picked at the remains of the Chinese food and had a beer for breakfast. After a careful glance at the parking lot, he slipped out into the late morning July sun and hurried off in Philip's red Volvo. Faith had rented a car for herself that morning.

He headed off through the Everglades to Miami. He needed a gun, and though Miami was two hours away, it was the only place he knew of to get a handgun on such short notice. During his days as a prosecutor in Miami, Geddy knew about a man by the name of Carlos Carrerras. He was a guy that could get anything. Guns, drugs, fake passports, with no questions asked. The police and the state attorney left him alone for two reasons: he put a lot of his dirty money back into the neighborhood in the form of homeless shelters, health clinics, and playgrounds. More importantly, he always knew what was going on and wasn't afraid to let the police in on it if it didn't conflict with his business interests.

Carlos's "office" was in a dilapidated Miami warehouse where he ran a boxing gym—just one of the many ways he gave back to the community. Geddy weaved his way through the hard-luck fighters and the cracked-leather heavy bags without noticing them until he came to the far end of the large, wide-open room. The gym was sweltering, and he was already sweating. He knocked on the door. A huge, well-dressed Cuban opened it and looked at him.

"I want to see Carlos," said Geddy.

"You a cop?"

"No."

"I've seen you before."

From inside the office came a voice. "Who is it, Raul?"

Geddy answered for himself. "It's John Geddy."

He heard a drawer shut closed, then a shade was drawn. "Let him in."

Geddy was allowed to enter the office, a spartan, whitewashed, square room with a single window. There was a small desk and about ten chairs, none of them matching, scattered about haphazardly. Behind the desk stood Carlos. He was short, stocky, and dressed modestly for a man of his wealth. When he saw Geddy, he flashed a smile which revealed a missing tooth.

Raul closed the door behind Geddy. "I thought you'd have a gold tooth by now," Geddy said to Carlos.

Carlos' smile disappeared. "Do I know you?"

"I need a gun."

"Do I know you?" asked Carlos again.

"Don't give me that shit. You know who I am." Geddy tossed a thousand dollars on the desk. "It's all I have on me. Get me whatever you've got on hand. I'll need ammunition too, of course."

"Of course." Carlos didn't look at the money. "Usually I charge extra when a man's on the run."

"I'm in a hurry."

Carlos Carrerras thought for a moment, then motioned to Raul, who left the room. Carlos walked out from behind the desk and stood directly in front of Geddy, staring up at him, the sweat on his prominent forehead running down into his dark eyebrows. "There's a fifty-thousand-dollar reward out for you."

Geddy met the smaller man's stare. "That's nothing to you."

"Fifty thousand dollars is not nothing, my friend. Do I look rich to you? Is my office so lavish that you think I couldn't use fifty thousand dollars?"

"Your house on Star Island's decorated a little more . . . lavishly."

Carlos frowned. "I don't know what you're talking about. I live upstairs, I work here in the gym. I train boxers. I've got a boy who's got a chance, my friend." Carlos laughed. "If he becomes champion of the world, then maybe I get a house on Star Island, eh?"

Raul came back into the room carrying a gun. Carlos made another gesture with his hand, and immediately Raul had Geddy in a headlock with the gun digging into his right temple. Geddy didn't bother to struggle.

Carlos was in Geddy's face. "You make threats? You trying to be cute, you think you know my business? You're in no position to make threats, my friend. I should hand you over to my police friends just as a gesture of goodwill to them. Why you want to threaten me? Maybe I should have Raul blow your fucking skull to pieces, eh? You like threats? You like when I threaten you?"

Geddy had to struggle to breathe as Raul tightened his hold

on his neck. The gun pressed harder into his temple. "I need a gun," repeated Geddy. "I'm in a hurry."

Carlos did not reply right away. He watched as Geddy gasped for air. Then he patted Geddy down, looking for a wire. Carlos was a cautious man, and the news reports that Geddy was on the run could have been part of a setup. There was no wire.

Carlos looked at Raul. "What do you think? It would be foolish to sell an unlicensed gun to a former state attorney, especially *this* former state attorney, eh?" He looked closely at Geddy. "You know what I think, Raul?" Raul knew not to answer. With a gesture of his hand, Carlos signaled Raul to release Geddy. "I think he really just needs a gun."

When Geddy caught his breath, Raul handed him the gun and a box of shells. Carlos walked forward and picked up the money. He handed it to Geddy. "People say I'm paranoid, but I'm not. Just smart. All you had to do was ask. Take the gun, it's yours. You're a special case, no charge. A gesture of goodwill, maybe someday you can help me, eh? But always remember, no threats, never threats. Threats make me nervous, okay? I have to watch my own ass."

Geddy checked to see that the gun was loaded. He stuck it in Raul's sweaty face. "Did you call the cops?" Raul backed up against the wall, his eyes wide with fright. His mouth dropped open, and Geddy shoved the snubbed barrel of the gun in it. Geddy looked at Carlos, who stood back nervously by his desk. "Did he call the cops on me?"

"No, no, he was just getting the gun. Fifty thousand is nothing to me, you know that. What do I care if you killed your girl? She was a rich bitch, eh? She probably deserved it. What do I care about fifty thousand dollars? Fifty thousand is peanuts, eh?"

Geddy left the barrel of the gun in Raul's mouth. His eyes never strayed from Carlos's. "I want to know about Hoffer."

"Why do you care about . . ."

"Was he involved with drugs? Was he a hit man? Was he crazy? Don't fuck around, I'm already wanted for murder."

"He was a bodyguard, for some Colombians," said Carlos finally. "He was stupid, not crazy. He killed a cop, a dirty cop. Everybody knew about it, but nothing could be done because the cop was dirty and everything would come out if some smart-ass defense lawyer started finding out about what the dead cop was doin'."

"So he was set up as the South Beach Butcher?" asked Geddy. "They couldn't get him for killing the cop so they pinned the South Beach Murders on him? Why didn't he talk? About the cop, the Colombians? Why didn't he go to the press with it?"

"Because then he'd be dead. The cops, the state attorney, even the mayor, they were all dirty. Everybody would go down if the scandal hit the papers. Hoffer knew if he breathed one word they'd kill him. But they had another problem, too. They couldn't catch that serial killer, so they decide to kill two birds with one trial, you understand? They can't catch the real serial killer, they can't put the cop killer in prison. They set him up so the pressure to catch the serial killer is off, and Hoffer gets what he deserves, and they know where he is if they have to kill him. He can't talk and run off, he's in jail, see? Even if he did talk, who would believe him? Everyone thinks he's a serial killer. So they all save their jobs, and everybody's happy. Except I heard about you, my friend, snooping around too much. You made everybody very nervous. They were going to kill you, but your old buddy the state attorney convinced everyone that he could get you to go away quietly. It was a good thing you left town."

Geddy's face twitched as he faced Raul again. He held up the gun and gave a warning. "If I see you follow me out, you'll get another mouthful."

Geddy backed off slowly and opened the door. He threw the thousand dollars on the floor. "This was just business, Carlos."

"What do you care, huh? You got your own problems without makin' trouble here. Why you care about Hoffer?"

Geddy didn't answer. Raul looked at Carlos, waiting for a hand gesture which never came. Geddy backed out of the office, hastily recrossed the long gym floor, and ran down the steps onto the street, then around the corner to the red Volvo. In a minute the gun and the shells were in the glove box, and he was heading for the highway.

• • •

The red Volvo raced through the Everglades, right past Naples, and north along Interstate 75 for two hours until reaching Tampa. It was almost five o'clock. He found the office building he was looking for and parked a couple of blocks away. He took the stairs to the fourteenth floor, then hurried through the doors where the name GALVANO & HAWKINS was etched smartly into the frosted glass. A secretary greeted him suspiciously. He told her he was Mr. Kennedy to see Mr. Galvano. Several minutes later, he was seated in the office of a lawyer about his age, with thick black-framed glasses and an earnest manner. Geddy wouldn't let the secretary leave the room.

"What can I do for you, Mr. Kennedy?" asked Bruce Galvano in a helpful way, though the concern on his face was clear.

"You know my name's not Kennedy, it's Geddy." The other attorney acknowledged that he already knew. "I know you'll call the police after I leave, and that's fine. But since there's a fifty-thousand-dollar price on my head, I think you should know that I have no intention of being caught. Not today, anyway." Geddy lifted his T-shirt and showed the gun.

Bruce Galvano could not hide his surprise, but he didn't look overly alarmed. He was a cool customer, Geddy thought. That was good. He wouldn't do anything stupid, and Geddy wouldn't have to stop him.

"I'm sure you're familiar with my . . . situation," said Geddy. "What you don't know is that Morgan Gentry tampered with the Adam Gentry Trust, and I need to prove it. I can't stress how important it is to me. I need proof. I've gone through the trust records several times within the last couple of days, and I discovered that other than a copy of the trust recorded in Lake Forest, Illinois, which Morgan missed because it wasn't specifically mentioned in her records, there was only one other copy of the trust outside of her possession. It was the copy the attorney who drafted the trust in 1952 had kept. I need that copy, and Caleb Galvano, your father, is the lawyer who drafted the trust."

"Yes, I know," said Bruce Galvano.

"You know?"

"I once spoke with Ms. Gentry about it, so I've been following the case ever since you sued Curtis Dole."

"You spoke with Morgan?"

"She came to see me. She correctly assumed that I took over my father's old clients and might still have a copy of the trust in my father's old files. She explained she was the trustee and would like to inspect whatever documents I might have pertaining to the trust because she was having a problem with it. We looked through my storage vault and found boxes of records belonging to Adam Gentry. Real estate deals mostly, but a few personal matters as well. She seemed to find what she was looking for. A copy of the trust."

Geddy looked almost angry. "Please don't tell me she took it."

"She took more than that. At first she just asked if I'd let her look through the files, but, hell, I didn't even know I had them. I told her she could have them for all I cared. I hadn't even heard the name Gentry until that day."

"Did she take them?"

"Sure, she had them boxed up and hauled off." Bruce Galvano leaned forward. "Three or four years ago."

•   •   •

Geddy returned to Naples just after sunset. He drove directly to the beach at Fifteenth Avenue South, where the first Measuring Life had been murdered. He took off all of his clothes except for the swim trunks and ran down to the beach. He waded into the water and swam out to the boat Faith had rented and anchored just off the coast. It was nearly identical to Morgan's Mako. As they had planned, Faith left the keys under a cushion in the cabin. On top of the cushion was a large plastic bag Faith had packed for him.

Geddy floored the throttle, and the boat nearly leapt out of the night-blackened water of the Gulf of Mexico. He raced along the Naples beaches until he reached Doctor's Pass. He slowed considerably and made his way through Venetian Bay at an easy clip until coming to Venetian Villas. Then, not wanting to attract the attention of any police that might still be there by pulling into the slip near Morgan's docked Mako, he drove a little past the villas, turned around and clicked the rental into neutral.

He looked at his watch. It was nine thirty. Then he pushed the throttle forward slightly and retraced his route out of Venetian Bay, cruising at a moderate speed until he was through Doctor's Pass and in the gulf again. Geddy headed north rather than go back the way he had come, once again crashing over the choppy sea in the dark at full throttle. Ten minutes later, he was at the Ritz-Carlton. He checked his watch. Ten minutes to ten.

Wasting no time, Geddy quickly threw the anchor overboard. With the large plastic bag in hand, Geddy dove into the water and sidestroked to shore. He was on the dark, deserted beach in three minutes, opened the bag, pulled out a towel, and quickly dried himself. He threw on a sweatsuit and sandals and pulled on a cap. Then he took a small purse from the bag. He put the plastic bag down and partially covered it with sand to keep it from blowing away.

He hurried up the beach then walked calmly past the pool and into the hotel by the pool-side entrance. Immediately on his left was a stairway with a sign that read, "FIRE EXIT—EMERGENCY USE ONLY. ALARM WILL SOUND." He opened it and—as is usually the case—no alarm sounded. Geddy ran the eight flights as fast as he could, stepped out, and, being careful not to be seen, he found room 812. He looked at his watch. Six minutes past ten. Don't forget to tack on another fifteen minutes she must have spent in the room, he reminded himself.

Geddy rushed down the stairs as fast as he could, then out the door and back onto the beach. He stripped off the hat and sandals and the sweatsuit and put them and the purse back in the plastic bag. He waded into the water and sidestroked back to the boat, climbed in, started the boat quickly, pulled in the anchor, and raced south.

This time Geddy sped past Doctor's Pass and Venetian Bay and traveled all the way back to Naples Bay, then veered for the left shore which he knew to be Port Royal, and finally to Curtis's old house. He went right next to Curtis's old sailboat, stopped against it for a few seconds, then turned and retraced his route back to the gulf, through Doctor's Pass and Venetian Bay until he was in front of Morgan's villa. The time: 11:13.

"Call it two hours," he muttered to himself.

At the Islander Motel at midnight, Geddy's phone rang. He picked it up before the first ring ended.

"Faith? Nick?" he asked frantically.

"It's Nick," his friend told him.

"Nick! Where are you? I must have called every major newspaper in the country trying to locate you."

"I was in Colorado until this afternoon. Faith tracked me down and told me everything and had me fly to New York. I'm at LaGuardia."

"Perfect!" exclaimed Geddy. "That'll give you a good head start."

"Head start for what? How can I help you? More important, why should I help you?"

Geddy panicked for a moment when for the first time it crossed his mind that Nick might not help him. But the panic left him immediately. Nick wouldn't have gone to New York unless he was prepared to help.

"Nick, I wouldn't ask if I weren't desperate."

Nick grunted. "Yeah, all right. Who do I gotta kill?"

"Listen . . ." Geddy told Nick everything that had happened since he discovered the switched Measuring Lives.

"You're screwed, dude."

"No, Nick, I've figured it out. The cops won't buy the truth yet because they think Morgan's a victim. They won't believe she's behind everything. If I can prove she's still alive and skipped the country with the money, everything else will make sense."

"If she's dead . . ."

"She's not dead! She's left the country! It's the only explanation. She had to disappear."

"You want me to find her, is that it? Great, you've narrowed down my search to the entire world, other than the U. S."

"Listen, by tomorrow, I'll know where she is. Get yourself a hotel room at the airport, and call me back with the number. Tomorrow, as soon as I find out where she is, I'll call you. I'd go myself, but I'd probably never make it out of the country. You do have a passport, don't you?"

"Of course I do, but John, what do you want me to do if I find her? You expect me to drag her back to Naples?"

"Of course not. All you have to do is prove she's alive."

Nick thought for a moment. "What about Curtis?"

"What about him? I'll get him out of this mess, but I can't do anything shut up in a motel room."

"What about Curtis's money?"

"I don't know, Morgan's got it, she's gone with it. When Curtis gets out, I'll help him if I can, but short of finding her and making her tell us where the money is, I don't know how he'll ever get it back. The police already checked with the bank where I set up the numbered account. The money's been withdrawn."

"Word is you withdrew the money and set up your own accounts and killed her."

"Nick, you know I wouldn't do that."

After a pause. "Probably not."

"So will you help me?" pleaded Geddy.

"Yeah, I'll do it. But short of kidnapping her, I don't know how I'm supposed to prove she's alive."

• • •

Moments later Faith let herself into the motel room. Geddy had been seated calmly on the bed, watching television, but he jumped up at her arrival.

"Where the hell have you been? I thought the cops must have grabbed you when you went to see Philip Percy."

"Relax, I'm fine. The lab work took a lot longer than I expected. I paid a guy to stay tonight until it was done." She collapsed on the bed.

"Lab work? What lab work?"

Faith didn't move from the bed. "You said last night you needed to prove Morgan switched the Measuring Lives and not her father. I figured out how to find out once and for all. I took the trust to a lab to have the paper Appendix A is printed on date-tested. That way we'll know when it was switched, and therefore, we'll know who did the switching."

"You're amazing!" exclaimed Geddy. He had been counting on Bruce Galvano to help him prove Morgan made the switch. When that idea fell through because Morgan already got to those records, he didn't know how he would ever prove it. "You've solved our biggest problem. So, how old is the fake Appendix A?"

"Well, I got some bad news. The lab confirmed that the paper the trust was printed on was about forty years old, which is about right since it was drafted in 1952," she told him.

"Even Appendix A?"

"Yup," said Faith, smiling.

"Then why do you look so happy? If the paper is really that old, it means the Measuring Lives were never switched. It means somehow the ten Measuring Lives listed in the Illinois version of Appendix A are the phonies."

"Nope," she said, teasing him now.

"Then why are you looking at me like that!"

She laughed gleefully. "The paper the five New Moon Murder

victims were printed on was forty years old. *But,* the *print* was only three years old!"

It took him a few seconds to realize it. "Of course! With all of those trust journals and papers and documents, she'd be able to find an old blank sheet somewhere. When she made the switch, she typed the New Moon Murder victims names on that old sheet of paper, so it would look like the rest of the papers."

"There's more," she told him happily. "The letter from Mark Gentry to Curtis, the one which purportedly proved that Curtis knew who the Measuring Lives where in 1972? I had that tested, too. The second page, the one with Mark Gentry's signature. They dated the photocopy paper and the print at just over twenty years old. *But,* page one, the page which says all the stuff about Curtis requesting a copy and mailing one to him? Just like Appendix A, it was only three years old."

"It was Morgan! She made that up to make it look like Curtis knew who the Measuring Lives were. We can prove it!" He hugged her and swung her around happily, getting carried away. But when he put her down, she looked serious. "What's the matter?"

"All of this is well and good, but it doesn't mean that you didn't kill Morgan. The police will still be looking for you."

"That's all right, Nick Farley is going to prove that I didn't kill her, that Morgan left the country. I just need to hold out one more night, then make one stop tomorrow, and Nick will do the rest."

She shook her head. "John, this is too much. There's too much going on. And there's something else that's been bothering me all day which throws another curve into this whole mess. I think you have to consider the possibility that Morgan killed Cynthia."

"I already have, and I know how she did it. I figured it out when I remembered something from the night I told Morgan she was going to inherit the forty million. Before we went out on her boat, I noticed it was low on gas. That's always bothered me because I was sure there should have been more gas, unless she took the boat out alone, which she never did. That's why I needed you to rent the boat for me—to see if the time and distances worked out. Morgan used her boat the night she killed Cynthia. I know she did it."

Faith ran her hands through her short black hair. "John, you've got to go to the police. They don't know what we know. They think you're a killer. You should see downtown Naples, it's like a war zone. There's a bounty on your head. People are running around with guns looking for you, rednecks from Fort Myers are forming posses. You don't know how dangerous it is for you out there . . ."

"Don't panic, Faith. Together we've almost got it all figured out, but I need one more day." She brushed away a tear and tried to look unafraid, but he could see right through it. "Look Faith, I know I've been asking a lot of you. I think I can handle it from here on. Why don't you go home, try to forget about everything . . ."

"Stop it!" she shouted at him suddenly.

He looked back at her uncertainly. "Stop what, Faith?"

"Stop pretending you don't know I love you!"

He didn't respond because he was completely surprised. He knew she had once been interested in him, perhaps, but certainly not in love. He had been so wrapped up in Morgan and then in his own problems. Now he saw her as if for the first time. He brushed away the short black hair that just fell over her brown eyes, welling with tears, and saw as if for the first time the button nose and smooth, unblemished skin. He knew he felt something for her. In a way he always had, but now things were so intense, he couldn't be sure what it was. All he knew was that at that moment it felt like love, and he wanted to tell her he loved her but he couldn't, not yet. He couldn't be reckless with Faith's feelings. He couldn't say something he wasn't sure of. Besides, she knew the score. He could see by the longing in her eyes that she didn't need to hear words. She just needed to be kissed.

Slowly he bent to kiss her lips and she pulled him down by the neck to meet him, but just at that moment the telephone rang.

He pulled back and so did she, and they stared at each other for a long moment. The phone kept ringing. Reluctantly, he picked it up. It was Nick.

"I just checked in at the Holiday Inn at LaGuardia." He gave Geddy the number.

"Good, Nick." He was still looking at Faith.

"Believe me, it's my pleasure. I figured out how to fix everything."

Faith had turned away from him now and stood by the door. He knew she was wiping away a tear. He shouldn't have answered the phone, he shouldn't have let the moment pass. Once more, he had caused another little heartbreak, if there was such a thing as a little heartbreak.

Nick was talking but Geddy said, "Thanks, Nick," dropped the phone, and rushed to Faith. She was crying and he wanted to tell her he loved her but he couldn't, so he kissed her. He kissed her like he loved her, and he held her like he loved her, and that night, he made love to her like he loved her.

At nine the next morning, Geddy walked into Higgins Travel Agency, located only blocks from his first motel, in the part of town where the less fortunate toiled. It was a small, narrow office with old, fading posters of exotic locations lining the dingy walls. Seated on a plastic lawn chair behind a metal desk was a man in his early forties wearing a wrinkled short-sleeved dress shirt and a tie. He was just what Geddy had expected, except that he was clean shaven and his desk was neat. The man seemed to be working hard at his computer. He was talking with someone on the telephone.

"Excuse me," began Geddy, but the man held up his hand as a signal that he'd be right with him. Geddy sat down and waited for a moment, growing impatient. He took out the gun he picked up in Miami and tossed it on top of the metal desk. The man looked at it then at Geddy. He hung up the phone without saying a word. The gun lay between them.

"You know who I am?" asked Geddy. The man's eyes told him

the answer. "How would you like to make fifty thousand dollars?"

The man didn't know how to respond. He looked at the gun, obviously considering a grab for it. Geddy watched him, waiting to see if the man would go for it. The man looked back at Geddy, who sat calmly. The man looked back at the gun, wiped his sweaty hands on his trousers, and thought some more about the gun. After a moment he sat back in his chair. "I don't want any trouble. I won't tell the police . . ."

"Yes you will," interrupted Geddy. "The gun's not loaded, but I'm giving it to you. Call it a gesture of good faith."

"Not . . . not loaded?"

Geddy reached into the pocket of his Levi's and slapped six bullets onto the desk next to the gun. "Now, why don't you draw the shades and put up the closed sign. This could take a while."

For three hours Geddy and Stan—in no time they were on a first name basis—narrowed down the possible flights Morgan could have taken to get out of the country. Then they had the passenger lists faxed over from a connection Stan had at the Fort Myers airport. Geddy scanned the passenger lists hopefully, but there was no sign of Morgan Gentry's name. He knew it was likely she would use an alias, so he checked the lists again, not quite sure what he was looking for. After thirty minutes of going over the passenger lists, he found it.

"All right, Stan, my man, all I need now is to use your phone."

"Yeah, go ahead, John," said Stan as he casually pushed the gun and the bullets out of the way to make room for the telephone.

Geddy called Nick. "You ready for this?"

"Go ahead pal, I've been waitin' all day."

"She's traveling under the name Nicole Didier. She flew out this morning. Miami to London to Zurich."

"Switzerland," Nick said. "Makes sense. That's where her money is."

"Yeah, and more than that. Her old friend Dick Didier has a house in Zermatt. It's a ski resort in the Alps. She used to talk about it all the time. I'd check Zermatt first, Nick."

"All right, I'm off. What about you? You won't go doing any-thing stupid now, will you?"

"How can I?" said Geddy with a wink to Stan Higgins. "I've been captured."

•   •   •

An hour later, Geddy was led into the Naples Police Depart-ment Headquarters at gunpoint.

"Stanley, don't touch that safety, you understand? And keep the gun in my back, but don't put your finger on the trigger. Most of all, don't get nervous when the cops see us. They're gonna freak, but just be cool."

Stan Higgins nodded his assent, too nervous to realize Geddy couldn't see it. Stan continued to follow Geddy right up to the main desk in the police department lobby. They still had not been noticed. The man behind the desk was doing paperwork. Geddy and Stan Higgins stood there for five, ten seconds, before Geddy gave Stan a backward kick in the shin.

Stan cleared his throat and suddenly came to life. "Uh, excuse me officer." The officer didn't look up. "Um, I've come for the fifty-thousand-dollar reward for this man."

It took a few seconds for it to sink in, but soon the officer jumped off his ass, drew his side arm, and started calling for help. In no time at all, eight uniformed officers surrounded them. From there things moved quickly. Geddy was thrown down on the hard floor with three cops on top of him. Then they whisked him off amidst much shouting and excitement.

Fifteen minutes later, he was sitting handcuffed in a drab interrogation room with two chairs and a table and a long two-way mirror on the wall. There were four detectives standing behind him and he didn't know how many on the other side of the mirror. Charles Warren, the bloated Naples state attorney himself, was seated on the opposite side of the table. Naturally, all they wanted to know was, "Why did you kill Morgan Gentry."

Geddy spoke in a tired, almost bored voice. "Guys, I've had a tough two days, and this whole scheme is probably going to be way over your heads as it is, so do me a favor and shut the hell up."

He began at the beginning, with Morgan switching the Measuring Lives. To get their attention, Geddy told them about the lab test results that confirmed the Measuring Lives on Appendix A of the trust had been switched sometime about 1990. Then he explained how Morgan and Cynthia had conspired together.

In 1990 Morgan became trustee, and they finalized their plan. Morgan switched the Measuring Lives, which meant the trust would vest in 1993, so Cynthia was guaranteed twenty million dollars, which she was to split with Morgan for making the switch. But by making the phony Measuring Lives the New Moon Murder victims, they could make it look like Curtis was the killer. That way, Cynthia could receive the entire forty million, which meant twice as much money for Cynthia and Morgan to split. They had almost no additional risk. If Curtis were found innocent, they would still split Cynthia's twenty million dollars.

They had only one problem to overcome if they were going to get it all. Curtis had to be proved guilty of the murders.

Geddy told the police and the state attorney how Cynthia had insisted that Geddy handle the matter personally. It didn't matter that he was new to civil law or that he knew nothing about trusts. The important thing was he had just won a high-profile multiple-murder trial. He was made to order to handle their circumstantial case against Curtis. Morgan and Cynthia handpicked him to prove Curtis committed the murders.

With the switched Measuring Lives and Cynthia's inability to have committed the murders, Curtis was the most natural suspect. Morgan knew that when the case went to trial she could show she had no reason to tamper with the books because it would appear to be against her interests to terminate the trust. She made up that letter from her father to Curtis to make it look like Curtis had a copy. Curtis would look like the only person other than her father who knew the identities of the Measuring Lives. The letter to Curtis contained her father's signature but only on the second page. There were plenty of letters from Mark Gentry to

Curtis after Victoria Dole died, so Morgan just found a two-page letter dated around the time she wanted her phony letter to be dated, retyped the first page, and made a photocopy, then stapled it to the second page with her father's signature.

When she first began putting the plan into action, shortly after becoming the trustee in 1990, she had been careful to obtain the copy of the trust that the lawyer who drafted it in 1952, Caleb Galvano, had in his files, and she probably destroyed a few others that turned up. But there was one thing she missed. She never knew there was a copy recorded in the public records in Illinois. In Florida it wasn't necessary to record a copy of the trust to a deed to land owned by a trust. It never crossed her mind, but that was her biggest mistake. Apparently, it was her only mistake.

Nevertheless, once the trial was over, Cynthia received the forty million dollars. It was hers free and clear. But rather than settle for her share from Cynthia, Morgan plotted to get all of the money for herself. She could have killed Curtis and Cynthia and then been the next relative in line to inherit, but that would make her the obvious suspect. So she killed Cynthia but framed Curtis. That way Cynthia was out of the picture, and Curtis, charged with her murder, would be disqualified from inheriting from his sister. Morgan, as the next heir, would inherit and she'd never be suspected of Cynthia's murder.

The police were skeptical that Curtis didn't kill Cynthia, since it appeared so clearly that he had. But that was exactly the point, Geddy told them. If Curtis was going to kill Cynthia, he wouldn't tell Philip he was going to the Ritz, have a valet park his car, ask for her room number downstairs, walk right through the lobby and take the elevator, kill Cynthia in her room, and then go out the same way he came in. Then he certainly wouldn't hide the gun in his boat. Not with canals and bays, the Gulf of Mexico, and the Everglades all nearby easy places to get rid of the weapon.

Geddy explained what Morgan had done. At seven o'clock last March, after they had won the Dole trial, Geddy, Morgan, and Faith had finally finished answering questions from the reporters and gone their separate ways. Geddy and Faith both went to the office, then home to wash up, change, and were at the Ritz-Carlton by about eight o'clock, where Cynthia was treating the firm to a victory celebration.

Morgan Gentry was conveniently not invited. At seven o'clock Morgan went straight to Venetian Villas. She arrived there at about seven twenty, which Faith verified with the security guard at the gate. Morgan went directly to her boat, just out of view of the guard station. It was already dark. In addition, the guard could not have heard her because he was in his glass-enclosed, air-conditioned guardhouse. Morgan left Venetian Villas in her boat at seven-twenty, cruised out of Venetian Bay through Doctor's Pass, then was just off the beach at the Ritz by seven forty. She swam to shore carrying a prepacked plastic bag complete with a change of clothes and, most important, a gun inside a small purse.

Morgan changed, went up the fire stairway through the pool-side entrance of the Ritz and up to the eighth floor, where her partner, Cynthia Dole, let her in. That would have been at approximately seven fifty-five.

Once in Cynthia's room, Morgan must have persuaded Cynthia to invite Curtis Dole over to discuss a settlement. Geddy had learned of the invitation by having Philip Percy visit Curtis in prison for the sole purpose of answering some questions Geddy had that only Curtis could answer. Curtis told Philip that Cynthia had called and asked him to come over to discuss a settlement in return for Curtis's agreement not to appeal the decision. The police had already heard this from Curtis after he was arrested. Of course, at the time they didn't believe him, since he looked so clearly guilty. As Curtis had also already explained to the police, he reluctantly agreed and it took him about twenty minutes to get to the Ritz, meaning he arrived at her room at about eight twenty. When he knocked on her door, there was no answer. Cynthia was already dead, and Morgan was gone.

Morgan had waited until ten past or maybe a quarter past eight, took a gun equipped with a silencer out of her purse, and

fired two shots into Cynthia's head. She rushed down the fire
stairway, stripped down to her suit, and swam back to her boat,
then drove all the way down to Naples Bay. Now, here is why the
boat was so important. Curtis had two Dobermans that patrolled
the grounds, making the sailboat the only place someone could
safely plant the gun on his property. Morgan had cruised by his
boat and stopped just long enough to dump the gun into the first
storage compartment she could find. Then she drove back to her
villa, where she arrived at approximately nine thirty in the evening,
plenty of time to be home by ten o'clock, when Geddy had called
her from the police station.

How did Geddy explain Curtis's supposed "attack" on him on
the dock at the villa? Curtis was on the run. He knew he didn't kill
the Measuring Lives and he didn't kill Cynthia, so someone had to
have set him up. Curtis didn't realize that Morgan was getting the
money from the trust, so he didn't suspect her. He probably
thought Geddy and Cynthia were up to something, especially
since it was Geddy who found Cynthia's body. Curtis must have
thought the plan went bad, and Geddy killed Cynthia then somehow framed him. So Curtis confronted Geddy hoping to find out
what was going on. Curtis was no killer. He didn't even load his gun.
He just wanted to scare Geddy into admitting what he thought
Geddy had done.

The police were speechless. It was all certainly possible, but
they still had an unanswered question, the most important question as far as Geddy was concerned: Why did Geddy kill Morgan?

Geddy explained that Morgan was not dead. Once the probate had been completed, Morgan had dumped him. She no longer
had any use for him. But before she got rid of him, she had him
consolidate all of her inheritance into a single, numbered, Swiss
bank account. She knew that something could still go wrong, so
this was a safeguard. If any part of her plan was discovered, she
had the money safely out of the country. In addition, she had the
Swiss passport of her lover's dead wife. She could leave the country easily under the name of Nicole Didier.

Geddy told the police how he had discovered the switched Measuring Lives and confronted Morgan at the house in Port Royal during her party. They argued out by the dock, then Geddy threw her into the bay, ripping part of her shirt in the process. Dick Didier saw Geddy go, then rushed out to the dock where he found Morgan. They decided this was the best time for Morgan to disappear. They smeared some of Morgan's blood on her shirt, she swam across the canal and found a spot to wait until Dick Didier was finished with the police. They met at a prearranged place, Dick drove her to Miami, and the next morning she flew from Miami to London to Zurich under the name of Nicole Didier. The police could easily verify it.

The state attorney was impressed, but he pointed out that there was no proof that Dick Didier was involved, and no proof that Morgan Gentry was the Nicole Didier who took that flight out of Miami. Geddy told them to be patient. He was working on that.

• • •

It was his second day in jail, and he was finally allowed a visitor. Faith rushed into his cell. They held each other for a long time without speaking. When she finally pulled away, he could only smile as she scolded him for being caught by a travel agent. The police, she said, were verifying everything he had told them, and the state attorney was making preparations to petition for Curtis's release from prison. The problem was, the police still thought Geddy killed Morgan. Nick had contacted Faith the day before. He couldn't find Morgan. Faith told Geddy she was going to fly to Switzerland to find Morgan herself, but he told her to be patient.

A uniformed officer opened the door to his cell and the substantial figure of Charles Warren appeared on the threshold. "This just came in from authorities in Zermatt, Switzerland," began Charles Warren, who was clearly blown away, as he handed Geddy a fax. "They believe they have the body of Morgan Gentry."

"Body!" repeated Faith.

"You were right, she was traveling under the name of Nicole Didier, wife of Dick Didier, a noted surgeon. Morgan Gentry's neck was slit wide open. The police found the murder weapon in the woods behind the house. It was a scalpel. Dr. Didier killed her. She was discovered in his bed."

Faith could hardly speak. "Why would he kill her?"

"They think that since she was masquerading as his wife, he killed her in order to get at the forty million dollars," the state attorney explained. "She had deposited the money in several Swiss accounts under the name of Nicole Didier. He thought he could inherit it, I guess, but about an hour ago your friend Nick Farley identified her to the Swiss police as Morgan. They've got Didier, he's in custody."

Faith was expressing her disbelief. Geddy didn't say a word.

Charles Warren continued. "They want us to notify the next-of-kin of Morgan Gentry's death. They recommend that her next of kin hire a Swiss lawyer to begin making arrangements for an inheritance of nearly forty million dollars."

"That's Curtis!" exclaimed Faith. "Curtis Dole is Morgan's next of kin!"

"I hate to say it, but this is actually the best thing that could have happened for you and Curtis," said Charles Warren. "It proves you didn't kill her, and it makes it simple for Curtis to get the money that's rightfully his."

"Then it's over," said Faith to Charles Warren. "You have to let John go."

Charles Warren grunted in agreement and watched her smiling up at him, proud of herself. He walked directly in front of Geddy, not hiding his dislike of him. They were standing nose to nose. "Yeah, he can go. But first I want to hear him say it."

"Say what?" demanded Faith.

"Over a year and a half ago, this cocky bastard marched into my office and told me he had the key to finding the New Moon Slasher. After I looked into it and told him he was out of his mind, he called me a coward, said I was a worthless public servant who didn't have the guts to do his job. Well, hotshot, I want to hear you say it. You were wrong. You don't have a clue who the New Moon

Slasher is."

Geddy kept his eyes locked on Charles Warren's but resisted the temptation to tell him he was wrong.

Geddy awoke as the old electric train rambled into the station. He looked out the window and watched as uniformed Swiss train workers loaded automobiles onto the last car of the train traveling in the opposite direction. That meant this couldn't be Zermatt, because cars were not permitted in the mountain resort. He looked about until he found a small wooden sign, white with plain black letters that read *Täsch*. He started to pull himself together after his long journey then checked his train schedule. Zermatt would be the next and final stop on this line. He felt the left inside pocket of his brown leather jacket to make sure the gun was still there, to reassure himself. Then he checked the right inside pocket, where he kept a Swiss army knife he had bought at the airport in Zurich.

After five minutes, the ancient train continued its slow climb through the Swiss Alps. The green rolling hills turned to severe sloping mountains, with gray rocks from past avalanches scattered alongside the tracks. He stood finally, having had enough of the hard wooden seat, walked out the door and stood between two coaches on the loud and windy metal landing. It was cool in the Alps, even in the summer, and he expected it to get much colder once the sun fell behind the mountains. He shoved his hands into his Levi's and watched the countryside roll by, trying to take his mind off the last few days. But his troubled mind's reprieve was short. When the train pulled into Zermatt station, Nick was there to greet him.

After a typically off-color joke and a hasty welcome, Nick demanded to know why Geddy had told him to wait for him in Zermatt.

"We're going to catch a killer," replied Geddy.

"A killer?" Nick repeated. "They've already got Didier in custody. They charged him for Morgan's murder."

"I'm talking about the New Moon Slasher."

"The *what*!"

Geddy threw his duffel bag over his shoulder and grabbed Nick by the arm to lead him away from the crowded platform, through the wide open station onto the street. It was raining lightly, so they ran across the street to the lee of a hotel, where Geddy explained.

"The police know Didier killed Morgan. What they don't know is that he's the New Moon Slasher. I think he might even be the Super-Killer Dr. Holmes was talking about during the trial."

"You're crazy."

"We'll see. You and I are going to have a little talk with the eminent surgeon tomorrow morning. Right now, I'm starved, and I have to call Faith. This is me," said Geddy, meaning the Hotel Gornergrat, which was directly across the street from the train station. "Grab a beer. I'll check in and call Faith. Then I'll buy you dinner and explain."

• • •

Two hours later Nick and Geddy were seated next to an enormous window in a restaurant a third of the way up the mountain, looking out over the white-peaked majesty of the Matterhorn while it faded from view as twilight turned to darkness. It was a Friday night so the restaurant was crowded with tourists, mountain climbers, and those avid Alpiners who came to ski the glacier in the shadow of the Matterhorn. Geddy had already told Nick his theory about Dick Didier being the Super-Killer.

"Your little Dr. Jekyll and Mr. Hyde theory won't hold up," Nick told him. "Didier's not crazy. He saw an opportunity to get his hands on Morgan's forty mil, so he went for it. He was no serial killer. He even used a scalpel to kill Morgan. He was no expert on murder. How stupid could he be? He was a doctor, for chrissakes. The Super-Killer is probably the most clever, efficient killer there's ever been. With all this modern law-enforcement technology, they still haven't caught up to him, even after all these years. He wouldn't use a weapon that would point to him so clearly. He would never make such a big mistake."

"I think he did make a big mistake. He never should have killed Morgan. He got too cute." Nick didn't reply. "Look, Nick, you're gonna have to bear with me. First things first. We need to figure out how he committed those New Moon Murders. I thought I pretty much figured out how they were done by Curtis, but obviously I was wrong. Let me hear your theory of how a serial killer would have carried them out."

They had had disagreements along the way, but Geddy had never really cared much about Nick's theories on the murders. He had wanted Nick to help him prove Curtis guilty, not be told he was wrong. But now he was finally asking Nick what he thought. Nick Farley cleared his throat and cracked his knuckles, for dramatic effect.

"Anybody who's gonna to commit a murder knows to get rid of fingerprints," Nick began. "You learn that by the time you're in grade school. The slasher was smart. He either wore gloves or wiped his fingerprints off the knives with his shirt. Curtis's riding gloves are one possible explanation, but there are a dozen others."

"What about the motorcycle headlight?"

"You mean what Mrs. Keenan saw behind the real estate office? Well, a motorcycle headlight is one possible explanation, but it's much more likely that it was a flashlight."

"If the killer wasn't wearing gloves during the first murder, how come he didn't leave fingerprints on the heroin needle? Remember, he couldn't have wiped them off, because the victim's prints were still there."

"I don't think the killer did heroin with the first victim. All Gabby Smith said when she left the bar that first night was that she made a score. She didn't say she was goin' with anybody to the beach to shoot the heroin, although that's what you made everyone think. I think she got the heroin, but then, like the selfish heroin junkie she was, she went off by herself to the beach to shoot up. That's when the killer found her, all alone. He initiated a conversation, she asked for his belt, and the rest is history. That explains why her fingerprints were on the needle but not the killer's. Since the killer wasn't shooting heroin with her, he never even touched the needle."

Now Geddy sat up a little with a look of excitement in his eyes. Nick anticipated what Geddy's next questions would be so he resumed his argument. "All right, so Curtis wore a thirty-two inch belt. So what? It's probably the most common waist size for a twenty-year-old, and the killer was probably close to the same age as the girls because Julieanne Cherube went off with him down the beach as if he was boyfriend material. I used to be that waist size, and I bet you were, too, along with half of the other twenty-year-olds in Naples back then. Same thing with the size ten-and-a-half shoes, a very common size. So again, it doesn't really narrow the search.

"Even the fact that the last girl, Debbie Moore, wouldn't ride a motorcycle doesn't really mean anything. We don't know that the killer rode a motorcycle. Maybe the killer knew her and was stalking her or peepin' in her window when she snuck out that night. Then he just walked up to the end of her driveway and pounced on her. We also don't know for sure that the guy she had a date with killed her. When her date arrived, he just left, thinkin' that she was standing him up. Her body couldn't be seen at night in the bushes. Again, your explanation about her being afraid to get on the motorcycle was only one possible explanation, and it's not the most likely."

"I suppose when Sally Baumgartner's date arrived he couldn't see her either, even though her body lay right in the middle of that dirt parking lot behind the restaurant."

"I'll stand by what I said in my stories. Do you remember?" Geddy didn't answer. "I concluded that Sally was waitin' for her date when the killer showed up and opened her car door. By now he was stalking his victims and was probably wearin' gloves, so he opened the door with a gloved hand, which smudged her finger-prints on the door handle. Then he pulled her out and tried to force her into the back seat where he was gonna kill her, but she fought, and while they struggled she dropped her purse back there. It's stupid to think she left her purse in the back seat during the drive to the restaurant. She would have left it in the passen-ger seat with her library books, not on the floor in the back seat. The killer tried but he couldn't get her in the back seat, so he threw her against the side of the car, pulled her head back by her hair and was gonna slit her throat right then and there, but she pushed off with her foot and they fell on the ground. They strug-gled and the killer stabbed her a dozen times before slittin' her throat. Then he left."

"Very clever, Nick, but you didn't answer my question. How could her date not see her body?"

"Remember the anonymous telephone call the cops received informing them there was a body in that lot? That was the date. He pulled up, saw Sally bleedin' all over the place and took off like a bat out of hell and called the cops to tell them. He didn't leave his name because he was scared to death."

Geddy thought for a long moment. "What about Julianne Cherube? Was she actually making out with this serial killer on the beach before she was killed?"

"No. I think the killer slit her throat first and then kissed her."

"That's sick, Nick!"

Nick laughed at himself. "I'm a sick guy."

Geddy shook his head. "All right, that's enough for now—it's all I can take, actually. Let's get out of here. We'll try to talk to some cops tonight before we see Didier in the morning. Just let me give Faith a call. I'll be right back." Geddy's leather jacket with the gun stashed inside hung on the back of his chair. He considered taking it with him to make the call, but thought it was safe enough to leave it.

"What's up with you and Faith?" Nick asked with a devilish smile before Geddy walked off.

"Yeah, it's what you think, Nick. Me and Faith. I guess you were right about her all along. I think she's great."

"If there's one thing I know, it's people," Nick congratulated himself. "So, you think you'll be able to work alongside your girlfriend?"

"We won't be working with each other. We're leaving Naples. We've had enough. I guess you were right about that place, too."

"Yup, I warned you about Naples over a year ago, but you didn't listen. Where are you two going to go?"

"I don't know. We haven't had time to talk about it. All we know is we want out of Naples. I'd like to go back to New York, but I think she'd like to move home to Knoxville. Maybe we'll settle for someplace in between."

Nick smiled. "I guess that would put you somewhere in the mountains of West Virginia."

"I was thinking someplace more like Washington, D.C. I used to work under Attorney General Reno a few years ago when she was the state attorney in Miami. She liked me, so maybe I'll see about getting a position with the Justice Department. If all goes well and I can explain away my handling of the whole Dole mess, I'll be prosecuting again. And once I'm a U. S. attorney, I'll have the power to find out exactly what's going on in the Miami state attorney's office."

Nick nodded. "Well, you always did make a federal case out of everything."

• • •

Geddy and Nick stepped into the six-person gondola, a small enclosed ski lift used in the winter to haul skiers up the mountain, for the return trip to town. They sat facing each other, Nick looking back up at the mountainside lodge and Geddy gazing down at the twinkling lights of the village below. It was raining hard now, and wind whistled outside the window. The sounds of the raindrops pelting their bubblelike capsule echoed in the silent darkness between them.

Finally, Nick broke the silence. "You know, John, I've been thinking," he said after they had begun their descent. "Dick Didier did you a favor. Maybe you should just let him be. You owe him one."

"How do you figure?"

"His murder of Morgan was the best thing that could happen. Really tidied everything up. It proved that you didn't kill her, and it made it easy for Curtis to get the money that's rightfully his. I mean, I know you're pissed at him because he was doin' your girl. . . ."

"Maybe."

"Come on, don't be naive, John-Boy. Didier must have known what Morgan was up to, don't you think? Didier must have been the one to get Nicole Didier's passport for her. Then when she came here, she was stayin' with him, and people who knew them in Zermatt say he was even calling her Nicole. So you gotta admit that Dick knew what Morgan was up to. I'll bet that he was seein' Morgan on the sly even while you were dating her."

Geddy stared at Nick impassively.

"But then again, maybe you should go after him," Nick said on second thought. "He deserves it all right. It's funny though. I came here to prove that Morgan's alive, but by the time I get here, she's dead. There are some pretty sick people in this world."

Geddy nodded his head thoughtfully. "You ought to know."

Nick didn't look up. "Yeah, I oughta know. I've seen the worst of 'em. From the New Moon Murders to the South Beach Murders to Morgan's murder. There's lots of sick serial killers out there, lots of sick people."

"You ought to know," repeated Geddy.

"Yeah, I oughta know." Nick craned his neck to get a better look at the view.

"It's really funny, Nick, that wherever you go lots of people start getting their throats slashed or their heads chopped off."

"Hey, I know it. That's what they pay me for. Go where the killers are. Write about the latest serial murderer. Get pictures if I can."

Geddy waited until Nick looked at him before speaking. "No, I mean you get somewhere first, *then* people start dying."

"I don't think I follow," Nick said casually.

"Take the New Moon Murders for example," said Geddy. "You go to work for the *Naples Daily News* in January of 1972, and eight months later, five girls are dead. By November, you moved to San Antonio. Three months later, seven girls there are dead."

"No shit," Nick said good-naturedly. "Hey, that's how I got into this line of work."

"You were brought up in a foster home, but you never stayed in one place too long. By the time you were seventeen, you'd been arrested three times, each time for cruelty to animals. One time you snapped their necks and then dismembered them. Another time you were caught throwing kittens off of a bridge. By eighteen you were on your own, an alcoholic, living out of your car. You had no college education and had a crappy job as a gofer at the *Norman Examiner*. You never would have become a reporter, except that, not coincidentally, a serial killer went on a rampage killing college girls, and you were the only person at the newspaper who could dig up any information, including obtaining the most secret details from the police. Just like with the New Moon Murders, you were the only person who seemed to know the details."

Nick laughed but not sincerely. "This is one of your best theories yet, John. I'm a serial killer." He shook his head in disbelief. "Why would I kill these girls and then start writing about them?"

Geddy didn't hesitate. "They were your trophies, Nick. I don't even know if you realize it, but that's what it's all been about.

You hardly make enough money to survive by freelancing. You live out of a fucking van, for God's sake. You don't write for the money or the love of writing, you write to exalt yourself. Experts think that the Super-Killer took no trophies, but you did. You glorified your murders by writing the most explicit, shocking stories about them and had them printed throughout the country for all to see."

Nick was very calm in his defense. "John, I simply made my living writing about serial murders . . ."

"You've been *committing* serial murders!"

Nick didn't even blink. "Just like Curtis was the New Moon Slasher, huh? Then you say it's Dick Didier. You thought Hoffer killed those whores in Miami. Now all of a sudden I'm responsible for all of it. Make up your mind, will you."

"I was wrong about Curtis, but that's because Morgan set us all up," said Geddy. "I was wrong about Hoffer because the police manufactured the case. Of course I know Dick Didier didn't kill Morgan. I just said that to get you up here. Of course he didn't kill anyone. I only asked you how you *thought* they were committed because I wanted to know how *you* did it! *You* killed those five girls in Naples, and *you* killed Morgan!"

"Bullshit!

"Once I discovered for sure that Hoffer was innocent, I realized you might be responsible for killing those seven prostitutes, too. I had Faith look into it, and she discovered that you got a parking ticket in Miami three days before the first victim was killed. You didn't show up in Miami to cover those murders, you were there days before the first girl had her throat slashed!"

"You're the one who proved Hoffer killed them."

"I was wrong. Hoffer was set up, and so was I. You've been traveling the country for years taking victims along the way, and every now and then you watched innocent men go to jail for murders you committed! You were everywhere the Super-Killer was. Colorado, Alabama, Miami, Texas, New Mexico, Oklahoma—and you were always there *before* the victims starting popping up! I know it's you, Nick, so don't tell me otherwise!"

Nick did not reply. The shouting stopped but the tension remained. Both men were staring at each other. Suddenly, Geddy reached inside his leather jacket and pulled his gun. "How many have you killed, Nick? A hundred? More?"

Nick shrugged casually. "I lost track a long time ago."

"Why did you come after me that night after my softball game?"

Nick calmly explained. "You told me on the phone that you knew who the New Moon Slasher was, but you wouldn't tell me who. I was afraid maybe you really did know, and you were just waitin' for me to show up so you could catch me and be a hero. You got away from me, so I called you later in the night and got you to tell me what you thought was goin' on. I told you I was in Alabama, but I lied. I had been in Naples, stalking you all day. After you told me all about the trust connection, I realized you didn't know it was me, so I thought I'd hang around for a while, watch you hang Curtis."

There was a long silence before Geddy's next question. "Why do you do it, Nick?"

"Didn't you hear Dr. Holmes, the 'serial-killer expert,' and all of the reasons he gave?" Nick said derisively. He laughed. "Serial-killer expert, my ass. They have no idea why serial killers kill. Sure, some are abused and neglected and generally fucked over by society. But look at you. Your childhood sucked, and you're honest to a fault. I don't know why I kill. But I'm not dumb. Don't ever think that I'm an idiot, because to kill as many people as I have and get away with it, you can't be some raving psycho. I just . . . feel it. When you sent me over here to find Morgan, I had an idea to kill her. I even picked up a scalpel to make it look like Didier might have done it. But I hadn't made up my mind yet. It was a lot riskier than killin' a stranger. But when I saw what a fuckin' slut she was, carrying on in Zermatt and sleepin' with that scumbag doctor—I just *wanted* to do it. So I did it. It was an impulse. Call me impetuous. There doesn't have to be a reason. And I'll tell you somethin', I don't feel bad about it afterwards. I feel the need and

I like it, so I do it and I don't feel guilty, and then I write about it. While I'm coverin' the murders, I find out everything the cops know, and when they get close, I move on. I'm not an imbecile."

Geddy thought that was true, to a certain extent.

Nick stared out the window. "You know I'm gonna have to kill you now, don't you?"

"I'm going to kill you," replied Geddy matter of factly.

Nick laughed at him. "No, no, you mean take me in, don't you? You know I'm a killer. I'll be sent away for life or they'll execute me. You can't kill me. That's murder."

"I don't care."

"You won't do it, John. You don't believe in killing. You believe in good triumphing over evil and in a fair trial."

"I've become more realistic." Geddy said it in a clear, strong voice.

"Are you worried that I'll get off?"

"You might. All I have is circumstantial evidence. It's no sure thing, and I can't let a fucking psycho like you get away."

Nick ignored the insult. He just shook his head. "You're not going to kill me."

Geddy cocked the gun. "For once, Nick, you're wrong."

"No, John." Nick reached into a pocket and pulled something out, something hidden in his fist. "Once again, *you're* wrong." He opened his hand and slowly let six bullets roll off his hand. One by one the sound of the bullets hitting the metal floor echoed in Geddy's ears.

"Two calls to Faith in two hours?" Nick said. "You never kissed Morgan's ass. There's no way Faith could have had you under her thumb so fast. You were callin' her about me, confirmin' that you had enough evidence on me so that after you killed me, you could tell the cops I tried to kill you first, that I'm a psycho. While you were flyin' over here to make sure I don't get away, Faith was the one checkin' into my past, finding out more about the Super-Killer's movements. She was provin' what you had already figured out: that I'm the killer."

Geddy cursed himself for his mistake. He'd left his jacket at the table when he called Faith from the restaurant because he didn't want Nick to get suspicious. He didn't think Nick would go through his pockets. The gun was too heavy for Nick to take without being missed, so Nick took the bullets instead. A sickening feeling came over Geddy until he remembered the Swiss army knife. He reached into his pocket and searched frantically for it. It was gone. When he looked up, Nick was holding the knife in his right hand.

"You're so fuckin' stupid, John. Even when you finally figure it all out, I'm still way ahead of you. I've been playin' games with you since we met. Do you know how easy it is to string you along? You were so fuckin' high on yourself, you never wanted to listen to me before, but how many times did I tell you that you were wrong about Hoffer and wrong about Curtis? All you did was laugh at me. You've been laughin' at me since we met. I'll tell you who's the real hotshot here, John. It's me. I've been three and a half steps ahead of you the whole time."

Geddy looked longingly at the bullets as they rolled about on the floor. He had no time to pick one up, load the gun, and shoot Nick. Nick was right. He had been toying with Geddy the whole time, and now Geddy found himself stranded at knifepoint forty feet in the air in an enclosed cabin with a psychotic.

"You're going to have to kill me, Nick," he said as his mind worked. He had thought his way out of jams before; he just had to keep Nick talking long enough to think of a way out of this mess.

But Nick didn't give him that chance. He lunged at Geddy's chest with the knife, and Geddy barely reacted in time to snake away from the stab attempt as it sliced through his shirt and took a small chunk out of his left side. The knife tangled in Geddy's shirt, allowing him to catch Nick off balance. He pushed Nick against the door of the gondola as hard as he could, causing the door to buckle. Nick was up in an instant, still holding the knife. He was transformed, his red, twisted face exhibiting all the rage that he carried within his depraved heart. Slashing the knife deftly about, he came at Geddy again. The space was small, and Geddy had nowhere to go. He was cornered. Nick had to be good with a knife. Geddy couldn't expect to hold him off. He had only one chance.

He hurled himself at Nick and tackled him around the waist, exposing his back to the knife. The force of the tackle drove Nick backwards towards the door. Geddy was betting on their bursting through it and plunging to the rocky slopes below before the knife-point was sticking out of his chest. It would only take Geddy a second. Nick had to hold off delivering the fatal blow for just one second. Geddy expected to feel the burn of pain in his back, but it didn't come, and when he drove Nick's back into the door, it ripped open with a crash. The pouring rain and the rushing wind roared in his ears as he fell to the floor of the gondola, his upper body hanging out over the dark slope below. He couldn't see Nick. He must have fallen.

Suddenly Geddy felt a crushing blow on the back of his head which almost sent him over the edge. Nick had grabbed hold of the top of the door and swung out to the side of the gondola. He kicked Geddy again, causing him to fall forward even further. Nick was still hanging outside the gondola, but he was able to deliver yet another kick, this time to Geddy's back. Geddy started to slip away. Soon he knew he would be falling like the rain onto the mountainside.

Just as he was about to go over the edge, Geddy reached to the side and grabbed the metal ski rack welded to the exterior of the gondola. His legs slid out, and he was hanging by one hand as the gondola continued its uninterrupted journey down the mountain. He looked down but could see nothing. He might survive the fall if he went feet first, but he couldn't let Nick get away. He had to hold on.

By the time Geddy looked up, Nick was safely back inside the gondola. Nick inched to the edge and tried to smash Geddy's fingers with his work boots. Nick missed three times, but then moved out a little further and grabbed hold of the door with his hand.

Geddy was soaked now from the driving rain. His legs swung out behind him from the force of the wind. Nick readied himself for the decisive kick, and this time his heavy boot found its mark, slamming down onto Geddy's hand. Geddy screamed in pain but managed to hang on by a few fingers as Nick readied for another kick. Geddy reached up with his free hand, and just as Nick's foot came crashing down again, he grabbed hold of Nick's leg and let go of the ski rack.

Geddy's hands slid down to Nick's ankle, but he held on and soon all of his weight was on Nick. He reached once again and snatched Nick's other ankle, then curled his knees to his chest and swung his legs up like a gymnast until his feet were planted against the edge of the gondola. He looked like he was playing leap-frog upside down. Then with all his might he pushed off with his legs and, still holding on to Nick's ankles, he yanked Nick's feet out from under him. Geddy felt them both falling.

It was a brief fall, since Nick managed to grab hold of the ski rack with both hands as Geddy held onto his ankles. Now they both dangled perilously from the side of the moving gondola.

Nick tried to shake Geddy off but couldn't. Geddy could feel Nick's baggy pants giving way a little, slowly beginning to slide off. Geddy reached with his right arm, pulling himself as high as he could and dug his right hand into Nick's back pocket. The pants were still sliding. Geddy held the pocket securely and with his left he grabbed hold of the other back pocket. Nick was struggling to hang on. Geddy felt the pockets giving way, he felt them ripping, he felt the pants sliding off Nick. The pockets were about to tear completely away when at the last instant Geddy grasped hold of Nick's belt. The pants were still sliding off Nick's hips.

The gondola continued its steady descent, the rain-streaked wind whipping past them as Geddy continued his climb. He had his legs wrapped around Nick's legs now and climbed Nick like a child climbs a rope in gym class. Soon he had both hands on Nick's shoulders with his legs wrapped around Nick's waist. With one last pull, he had his left arm up and around Nick's throat.

When he had Nick in a secure choke hold, he stopped climbing. He could have made it back inside the gondola, perhaps, but the thought never crossed his mind. He clasped his arms around Nick's neck as hard as he could and let his legs hang down, allowing all of his weight to fall onto Nick's neck.

At first Nick made gurgling sounds as Geddy squeezed with every ounce of energy he had left. He knew once Nick was dead, they would both fall. The fall might or might not kill him, but Geddy was resolved. To let Nick Farley escape would be to allow him to continue his twenty-year rampage. If all of the murders attributed to the Super-Killer were committed by him, that would make Nick the most prolific serial killer of all time. Geddy could not let him get away. He had to be killed.

No sounds came from Nick; Geddy was holding too tightly onto Nick's windpipe. Geddy groaned with the effort, trying to break his neck if he could. Their heads were side by side, no more than an inch apart. From this close, Geddy could see the veins in Nick's head bulging and his mouth wide open, gasping for breath. Just a little bit longer, and Nick would be dead.

Suddenly they dropped into the darkness below. Geddy instinctively let go of Nick and tried to ready himself for the impact. Geddy cursed aloud as he realized that Nick must have let go intentionally, because Nick was definitely still alive. Geddy could hear him screaming on the way down.

• • •

Geddy's feet hit the muddy slope and slipped out from under him. The rest of his body landed with a thud, but his legs had taken most of the impact. He felt his bad ankle turn a little. There was some pain, the wind had been knocked out of him, and he was sliding down the steep slope, but he was conscious. He knew he had survived.

He was on his back hurtling down the steep mountainside, at first with his legs in front, until he came over a rise, went airborne, and landed head first. He rocketed downward with his hands held over his head, gaining speed as the mudslide seemed to gain force.

He felt he was taking half the mountain with him. He tried to dig his toes into the earth and then his elbows and finally his fingers, but he couldn't slow down. The trail must have curved away because Geddy suddenly flew off the side of the slope and was flying through branches. He landed in a thicket and rolled on his side for several rotations before coming to a stop. A generous amount of mud had followed him into the forest and now poured over him. For a frantic moment, he couldn't breathe and had to dig furiously until he could push his head up through the mud.

He pulled himself out of the mire and held his face up to the rain to wipe the mud from his eyes. When he could see again, he collapsed onto his back, his chest heaving and his ankle throbbing, the jolt from the fall still radiating through his body.

It was quiet in this wooded patch near the bottom of the mountain. He strained to determine where the village should be. Through the trees he could see a few lights from the chalets and hotels closest to the mountain. He let his head fall back onto the mud, and he began to breathe more easily. He listened. He heard nothing but the rain, sounding like static as it beat against the leaves of the trees.

It was over. He did it. Nick didn't make it. Nick must be dead. He cautioned himself and listened some more, but other than the steady patter of the rain, not a sound was made in the forest. He laughed. He laughed until it hurt his ribs, which he couldn't remember injuring. He held his ribs and laughed hysterically until he heard the crashing sounds of Nick desperately racing through the thick woods.

Geddy didn't give chase right away. Nick must have been forty yards to his right and below him now, hurrying towards the village. He was obviously not trying to be quiet. He must have thought Geddy was dead. He'd have an advantage in the dark. Geddy fingered the scar on his cheek unconsciously, then slowly pulled himself into a sitting position.

He wanted to give up, to let Nick go. He'd had enough. He tried his best, and that's all anyone could ask. He knew this was the last chance anyone might have to catch Nick for a long, long time, but Geddy had already gone above and beyond what anyone could ask. He just couldn't do any more.

Well, the least he could do was get to the police, help them search the town. But he swore that if Nick got away, he was out of it. He and Faith were starting over and someone else could catch Nick.

But if he got away now, how many more victims would he take before he was caught?

Geddy pushed himself to his feet, covered in mud from his hiking boots to his normally golden hair. Only his eyes could be seen from his blackened figure in the dark forest. He started to run but pain shot up his ankle and he fell. He stood up almost immediately and walked gingerly on it, pushing invisible branches out of his way, never knowing where to step because it was too dark to see, the full moon obscured by clouds and the density of the branches overhead. Eventually the ankle loosened up enough for him to run, with a limp. He fell several more times on the steep terrain, ran into trees, and nearly had his eye taken out by a branch, but in ten minutes he came out of the woods into a shallow creek which ran alongside a slope-side hotel. He let himself fall into the clean mountain water and could feel the weight of the mud washing away. The water was cold. He dragged himself out of the creek and sat for a moment at the water's edge to listen. He couldn't hear Nick. With the head start Nick had on him, he'd be in town by now.

A half hour later the police were combing the narrow, winding streets of Zermatt on foot, in little electric carts, and on motorcycle. Geddy was on the back of a motorcycle as a young patrolman zipped through the streets in the rain, beeping a shrill horn to get pedestrians out of the way while Geddy searched their faces. There are no sidewalks in Zermatt and no cars, so the people usually walk carelessly about in the middle of the street. Geddy looked up and noticed a police officer perched on the roof of an A-frame chalet. Another hurried out of a side street and immediately dashed into an alley behind a watch shop. The entire ten-man force had been mobilized.

Outside Geddy's hotel was the chief of police and several officers. Geddy directed the young police officer to pull up next to them. *"There is nothing?"* asked Geddy in French as he got off the motorcycle. Geddy was a mess. Even his plunge into the creek and his time in the rain could not remove all the mud.

The chief, a stout gentleman with a black mustache and a

meticulous uniform, shook his head and replied in French, their common language. *"Your man is nowhere to be found, Monsieur. We have been discussing the idea that he climbed the gondola tower and jumped aboard a gondola and is trying to make it over the mountain to Italy. Do you think it is possible?"*

Geddy struggled with the French, but he basically understood. *"No. He came down. Of that I am certain."*

The chief frowned. *"If he is in the town he must be hiding indoors. We will have to conduct a room-by-room search. Are you sure you are not mistaken?"*

"As I have said, I am certain."

The chief immediately began barking orders in German, which Geddy didn't understand. The officers went off in different directions, presumably to begin searching the innumerable hotel rooms, chalets, taverns, restaurants, and shops. When they were gone the chief turned back to Geddy. *"Wait in your room, Monsieur. If we find him, we must know where to find you to identify him."* He patted Geddy on the shoulder, smiled and said in broken English, "Not to worries. If he is among the town, he is found."

Geddy watched the chief go. He felt a little better now and didn't want to wait in his room. He wanted to help find Nick. He gazed once more up and down the streets. He thought about checking the train station, but he knew the last train left the station a half-hour ago and was searched by the police before it departed. Nick was not on board. The chief was right, he had to wait in his room. They needed him to identify Nick if he was found.

Geddy was walking up the stairs to his hotel when something made him stop. He heard a faint sound on the wind. He turned his ear to the north and listened. He couldn't hear it anymore. Suddenly he noticed a woman standing behind him, waiting to get past him and into the hotel. "Sorry," he said to her in English, stepping out of her way.

"It is the train," she said to him, showing her crooked teeth.

"It is in Täsch. It is leaving."

He looked at her with a puzzled expression. "The train left here twenty minutes ago. Täsch isn't that far."

She was surprised at his urgent tone of voice. "No, sir, it is not far. Only three miles, but they must load the automobiles onto the railroad cars. It takes time."

Geddy was off like a shot. The police searched the train in Zermatt, but they didn't consider that Nick could have made it to Täsch and gotten on the train there. Once safely away on the train and out of the mountains, there was no telling where Nick would get off.

Down the stairs of the hotel and around the corner was the police motorcycle. He kick-started it and a second later was screaming across the street, into the deserted train station, gathering speed. He didn't know the way to Täsch by road, so he would have to follow the tracks. As he approached the end of the platform, he pulled up on the handlebars and flew off the edge, the wheels shrieking as they spun in the air. He landed squarely between the two sets of tracks, but the motorcycle almost slid away from him on the loose gravel until he regained control. Geddy gunned the throttle, hit the headlight, and was racing alongside the railway like he used to do in the Bronx on his friend's dirt bike, squinting through the rain which slapped against his face. The sides of the tracks were strewn with the rocks which occasionally rolled down from the mountains. A few times when he drove over one, he almost lost control, but he managed to remain upright and charged ahead.

In five minutes, he passed the well-lit station at Täsch where a few station workers watched in utter befuddlement as they saw what looked like a crazy American in a brown leather jacket, blue jeans, and hiking boots racing by like a daredevil, crouched low over the handlebars with a determined look on his face. He was past the station and in the distance could see a light that must be the rear of the train. Everything else was black. After Täsch there were no towns for a considerable distance, just mountains and valleys and farmland and pastures. He was racing to close the distance between himself and the train.

Finally he had the last car in sight, a flatbed coach hauling automobiles out of the mountains. He was alongside the auto coach, but raced onward. He was passing the first passenger coach, when he looked up and saw Nick, standing and staring with his face against the window, shocked to see Geddy not only alive, but hot on his heels. Geddy gunned the engine and was soon alongside the front of Nick's coach. He stretched his left hand toward the train, but it was just out of reach. He took his time. Nick couldn't get to the cars ahead of him without passing right by Geddy. Geddy knew that if he could just get on the train, he would have Nick trapped in the last passenger coach.

He tried again, this time noticing a handle on the side of the train to help passengers get on and off. He reached but could not quite touch it. He couldn't get closer without driving over the ends of the railroad ties as they protruded from the rails. He would have only one shot at it.

Geddy drove as close as he dared, then let himself and the bike lean drastically to the left. Soon it was falling toward the train. If he missed the handle, he would fall onto the tracks. His left shoulder was heading toward the ground and the bike started to slip out and away from under him, but at the last possible moment, he let go of the handlebars, reached out with his left arm, and grasped the handle just as the motorcycle bounced away behind him. He made a stab for the handle with his right hand, too, and found it, but he was still dangling with his feet just off the ground. His body twisted in the rushing wind. He desperately sought a foothold. Finally he was able to get a foot onto one of the steps. He swung the rest of his contorted body around and collapsed in a heap on the short metal walkway between the two coaches.

He had no time to admire his stunt. He was up in an instant, bursting through the door into Nick's coach. The passengers looked up with a start. Nobody spoke. Other than the sound of the train rattling along on its steel wheels, it was completely silent.

Not one person moved. To Geddy, every person in the coach looked as if they were hiding something. He scanned their faces one by one. No Nick. Everyone was staring at him, soaking wet, clothes black with mud, a few cuts on his face from the branches, and his shirt stained with blood where Nick's knife had stabbed him in the gondola.

He dragged his right foot behind him as he made his way down the aisle, searching every face, until he was halfway through the coach. Suddenly a little boy near the back of the train stood up, said something in German, and pointed out the back door. His mother jumped up instantly, pulled him down, and clasped her hand around his mouth. Geddy realized they were afraid of him. His surprise caused him to hesitate, but then he was out the door the little boy had pointed to and was standing on a metal platform in front of the auto coach. Nick was nowhere to be seen.

Geddy jumped up and caught the roof of the passenger coach, pulling himself up until his chin was over the roof. He could not see Nick, but he could tell it was wet and windy and the roof slanted severely to the sides. If Nick went up there, he wouldn't get very far.

Geddy leapt onto the auto coach. Seven cars were lined up single file on the open flatbed. He dropped to the floor and looked under the cars. As far as he could tell, there was no one there. He cautiously slipped past the first few cars, peering through the windows as he went, in case Nick was hiding inside one of them. On guard and ready for Nick's attack, he looked under the cars again. Nothing. He made his way to the end and dropped down next to the gate at the rear of the train. There was no sign of Nick. That could mean only one thing: he must have jumped off the train.

Geddy looked out at the darkness and admitted to himself what he knew to be true. Nick was gone. Geddy couldn't find him now, even if he jumped off, as well. Nick would be hundreds of yards south and have a whole night's worth of darkness to get away. They would probably never catch him. Nick would soon be killing again, and there was nothing Geddy could do about it. In a minute, he would work his way to the front of the train, and the conductor could radio the police, but Geddy knew it would do no good. He sat down on the bumper of the last car and pushed his rain-soaked hair out of his eyes.

Far off, about a half mile behind the train, a light suddenly appeared. He had to squint to make sure, but yes, now he could tell what it was. It was moving. It was the only light he could see and it was faint, but it was moving. Geddy felt suddenly ill. Things were even worse than he had imagined. Nick had gone back for the motorcycle.

Insult was added to injury as Geddy watched the light get fainter. On foot maybe Nick wouldn't get too far and the police would have a chance, but now Geddy had provided Nick's means of escape. There was no stopping him now. He would be far away by morning.

The train rounded a curve and for a moment the car Geddy was sitting on shifted its position. He jumped out of the way, fearing his legs might get crushed between the last car and the gate. That gave him an idea.

He leaned over the rear gate, searching for a way to open it. Not finding any, he climbed over the gate and got a foothold on the outside of the coach, groping desperately just a few feet from the tracks until he found a latch. He pulled it up and felt the gate give a little. He scrambled over to the other side, and this time stood along the side of the coach until he found another latch and pulled it up. The gate swung down on its hinges so that it dangled a foot from the tracks.

Geddy got back on the flatbed coach, pulled a set of skis from the rack on top of a little European car, and plunged the back of the skis into the driver's window, shattering it. He threw the skis off the train and opened the car door. He was relieved that the railway men had left the keys in the ignition. Geddy hadn't hot-wired a car since he was thirteen years old and wasn't sure if he could still do it. He started the car, put it in reverse, and jumped out.

The little car went crashing to the rails and disappeared into the darkness as the train kept rolling.

He hurried to the second car, a two-door BMW. It was unlocked, with the keys inside. He repeated the drill and rolled it off the edge of the flatbed. He hurried to the next vehicle, a Land Rover.

Geddy jumped inside and started the engine. He kept the lights off, pulled the seat belt over his shoulder, and made note of the gears. He revved the engine, making sure it was warm, making sure he knew what he had underfoot. He looked behind him. Twenty feet. Twenty feet to the end of the flatbed coach. He let the engine idle. He checked the seat belt one more time, took care of the emergency brake, said a silent prayer, and slammed the vehicle into reverse.

Giving it as much gas as he could, Geddy popped the clutch. He pushed his head back hard against the headrest and looked down at the steering wheel, making sure he kept it straight so he wouldn't rub against the sides of the auto coach. He braced himself, holding his arms straight out against the wheel with his elbows locked and his teeth clenched. He closed his eyes as he went flying off the back of the train. He could hear the wheels spinning in the air, so he let off the gas and hung on, bracing himself for what was coming.

The Land Rover hit hard, the rear bumper first and then the rear wheels. It bounced several times and for a moment felt like it was going to roll, but soon it was on all four wheels, and Geddy could hear the engine still running. Without thinking, he shifted to neutral and slammed on the brake. He gave himself a second or two to regroup once the Land Rover settled, then threw it into four-wheel drive, bounced over the rails, and sped down the incline next to the tracks, crashing onto flat land. Geddy turned his vehicle south and looked out over the black horizon for the motorcycle headlight. He couldn't see it, so he risked turning on his lights for a split second, just to make sure he wasn't on the edge of a cliff. He could see he was in a lush, rolling, green valley.

He punched the headlights off, turned on the wipers, and, after initially spinning his wheels in the mud, was soon cruising along in the darkness, navigating by hope.

●　●　●

For three minutes, Geddy gazed into the black night searching for Nick as he charged onward. Once he hit something. He wasn't sure what it was, but it was white so he assumed it was a sheep or maybe a goat. It made him think he was probably in a wide-open pasture. He knew there were mountains all around, so he was gambling that Nick would be coming his way. Nick surely would not head back toward Zermatt. Since Geddy figured that since the train tracks would take the easiest way through the mountains, the odds were that Nick would be following alongside of them.

Geddy bounced along at only thirty miles an hour, a bit tentative in the dark. Suddenly he saw a light. It was as small as a pinpoint, and it was the only light on the horizon. Geddy sat up in his seat and gripped the wheel more tightly. He gave the four-by-four more gas. In fourth gear now, gaining speed as the grass turned to mud beneath his wheels, he could see nothing ahead of him but that light. He headed directly toward it. It was now a ball of silver dancing along the black stage in front of him. With each swipe of the windshield wipers, the light grew brighter. Geddy bored in. He shifted into fifth. Fifty miles an hour. The Land Rover started sliding from side to side. He struggled to keep a straight course but refused to let up on the gas.

Now the motorcycle was only about a hundred yards away. The ground between them was falling away fast. Sixty yards. The light didn't stray. Forty yards. Geddy almost lost control and almost slipped off course, but he frantically worked the wheel and his course remained true. Twenty yards. He knew by now he must be in sight. He pulled on the Land Rover's lights and now, ten yards away, he saw Nick clearly for an instant. Nick yanked the handlebars hard to the right, but the front tire just slid sideways in the mud. With five yards to go, Nick's hands were held out in the air in front of his face. Geddy had him, and he held on tightly because he was going to destroy Nick and any second he should hear the *Crash . . . !*

As the first rays of the sun drifted over Geddy's face, he awoke with a start. On his lap was the deflated air bag. Still across his chest was the seat belt. The back of his head ached where it had bounced off the air bag and into the headrest, but his arms could move. Next he tried his legs. They seemed fine. The windshield looked like a maze of spiderwebs, streaked with blood. The lights had been left on overnight while Geddy lay unconscious at the wheel. He tried to start the Land Rover, but it wouldn't turn over. The battery was dead. He unbuckled the seat belt, opened the door, and carefully slid down out of the four-by-four, keeping the weight off of his right ankle as much as possible.

He was in a long, narrow valley surrounded by mountains, the orange sun flaming not quite halfway over the white peaks. On the horizon to the north, where the tracks of his Land Rover were etched conspicuously in the earth, he could see a herd of sheep grazing contentedly. Nearer to him was the wreckage from the motorcycle. The gas tank was burned out, the twisted handlebars stuck in the ground. A tire was forty feet away toward the tracks. Fifty feet directly behind the Land Rover, Geddy saw a small mound lying like trash in the dirt.

It took him a minute to get there. He knew by then what it was, so he wasn't surprised to see the remains of Nick's body. The head, torso and arms were there, but only one leg. Geddy was sure the other leg would be underneath the Land Rover or maybe stuck in the front grill. Dried blood ran out of holes in Nick's skull and lined his face. His eyes were open, wide open, as if still surprised to see the Land Rover racing toward him, surprised even in death. His clothes were black with mud, like Geddy's, and a couple of ribs protruded from his shirt.

Geddy didn't know how long he stared at Nick's body, but he

sat cross-legged next to it and might have gone on staring at it all day if he hadn't heard the train whistle blowing. He looked up and realized it must be coming from around the bend. He took one last look at Nick, thought about spitting on him in disgust, but his mouth was too dry. He struggled heavy footed through the muddy field until he was on the track. Then he headed north, where he was sure an inbound train was halted by one of last night's automobiles lying wrecked on the tracks.

As he limped along in the quiet of the new day, Geddy felt no guilt over Nick's murder. Maybe for Morgan's, but not Nick's.

Nick Farley was a serial killer. How many victims had he taken over the years? It was impossible to know for sure, but it was probably somewhere around a hundred. Could he prove that in a court of law? Probably not. But the circumstantial evidence Faith dug up suggesting Nick was the Super-Killer, coupled with Nick's confession to Geddy that he had killed Morgan as well as God knows how many others, would be more than enough to clear Dick Didier of Morgan's murder.

It would also be more than enough to make Nick Farley the latest serial-killer sensation. People like Dr. Holmes would write books about Nick Farley. They would make up a trading card for Nick Farley. Someone would tell the families of the New Moon Murder victims about Nick Farley. Those families had counted on Geddy when he told them Curtis was responsible. They must have cursed him when they learned it was a hoax and that Curtis wasn't the killer. He wouldn't tell the families himself because he didn't feel that he deserved to, but the police would tell them and they'd know the New Moon Slasher was dead. Maybe they'd even learn that Geddy himself killed Nick Farley, and they'd forgive him.

But the truth was, he didn't much care anymore.

40

Geddy drove Morgan's vintage white roadster through the opened gates of Curtis Dole's chateau on Green Dolphin Drive. By the time he was at the door, Philip was there, waiting for him.

"Come in, John. Curtis is doing some work on the sailboat. He's expecting you." Philip led Geddy through the house and onto the veranda. Curtis was in the boat, sanding down a part of the teak deck. "Look, maybe he's not ready to forgive you, but for the record, I say you deserve a little credit for making it all right in the end. I realize that what Curtis went through wasn't your fault. Who would have thought those two women could play with so many lives merely by replacing a piece of paper?"

Geddy accepted Philip's hand and nodded thanks. Then he limped across the lawn and stood on the dock next to the sailboat. Curtis's Dobermans were sitting at attention on the dock on either side of Geddy. When Curtis finally looked up, he waited for Geddy to speak first.

"Faith and I are leaving town tomorrow. I'm dropping off

your car."

Curtis threw the sandpaper on the deck and wiped his hands. Geddy tossed him the keys.

"You keep the car," said Curtis.

"I don't want it."

"You keep it."

"No," insisted Geddy.

Curtis took a beer out of the cooler and offered one to Geddy. Geddy was going to say no but changed his mind and accepted it. Curtis offered Geddy a seat, but this time Geddy shook his head no, so Curtis remained standing as well.

"You can't stand to look at it, can you?" asked Curtis.

"Can't stand to look at what?"

"Morgan's car."

"Morgan's dead. It's your car now."

"Yes," agreed Curtis thoughtfully. "And you can't stand to look at it. Guilty conscience?"

Curtis tossed the car keys back to Geddy, who looked at them for a moment before closing his fist around them. Geddy took a long pull of his beer. "Thanks for the beer," he said and turned to go.

"When did you figure it out, Geddy? When did you realize that Nick was a killer?"

Geddy kept walking.

Curtis continued to call out to him, with a trace of laughter in his voice. "You knew Nick was a killer before you sent him to find Morgan, didn't you? You weren't surprised he killed her. You expected him to. You knew it would get you off, and it would get me my money back. I know it's true, Geddy." Curtis laughed heartily as Geddy neared the house. "She deserved it! Take the car, Geddy, there's no reason to have a guilty conscience! She deserved it!"

Geddy let himself in the house and left his empty beer bottle on the front stairs. He walked outside and stood in front of the vintage white classic, shining spectacularly in the spotlights of

Curtis's front courtyard. He tossed the keys onto the driver's seat, limped through the gates of South End, and began the long walk back to town in the twilight.